RIVER TO THE OCEAN

RIVER'S END SERIES BOOK FIFTEEN

LEANNE DAVIS

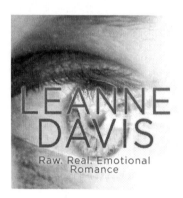

LEANNE
DAVIS
Raw. Real. Emotional
Romance

This is a work of fiction. Names, characters, places, and incidents are either the product of the author's imagination or are used fictitiously, and any resemblance to actual events, locales, or persons, living or dead, is entirely coincidental.

River to the Ocean

Contact Information: dvsleanne@gmail.com

River's End Series, Book Fifteen

Print ISBN: 978-1-941522-85-1

Edited by Teri at The Editing Fairy (editingfairy@yahoo.com)

Copy Editing: Joan Nichols: JRT Editing

Cover Designer: Steven Novak (novakillustrations@gmail.com)

For all the boating/camping trips to (and on!) the Ocean.

CHAPTER 1

"*W*HO? JACK RYDELL?"

Mathias Griffin repeated the name under his breath. *Rydell?* Where had he heard that name before? Glancing up, he squinted at the source of the voice, as if narrowing his tunnel of vision could allow him to better hear the conversation at the next table more clearly. But the man merely said the name and then leaned forward, hunkering over his beer.

Finally, Matt jumped to his feet. Hell, why not just ask? "Pardon me?"

The older man glanced up, his flannel barely spanning his pot belly and his silvery hair long and regal. "Yes?"

"You mentioned the name Rydell. May I ask if… ah… you're referring to a person who lives close to here?"

The man leaned back and snickered. "You shitting me? Which one? 'Bout two or three dozen live right there." He waved his hand out the front window of the small River's End Tavern. "Right smack dab across the river."

"Right. I just… ah, have a short message for them.

1

Thanks." *River. River's End. Rydell.* It all meant something to him once. But what?

He flopped back down. The two men finished their drinks and lumbered to their feet to leave. Alone, Matt kept flipping the name around his head, straining to seek the thread that explained it. There was one. He knew there had to be. But what was it? The guy said lots of Rydells lived nearby, like any idiot should know that. But why would Matt know?

Finally, after tossing a few bucks on the table, he rose to his feet. Stepping out, he started to amble towards his truck when it hit him. Yes! That was it.

Lillian Rydell.

That was the one Rydell he knew. She lived by a river. She talked a bunch about her family's ranch and the river nearby.

Fuck. He smiled. Lillian Rydell. Someone from a long time ago. Someone he hadn't seen in years. Someone he knew in some ways but not others. No one he really thought about either. But... she was right there? Smack dab across the river? What would she think if he showed up?

Well, that depended on the situation. If she were married or happily dating someone, no way would she want this blast from the past showing up outta nowhere to ruin that. Possibly even destroying an ideal image of herself. But if she weren't, would she mind? Now that he was physically there, so close, his curiosity rapidly piqued. He wasn't happy with how they ended up. A major regret in life that he often contemplated was *what if?* What if they had actually spoken the next morning? What might they have said or done? Would their paths and company have parted forever as they did? Or what if they instead shared an actual connection? Sure, it was a one-night, drunken hookup, but it stuck with him. He remembered her name. He often wondered what if things happened differently?

In his mind's eye, his thoughts of Lillian were familiar, although he never added her last name. However, it all came together at that crucial moment.

She was gone the morning he woke up after their wild night, and he had no contact information to reach her. It never occurred to him to look her up in River's End. But duh! And now, here he was. His travels brought him here so why not take a small detour across the river and ask for her at the Rydell River Ranch?

SUN STREAMED above the river in angles, making the golden, web-like shapes shimmer above the sand-and-rock riverbed. The clear water became a lush green and gold in spots. The surface rippled with the dancing, shimmering glitter of white-gold rays from the sun. The searing blue sky was only tolerable with a strong pair of dark sunglasses. Irrepressible light flooded everywhere. The brown mountains clung to tall grasses of gold and beige that were only interrupted by the stark contrasts of the bright green pine trees. Hugging the river along the valley floor, the rich green shrubbery adorned the cottonwoods, wild rose bushes, aspens and myriad pine trees, all tangled in lovely swatches that contrasted with the endless distance the valley offered. Free, unobstructed space characterized the land and sky. Hot sunlight. Warm breezes. Summer revealed the valley in all its glory.

Lillian Rydell waded in the river as her various family members swam, floated, and meandered around the swim-hole. A few others lay on the beach, sunning themselves while their kids played in the sand. It was a menagerie of cousins, aunts, uncles, one sister, brothers, kids and parents of cousins that comprised the Rydell spawn and those who married them. Today, the Rydell family gathered to play and frolic at the beach. A lazy ambience persisted on this too hot Saturday afternoon. All in attendance seemed to enjoy the space they owned and loved as proud members of the Rydell family. This was a perfect summer to Lillian. The ideal definition of it. Glad to feel the sun's rays on her body, she raised her head and let the shimmering heat beat down on her upper body as the river flowed around her, cooling her lower body in glorious, silky persuasion.

That's what Lillian Rydell always loved and enjoyed most while growing up here in the Rydell River Valley. She watched her son float on an inner tube in front of her. For at least a century or more, her family were considered the founders of the whole area. The river and valley were named after Clint Rydell's family; and now, so many generations later, here she was.

Her grandfather, Jack Rydell was still the patriarch of the family, as he was in the past. Jack's brother, Ian, and his wife, Kailynn, took more responsibility now but most people still associated the Rydell Ranch with Jack.

Lillian's six-year-old son splashed and swished around in his inner tube, pushing away from her, and paddling beside the shoreline. Struggling when his life jacket lifted him too high off the tube, his short legs strained to reach the water so he could kick for propulsion. But he managed. Ever since he was six months old, he had no fear of water. Lillian smiled at his early signs of independence, until, two seconds later, he floundered awkwardly. His confidence in knowing she was always right there, as she tried to be when she wasn't working, boosted his courage. Only her job tore her away from him.

Lillian worked as the town's large-animal veterinarian, and her biggest client was her own family's ranch. She devoted her skills to the numerous horses they owned and boarded. She often spent entire days working only on the ranch. Her mom and younger sister eagerly babysat for her son, Benny, along with her grandma, Erin. No need for outside daycare or commercial babysitters, a luxury that also made her job as a full-time veterinarian and single mom very doable. When she occasionally became overwhelmed, she tried to remember that. She had so much help around her. So much access to anything she required, that there was no reason to expect her career to lapse. Her son would always be fine. He'd turn out better than fine. Lillian's dad, Ben, served as his role model, and also worked at the ranch. The little boy simply followed his grandpa around, shadowing him, and Ben handled him with a patience that was tolerant and admirable.

As her father's veterinarian, Lillian laughed when her dad often winked and called his services "payment" for all the pro bono work she provided on the ranch.

"How the hell we survived so many decades without our own personal vet on the premises is a puzzle, and now, well, you're the best addition to our team." Her dad often said that while beaming with pride at her. He was in awe of her advanced degrees. And especially proud of the *Dr.* in front of her name.

Ben lacked advanced education. Following in his father's footsteps, he enjoyed working on the horse ranch and being with Jack. Ben took extreme pleasure in observing Lillian's quick mind when it came to her studies and he encouraged her strong desire to pursue veterinary medicine. When she was relatively young, during middle school, she decided to become a veterinarian because she so loved animals. In sixth grade, she started an animal club with only three members: Lillian, her best friend, Britney, and her little sister, Jade, who was barely four. Despite having no idea what they were doing, Jade was eager and grateful when Lillian insisted she participate in the club.

Meeting weekly, they treated any animal in need of care, usually some kind of insect or another. Keeping them inside jars and little bug catchers, they probably killed more creatures than they saved, but all three desperately took their work seriously.

They also sold lemonade and cookies to raise money they donated to animal welfare organizations. Later, she realized only her family bought their offerings, despite overpaying for them. Still, it became a source of money that they could earn and donate in the name of their club. Every wounded bird, rodent, and cat landed on the list of victims Lillian hoped to save and help. Even as a kid, she cringed at seeing dead bugs splattered on the car windshield. To her, all creatures deserved to live out their lives as well and as fully as anyone else.

Growing up on the ranch, Lillian understood farm animals. Luckily for her, none of their animals were raised for food. If they were, she'd have probably released them before they could be slaughtered. Many of the men in her family hunted and fished. That made her stomach sour. Long ago, she became a vegan after hearing the horrors (to her) of killing game and being on the receiving end of subsequent ribbing from Grandpa Jack and her own dad. She stuck to her principles. Animal care was her joy, her passion, and her excitement; the icing on the cake was getting paid to do it.

Beyond that, of course, was the unconditional love she had for her son.

She smiled when her thoughts drifted back to him. He stopped floating to dig in the wet sand on the sandbar. He was digging a tunnel deep into the side of it as the river water gently immersed everything he carved out.

The joy of simple activities. She remembered herself and Jade doing the same thing. The ranch was an idyllic and exquisite place to grow up. Naturally, it was not spared from drama, hurt, betrayal, drug abuse, fire, or devastation; even a rape occurred there. The terrible fire that nearly destroyed it and the loss of some family members who unfortunately died could not diminish the wonderful memories Lillian had. Nothing was perfect or immune from the frailties of life and humanity. But Lillian was always grateful for the river, the valley, the family and the home she inherited along with all the love she received. It was their own community and something she treasured highly.

Her education briefly took her away from River's End, but she always planned to come straight back and set up her practice in town just a few miles from the ranch. She accomplished exactly what she expected and chose for her life. All the exacting, lofty goals she assigned for herself were eventually achieved. Always. She exceeded her parents' expectations. Her motivation was internal. She followed concrete plans and goals and her entire focus remained centered on those things.

The only interruption in her career trajectory was her son.

He was the one unplanned commodity. At the time, she considered him a horrifying mistake.

But he truly turned out to be the greatest accomplishment of her life.

Go figure.

The roar of a two-person side-by-side buzzed down the beach trail. Glancing up, Lillian expected to see a family member or friend. They often came to their private area of the river for its wonderful, big beach where they could swim, sunbathe, relax, and socialize. It was her uncle, Ian. His gaze scanned the small crowd, and he absently exchanged the usual pleasantries to the few who engaged him. When he spotted Lillian, his gaze zeroed in on her. He waved her over.

Oh, he must have needed her for one of the animals at the ranch. She nodded, already crossing the small stretch of river. Someone was in need of her expertise. Not the first time. She took emergency calls at all times of the day and night. The nearest emergency vet was located in town, a good thirty miles away, so Lillian was fast becoming a well-tapped resource at this end of the valley. The river water reached her thighs as she crossed quickly. She took Benny's hand in hers. "Okay, buddy, some critter or another needs your mama now, so I'm going to leave you with Grandma."

Familiar with her "critter helping," as he called it, Benny watched her wave at her grandma. Erin nodded and came closer, squatting beside Benny. Surprisingly, Erin was Benny's great-grandma and to many onlookers, her fresh-faced beauty and youth were still evident despite being called *Grandma.* "Thank you, Grandma, I don't know how long I'll be..."

Erin waved her hand dismissively. "I know the drill by now, little Lil. Go and take care of it. It might be one of Jack's horses, for all you know. He's gotten way too spoiled with having you so close at hand and his old age makes him finicky. He's becoming such a worrywart with his rescues. Thank goodness you manage to ease the burden. And besides, Benny loves me. He's our first great-grandbaby and although it's horrifying to reach age sixty-three, since it means I'm officially old, I love any time I get to spend with him while I'm still relatively mobile."

Lillian scoffed. "Relatively mobile?" She leaned over to kiss her grandma's cheek. "You can probably still out-walk me." She squeezed her grandma's arm with clear affection. "Thank you."

"Go now. See you when we see you."

Grabbing her towel and phone, Lillian slipped on a coverup over her swimsuit. She slid into the seat beside her great-uncle Ian, who gave her a nod. He was a man of few smiles and words, but so intense in his care for animals, she always knew each one was very special to him.

"Well, what's the animal emergency?"

"None." Ian slipped the vehicle into reverse and glanced backwards for a clear path. "Someone came to the front desk of the inn, asking for you. Claims to be an old friend. Thought I better let you be the judge of that."

"Old friend?" Her eyebrows rose in unmasked curiosity. *Who the hell could that be?* "Any name?"

"They were very busy and didn't ask; they just radioed me to find you."

She wasn't sure who was working the desk at the Rydell River Resort today. Her great-uncle Joey and his wife, Hailey ran the resort and often one of their grandkids worked the desk during the summer.

"Okay. Drop me off at the house and let me change."

Ian stopped the UTV and released her before she entered her small, quaint house. Down by the river, her only neighbors were family members. Uncle Joey and her grandparents lived across the small road, while Ian and his wife, Kailynn, along with several cousins lived a bit beyond that. They divided some of the land decades ago so it would be available for them and any future Rydells to build if they chose to. Her parents preferred to reside in a luxury apartment over the main arena. Lillian appreciated her humble privacy and recently built a small, three-bedroom rambler to accommodate her and Benny. She quickly shucked her swimsuit and flip-flops for a pair of shorts, a tank top and sandals. Brushing her hair, she shrugged at her reflection. The mass of long chestnut hair, with reddish highlights that reached her waist and the bluntly cut, thick bangs accentuated her dark eyes.

Ian waited in the side-by-side and zoomed her down the recently paved road towards the resort check-in office. The ranch was renovated, and many impressive changes and upgrades occurred over the last decade. Paved roads, new buildings, and a total revamping for some of the older ones, with an eye towards modernization and warm ambiance improved the ranch substantially. It kept the authenticity of a working horse ranch, but now, it had become more of a vacation place than what her dad experienced when he grew up there.

Ian dropped her off and drove the side-by-side away with a wave as she entered the cool, air-conditioned foyer of the resort. It allowed the guests to check in or visit a gift shop that supplied sundries and souvenirs like keychains and whatnot. Advertising and marketing ploys were part of the changes that were added over the years. A small café featured a simple, but delicious menu of homemade donuts, quality sandwiches, and gourmet coffees and lemonades.

She glanced around, curious to see who asked for her, making her gaze quick and darting. Who the hell could it be?

The woman with two kids clinging to her legs? No. No recognition there. The older man having a sandwich in a bay window of the café? No. No!

She walked over to the reception desk and found Blake Alexander working the counter. "Did someone come here and ask for me?"

"Yes." He was busy typing on the computer and began biting his lip. "I think he stepped out momentarily to look at the view."

Lillian's gaze lifted towards the hallway that led to the French doors and deck outside. It offered a majestic view of sloping land, sprinkled with tranquil horses, surrounded by neat, prim, white fencing that showcased the winding, blue ribbon of the river. The right, high side was where the Rydell barns and horse arena were located. To the left lay the mini cabins with a waiting list of guests; everyone rented those first mostly because of their close proximity to the river.

There indeed was a man. His back was to her, leaving only his left side visible. She noticed his t-shirt, shorts, and wide shoulders that tapered down to a slim waist and a pair of powerful legs. There was something so strong and visceral about him, as if a bolt of energy shot out from him that nearly launched him right out of his sneakers. He rocked slightly, appearing unable to stand upright.

Man. Okay. Younger, judging by his physique.

Who could it be?

She stepped closer to the glass doors until she had a full view of his back. It was a fine body, but she still wasn't sure. Perhaps a previous client she helped out with a horse or a cow or a chicken or hell, a dog? Who knew? She encountered many people in the course of her services. Perhaps a tourist whom she once assisted had returned to the area and decided to look her up? Could be. Not the first.

Then, he turned his face to the side.

That was all it took. A glimpse of his profile and she instantly recognized him. Even after all this time. All these years.

Mathew Griffin.

Dear God, it was no mistake, *Mathew Griffin.*

Her heart skipped a beat, and she gripped her fingers in a tight fist. Oh, no. Not Matt. Her heart began to race as she tried to swallow the lump of dread that filled her throat.

Wearing dark aviator sunglasses, his only defense against the brutal sun's glare, the sweat from the ninety-plus temperatures glistened on his forehead as he looked out at her family's land. She remembered the dark chestnut, curly hair. There was no mistaking this man. Ever. Although she didn't know him. His image remained with her in a way that no one else's could.

The same face that she saw every day staring back at her, the face of her son.

She stepped back.

No. Oh, no. What could she do? Confront him? But how? After all this time? After what happened? How could she admit the secret she kept? His secret? His son? How could she just say hi and make casual conversation? Naturally, he had no idea. None. She almost wilted with panic. Thank God she left Benny at the river, far from here, with Erin. There was no reason to think they might wander up here, not onto the deck of one of a dozen outbuildings on the ranch. Concealed from the main driveway, as well as the road to the beach, she hoped vehemently that her family remained at the beach.

How could she not confront him?

How could she avoid telling him the truth?

What in the living hell was he doing here? Here? After all this time? Why? What could have motivated him to come here? Why on earth would he now?

It was a random, ordinary Saturday afternoon in the middle of July. Why would he suddenly materialize here? Her brain struggled to find the words. Nothing fit. There was no explanation. How did he even know where to find her? More importantly, why?

Did he know or suspect anything about Benny? No way. How could he? There was no possible way. Indecision and confusion paralyzed her. Childishly, she fought the urge to turn away and leave the premises with undetected, swift steps. She imagined herself telling Blake to ask him to leave and swear that she wasn't anywhere near there. Ever. But—

Matt fucking turned around right then as if he felt her eyes riveted on him. In that moment, their gazes met and locked over the small span of twenty steps and two panes of glass. They stared as the time melted, but also sizzled.

Holding her breath in her lungs, she experienced a visceral, full-body response to him.

Like the very first time she laid eyes on him. Her reaction temporarily derailed her intended life's plan. It almost ruined it. Coming home early, filled with shame and embarrassment, Lillian took some time off school to give birth to a child she didn't want initially but subsequently had… and it was Matt's.

Of course, her guilt and shame at the surprise pregnancy were long gone and far behind her. On the day Benny was born, all her misgivings faded to a purple, hazy mist before vanishing into the ether. Until then, a dark, angry cloud hovered over her and her beloved career, which she feared would forever be disrupted.

Seeing this face again and that body? The freaking instant chemistry consumed her then and now, or so it seemed. Why? She had no answer to that. Or why what happened that night permanently marked her life's direction.

Did she ever expect to see him again? No.

Her eyes were rounded orbs of horror and shock. She couldn't smile when her lips instantly tightened.

Panic stirred in her guts before lodging into a lump in her throat. Benny! She had to protect Benny. Always. Whatever the costs. Right now, Benny was her number one priority.

It didn't matter how Matt came here. All that mattered was he stood directly in front of her. She needed to stay calm, cool, and casual in order to persuade him to fucking leave. Right? Sure. Naturally. That was the only course of action. The only one she could see. Her son was hers, alone. Not his. It was too late.

For one full year, Lillian searched for the mysterious man who helped her conceive a son. however, she never learned enough about him to actually find him. That horrifying reality was later reluctantly shared with her parents as well as her freaking grandparents. Everyone knew the story now. It was both humbling and humiliating. Mostly, it was so uncharacteristic of her. Truly. Just one time was all it took, and God's sense of humor was sharp and awesome. Sure, she learned a lesson. Mathew Griffin was nowhere to be found and she quickly realized she was about to become a single mom. The identity of her child's father remained a total mystery to her until the next step in her downward spiral of regret and humiliation: someday her son would have to hear her awful confession.

And now? Matt was here?

Shaking herself from her catatonic reverie, she gripped the door lever and pressed it down, stepping out to meet the gaze that still held hers. The father of her child. What was she supposed to say to him? Hello? How are you?

She pressed forward, her steps slow and measured as his gaze slowly took all of her in. And then she stood before him.

Almost dizzy and feeling slightly surreal with the knowledge after all this time, a matter of years, and all the subsequent distance, here he stood. Her chance to do right by him for Benny crossed her mind. But her brain was too fuzzy and stunned. What should she do? What would he do if she told him about his son? Would he run the other way? Never to be heard from again? Was Matt mean and insensitive? Or warm and wonderful? She didn't know. That was the problem. That was the source of all the other problems. How could she trust a complete stranger with the most precious person in her life, her son? He was all hers. She owed him her unconditional protection and safety before giving him a father. Forti-fying her resolve, she chose not to tell this stranger the truth. She could not bear to hand over her son to a complete and utter outsider. She had to protect Benny first. Always. Forever.

Convinced she was right, she pasted a small smile on her face and said softly, "Hello?"

CHAPTER 2

*T*URNING WHEN HE SENSED a pair of eyes on him and... what? Energy? Something very potent was at work. The same sensation that happened the night he met the woman he came there to see. Lillian Rydell. The receptionist at the front desk didn't bat an eye or act like it was a strange request or even unusual when he asked for her. He nodded like it was freaking normal. She called someone and said it could be a while because Ian had to hunt for her down at the beach. *Go ahead*, she urged him, *and take in the view*. So, he did while wondering who Ian might be. His real reason for being there still eluded him. Especially after all this time.

But glimpsing a presence behind him, he turned and found her. She was why he came here. The living image of the woman he remembered was quite shockingly correct. Something new and irresistible overcame him the first time he saw her. His reaction to her grabbed his heart and twisted it all up in a weird way, leaving him almost tongue-tied.

She was indeed lovely, as many women were, although there was something exceedingly lovely about her. Her brunette hair was very much like his own. She had big, dark eyes, fringed in long lashes. Her small, pixie face had sharp cheekbones, a small, up-tipped nose, and rose-red lips. She was a small woman with narrow, slim shoulders and nicely toned arms and legs. There was something both fearful and delicate about her. The combination created a contrast that made her seem like a firecracker ready to go off.

When Matt first met her, he approached her and became a bundle of nerves. Why would this gorgeous, interesting woman allow him to buy her a drink? But she did. And they talked. For hours. Many drinks later, Matt was drunk and having the time of his life. They went back to his motel room. She, then a student, was finishing her bachelor's degree. Not only did she appear intimidating, she *was* intimidating. Bold, daring, smart, oh fuck! She was smart as a whip and just as cutting in her retorts. The mental gymnastics required just to keep up with her invigorated and humbled him.

Hot. So hot. He managed to remember that despite his drunken haze. He flashed on images of the night they spent together. Sensual, wonderful images that were also familiar as they often integrated his thoughts. To his surprise, she was very unexpected and extremely interesting.

Then… she vanished. The next morning, there was no trace of her. He almost believed he dreamed her up. The perfect woman and the perfect night. But without any more than a name, he had no way to find her again. Yet, they talked for nigh eight hours without any pauses or problems. It turned out to be the most unusual meeting and night of his life. Yes, it was technically a one-night stand, but it felt way nicer than that.

And he never told anyone about it. Least of all, her.

Eventually, he forgot about it and moved on, pursuing his own damn life. But upon hearing her name, in a matter of seconds, sexy images of her flooded him. And now here he was. Drawn from his visions of a night so long ago, she was just as he remembered.

She looked exactly the same. Shorts that exposed her strong, tanned legs. Tank top revealing the attractive combination of strength and toned muscles inside a feminine and totally seductive frame.

She finally broke their hypnotic, intense stare and came closer, stopping just shy of him. He swallowed and his nerves made his hands clammy as he clenched them anxiously. Lifting his hand to his sunglasses, he slid them up his forehead into his hair. Her gaze followed his movements and dropped back to his eyes. Staring, she didn't smile or comment. After a long moment, he said, "Do you... remember me? I... I'm not sure—"

"I remember you, Matt."

Her voice had the same low, cool, sexy tone. No doubt, it would be calming in the midst of an emergency to both animals and animal owners. He hoped she became the vet she so passionately spoke about.

"I wasn't sure. I... Is it a problem for me to be here? I mean, if you have a husband or... or anything, this might be..."

"No. There is no one." She cut him off tersely.

He nodded. His throat went dry. No simpering from this one. He distinctly remembered that about her now.

"How... what brings you here?"

"I didn't know where I was, quite honestly. I stopped across the river for lunch and a cold beer on my way through the town and literally overheard someone saying the name Rydell... and it triggered..."

She nodded. "That night."

"That night." He finished at the same time she did.

"That's uncanny. The timing, I mean."

"I thought so too. I debated whether or not to try to find you and decided to check it out and the kid at the front desk knew exactly who you were and wasn't at all surprised when I asked for you…"

"I get calls from strangers as well as the townspeople whenever they need animal care. So no, no one would think twice of someone asking for me at the reception desk."

"So, you *did* become a veterinarian?"

"Yes. I did."

"And the family ranch that you hoped to start your practice in worked out too?"

"Yes, that too."

He glanced away from her, though it was hard. Holding his breath as he kept staring at her, she became so compelling. Small in stature and presence, she swiftly managed to drain the air around her of oxygen. Tearing his eyes from her attractive face and body, Matt turned to the equally amazing views of nature surrounding them. "This isn't what I pictured when you called it 'the family ranch.' This is more like a showplace for some giant corporation."

"It became far more than anyone ever dreamed it could be. Which is good and bad. Commercialization draws many tourists who want to stay in the cabins, or at the small hotel up that way, and eat at our gourmet restaurants and use my cousin's golf course. Rydell River Resort offers horseback-riding and all the usual river rentals of kayaks, rafts, floaties and inner tubes, so it's become kind of a huge thing. But despite all that, the horses are the primary reason for the ranch and most of its improvements. They remain the basis for the entire place."

"And that's where you come in."

"I'm just one of many." A small smile touched her lips. She stepped back toward the only small sliver of shade the corner of the deck received from the building overhang. He followed her and they shared a small smile beneath the cooler, less glaring spot that was smaller and cozier.

They exchanged long looks again. Being so close, he managed to see the unique gold rings that edged her irises. "I know this must seem strange. I didn't think it out completely. But it was such a coincidence that I had to know if the Rydell name I overheard at lunch was actually related you. By sheer accident, I arrived in the infinitesimal town you told me you were from without grasping I was even here. And yet, I still found it."

"I'm shocked you actually remembered me."

"Of course, I did." His gaze found hers. A blush heated her neck and cheeks. Darting her eyes away from his made him smile but he kept it to himself. Sleek. Strong. Cool. But the awful fact that she had sex with him on the first night they met made her suddenly feel embarrassed and unsure.

"I've never spent another night like that one," he said softly.

She cast a glance at him and then looked away. "How so? I mean, are you referring to it being a one-night stand or… what?"

"No, I was referring to you. I've never been with anyone like you before or after that night. No, it was not my usual thing, but I meant it more in the way we—"

Connected. At the time, it seemed as if they knew one another; that, combined with a giant flashpoint of chemistry was a new phenomenon. No woman ever grabbed him in the guts before turning them inside out with just her looks, never mind her cool, husky voice. Once he started engaging her, it all became crystal clear.

She was so much more than him. Smarter. Classier. Better educated. More widely read. Richer, too, if her family's ranch were any indication.

She never acted like she was a rich girl. It made sense

though, judging by her class and sophistication. Matt found her goal of becoming a big-animal veterinarian extremely fascinating, especially when he considered her tiny stature and incredible figure. She intrigued him at once after he discovered the horse ranch that her family owned was her final destination spot.

Matt never pictured the scope of such a giant operation to be her "family horse ranch."

Her expression seemed kind of standoffish and he wished he could slink away. He also wondered if he pissed her off by showing up so unexpectedly. But he understood. Seeing a one-night stand from her past after what? Five or six years? Maybe even more. The passage of time wasn't clear. Just weird and disconcerting. He didn't really expect to find her. The same exact person he remembered so fondly. "I'm sorry for disrupting your life so suddenly. I didn't think I'd really find you and I never intended to put you on the spot like this."

Her face morphed, going from kind of perplexed and cool to another blush. What was that all about? Regret? "I just… I remembered you… and…" He looked away, his cool demeanor quickly fading. Damn it. Why did he come here? So lame. Of course, he couldn't charm such a strong, inter-esting woman. Even when he tried to years ago.

Besides, what did he expect from her? He had no concept. On impulse, he came there without articulating his motiva-tion. At a loss for words, he shrugged and finally threw his hands up in helplessness. "I've no clue what I'm doing here. I just remembered you and wanted to see if it was really you. I had no agenda after that."

She smiled finally. Wow, that sweet smile. It gripped a guy's heart and shredded it. "Rydell is the name of the valley, the river and the ranch. Not exactly a secret."

He chuckled then. "True. I didn't connect it though. Not

until I heard the name, Jack Rydell. You must have mentioned it to me. Then it clicked."

"I probably did. He's my grandfather. Very well known around here."

"I think I recall you saying that. My granddad is close to me as well—"

She nodded. "We talked a lot about that too. I remember." She shifted her weight from one foot to the other.

"I remember it too. But it was a long time ago." Matt added.

"I was sorry we didn't share our information. And then you disappeared…"

"I was horrified," she rushed to explain herself. "I'd never done anything like that before. And I also wished we exchanged numbers or had some other way to find each other again. Incidentally, you have zero social media presence, which is insane nowadays."

"And I didn't try to use it to find you because it never occurred to me. I was raised by my grandfather, remember? He disdained modern technology and so did I. Didn't even get a smart phone until a few years back and that was only for business purposes."

She smiled with genuine amusement. "Still as weird as you were back then. It would have been appreciated… And it certainly would have made it easier to find you."

"Did you want to find me?"

"I guess so. At first maybe. It was so beyond my usual behavior and I felt a bit confused after it happened."

"Me too."

She gave him a raised-eyebrow look of *sure* and he grinned. "No, really. It was so unusual for me."

"Well, God, same for me. I was pretty drunk."

"I believe we got that way together."

She smiled softly. "We sure did."

He smiled back and that fast, the same initial spark they shared re-ignited between them. That fast! That night from so long ago happened fast and furiously too. Ridiculous. Older and wiser now, he grabbed his sunglasses to cover his eyes. No. There was no such thing as an instant connection with anyone. It was sheer lust. So what? No reality to that.

"Look, I realize how rude and weird it was for me to show up like this. But would you mind having a longer conversation? Would you be open to having dinner tonight?"

"Are you staying in the area?"

"For the night." He wasn't, of course. Not until now. The instant decision to change his plans was more of a reaction than a desire. Stay overnight for what? He didn't know. Sure, he liked her a whole lot back then, and he started to feel the same way now. He had to hurry back to book a room at the dumpy, little roadside inn he passed in River's End. It looked as decrepit and shabby as the wagon wheel relic and time capsule they displayed in the town square. "I know I sprang this on you without any notice…"

"I'm sorry. I have to leave soon to go out to a farm in the hills to administer the annual vaccinations and health check-ups. We were just waiting for the heat to die down."

Her job. Duh. Matt pictured her wrangling a giant cow or a horse and he smiled. Not your usual woman, he had to give her that. "Right. Of course, you do."

"I wish we could have more time to talk…"

"But who knew I'd be dropping out of nowhere almost five years later?"

"Seven." She flushed red. "Almost *seven* years later."

"Right." Something was rapidly deflating inside his chest. He suddenly felt lost. No, he never had her for more than a night. They had one connection. She didn't have time for anything but her education. He didn't live there. An odd sense of lost opportunity made him sad. Like he failed to grasp something special that could have turned out to be… real. Something big and different and interesting. Seven years? That was way too long. They were still kids in many ways when they met. Twenty-three years old. It was okay to engage in one-night stands at that age. It was all about exploring and discovery. That was before it turned into a sad, lonely way to be with others. "I just wanted to see you again and say hello. I'll let you return to your life."

Feeling stupid and strange for his spontaneous visit, he wondered if she felt the same way. Obviously, seven years after a one-night stand was not like celebrating an anniversary. Especially when it ends without a parting word and no phone numbers.

Matt suddenly recalled a mole on her upper left thigh that he licked and sucked on while she laughed and giggled because it tickled her. She was so adorable.

But now it was time to make his exit after an awkward reunion. One he should not have initiated.

He nodded and started to pass her. A few steps later, her voice called out and stopped him dead. "Can I ask you something before you leave? Where exactly are you from? If I'm ever traveling through there, wherever it is, maybe I could stop by and say hello like this."

His heart thudded with longing. He was actually wishing she would. Hell, yeah. He was really wishing for that to happen. He turned back. Slipping his wallet from his back pocket, he handed a business card to her. "There is all you need to know to contact me. If you ever want to say 'hi,' I hope you do."

A sinking feeling crept over him, a sense of knowing, *nah, that'll never happen*. It was a kick to see her again though. She lived up to everything he believed and remembered about her.

Taking the card he offered her, she smiled, obviously

amused. "Paper again. You really are a relic from the last century."

"Why change a good thing?" He flashed a warm smile. He was good-natured. God, the comfort and ease he displayed; why didn't she feel that? "Besides, lots of people still use business cards."

"Sure, Grandpa." She grinned and glanced down before frowning. "Westport? Is that next to the ocean? You live all the way out there?"

"Yes. I run my granddad's charter boat business." How did that remain undisclosed during their infamous night? Maybe because back then, he was still vacillating over what to do for a living. After working some odd jobs, he wasn't sure he wanted to commit to the lifestyle of his granddad, but he soon went all in and never regretted it for a day.

"The ocean. That's pretty far from here. What brings you so far inland?" Her words were said in jest, but a high-strung tension was attached to it.

"Vacation actually. I've got a friend who lives on a river in Idaho. He boasts about the excellent fly-fishing so I'm on my way over there for a week of fishing and relaxing."

"A fishing vacation? I thought you fished for a living?"

He grinned. "Yes. It's sort of a calling. Can't explain it. Everything I do seems to revolve around it, I guess."

She nodded and stuck her hand out in parting. He set his hand in hers. Their gazes explored each other, drawing them closer together. She glanced down to read his business card.

Didn't she feel the magnetic draw? It was so damn strong, it was shocking.

"Mathias? Your first name isn't Mathew?"

"No."

"Oh, I just assumed it was."

Her frown deepened. Apparently, she didn't like knowing

25

his name was actually Mathias. "Well... It was nice to see you, Matt."

He released her hand. "You too. I wish you all the best, Lillian."

She gulped. "You too."

Then he stepped past her and left.

GOOD GOD. The same freaking attraction that led to so much trouble for her was still there. How could it be? After all this time? Especially after what happened last time.

But the zing! in her fingertips when they touched was not imagined. The strength of his gaze emitted strange sensations that she sensed throughout her body. Like something physical were caressing her skin. It extended to the areas it should not have reached. So what if he was still handsome? Lots of men were that good-looking. Why did she have such a reaction to him?

It was about the son she had. His son. Matt was her son's mirror image. It was more than disturbing. She never realized how much Benny looked like his father until Matt showed up in a vibrant, refreshing manifestation just now.

The grip of ancient guilt all but suffocated and alarmed her.

He was her son's father, and the man had no idea he even conceived a son. No more than half a mile away, Matt's son frolicked in the water with his great-grandmother.

Her son had no idea that his father was there. Right there on the ranch.

In the end, she knew she was avoiding the truth. By denying her son the chance to meet his father, she was ignoring any wishes Benny might have to know his dad. She had become the problem. Before now, she had no way to contact his dad. She tried to trace the name *Mathew Griffin* and *Matt Griffin*. But she never tried *Mathias Griffin*. She felt like slamming her head against the wall. How could she not try another version of his legal name? For seven years, she simply failed to find him because she had the wrong name!

A new wave of guilt for not knowing her baby-daddy's first name made her shudder. Lord, that sounded so bad.

His last name, Griffin, was common and hundreds of them came up on the internet searches she did. None, however, were the "Matt" she sought. She never found his picture or any other reference that connected him to her child's father. Not until she strolled up behind him today. Until that moment, she wasn't betraying Benny or Matt. She didn't know. Now? She did. She knew the truth. She had his business card. She had his name. Three phone numbers. An email address. A business name and location. She finally made contact.

Staring down at her shoes, her heart sank like heavy river rock inside her chest.

He lived somewhere on the damn Pacific Ocean coastline? That was about as far across the state as it was from New York. It wasn't a matter of driving Benny an hour away to visit him. It was totally unworkable. She wondered what might be workable. Did she expect Matt to hear the news he had a son and just what? Suddenly decide to spend summers and weekends with him?

Her worst fear and greatest desire clashed. Who wouldn't want to know her son? Meeting him once, and seeing his sweet, toothy smile or hearing his funny words were priceless. How could Matt not want to know her son? Their son? She shivered. *Their son.* No. She wondered if she could handle that. She never had to share her son with anyone. He was all hers. First and always. Sure, her friends and family members loved, adored and helped care for him. But Benny was all hers. She made the final choices. She provided for his needs, wellbeing, and physical, mental and emotional happiness. Now she had to share that? Her brain began to shrivel with doubt. No. The very idea of having to ask or consult with anyone else was repugnant. Ugh. No way. She liked being the boss of the entire situation.

Once terrified and scared, due to being so young, Lillian lacked self-confidence at first. But her commitment to motherhood was vigorous and her love for her son made her sure she was destined to be the sole source of Benny's upbringing. In only a few weeks after his birth, Lillian considered it a blessing she could not locate his father. That meant Benny was exclusively hers.

Of course, she could not tell Matt the truth. She didn't owe this stranger anything. Never mind, her son. HER SON. He was hers, alone. No. That was the reason she swiftly dispatched Matt. Even lying to get him out of there. Acting standoffish, she hoped he would feel odd and strange for seeking a random partner in a one-night stand that never mattered.

She made him feel worse than weird. Not unwelcome, but definitely strange.

What if she were married, with her own family? Or dating someone exclusively? And what spouse would allow a freaking one-night stand to visit out of the blue? No one. He took an odd and unsolicited gamble by showing up like that. So unexpected. He should have felt weird, and she was glad he left. It was thankfully over and done.

She tried to ignore their almost-instant connection. That fast, the night he asked to buy her a drink in the bar flashed back into her mind. A totally natural and common occurrence after meeting someone. Nothing original or cute about it. Even the anonymous sex.

But the warmth they both felt re-emerged. The instant

appreciation of humor and the way he so easily understood her without any explanation were uncanny. It never happened before or since that night. Celebrating the end of the classes required for her bachelor's degree, Lillian went out with friends to release the pressure and steam and there he was. Across the bar. They made eye contact and the obvious interest they shared could not be repressed. "Hi, can I buy you a drink?"

Lillian said *sure*, and they spent five or six hours just talking and drinking. They both got drunk before they shut the place down.

Back at the motel, they had sex. Snippets and details were blurry. Some images were startlingly clear. She woke up early, horrified at herself and overwhelmed with shame, she had no option in her mind but to vanish. Go. Her humiliation forbade her from giving him any more identification. Knowing his name was all she had. So, she vacated the premises as fast as she could and went back to school.

In the next few months, she realized she was pregnant. There was no mistaking who the father was. The idea of coming home in disgrace to confess to her family she was pregnant and didn't know how to contact the father was the lowest point in her life. But now she loved her son, so it didn't matter how Benny came into the world; she was just grateful he did and shared his life with her now.

Her parents were not judgmental and fully understood her predicament. Lillian's birth was also unplanned. Her shattered self-respect and belief in herself were soon restored. Her parents were always honest with her and never failed to convince her of their unconditional love. That's exactly how she instantly felt with Benny.

Her parents, Jocelyn and Ben, conceived Lillian on the one night they had sex. A terrible forest fire broke out subsequently. Her father, Ben, was unhappily married to another woman named Marcy. Tragically, Marcy died from smoke inhalation in the same fire, on the same night. Ben freaked out and left town, temporarily turning to drugs and alcohol to cope with his losses. Jocelyn also left, preferring her privacy during her pregnancy, which she endured alone. When her labor started, she called the Rydell River Ranch for help and Jack summoned an ambulance. But Lillian came before the ambulance arrived and they found her on the floor of the shack her mother lived in. Jack left to look for Ben, whom he eventually managed to bring home to Jocelyn and Lillian. It was a tense time, but they all worked through their issues and married one another. Several years later, Jade was born. The ensuing years cleared up most of the misunderstandings between them.

Lillian's "indiscretion" was easily tolerated and forgiven. They were eager to help and support her. They never blamed her for changing her scholastic path temporarily.

"This is not supposed to happen to me. I'm supposed to be a doctor! My purpose is to help animals. That's always been the plan!" Lillian cried, sobbing against her mom's chest before Benny was born.

Her mom patted Lillian's back, being taller and stronger than Lillian, Jocelyn easily held her tightly against her chest. "You will continue on your path. This baby will simply be a new feature of it. A new highlight in the plan. I promise you: it will be okay. When I found out I was pregnant with you, I believed my life was over, but as it turned out, your birth was the start of it all."

"That only worked out because Dad knew. He was a decent man; he was just mixed up. I don't know the first thing about Benny's father. I was careful. I swear I was. We used condoms. I don't understand how it happened... and please don't lecture me about the logistics. We were careful."

Lillian cried a lot during the next several months. She

received her bachelor's degree and after Benny was born, began her first year of vet school, all while caring for her newborn baby. Benny arrived in the summer, so she moved back to school with him in tow. She received lots of help from her family and plenty of money to afford adequate childcare. They eagerly contributed their time and money to ensure Lillian could manage to attend vet school while raising her dear, little toddler. It was hard for Lillian, but somehow having Benny gave her a stronger sense of purpose and actually made her work harder.

Her family's support was invaluable and spared her from the travails of the average struggling single mom, but Lillian liked and needed to be responsible for Benny.

After receiving her Doctor of Veterinary Medicine and taking the state exam, Lillian returned home. Contented to be back where she always intended to practice, she began her chosen career. Her first clientele, i.e., her grandfather and father, remained her biggest clients. Her dad operated the boarding, training and breeding programs at the ranch. Her grandfather, Jack, ran the River Rescue, which required an entirely different line of equipment. Rescuing abused and neglected horses, most with both emotional and physical injuries and scars, Jack had to employ various innovative therapies. Lillian had long ago proven her incomparable value, which included several emergencies where her close proximity turned out to be a lifesaver.

"Always knew we needed a live-in vet here, little Lil. Seeing that it's you, makes me so proud every time I watch you work your magic." Lillian never forgot her Grandpa Jack saying that to her. It helped her manage the strain and stress of being a single mother and trying to set up a new veterinarian practice. Lillian never lost sight of her goals. She adored seeing that sparkle in her beloved grandfather's eyes and hearing the pride in the tone of his voice whenever he spoke about her.

"You expected Dad or Charlie to be the vet though."

"I thought Charlie might take that path, but his life took him in a far different direction than animal care could offer. Ben wanted to be like me, doing the job I do and carrying on our legacy, while Charlie saw things so differently, and had to seek his happiness far from here. Now, seeing my granddaughter is here again, trained to do this wonderful profession, is nothing less than excellent."

She laughed but saw his eyes tearing up. Being such a sedate, gruff man, Jack rarely expressed himself. When he did, one listened.

Lillian never had a discussion with her grandparents about the father of her surprise pregnancy. They knew. Her mom told them and let her know she did. But to their credit, not once did a disappointing glance land on her. Not once did they ask her about the sketchy deadbeat who sired Benny. They simply were loving, supportive parents as her parents were to her son.

"Benny Rydell represents the fourth generation," was all Jack said with a gleam of pride.

Benny didn't resemble any other Rydell. He was his father's clone. Only Lillian saw that. Only she knew that.

Benny had no father in his life.

Not until today.

CHAPTER 3

$\mathcal{W}$HAT TO DO WITH the knowledge of learning the whereabouts of her child's father?

Walking back to the beach, she found her grandma holding Benny's hand as they trudged up the road. His wet hair clung to his scalp and his beach towel was wrapped around his shoulders, being so large it trailed behind him. "That didn't take long," Grandma said as she drew closer.

Lillian smiled at them. "No. It was simply an old friend who wanted to say hello on his way through town. Someone I met in college."

Grandma Erin shared a look with Benny and Lillian caught it. "What are you two cooking up?"

"Well, we thought you'd be a bit longer so I might have promised Benny some chicken nuggets and French fries and his choice of a movie…"

Lillian cringed. She never allowed chicken nuggets in her domain, but Benny loved many meat products that various family members offered him. Long ago, she quit fighting for him to be exclusively vegan or even vegetarian. Benny ate meat on occasion, but only with the family. Still… it made her cringe. The time Benny spent with his great-grandparents was precious. How many kids had healthy, youthful, vibrant great-grandparents to interact with in their daily lives? Not many. She always encouraged these special times, trying to pack her son full of them, as she remembered herself receiving. She knew how these simple, ordinary, and extraordinary times became etched into her childhood memories. Her loyalty to Jack and Erin Rydell bordered on being their fan-girl. She adored her grandparents and believed they hung the moon and stars when she was growing up. Her reverence for them never faded. She remained Grandpa's enthusiastic fan-girl even if she were freaking thirty years old.

"So basically, I'm on my own for the night?"

Grandma grinned. "You are."

Benny giggled. "I get to eat ice cream too."

Grandma cringed and pretended to give him a stern look with a finger to her lips. "That was supposed to be a secret."

Lillian played along. "Well, I can't compete with chicken nuggets, fries and ice cream. Besides, I'd never let you eat all that."

"That's what great-grandparents are for."

"Between you two, his teeth will rot out by the time he's ten."

Benny snorted. "Not with all the green stuff you feed me."

Lillian laughed as his face twisted into a sneer. "Well… I guess my job as a mother is done here." She leaned over and kissed the top of Benny's wet head. "Okay. I'll let you guys go off to rot your teeth." She glanced up at her grandma and mouthed a *thank you*. Erin smiled and winked back in reply. Setting her hand on Benny's again, they continued walking towards the house.

Lillian's evening was unexpectedly free. Usually, that was

a welcome break; but now, she wanted to cling to Benny's little body and reassure herself he was there and safe and still all hers. His father had no clue about him. She wasn't prepared to be swallowed by a terrible, dark feeling that she was doing a very bad thing. She wasn't really denying a parent the knowledge of his child.

Imagine if she knew nothing about Benny? She shuddered in horror. Her biology demanded that she carry him to term and give birth to him so the knowledge and connection between them existed almost from the beginning. It wasn't Matt's fault if he didn't have it. It wasn't hers either. It was a fact of life and biology. Without contact information, neither party could reach the other. At the time, she believed he attended the same school. She never asked, which turned out to be an obviously, stupid oversight. After fleeing from the motel that night, she looked for him on campus only to learn there was no Mathew Griffin. From there, she relied on the internet for her searches but never managed to locate him.

Until he found her.

The heat shimmered on the pavement and sweat rolled off her brow. Walking a little further, she came to one of her favorite spots, the barn. Grandpa Jack was almost always inside one of his rescue barns. Tending to the injured, neglected, and unwanted horses, he nursed them back to health, using any means necessary for each case. It was a passion that became a project and eventually, turned into a successful business that flourished by doing so much good.

She entered the space and the cool air rushed over her. Fans blasted the chilly air and dispersed the incessant midsummer heat.

She passed Finn Alexander, a relative by marriage who worked in the barns with her grandpa for as long as she could remember. Finn was deaf and didn't hear her, so she waved to let him know she was present. She wandered further inside until she saw her grandpa. He was bending over one of the horses, its hoof resting in his hand. He looked up and a small smile of pleasure crossed his face. "Hey there, Lil."

"Hey, Gramps." She wandered closer, running her hand along the saddles that projected from a wall.

He stopped trimming the hoof of the horse and leaned back on his heels, looking up at her. Then he asked, "What's going on?"

"What do you mean?"

Standing up, he set down the file. "From the time you were a little girl, whenever something bothered you, I'd find you wandering in here and touching my saddles or playing with the horse tack until I asked you why."

"I did not. And I'm no longer little or young."

He laughed softly. "To me you are and always will be. So, what's going on, my girl?"

She took comfort in his kind words. His wrinkled, weathered, tough face reflected a compassion that was both gruff and constant. His red hair was faded to white at the age of seventy-two and he wore the same rough jeans, t-shirt, cowboy boots and hat as he did when she was a little girl. In a changing world, the steady image of her grandfather, in his looks and actions and even the timbre of his voice were as constant and predictable as the stars in the sky.

Jack was also correct. She felt like a child in need of a grownup's advice. She was lost in her thoughts and needed to be told what direction to take. What was best for her son? That was what mattered most.

"Well... yeah. I'm having a crisis of conscience."

"What's it about?"

"I... I don't know. I'll eventually figure it out."

"Clearly you will... eventually. That's why you're staring at the wall of saddles as if you've never seen a saddle before."

She could not repress a small smile.

He persisted as she hoped he would. "Out with it."

"It's… hard to talk about. To you."

"And yet you came here, knowing where to find me. On purpose."

Chagrined, she sighed. "Benny's father… I never told you who he was."

He gave her a crooked grin. "Well, I have some knowledge about that."

She freaking blushed, and cleared her throat. "Yes, right. But well, at the time, I didn't really know his father."

"Yes. I'm guessing that pertains somehow to something that happened today, after all this time. Until now, you've been more than careful not to discuss Benny's gene pool with me."

Blushing again, despite her age, Lillian replied, "He… Benny's dad just left here."

Her grandpa didn't gasp or even react to her information. He nodded only once. "You never knew how to find him, right? Not until this day."

"No, I didn't. I looked and tried to find him before Benny was born. And later, I just let go of any urge to tell his father because I moved on. I was prepared to have Benny alone. And with all the family situated right here, I had all the advantages and support to make it work. It has worked well. Even down to Grandma having him right now. I didn't tell Benny's father about him. I strongly persuaded him to get out of here. He said he was passing through, overheard the Rydell name and came to the ranch to see if I were one of the Rydells. He wasn't really searching for me or anything, except to say hello, I believe.

"I rejected his invitation for dinner, and he took it with grace and got the hint and left soon afterwards. I asked for his number to contact him later… and he didn't seem to think it odd. But I didn't tell him about Benny. The words got stuck in my throat. I don't know how he didn't sense something was wrong with me. But he didn't. He left, never knowing my secret even though it's something that might change his life forever. Or maybe he'd do nothing and never try to seek a relationship with Benny. But how could I know? I never really knew the guy, so I have no way of guessing or predicting how he'd react."

She all but wilted after the rush of words slipped free. Her strung-out emotions were visible. Grandpa nodded and she continued. "I don't know what he's like. He lives in Westport, next to the Pacific Ocean. He and his grandfather charter a fishing boat. He's not close-by at all. Doubt he would ever run into Benny, who looks just like him. How can I trust him with Benny? My son. A stranger who has no legal right to him? Poof. Am I supposed to accept that and suddenly share him if Matt's interested? How do I know what Matt's like? I don't even know him. What if he's a narcissistic asshole or a serial killer? Benny is only six. I can't risk his safety and health. His emotional wellbeing. He is fine. Just fine. No, he's great. With us. The fourth generation Rydell. He has Dad and you, Ian, Joey, and Charlie to fill the role of a father figure. He doesn't *need* a stranger intruding on his life just because he's being raised by a single mother. He has anything he desires in spades. He's happy. He's so happy. I am too. Why would I ever risk sinking that boat by inviting something I don't know anything about onto it? He's someone I don't know the first thing about. I just can't do that. And freaking A! The guilt is already gnawing at me. What if... Benny hates me in the future for doing that? Do I have the right to keep Benny's father from knowing him? What if... they both hate me for it?"

Exhaling a whoosh of breath, she plopped down on an overturned bucket near her. She finally glanced up at her grandpa. He came closer, grabbing another bucket and setting it near hers. "Well, that's a lot to mull over, huh?"

"Yes," she agreed. "I screwed up, Grandpa. Having a one-night stand that resulted in an unplanned pregnancy. Weren't you always shocked by me? You must have been appalled."

He chuckled and nodded. "Yes. But it didn't change you, not in my mind, Lil. You were and are a smart, funny, strong kid and then you became a woman. You inherited your mom's fire and strength; and you know how much I adore your mother. I helped bring you into this world. You were and are very special to me. So, of course, I wasn't appalled. I took it in stride because I completely trusted you to rise to the occasion and become the best mother. Just like your mother did. She had a hard time but rose above her situation."

"I guess they can't be too harsh in their opinions towards me."

"No. Ben did something wrong by leaving like he did. He had a lot to atone for, which he did and now, look at the family and life they built. Beginnings don't determine the whole story of the journey and they definitely cannot predict the end. Remember that."

"But shouldn't I tell Matt? Or should I just be silent and selfish and…"

His hand touched her shoulder. "Lillian, it isn't selfish to take a long pause, a few days or weeks, whatever you need to decide the best route to promote the safety and highest potential of your child. Of course, you shouldn't rush out and tell a stranger this. You rightly deserve all the time you need to evaluate the entire situation from all angles. It's exactly what I'd do."

Her guts twisted up and seemed to relax at receiving his permission to admit her doubts. Not knowing wasn't a bad thing. Tears streamed from her eyes. "I don't know what to do."

"I think that's what makes you both human and the best mother. You want Benny to live the best life he can, and you're willing to make a hard decision for you if it's best for him. But you don't have all the information yet to decide. So, of course, you need more time. And feeling guilty and unsure just means that you're the best mother you can be."

She leaned over and rested her head on her grandpa's shoulder. Taking in a deep breath, she said, "Thank you. I needed to hear exactly that. My head and heart are spinning and shooting mean thoughts, stabbing my own brain with so much indecision. But I dare not be wrong about this. Not when something is so important… or at least, it has the potential to be that important to Benny."

Jack leaned down and kissed the top of her head. "You should consider visiting where he lives. Get together with him. Check him out and see what he's like. What his life is like. What his family and friends are like. Get a better feel. Don't even contemplate telling him about Benny until you're convinced he isn't the culmination of your worst fears that you told me about. Or a terrible person who would try to sue you to take Benny from you. Understand this, being with you, his mother, will always be the primary factor in determining Benny's mental, physical and emotional health in general. So, it's perfectly legitimate if you choose not to tell this Matt person because he can't enhance Benny's life. If there's a chance he could make it worse or drastically different, fuck no. Don't tell him. You play it off by saying you were curious about dating him or something like that. Then you leave and never return; especially if the guy is anything less than what I expect from a man and a decent father."

She smiled and leaned her head against his arm. He was so sure. She relished his dose of confidence. "That is actually a perfect solution. It lessens my guilt without letting me ignore the shocking development in the situation. But you're right. I am the most important part of Benny's life right now, so if any person tried to take him from me in any way, then fuck him."

Grandpa patted her arm. "Exactly."

"I love you. You reveal the truth and also ease my awkwardness in this."

"You can always come to me for advice. If I ever get so old and senile, I can't support my kids or grandkids, well, then it's time to put me out to pasture."

"And say fuck with the best of them."

He chuckled. The first time he said that in her presence was when she was in her twenties. He shocked her at first, but she also knew she reached adulthood in Jack Rydell's eyes. He didn't swear around the kids, but he did with his sons and other adults. Now it was okay to do around her. She was one of his people. "Sometimes it's the best word to describe something."

"For this. Kind of. I can't believe this day."

"Matt, you said? What did he seem like?"

"Honestly? He was nice enough. Friendly. Asked if I were married or with anyone in particular and hinted that he'd leave right away if that were the case, considering our past… connection."

"There was a connection though?"

She groaned. "Oh, Grandpa…"

"Well… I'm still well aware of how biology works."

"I… yes…. I mean, I'd never have done what I did unless there was a strong connection. It came back today."

"Then maybe you should go and check him out. Interview him if necessary. Find out if he's worth introducing to your son. Don't give in from guilt. Tell him but only if it's absolutely clear that Benny's life will be better if he knows. I give

41

you my permission to make that decision for Benny. You know him. You be the judge as to who gets access to him. Even his father. For now, he doesn't know about him so it's no loss. And if someday Benny finds out about this, you tell him what I said."

She laughed. "Grandpa…"

He waved a hand. "Yeah… sure, I'll be dead. But you can still tell him…"

"Oh, don't even…" She shuddered against his strong and wiry physique. She could not imagine a day in the world without Jack Rydell being in it.

"If Mel did this, what I did, would you react so coolly?"

"I would. My son cheated on his wife and hightailed it out of here, leaving me to deliver his child. Forgiveness came easy to me, all of us make mistakes. Bad judgments. Lazy decisions even. Selfish actions too. It's what we do about them that matters. And look what you did with this, Lil."

She lifted her head and searched her grandpa's weathered, wrinkled, dear face. "You really mean that?"

"Always. Even after I'm dead. You remember that."

She nodded.

"I will. Always. But you will never die. You will live always… inside me forever. You know that, right?"

He turned her in a hug. For the first time since Matt showed up, her panic started to wane. Like a freaking spider, it climbed up her esophagus and lodged in her throat. She relaxed into Jack's arms, trusting his strength and guidance as always. He didn't say things she didn't believe were true. So, he must have believed in her. And what she said. He also admired her judgment.

"Now I should probably repeat this with my parents. Boldly reliving the embarrassing circumstances surrounding my child's conception."

"Well..." Her grandpa laughed outright. "Remember they better not cast stones, considering how they created you."

She laughed and let it sink in.

Grandpa Jack continued, "I know you'll make the right decision for you and Benny. Don't let your guilt con you into giving away any of your power. Okay? Only include this Matt if you're damn sure he will enhance Benny's life and not infringe on yours. That is number one priority. Guilt you can live with. Losing Benny to someone who doesn't deserve it? That's something you can't live with."

"Thank you. This is what I failed to say but fully intended to decide. You're right. Benny is the only priority. From there, I can live with anything."

"Exactly. I love you, Lillian Rydell."

"I love you too, Grandpa."

Lillian started to plot her strategy. Telling her parents, getting their support and advice and then making plans to visit the father of her child... But to what end? She had no clue yet. Two weeks later, she hired a trained professional to cover her vet practice and she set off to find out.

CHAPTER 4

$\mathcal{L}$ILLIAN KNOCKED THREE TIMES. Softly. She almost hoped no one would answer. But she'd come this far, enduring a gut ache for days to make the decision to come here. After traveling for half the day, she settled into a seaside motel, although she actually had not seen the ocean yet. The Pacific Ocean was something mystical and new to her.

She tracked his home address from his business card using GPS. She imagined how shocked he'd be when she suddenly arrived at the small, modest, square, one-story building. The neighborhood, if you could call it that, consisted of a long road, scattered with ramshackle properties, outbuildings and weather-worn residences. Most appeared to be built during the late nineteen sixties and early nineteen seventies. Some might have been constructed as late as the eighties, but they were all dated and looked tired. The one that matched the address on the card had blue paint, white shutters and a black roof. A small porch with barely enough room for two people to stand on it surrounded the front door. On each side of the door was a window.

The front door opened, and Lillian's heart thumped so hard she could have sworn she heard it. An elderly gentleman answered. *Granddad?* Most likely. If she were at the right address.

"Um… hello, I was looking for Mathias Griffin."

"He's out on the boat. Whom shall I say is asking?"

She hesitated, unwilling to answer or identify herself to a stranger. But she could not back down. She planned to meet up with Matt and feel him out. She had to search his life for clues about who he was and the caliber of person he could turn out to be. Only then could she make the great, huge decision of her life: revealing the truth that he was the father of her child.

Her heart sank at the mere thought of it. She fought the urge to turn around and leave. Granddad could describe her, although Matt wouldn't really know it was she that showed up here. She could go back home to the ranch and leave instructions that a man named Mathias Griffin was unwelcome there for the family and staff, including all of the workers of the ranch, resort, rescue, rentals and golf club. She knew they would adhere to her wishes. Matt would be forever banned from their world and her son would remain safe.

But… what about the plan?

She had to see.

"Um… my name is Lillian Rydell. Matt and I are old friends and I hoped he might want to grab a coffee with me as I just got into town…" Her voice drifted off. Granddad would not recognize her name… right?

"Oh? Well, come on in. Wait here. He should be back in less than an hour now. He's probably already back in port and most likely disembarking the clients and their catch, or else he's cleaning the boat up. Please…"

He swept open the front door and offered Lillian a

welcoming gesture with his palm up and a kind smile. He noticed her hesitation. "Oh. Pardon me. I'm Matt's granddad, the name is Jefferson Griffin. We bunk together. He was bringing home fresh crab for dinner, so I know he'll be here in no time at all."

She decided to take him at his word and stepped inside. She was at the right place and she knew it. Matt mentioned his beloved granddad to her that night—it was all she knew about him though. She had no doubt she was physically safe. "Thank you, Mr. Griffin. I hope I'm not interrupting you or anything?"

"No. Not at all. Just watching my daily dose of talk shows. Almost time for evening news. I enjoy staying informed and the talk shows discuss all kinds of stuff I never knew about back in my day. Come sit down. Please. If you don't mind keeping an old guy company."

She stepped over the threshold onto the linoleum square that served as the entryway. It led to the small living room. The floor was covered with worn, shaggy, dark carpet, and a matching dark couch that was lumpy and droopy in spots. A large coffee table made of particle board matched a single sidetable that was wedged between the couch and a brown recliner. Obviously, that was Granddad's spot. Lillian noticed a pile of magazines and novels sitting in a basket. A TV tray held various items ranging from a glass of water, to his spectacles, to a TV remote and a small flip phone. She detected a small limp on his right side when he walked. Dressed in dark slacks and a button-down shirt, he could have been ready to go to a town meeting or church rather than just sitting here. He sat down and indicated she should sit too.

"Please make yourself comfortable. I'd call Matt and tell him to come home now, but there are certain things you have to deal with on a charter boat. You can't just leave it all willy-nilly and expect someone else to take care of it later on."

"I don't mind waiting at all. I showed up here unannounced without any expectations he'd be at home, so already it's been a success since I got to meet you."

He beamed at her flattering comment. "So where do you know my grandson from?"

She described their introduction in more polite and pleasing terms, describing the college town bar from seven years before. Thank God, Granddad didn't press her as to why their one-time encounter would bring her there now. Obviously, there was more to the story, but Granddad gracefully turned the conversation to a more generic one, much to Lillian's relief. He was an articulate, well-spoken man. Delightful company, actually.

"Have you been downtown yet?"

"No. Not yet. I plan to go there though. I've never seen the Pacific Ocean, so I intend to do that too while in town."

His white eyebrows pushed upwards, and his mouth turned down. "You've never seen the ocean? Never been on it? Wow."

She bit her lip at his unmasked astonishment. "No. I grew up inland, on the other side of the Cascade Mountains. I visited the Puget Sound area before, which has salt water, but it was mostly calm without any waves or surf. I've never actually witnessed the open ocean or waves crashing on the beaches."

"My whole life was spent on it. I was more at home on a boat than in any house." He waved his hand to the building surrounding them. "Bought this for my bride, Mona, when we first got married. She needed roots and a place to raise our son, somewhere to call home. But I was always more comfortable out at sea, traveling on the open ocean."

"What did you do for a living? Were you chartering boats then as well?"

His smile was strong and sentimental. "Everything I could. There is probably no job I haven't been assigned to do on a ship. I became a sailor when I was sixteen and never left it. Mona dealt with my long trips at sea. But I had long stretches at home too. I think she gladly accepted it all in the end. I lost her about a decade ago. Then my health started to act up, and one hip had to be replaced… so now it's for sheer pleasure when I return to the ocean. Matt provides a lot of relief…"

His eyes sparkled with loving care. Okay, that was something important. He stood out as a moral compass for Matt. His grandfather obviously valued him. Immensely. And he also needed him. So, it wasn't likely Matt would ever leave this place. He had to remain in this area as the captain of a charter boat. Good God. What a clash to her life and environment. How much further apart could they have been?

"That sounds fascinating."

"Didn't seem so at the time. But I think it's fascinating you never saw the sea before. The power and sheer size of it with the endless pounding of the waves on the shore. It calls to the soul."

"Or urges one to stay more firmly rooted on the land. Rivers are more my speed. I feel more comfortable if I can touch the bottom, or at least see it. It's not so wide and vast that I can't fully see the other side of it or navigate through it. I grew up on a crystal clear, cool, fresh-water river, which is the next best thing to heaven. That's my kind of water feature. Controllable, smaller ripples, and narrow enough to see the other side."

"Oh, my girl. A river is like a wandering weed, while the ocean comprises an entire forest. Ahh, Matt will have to get you out on the open ocean to rewire you for your sea-legs."

His smile was good natured, and his tone was affable in his teasing.

She smiled, enjoying him immensely. "Sea-legs? Oh, I seriously doubt that. The thought of being on the open ocean with its infinite depth terrifies me. Never mind all the sharks, whales, and other dangerous creatures living there… no, thank you. I prefer the small trout and suckerfish that inhabit my dear, little river. That's enough underwater life for me. And the salt sticks to your skin, right? Isn't the water pretty cold here too?"

"Yeah, it is. Being the largest ocean in the world, it does get cold. But this is our mild season."

"Mild? We have to endure triple digits daily where I'm from during the month of July."

He shuddered. "Oh, no way does that happen here. The best we can hope for is cloudy skies and a high of sixty-five. That's nirvana for me and luckily, it happens quite often here."

Their conversation rambled on, alternating between comparisons and teasing. One-upping the other in stating the pros and cons of rivers and oceans. Until the front door opened.

Suddenly. Without any preamble or warning. No sound of a car pulling in or the garage door opening. It was like Matt teleported himself into the entryway.

Opening the door, he started to say, "Hey, Gr—"

But the words died on his tongue. His head shifted back a tiny amount, and the whites of his eyes widened. Glancing at his granddad and then at Lillian in amazement, Matt watched Lillian jump to her feet. Clasping her clammy hands together, she twisted her fingers and tried not to fidget. She smiled feebly.

"Lillian?" Matt said with undisguised shock in his tone.

"Hey… hi… yes. I—I hope it's okay that I stopped by…"

"Stopped by? Aren't you about three hundred miles from your home?"

"Yes... yes... um..." Glancing towards Granddad, who made a face at Matt, Lillian was speechless.

"Matt, she stopped by to see you. She must have had some business in the area. Don't be rude."

Matt's face immediately recovered from the shock, but a tiny bit of suspicion remained in his expression. He nodded and a smile touched his lips. "Right. Yes, you're right, Granddad. Welcome to our home, Lillian. It's a pleasant surprise."

It wasn't at all. But for Granddad, Matt concealed his alarm and displeasure. No, maybe not that bad, but his puzzlement persisted. She randomly showed up at his house after he got home from work. Yes, it was quite strange. She understood his hesitancy. Honestly, she'd be much more put off if he were *inside* her house. At least he approached their family business where guests and strangers were allowed. Not like her visit. She invaded his space. And met the most precious person in his life, his granddad.

Setting his mouth into a straight line, Matt did not welcome her but neither did he display his anger. His hesitancy bothered her. She had to do some mental dancing because it was weird she came there. Especially after the way she brushed him off at her place without making any plan to connect beyond the moments they shared on the deck of the resort check-in office. She didn't suggest seeing him again or anything. Her polite demeanor could not discount the sparks they both experienced, but not asking to see him again was pretty obvious.

Now, he comes home from work, more than two weeks later, and surprise! There she was with his granddad, in his house. Out of nowhere. Naturally, he felt suspicious and cautious, but most of all he was wondering *what the hell?*

No, she couldn't tell him the truth of her purpose for

being there. It made sense and could explain her presence at once, but she swiftly formulated an excuse in order to dance around the truth. She had to attend a conference in Olympia, and since he recently showed up at *her* ranch, he was still on her mind. Having never seen the ocean before and taking a week off for vacation, she spontaneously chose to spend it on the coastline, a mere few hours from where her conference took place. Yes, she probably overstepped her welcome in coming here. But here she was.

She hoped he wouldn't kick her out.

"Mrs. Rydell?"

"Doctor. It's actually Dr. Rydell," Matt corrected his granddad.

Granddad turned to her. "Really? You didn't mention that."

"Well, I don't insist upon it. I prefer you call me Lillian, actually."

"Doctor, huh?" Granddad's eyes gleamed. "That's most impressive."

"Doctor of veterinary medicine. Not humans."

"Well, it's just as impressive. What a wonderful calling."

"Thank you," Lillian replied, her tone as sincere as her smile. Granddad Griffin was a delightful man. Not at all like her Grandpa Jack, but his sincerity, quality and decency came through as clearly as a cowbell.

"Anyway, Dr. Rydell confessed she'd never seen the Pacific Ocean and of course, that means she never rode in a boat on it either. You'll just have to remedy that, Matt."

"Never?" His gaze landed on her. Strange shivers broke out over her skin. Crap, she was way too aware of his eyes on her.

"Never. No. Just the ocean at Puget Sound. I've never seen the open ocean, or waves or sandy beaches. Definitely never went out on it." She shuddered.

"Dr. Rydell was explaining to me the unique value of rivers and I was trying to describe the epic glory and vastness of being on the open ocean."

Matt entered the room further with a genuine laugh and his shoulders seemed to visibly release the tension when they dropped a few centimeters. Was he accepting her presence? Maybe. Mostly owing to Granddad's charm. The man was wonderful. Without him, she could not ignore her fear that Matt would not welcome her unexpected arrival.

Moving fully into the room, Matt looked more closely at Lillian and said, "So you were in the area? Or nearby, that's it?"

Oh, come on, Lillian, keep your game face on. Her nerves rippled inside her, but she kept a generic, pleasant smile on her face. Her glance darted away at the last moment and then came back. "Yes. Vacation. Had to attend a regional conference in Olympia. I drove out through the rain forest and decided as long as I was already this far, I should see the ocean up close and personally. Honestly, that's what really drew me here. I remembered the name of the town where you said you lived, Westport. It's just a short distance from there and well…" She let her statements drift off with a shrug as she pursed her lips and became pensive.

"Well, um… this is truly a shock. I didn't think I'd ever see you again." Matt's gaze dropped to Granddad before it returned to her.

"Well, neither did I, considering the distance. But strange circumstances drew me out this way… maybe you experienced the same thing when you dropped in on me." She gave him a subtle mental nudge.

He grinned finally. "True. I did do that."

"So, surprise. I did that." She replied in the same tone with an eyebrow lift… Yeah, Matt didn't miss that tiny flirtatious edge in her voice. God, what was it with her and him? She wasn't really a flirt, not usually. Rarely did she connect with men in any kind of romantic way. Her work demanded her professionalism at all times. There was no nonsense allowed during her examinations of animals. She dealt with pet owners, farmers, ranchers and everybody else, all the time. She could hold her own with any foul-mouthed, ill-tempered, cocky, know-it-all alpha male. She'd heard all of their insulting names and experienced plenty of condescension, so she knew exactly how to put such men in their place. She was small, but there was nothing petite or miniscule about her. Certainly not in her attitude, intelligence, mouth or self-confidence. But with this man? Those undeniable, damn flashes of chemistry and mutual flirting and… (oh, God help her!) girlie retorts, seductive smiles and brief eye-locks before looking away, occurred in just the few *minutes* they were together.

Right now, however, he could be her enemy and someone she needed to be very cautious around.

"So, I wondered if you'd mind maybe showing me your favorite beach? I can obviously find one myself, but it's more fun to do it with someone else. Perhaps we could get a coffee or something."

He glanced at her, studying her for a long time and gazing deeply into her eyes. Then his attention switched to his granddad and he asked him, "Do you mind eating alone tonight?"

She stiffened and interjected, "Oh, no. I didn't mean tonight. I wouldn't dream of asking you to change your dinner plans. Not without any notice and your granddad was so gracious…"

His granddad scoffed. "He'd rather gaze at your lovely, *young* face than my old, wrinkled one, which he sees almost every night. Go, you two. Have some fun tonight. It will do you good to see someone your own age for once. We'll have

53

that crab you brought home tomorrow night. There's all kinds of stuff in the freezer and I'm a mean microwave chef."

Granddad's reply suggested Matt didn't have a girlfriend. Or at least, no one he regularly saw. Good. Right? Wrong? She didn't know.

Matt smiled and replied, "Okay, if you're sure you'll be fine…"

"Always am, kiddo. Lord, you're not my babysitter. I'm not quite that senile yet."

He was easy to laugh with and Matt glanced at her. "Let me quickly change and wash up."

"Of course." She shifted around, suddenly uncomfortable with herself. In her usual Lillian Rydell mode, she would never have shown up unannounced at a stranger's house, or a near stranger and expect to eat dinner. Not without an invitation. Now here she was. She hated imposing on them like this.

Sitting back down, she waited quietly for Matt. He wore jeans and a sweatshirt that was well worn and very old. She caught the slight smell of… what? Sea life? Fish? However, it was not overwhelming.

He stepped around them before disappearing down the small hallway.

"My grandson is acting uncharacteristically bashful and confused. I think he might like you, Dr. Rydell, but don't tell him I told you that." He winked as he said it with a conspiratorial eyebrow wiggle. Lillian blushed. Did she actually want him to like her? No. Oh, no. She wasn't there to seek a boyfriend, or to flirt with him or even see the stupid beach in person. She came there solely for her son. And a chance to interview her son's father and see if he was the kind of man she approved of when it came to spending any time with her son. But her nerves felt strung out now, so she sort of forgot that.

In only fifteen minutes, Matt came out again. Freshly showered, she watched the moisture dripping from the dark brunette strands of his hair. His new clothes were a freshly laundered pair of jeans and a dark t-shirt. Handsome, casual, and refreshed. She still caught the earthy, work-weary look in his demeanor.

"Well, if you're ready to eat then..." he said with a quick glance at her and then away. She rose as he re-entered the living room.

"Thank you for the gracious welcome and delightful company," Lillian said to Granddad. There was no sucking up, and she was truly grateful and meant it. His kindness and warm greeting when he invited her to wait for Matt was reassuring. She was prepared to turn on her heel and run back to the car before driving straight home. But doing that would fuel her guilt to unbearable levels. This way, she'd know for sure whether or not to tell him. By the end of her trip, she would know if Benny's father deserved to meet his son.

Matt's granddad only made her more eager to find Matt. So, she thanked him for that.

Her stomach was roiling in knots as she followed her "date" out the front door.

CHAPTER 5

"WELL, IT'S NOT AS fancy as your car, but would you mind taking my truck?" Matt's words interrupted Lillian's fleeting, panicky thoughts.

Lillian let out a genuine laugh. "I grew up on a working horse ranch operated by my father and grandfather, so of course, I'm used to driving in trucks."

She settled into the cab and he started the ignition before shifting into reverse as he looked over his shoulder. She caught a glimpse of his well-sculpted profile, the slope of his nose and his thick eyelashes that were so long and black. Ooh... he was a handsome man. No wonder she made an exception to have her one and only one-night stand. Any indiscretion with this incredibly hot man would have tempted her.

Once on the street, he shifted into drive and she found herself unreasonably drawn to watching his exposed hairy forearms. They looked so strong and manly as he steered the vehicle. A simple action that rose to become a manly endeavor as if it were sexual foreplay.

No. No, it wasn't. She was on a reconnaissance mission

and she needed to keep that in focus and clear. Totally, one hundred percent, crystal clear.

"So, you've never caught seafood from the ocean; do you enjoy eating it?" His question shattered the few seconds of quiet during which she was gawking at his freaking forearms.

"Um… well, no. I don't really enjoy eating any type of meat, from fish or other animals in general." Regret seeped into her tone. She knew how her preference toward vegan dining offended some people. Growing up, it was usually met with a groan and an annoyed eye-roll like *oh, you're one of those.* "Animals… well, they're my thing. I became a vet because I like to help and save and nurture them. I treat farm animals, of course, who are later slaughtered, but I try to provide them the healthiest life possible. I wish I could save all of them. Wildlife too. I just can't—"

"Eat them," he finished, nodding as he added, "that makes sense. So no to the seafood. How about getting deli sandwiches? You can order the vegetarian alternative."

"Oh." She was startled when he didn't roll his eyes or say a snarky comment, especially since he fished for a living. He caught and killed fish for clients. Fishing was an experience he used as a commodity to sell, so she expected him to reply with more disdain.

"Aren't you bothered by that?"

"Being a vegetarian? Well, no. I'm glad not all people are, or I'd be out of business. But I respect your choice."

"Thank you." She nodded and gave him a grateful, genuinely glad smile. "But I don't mind going to wherever you were thinking. I can always choose a salad or noodles or something. I swear. I'm not that difficult. I can handle seeing you eat meat too. I just can't."

"I appreciate that. If you're sure you're okay, it's a pretty spot that overlooks the marina. And it's very close to an ocean beach. If we time it right, you can watch the sunset and catch your first glimpse of what my granddad was trying to describe to you."

Wow, it sounded so romantic. No, spontaneous. Strange to be doing this. He was awfully quick on his feet to suggest that.

"I'm sorry to spring this on you. Are you sure you don't mind? We don't have to, you know, hang out together."

"I reached out first, right? I really didn't feel welcome and assumed I'd never see you again."

"I was just startled. That's putting it mildly. And honestly? I was also a little embarrassed. My whole family lives there and if they found out I once…" Her throat went dry, and she had to cough. Her nerves were ragged, and heat filled her cheeks. NO! She should not be this way. She simply had sex with this man. Years ago. Consensual, wonderful sex. But now, her hot sensations were rooted in embarrassment.

"Yes. I expected it to be startling. But I failed to see how much so."

"Unwelcome too?"

He slid a glance at her. "No. No, it wasn't."

"Do you think your granddad figured out we were a little more than old friends?"

"Maybe. But I doubt he cared. Or even bothered to contemplate it. Are we? Old friends, I mean?"

Blunt honesty. She remembered Matt often just stated things, even hard things to talk about and he didn't shy away now. She liked his honesty. Usually, in a pickup situation, people tried to appear charming and used games and lies to achieve their ends. Matt was friendly and honest. Perhaps just at this moment.

"I don't have a clue. It feels peculiar between us. Strangers, but…"

"But… yeah… we share a history."

"A history," she repeated with a glance his way and then back out the window. "You must realize that I don't do that. Usually. Never, actually."

"It might be hard for you to believe, but neither do I, which was why I remembered your name so clearly."

"I remembered yours just as clearly." She only conceived a son with him and tried to find him for several months. But did he remember her fondly? And their one night together? She really liked to think he did; especially since he had no reason to recall anything about her.

He pulled into a parking lot before a single-story building with glass front doors and huge windows that was obviously the restaurant. "Would you like to wander around the marina first or would you rather eat?"

"I would like to walk and see the marina. I really would." She hoped it might calm her nerves.

Wearing heeled black boots, she didn't anticipate doing much walking and hoped no blisters would form. Circling the building, Lillian got her first view of Westport Marina. It could have been featured on a postcard. At six o'clock, the hot sun was angled in the sky and reflected by the still water. The sky was a soft, pixie blue, not the bright, harsh, searing blue summer sky she knew at home. The street hugged the large marina, with bike paths and trails for pedestrians. There was a large, rock jetty that stretched as far as she could see. Rows of docks were lined up, giving it a street-like vibe except the large vessels that floated on the water replaced the cars. The docks were labeled alphabetically.

Each had a slanting gangplank that connected it from the street down to the docks. The edge of the harbor had countless slips and mooring spaces along it. Staring out at what seemed to be mostly personal watercrafts and small charter boats, Lillian was impressed. She saw several incredible sailing yachts with their large masts pointing high and standing out amidst the smaller sailboats. She had no clue how many kinds of boats there were. A large observation tower stood at the far end of the docks, butting up to the rock jetty that surrounded the harbor. It protected the anchored vessels from the pounding waves. The rumble of the waves on the shore was audible although Lillian couldn't yet see them.

That was what the ocean sounded like? That beastly roar? A thunderous rhythm of unbridled power? She knew what ocean surf looked like from movies and photographs. But hearing that visceral crashing on the shore stimulated all of her senses. The air seemed heavier and the saltiness and unfamiliar scents that were both foreign and pleasant drifted towards her. She was reminded of the seafood section at the grocery store, but it was not as overpowering. Seagulls perched and flew, landing on the docks and boats with unending movement. The boats dipped gently up and down as the small waves lapped their sides.

One entire side of the street had gangplanks, going down as far as she could see. The other side of the street was peppered with businesses and shops. Lillian walked down a large, wide sidewalk with symmetrically placed planter boxes, brimming with colorful flowers. The light poles that rose up from them held American flags that flapped in the gentle breeze. It was attractively quaint and idyllic when the afternoon sun made it glow with a golden sheen.

"Wow, this is unbelievably beautiful." Lifting her eyes from the exciting scenes before her, she glanced at her escort. Matt gave her a nod and his eyes gleamed with approval of her.

"I think so. For a small seaport, they've done a good job at making it pleasant and picturesque to draw in the tourists. You can't miss all the RV camping and motels on the neighboring streets. There are endless miles of beaches and several access points, including this marina, and all are within walking distance."

"You keep your ship anchored here?"

He tried hard not to smile and had to bite his lip to keep the laughter contained, but it still came out as an odd marriage between a snort and a grunt. She realized at once she said something wrong but wondered what it was.

"Um… I have a boat. And ships are much bigger vessels than what I have."

She let out a laugh. "Oh, like those cruise and cargo ships I've seen advertised on TV?"

"Yes."

"I feel like a green newbie."

He shook his head. "How could you know? You never did this before, right? You never saw the ocean and the seaside, so you probably never heard the lingo."

"No." She ducked her head when a little blush heated her cheeks.

"Imagine all the stuff I don't know about animal care that you take for granted. If we had a contest for general knowledge, we both know you'd far outscore me, so don't feel embarrassed. And ask away. There is nothing you can ask me that I wasn't asked before. And unlike most rookies, you are super intelligent so whatever question you come up with would make perfect sense." He then nudged her. "But yeah, to your original question my boat is moored on Pier D right over there. The one with our last name on it."

Her gaze scanned to where he pointed. Immediately she noticed the large, white boat with Griffin Family Charters written on the side of it. It had an enclosed cabin with multiple length antennae rising high up into the sky off of the cabin's rooftop. The front of the boat had a silver rail around it, and the back was a large open deck. There were three separate motors hanging off the back, two large and one smaller. It seemed an impressive boat.

But to spend all day fishing with strangers in that space would be tight quarters. She turned to him, head tilted and asked, "Wow. That is bigger than I could ever imagine handling. But you must get along well with people then? I never thought about it before, but your job requires that you have daily new client interactions."

"I do. Most of the time. Sometimes, I get repeat customers, but most of them are new. And I guess I'm not too terrible or I couldn't stay in business. The grizzled, old fisherman you see in movies won't do. I gotta be charming and engaging with my clients in order to make them feel welcome. We're thrown together in such a small space; we instantly have to cope with the cramped quarters, so you have to start talking and interacting. Then once we get out to the fishing spots, my clients are usually seasick, scared, or elated. Some claim to be having the time of their lives. I have to reciprocate their attitudes when I'm out there. But once we start catching fish, it's an instant ice breaker. I don't know what spawns it but using teamwork to extract a magnificent creature from the deep, rolling seas is something that makes people bond. They all say the exact same things. Honestly, I could play a video and record their common reactions. It's the best part of the job. The worst are the seasick clients who fail to respond to the seasick pills. They kind of hate me during the entire trip. Nothing I can do about that. But some of them look at me as if I'm Poseidon, the god of the sea. Some want to fulfill a lifelong dream of catching a certain fish or a certain size of fish. Others just like to be out on the open ocean."

He glanced at her and then away, rubbing a hand on the back of his neck. "I, uh, guess I am overly chatty from habit. Never realized it before."

She couldn't restrain the warm, huge grin that split her face in two. "I love hearing that you enjoy your job so much. You create special experiences that people can check off their bucket-list items or just throw up and feel miserable. So, your career is unique and interesting as well as ever changing. And apparently, you really do love it."

He gave her a grateful look. "I do enjoy it. At least you didn't laugh and snort like I did when you said I owned a ship. I'm sorry about that. I didn't mean to react that way, but it was so adorable coming from you. Not the first time I've had to make the distinction, but it always makes me smile when people call my boat a ship."

"Laugh then," she replied with her own huge smile.

He shook his head and a boyish grin appeared on his face. "Right. Laugh. Should we go eat and then I'll introduce you to the Pacific Ocean?"

"Yes!" she agreed, hating her enthusiasm for the plan. She dreaded what was next to come. Sitting down to talk some more to this man like it was the best first date ever was not her intention.

Oh, no. What was she doing? This was a reconnaissance mission. This was stealth-mode espionage. Not a freaking date. But her heart skipped with anticipation as they walked side-by-side and his hand grazed hers. Barely touching, but heaven help her if she couldn't feel the heat coming off it.

They walked into the dark entry of the restaurant. It was better than Lillian expected with dim lighting and deep, subdued colors for dramatic impact. The hostess asked them to follow her further into the room. Tables were set with crisp, white tablecloths and the high-backed booths created the illusion of privacy. They were seated beside the large windows that overlooked the marina. It was very pretty and somewhat romantic.

Sliding into their seats, they each took their menu and waited for the busboy to pour ice water in their glasses.

They both perused the menu choices and Matt set his menu aside before she did. Then they smiled over the place settings and the expensive glassware that caught the candlelight from the low votives. The ambiance told her it wasn't a cheap place and her guilt pained her. This wasn't a date. She showed up on a workday out of nowhere. Literally. And he was so kind as to bring her here? His response and greeting were so much nicer than what she gave him.

Matt had to deal with the public on a daily basis and his easy-going, sincerity and charm made it hard to find fault with his attitude and demeanor. She was encouraged by that, but it was no guarantee. One never knew the inner motivations of someone else, even the most pleasant, polite, funny, and genuine ones.

"Did you find a vegetarian option?"

"Yes, I'll have a simple chef salad without the bacon and ham bits. What about you?"

"Oh… the fettuccine sounds good."

"The seafood combo?"

"Nah. The plain sounds nicer."

He didn't choose the seafood he no doubt brought her here to sample and which she would probably have appreciated and loved. Given his profession and their location, sampling the local seafood would be the usual date. But not for her. Not for someone who didn't eat any of it.

"You can order seafood fettuccine. I don't expect anyone to avoid eating their true preferences in front of me if they have no problem accepting my preference."

He shrugged but gave her a warm, knowing smile. He was doing it only for her. Unusually sweet. "Nah. I just feel like it right now." He rested his elbows on the table and leaned a few inches forward to take the glass of ice water and sip it.

His gaze stayed glued to her face. He seemed to scan and memorize it. It should have made her uncomfortable, being too intense, and too knowing. But damn it. Lillian was doing the exact same thing.

He was so symmetrical in his build. She studied the slashes of dark eyebrows over his thick, dark eyelashes and the bright brown of his eyes and wide Roman nose. His high cheekbones and slender jaw were very masculine. But his crowning glory? That was the thing that first attracted her to Matt and what she adored about her son. Swirls of chestnut ringlets adorned Benny's little head. They twirled and flopped through her fingers and now she literally itched to dig into Matt's hair and grip the strands as she tugged his face—

No. Oh, no. She had to banish such thoughts. She was losing her grip on herself.

Yeah, anyway, she really liked Matt's curls. And her son's adorable ringlets melted her heart. Matt was the adult, mature version of her son's strong features and it was so uncanny to see that, which was why she couldn't stop staring. So rare and unique. Good God. Matt's gene pool must have been very dominant because he created a tiny replica of himself in their son.

Their son.

She grabbed the glass of ice water and downed two large gulps as the thought spun around her head with far too much power and magnitude than she preferred. Here she sat, enjoying a lovely restaurant and harbor view with her child's father. Technically, they were parents, yet he didn't know. The truth was both cruel and terrifying. To her. Cruel that she knew and he didn't. And meeting Benny was knowing her true purpose in life. It was also terrifying if she read him wrong. What if he was performing the charming niceties to conceal the inner asshole or even a child predator?

Not that she suspected that, but her nerves were so scattered that she didn't know. And before she could reveal Benny to him, she simply had to be sure. So, she sipped her ice water and swallowed and stayed silent.

She couldn't resist marveling how much their son resembled Matt.

God help her. A sweeping warmth started in her stomach, filling her up and flowing like warm honey throughout her entire body.

"So, if I remember correctly…" The urge to speak was prompted by the reminder that although Matt remained a damn stranger, she had sex with him and gave birth to his child. She kept her gaze fastened on his face. She refused to allow the images of his naked body fill her mind. Was he doing the same? Or letting those images run rampant?

So. Damn. Awkward.

"If you remember…" When she drifted off to her past thoughts, he prodded her, "You were saying, Lillian?"

"Right. If I remember correctly, you were still unsure about what to do with your life when I met you. I honestly assumed you were a student at the same school I attended. I only realized later you were not. You weren't working as a charter boat captain back then since you didn't talk about it. I assume that decision came later."

"You… you looked for me? And thought I was a student on campus?" His head tilted as his voice warmed with more pleasure and interest.

Her skin sizzled in what felt like a hot sheen. She worried that it was probably obvious to him. Lowering her gaze to the place setting before her, she nodded. "I did. But there was no Mathew Griffin enrolled there. When I realized I never asked how to contact you and had no other details except your name, I felt so lazy and stupid for not asking the most basic information, like where are you from?"

"Same here. We talked about so much that night but avoided the most direct and obvious topics. When you left so abruptly, I figured you probably regretted it and never wanted to know more about me anyway. I could have found you right off since you were enrolled at WSU, or at least I believed that. The thought crossed my mind several times, but my insecurity always stopped me. What if you hated me? Or really didn't want to hear from me?"

Didn't she know it?! The re-runs of that night haunted her mind for years. She kept looking for hints or clues as her guilt and confusion over what to do with an unexpected pregnancy and imminent baby crippled her. At the time, she believed it was hopeless, like looking for a needle in a haystack, so she let it go. But abandoning her search was never easy or guilt-free.

And now, here she was.

"I'm sorry I did that. I freaked out. It was not… my usual response. First one-night stand for twenty-three-year-old me. I usually avoid bar pickups actually, and never went there for any hookups. I freaked out and left, but later realized I did want to see you again despite the shocking results."

"It was pretty shocking to me too. I wanted to see you again too, but my insecurity kept me from doing that. I find it soothing to my ego now that you felt the connection too and didn't have regrets about it."

They shared a swift glance at each other before they both looked away. She wondered what all these snippets from the past meant. They had a little connection, besides the son they created that night, but talking and spending time together were nothing to base her hopes on. They weren't anything at all except perhaps a segue to a second date.

She kept her gaze on the flickering votive candle. "I felt it too. It confused me since I don't often experience such things."

Quiet descended on them for a moment and he cleared his throat. "So back to the start. When I met you at twenty-three, I was traveling around aimlessly, doing nothing. Visiting friends in the area. Figuring out my life. After leaving high school, I knew I wasn't programmed for four more years of education. I considered several trade schools but never fully committed to any. I was working odd jobs to figure out what I might want to do in the way of a career. I was born and raised in the house I now share with my granddad. My grandparents raised me. I was a late bloomer in my rebellion and being relegated to the charter boat business by my granddad was not encouraging to me at the time. It seemed... so common. By never leaving the town I was born and raised in, I could only wonder how to seek broader horizons. So, I decided to pursue a new life."

"Did it work? I get the small-town-confinement thing. My small town is far smaller than yours, even. But my perspective widened in college. I spent time away off and on for eight years. I never stopped planning to return home again, however. Practicing vet medicine on my family ranch with my dad and grandpa were a lifelong dream."

"Your family ranch is a five-star resort and golf course. It's a freaking destination travel place. Not exactly the kind of ranch I was expecting. I'm sure I wouldn't have dared come there to find you if I realized where you actually lived."

She let out a laugh that loosened her nerves. "True. So many people don't know what a ranch means... and being on the Rydell River is everything. My grandpa and his brothers expanded it to accommodate their own needs and desires, and the needs of a growing family. They always had hopes some of us would return to work there in varying capacities. Our family business was one we all expected to keep expanding and growing. My grandfather, Jack Rydell, is the patriarch and the one who least likes change, but his vision wasn't just about him. He realized that what fails to grow eventually dies so he sacrificed his own desires for us."

"Sounds like quite a man."

"He is." She smiled at her glass of water before dousing her parched throat. "A lot like your granddad. Family businesses need to be passed down and all that to the loyal grandkids."

"Yes. But he has only me and we have only each other. We are not wealthy either, and barely scrape by. So, not quite the same."

"I meant, his strength of character. It was obvious to me when I met your grandpa."

"Yes. True. He has that in spades."

"Yes, and wealth doesn't determine the character of a man or a person, I should say. Having money or not having it does not determine what any person is or becomes. Not in my experience anyway."

"Oh, how true that is. Assholes are rich and poor. Been my experience as well."

She smiled at his tone. "And are you an asshole?"

He leaned back and crossed his arms over his chest. "Well, I think I might have been one when I first met you. I was searching for a career and disdainful of my lot in life. A smelly fishing boat was all my future held? Being the bait boy for more than a decade, I kept thinking there had to be a better life for me. I provoked a fight with my granddad, which was a terrible thing to do. He always worked so hard, and I was so ungrateful... well, that's water under the bridge, but I left for a year. I traveled down the coast of Oregon and came up through Eastern Oregon to end up in Pullman that night we met. I believed I was searching for much more than a life like Granddad's and damn! I was surprised that you even gave me the time of day. Barely a month later, Granddad had a heart attack. It was a mild one, and he's taken better care of himself since then. But when the ER doctor called me to say my grandfather had a heart attack, well, that snapped my entire life back into focus."

"Oh my God, how scary."

"I knew Granddad needed me and that was where I belonged. Westport and the boat. I came home, nursed him back to health, and he fully taught me the business and being the boat captain. Ever so slowly, he shifted all the responsibility to me. From then on, I valued and cherished every lesson he gave me. I absorbed his vast experience from spending decades on the ocean. I lived each day, worrying that his heart would fail, but he fully recuperated. When I was twenty-six I took full charge of the boat and the business. I was finally reassured he wouldn't die on my watch and I relaxed slightly, but I still remain close and worry about him. He is everything to me. He's all I have."

That story of devotion to his granddad, despite his desire to seek unknown horizons, was totally understandable. Any youth feels the urge to pull away from their roots and discover new pastures. It was a plus to her. It showed his curiosity about life, much more than he could see or articulate. His intelligence motivated him to find his own path, but he recognized the precious roots where he came from and the place he already had. Plus, his heart made him come back home to care for his elderly granddad, just as his granddad cared for him as a child.

Matt instantly scored several points. All from asking if he were an asshole. And his answer reflected his high standards for honesty and compassion.

There was something very likeable about him.

"Can I ask what happened to your parents? No siblings? Aunts, uncles or cousins?"

"Of course, you can ask. Those are pretty normal questions. No siblings that I know of. My father was an only child. So, no cousins. I had a small family. My mom never factored into it. I never knew her. My dad was… flaky. An asshole who tried to find himself and never did. He left me with his parents, who raised me. Randomly, he'd show up at times. But the thing was: I had no desire to be his son. I know some sons would have tried to build a relationship just because he was their father. But I considered my grandparents were the only parents I had. He was just a jerk who randomly appeared for a few days, pretending to care, trying to be fun, buying me frivolous things and ice cream before he disappeared. Even as a young child, he never impressed me. He wasn't an honest person… ever. My grandparents were the steady rocks in my life. They were heartbroken by his callous behavior and lack of character. The deadbeat he turned out to be was his own choice. I never cared. I think maybe I helped alleviate some of the pain they endured from his total lack of empathy."

"That's beautiful they did that and always supported you."

"Yes. They were amazing. It was tough losing my grandma, and Granddad became everything to me. I was scared sometimes. You know, having only one older man for a family. And if he suddenly died like Grandma did, I would be all alone. What a big, scary thought. Instead of feeling closer to him, I think I tried to avoid him in my effort to ignore my pain and grief at losing Grandma."

The server came just then and placed their plates before them. After exchanging some niceties, she discreetly left. Lillian and Matt politely set the linen napkins on their laps and grabbed their forks. Exchanging smiles before they each took a bite of their vegetarian meals, Lillian thought Matt was sweet to do so in honor of her preference. Yeah, she definitely noticed it.

"Wow, this is great. The dressing is so tangy."

"They serve the best food here. So, it's not surprising."

They ate in companionable silence for a few moments. Then he asked, "So, what about you? You went to vet school and moved home after earning your degree? Any family or kids for you?"

"Umm, yes, I finished school and moved home. It took a lot of time and energy to set up my practice. I'm still establishing myself. The area isn't... well, progress is a bit slower out there. Sometimes I wonder if we're a whole decade behind other towns. I still surprise my clients when I show up and they realize that Dr. Rydell is, in fact, *a woman* as if it's a brand-new concept. But I'm used to disproving all the stereotypes." She hoped he ignored her swift avoidance of answering his inquiry about kids.

"That's hard. And pretty amazing."

"I've been too busy for personal relationships or even a hobby. I ride horses a lot for exercise when I'm not treating them. My grandpa is Jack Rydell, and he still rescues them. I also swim in the river quite often, like now, when it's so hot in the afternoons. But my life is pretty quiet, other than my interactions with family and childhood friends. My family is huge, kind of like being a whole city of people. Family reunions are a freaking trip, I'll tell you that."

"I can't imagine having that much family. Do you love it? Or do you find it stifling and overwhelming?"

"I guess I must love it because I came back to it. I don't ever think of it as being something to deal with. It just is what it is. Does that make any sense?"

"It does."

"Any outside relationships for you? Other than you and your granddad?"

He winced. "I hate to admit it but I'm kind of a date killer. Most of the time. Looking after Granddad has ended more dates than I can count. And what else can I do? He's my only family. I live in his house, but he calls it ours. He needs me now and there's no way I'd ever put him in an assisted living arrangement. No one else is qualified to take care of him. Ever. Period. Just me." He sighed. "So how can I pursue a relationship? Most women my age don't want to hang out with a former fishing boat captain in his seventies. So, I doubt I'll have a relationship anytime soon, not in my youth. But I do have hobbies and the boat keeps me busy. So, it's fine. I didn't grow up with a big family around me, so I don't know what it's like. I guess it's hard to miss what I never had. But I've always relied on Granddad and I'll take care of him until he leaves this world for the next. Always. End of story."

That was the most beautiful summation of a life she could imagine from a person their age. Matt showed grit, determination, integrity, strength, selflessness, and mostly love. It was the definition of unconditional love. Her heart began to melt in her chest. God. If he were half as wonderful as she sensed he was, Benny would be lucky to have him in his life.

And Matt would be lucky to have Benny in his too. He had no one but his granddad. He was unprepared for a woman, much less kids. He already had a kid. How could she deny him the truth when he showed so much devotion for his only relative?

But he lived in Westport with his granddad and that wasn't changing. He had to be beside the ocean because his business relied on it. His business was his legacy, which meant as much as the Rydell River Ranch did to Lillian. She couldn't begin to fathom the logistics required if she did decide to share her secret. Her stupid secret. She hated being that woman. One with a secret. Someone with ulterior motives. Matt seemed thus far honest, genuine, open, and transparent. Mostly, he was decent. So damn decent.

His business required him to have a boat and the ocean close by. How could she manage to ever make it work? Lillian required the Rydell River Ranch as her source of income and stability. They were hundreds of miles apart. She could not let her son be that far from her. Ever. Despite all of this man's genuine goodness.

Her guilt gnawed at her. She knew he deserved to know about his son. The only reason he wasn't engaging in her son's life was because he didn't know him. She knew, after this one evening, if Matt had known she was pregnant, he'd have tried to participate in his child's life from the very first, no matter what his relationship with Lillian was like.

Oh, shit. When did the chance to tell him about Benny become she *hadn't told him yet*?

The meal continued and they discussed the seven years since they last saw each other. They wandered over various subjects. Finally, the bill came, and Matt paid it without any hesitation. Then he gestured for her to rise. "Would you like to see the Pacific Ocean now?"

His grin was huge, and she could see he was thrilled to be doing this. He made it into such a grand gesture that she could imagine the excitement he would have in showing it to his son.

No. She could not romanticize the situation. Her interest in seeing her son develop a relationship with his father was still a fantasy that sounded idyllic. Average. Ordinary. Like everyone else. Unlike most others, however, she didn't really know her son's father. Not well enough to trust him. When and how the day would come when she could trust him enough to tell him the truth remained a mystery. She had a whole freaking week, which was laughable if she seriously considered risking the safety and custody of her son in only a week's time.

Matt charmed her after one meal. God, what did that mean? It was too much, too soon, just as their one and only night together was.

And look at how that ended up.

CHAPTER 6

S HAKING HER HEAD AT her internal terrifying thoughts, Lillian tuned back into Matt's question. "Yes, I can't wait. Let's go."

They rose to their feet. He gestured for her to walk first and followed her out. Once they were on the street, he said, "Let's leave the truck here. It's just a short walk."

Ambling down the sidewalk, the minimal traffic passed them along with several people. Coming up to the tall rock jetty, she stared and asked, "How many dump-truck loads of rock do you think it must have taken to build this jetty? Each rock is a quarter of the size of the truck."

"I can't even imagine how many," he agreed. "You want to walk down that way or climb up here?"

"Climb up here, of course." She grinned and he grinned back, flashing his teeth and a dimple of unconcealed pleasure at her answer.

They jumped from one large, jagged, black boulder to the next. The rocks fitted snugly to make a giant, solid wall that stood staunchly against the ever-pounding surf. The rock wall ran for miles. She could feel the vibration with each smacking crash of waves on the opposite side. The whoosh and crackles of spray from the relentless surf cooled her face and arms. The sky overhead was fading in color as the twilight settled in. It was a vibrant mix of blues. Finally, they managed to climb to the top and found a flat rock to stand on. She gazed out at the massive body of water and watched the swirling backwash flowing out, hitting another wave, cresting with foam and white-tipped spray before hurling into the jetty wall. The spray was a brilliant splash of water that sparkled in the sky. The intense sound and vibrations of raw energy seemed to climb up her body with each successive, rhythmic wave. To her left, the surf retreated to reveal a curved, sandy beach. It wasn't too long and would have taken perhaps twenty minutes to walk before ending in more jetty rock. Across the massive waterway, she spotted what looked like board game-pieces, but they were buildings. They were so small and minuscule, they appeared to be flat on the water.

The sun shone like a coin dipping into the sea where the ocean and sky met. Round, streaming, golden, wavering lines rippled across the shimmering water towards them.

"So magnificent," she finally said after a few quiet moments of appreciating the colors and water displayed before them.

"You know this isn't the real ocean, right?"

"What?"

He grinned. "The open ocean and surf are over that way. This is Gray's Harbor, a place where the deep water of the Pacific Ocean meets the shallower water of the harbor. The jetty works as the breakwater to protect the harbor. From the air, it looks like arms reaching out into the ocean or a spider-web that circles the whole harbor."

"What are the lights across there?" She pointed toward the flat expanse of water.

"That's a small spit connected to the mainland called Point Brown."

"It's pretty incredible."

"It is. Want to walk on the beach?"

"Sure."

They wandered into the deep, sinking sand. Splotches of sea grass and driftwood lined the light brown, soft sand. Waves crested and crashed as the sky's myriad colors reflected on the water surface. Daylight seeped away slowly, and the darkness descended. Still their conversation continued, filling the space between them with happy energy. It was a bond that surprised as well as delighted her.

They reached the far end of the small cove. "Beyond this sandbar lies the open waters of the Pacific Ocean. There're probably some surfers out there now."

"Surfers? Wouldn't it be freezing?"

"They wear wetsuits. Usually, it's quite crowded right along the jetty."

They walked to the far end of the beach, where yet another jetty wall jutted out into the ocean. Waves climbed and peaked, splashing down on both sides of the rock wall. This arm of the wall continued further out to sea. The open ocean lay on one side and Gray's Harbor on the other. She couldn't imagine the engineering required to build such a wall. It reminded her of a huge, grasping hand, clawing through the waves. On the left, the tall waves resounded down the long, sandy beach of the Pacific Ocean. Only a handful of people still walked or gazed out towards it. A few brave figures bobbed in the sunset's reflection on the water, the surfers Matt spoke of. The beach was a huge expanse of wind-swept grasses and sand dunes that extended as far inland as she could spy from this viewpoint.

The shorebreak made huge, loud, vibrational sounds that were much more ominous and intimidating than the ones that hit the inner harbor jetty. The wind tossed her hair, and the twilight seemed to linger over the water.

"That's Grayland Beach State Park. No overnight camping, but you'll find tons of pedestrians, sightseers and surfers who park down there and occupy the entire area. You can see why they come here with such a spectacular view and cozy ambiance."

"You can say that again. The Pacific Ocean is much more than anyone advertises."

"Good, huh?"

She tilted her head and found him watching her, not the view. He radiated an appreciation for her that she found in nature. "No, much better than good, it's great," she said as their gazes got hung up on each other. That energy between them was just as seismic as the waves that seemed to be temporarily suspended before they crashed on the sandy shoreline.

They stood together, staring out and watching the swells. Eventually, the surfers left as the sky lost all of its color and the twilight became too dark to see.

Sitting down on one of the large jetty boulders, they let their feet dangle. They sat very close with their butts only a few inches apart and their knees touching. They were quiet for a long while, both relishing the moment, she suspected, but mostly each other. She set her hand on the rock beside her and it only took a few moments before his slipped on top of hers. It was a soft, subtle gesture and very natural. She could have easily and gently freed her hand without much movement. But she didn't. She left her hand inside the gentle arch of his warm palm.

She was breathless and full of anticipation. An encompassing warmth and sense of pleasure and excitement overcame Lillian. From absolutely nothing. The seaside sunset was simply being shared with a man. A man whose hand seemed to scorch hers with its intense heat. It was so ridiculous.

But not imagined.

Same heat. Same energy. Same state of confusion. That was exactly how it happened when they were twenty-three.

Luckily, the hormonal, impulsive, lustful girl she was that night was seven years older now and wiser. She wouldn't act it out again, but she couldn't deny wanting to.

To mask her emotional urges, she remarked idly, "I never pictured surfers in Washington State."

"Southern California, Florida and the Gulf of Mexico are the first places you expect to see surfers, huh? But they're here too. They are all wearing extra-thick wet suits; since it's the Northern Pacific and icy cold. They surf almost all year round. I never got into it. I prefer being *on* the water, controlling where *I go* on it, not being tumbled around like a washing machine, never knowing which way is up. I have a few friends whose kids surf. They love it. Most get a bit fanatical about it."

A shiver traveled up her spine. He glanced at her, feeling it also. "Cold?"

"Getting chilly now that the sun is gone. At home, it's at least ten degrees warmer. We get the extremes, both cold and hot. So, I'm used to cold temperatures. But this is like a slow chill, fading into somewhere in between."

He chuckled. "Yes, the ocean air can't compete with dry heat, and can be very harsh at times. Even temperate climates dip down pretty low and go up in a swoop. Our average temperature is mid-seventies in the summer and mid-thirties in the winter."

"Does it rain as much as I've heard?"

He released her and rose to his feet, turning to offer his hand to pull her up. They were facing each other and staring too long when they spoke. Closer too. So much closer now. "Not sure what you heard, but yes, it rains a lot. More than half the year. The rest of the time, it's foggy and gray. Seeing the sun is glorious and its effect is greatly appreciated by all the residents. You can see how the abundance of rain makes everything sparkly clean. But the flip side is we have a lot of darker days and lingering clouds."

She shuddered. "I hate clouds. And rain."

He laughed. "I hate extreme heat and extreme cold."

"Dear God, how can people enjoy this weather?"

"Oh, sixty-five degrees and partly cloudy is my sweet spot."

She cringed as she rolled her eyes. "That's exactly what your granddad said. It must be hereditary. No way for me. Sunny skies and eighty degrees at least is my idea of a sweet spot. If I'm not working or trying to be productive, I can even enjoy a ninety-plus degree day where I can really enjoy a relaxing time in the river."

"Shoot me. My idea of hell on earth is to be boiled to death."

"Wow, we *are* polar opposites."

He reached up and lifted a stray strand of her thick hair before tucking it ever so gently, behind her ear.

She imagined how gentle his hands would be when tucking her son into bed. If Benny skinned his knee, she could see him lifting him up and gently treating the mild injury that would have put Benny in tears. There seemed to be a calm serenity about Matt, along with an admirable streak of tenderness and care. She knew she recognized it and was drawn to it that night in the bar.

Seven long years ago.

And now? The spark still flickered between them. He smiled at her comment. "Polar opposites can usually carry on the most interesting conversations." He paused, letting his hand dip down and take hers. "Like the kind of conversations I have with you."

She snorted. "That was the best line I've heard in a while."

His head shook. "The last woman I used a line on was you. It was cringeworthy then and it would be now if I were doing it to seduce you."

"How do you get your women then?"

He bit his lip. "Good question. I don't know. I dated a few women from the area that I knew from my youth. So, not really a pickup, just reconnecting. Sometimes I have dates with people I meet in my ordinary life. People with similar tastes and common interests. But using tired pickup lines in singles' bars? God, I gave that up after a small, dark-haired girl slipped away and broke my heart."

Damn! if her heart didn't thump. "You barely knew me. Only for a few hours."

"True. But we did more than I usually do in a year. We had sex and we got drunk and laughed together like old friends, which was awesome. But our conversation? That was also pretty stimulating."

"I didn't actually break your heart."

He stared deeply into her face, his gaze scouring her features. "Okay, maybe not. But perhaps I caught a glimpse of you easily capturing my heart. I never felt a connection like that before or since. What about you? Be honest."

"Honestly, I can't. It's all happening again too soon. Like it was then and now. I am not like that. Instant attraction is like a flash in the pan. It's over and done."

"I agree. But I am feeling something new and different with you. It's an undeniable energy."

She chewed on her lower lip. How honest could she be? He vocalized the exact thoughts she was thinking. "Okay. I thought it could have potentially been a good connection at the time. And it seems to have picked up where it left off."

He grinned. "I'll take that. Yes. The potential is there. I don't and haven't found that very often, if ever, with other people."

"Okay. I can admit to that. I don't like all people and can't suffer many for long periods of time. But you seem so easy to get to know. It's like a gift with you."

"It might be. But I find it easiest when I'm with you."

She didn't release his hand but turned and tugged him toward her as she hopped onto the beach below. He followed and they strolled, their hands linked. No words were necessary. "Careful, there you go again. That was a borderline line."

"Nope. Never. I will not admit it. That was the truth. Not my fault if guys use it to deceive others or play around with them."

He slowly walked up the sand dune to a slim trail in the thick grasses that dropped down to a paved walking path. It was a heavenly respite on Lillian's calves and feet after the soft, sinking sand. The path also had intermittent lighting. "The state park maintains this area." He told her more about it as they sauntered back towards the marina and his truck. When the trail went below the jetty where the water wasn't visible, the crashing sounds and thrashing vibrations still shot right through Lillian.

Finally, they released their hands and climbed into the cab of his truck. "Where are you staying?"

She rattled off the name of the small, cheap motel she booked for the night.

"I'm going to say something that you can totally decline without offending me. I just thought I would throw it out. As you know, I live with my granddad, so I hope that would buffer this if it seems creepy or weird. But you're welcome to stay with us for the week. We have a spare room and bathroom that locks, and Granddad is there too so I swear it's not a come-on, or a line and it's definitely not intended to sound creepy or weird. It's a safe place to stay and maybe I could show you around Westport some more."

Wow. She never expected that. Not so soon. So incredibly soon. But strangely enough, it wasn't creepy or strange even though she would never agree to it under ordinary circumstances. Plus, Granddad was there. She could literally see Matt in his own home and environment. She could also snoop through his house. Maybe find all the answers as to whether or not she should share her most cherished person with this stranger?

Leaping on her chance for a unique opportunity, she said, "It is strange. And normally, I would give it a hard pass and a loud no. But it's not creepy and your granddad is delightful. I would be grateful to have both of your company in this strange place. Okay."

He nodded without yelling a whoop of joy, as if he just duped her. And now she was about to experience living with him.

CHAPTER 7

SOON AFTER ARRIVING BACK at Matt's home, they found Granddad already in bed. Matt led her to the prepared small guest room. It was clean, neat and functional. They said goodnight before she tucked herself into bed. Lillian was not sleeping though. Staring at the ceiling, she relived every moment of their meeting today, from his utter surprise at seeing her to when he slipped his hand behind her ear to tuck in a strand of her hair. That moment created chills that raised the hairs on her arms. For God's sake. Even now, alone in bed, she experienced a physical reaction to him.

He was so handsome. So kind. So interesting and different from her, yet so similar.

She analyzed and tried to neutrally evaluate every story and every reaction she remembered with a more critical eye, seeking any flaws. What vices did he have? What were his innermost thoughts? She was scanning for a detrimental imperfection and the potential for him to be a bastard or someone who might betray her never left her brain. She needed some sign before she could tell him.

As of now, that sign had not arrived.

Morning came and she slipped into the small bathroom Matt said she could use during her stay. She showered and got dressed before coming out to the most domestic and innocuous scene she could imagine: Matt was serving his granddad eggs and toast. It instantly warmed her heart as it appeared to be their normal routine. It wasn't being done for her benefit or to make Matt seem sweet or impressive. Which was exactly why it *was* so sweet and impressive.

"Good morning, Dr. Lillian," Granddad said as soon as he noticed her.

She flushed and glanced at Matt, who gave her a warm smile. "It's okay, I told Granddad you're staying for the week with us so I can show you around the place."

"Yes. And good morning to both of you but please just call me Lillian. You certainly don't have to call me doctor."

"But it's something you worked so hard to earn. I don't socialize very often with doctors."

She loved this man and she smiled at him with a genuine, wide, toothy grin. "Well, then I shall gratefully accept it as a compliment from you."

"What do you like to eat for breakfast?"

"Anything. Guest. Good manners prohibit me from answering that."

He raised his eyebrows in challenge. "Host. Good manners demand that I provide you with whatever you prefer to eat. That's why I asked."

"I'm not picky with any kinds of food except animal products, which automatically makes me seem picky and hard to cook for. I start to worry you'll rescind the invite now that I reminded you of that."

He laughed outright and very loud. "I thought of it as soon as I asked you what you wanted for breakfast. Maybe some toast with avocado or peanut butter? I can also offer you oatmeal or some other brands of cereal, but we only have cow's milk, so...?"

Hearing Matt actually thought about it and tried to think of her possible preferences warmed her heart and flushed her cheeks. "A piece of toast with peanut butter actually sounds perfect."

"How about a cup of coffee?"

"That would be lovely."

Granddad nodded to the chair beside him. "Please sit down and tell me what you thought of seeing the ocean for your very first time."

Lillian sat down and Matt served her coffee and toast. Giving him a warm thank you, she turned to Granddad and embarked on a light, fun, heart-warming conversation. One thing that stood out to her and what she most appreciated from Matt was that he let them carry on their discussion and only interjected a few times. He let Granddad tell his long stories and patiently waited for them to end, as did she. Lillian observed his infinite care, respect and patience in Matt's interactions with his elder. The same way she treated her grandparents.

She saw something genuine and real about Matt. She doubted she was wrong.

Finally, only after their lengthy conversation ended, did Granddad rise to leave. He explained he had to begin his morning walk around the block, a ritual he insisted on performing alone.

"Gotta keep moving. It's like oil to these old joints."

"Always alone?"

"Heck, yeah, Dr. Lillian. I'm nearly as old as the ocean, and not yet in any need of babysitting. I can still walk just fine and until I get lost or confused, God release me from such a condition or day, I'll enjoy my morning walks as I always have."

Matt nodded his agreement. "Yes, he's sharper than I am most days."

"True, that, my son. True, that."

Lillian could not restrain a laugh at his hip answer, especially when he winked at Matt. She remained seated, having finished her morning meal. Matt cleared the table, washed the dishes and cleaned up the kitchen before he sat down too. They shared what was left in the coffee pot and Lillian noticed and appreciated their candor when they spoke to her.

Only after Granddad closed the front door did Matt turn to her with a warm smile and say, "Thank you for letting him tell his stories. They are long-winded at times, especially when you've heard them for decades, but they mean the whole world to him."

"I wasn't letting him tell them. I enjoyed hearing all about them. And I asked him to continue. I found his early days at sea utterly fascinating. I would love to hear more about it. Don't forget, sea stuff is crazy new to me."

His pleased expression at her answer should not have made her warm and fuzzy inside but it did. What? She was flushing with undisguised pleasure because she pleased him? Yikes. What the hell!?

"So, I asked our relief captain to take my clients out today. Maybe we could go back to the beach and enjoy a picnic. Walk around the marina and later… perhaps I could show you my boat. That is, if you're interested."

Her heart lurched with joy. He totally arranged his day around her. *For* her. After she popped up without any planning or warning. He could have been justifiably annoyed and unaccommodating. Instead, he catered to her vegetarian diet and canceled his workday. "I never meant to impose on you like this. When I showed up, I was thinking we could meet for coffee sometime this week, working around your schedule. I would never have expected to barge into your house, insist on eating a specific diet and keep you from your work. I'm the worst guest ever and I'm not even a guest."

He leaned forward to reply, "I can't tell you how welcome you are, or I would never bother to be so polite, so remember that. I want to do this. I want to spend the whole day with you more than anything else I can think of. I'm more thrilled than I've been in years just looking forward to this day."

Her heart swelled with pride. He said all the right things, but without any smarminess. She could tell he wasn't feeding her what she wanted to hear. "In that case, I'd love to spend the day doing what you just described."

He smiled with relief. She smiled back and damn! Her heart actually started to hurt now.

MATT STARED at the small woman beside him. The sun reflected its rays on her dark hair, shimmering in the strands. She was so lovely. Everything about her. Her smile was very sweet and yet, also confident. Commanding, and always in control, during these soft, intimate moments, Lillian seemed astounded and so grateful for the simplest kind words or deeds towards her. She seemed surprised that Matt was a decent human being. It was so easy to please her in such small ways and he loved watching her soak it up. His only goal was to keep bringing that incredibly wonderful look on her face and sparkle in her eyes.

Having her there, in his town, staying with him didn't compute. Lying awake for most of the night, Matt was trying to figure out how she ended up there. Sleeping over, in his town, in his house.

The more time he spent with her, the more he saw her

inner self and it matched her truly lovely, exquisite exterior. Of course, that was what drew him to her first, even during their second meeting at her family's ranch. And now? All the energy and heart he remembered about her came through. Tough and strong. Intelligent and so well-read on many topics. She could debate with anyone and never back down in her opinions. She had a gift when it came to arguing her viewpoint, based on lots of facts. She could have been a successful lawyer if she weren't so smitten with animals. She also knew how to listen. She could swiftly alternate from fierce advocate to sweet caregiver in a moment. The contrast fascinated and enthralled Matt. She had his undivided attention.

And his exclusive attraction.

He liked how she was kind, attentive, considerate and caring with Granddad. That might have been the most revealing part of her character than anything else. Her degrees and her fancy job and obviously wealthy family notwithstanding, her kind demeanor was all about her. The way she smiled and actively listened to his granddad's tales of the sea. Sometimes, he launched into lengthy stories that never seemed to end, but she calmly took it all in with humor and appreciation.

Matt was intrigued, interested and impressed. The heady combination was unique for him; no other woman he ever met in his nearly thirty years managed to do that for him.

They spent the day exploring the beach. The agreed-upon picnic consisted of vegan choices. Lillian was pleasantly surprised when he kept respecting her chosen diet without further commenting on it. Choosing a private section of beach where only a few walkers or joggers passed below them, they sat in the dry, warm sands near the sand dunes that were covered in long, thick grass. They later took their shoes off and let the sand tickle their toes as they ambled down to the edge of the surf. The small waves lapped and licked their feet. She cringed and laughed at how cold the water was on her bare skin.

They also brought and flew a kite that Matt stored in his garage. The coastal wind kept the daytime temperatures pleasant in the summer sun despite the extra heat. Lillian claimed that this was not hot at all compared to the heat she endured most summers.

They wandered through the entire marina, browsing the vessels from the pleasure crafts at one end to the commercial fishery and crabbing boats at the opposite end. The commercial area was closed off to the public. It was grimier, without any eye towards offering an appealing ambiance. It was all functional. The stench of crab, fish and all things harvested from the salt water was far stronger. She wrinkled her nose and tried to keep from gagging. Matt barely seemed to notice it although he knew it could be overwhelming to some people.

She covered her nose with her sleeve. "This smell makes me think that salt water is definitely not right for me."

"Ripe, is it? This is the ocean at work."

"How do you get used to that?"

"Don't even notice it anymore."

She shuddered. "Wow, I can't imagine that. It's pretty pungent."

Pungent. Oh, yeah, the words. She was so intelligent and well-educated that Matt actually liked how she spoke. All things about Dr. Lillian Rydell seemed to appeal to him. He really should not have missed a day of work today. Not on such short notice. Contrary to what he told her, his relief skipper was pissed off for the lack of notice and his lame reason. A good friend was in town unexpectedly and he had to show her around. *But,* Matt thought, *what if she were his freaking destiny?* It often felt very intense and different when he was around her. He didn't believe in romance, or love at first sight, or any other shit like that. But he had to admit in this one case, he sensed the potential for something bigger. And that's what drew him to her like a housefly to fly paper.

Matt wanted to be caught by her. And maybe she could wrap him around her finger.

"Someday you'll have to come out on the sea with me."

She shuddered. "I can't imagine being on the deep ocean. And the whole fishing part just makes me cringe and shudder."

"Oh, that's right. Of course." He almost hit himself and said *duh!* How could he fail to realize her love for animals would naturally extend to sea creatures? Of course, she found fishing morbidly distasteful. It was pretty gross, in fact. All the slime and goo involved. The odors were quite overpowering, and the rookie fishermen and women squealed and wrinkled their noses when the killing and cleaning and processing of the day's catch inevitably occurred. So, of course, Dr. Lillian Rydell would avoid doing such a terrible ordeal.

But when she set her hand on his arm and explained, "I didn't mean to deride or make a negative comment about what you do. You provide a necessary and much-valued service. People need to eat and most of them eat fish and other sea creatures. I choose not to. But I'm not against other people doing it. Right now, I'm just petrified at the idea of going out on the sea. It's just that really, and not because I'm against fishing."

Relief instantly flowed through him. She didn't disdain his job, his lifestyle or his reason for being. Fishing was all those things to Matt. A family tradition, it was the part of himself and his ancestors that he most valued. What if she'd been against it or disdainful toward it? Perhaps they could never—

Never... what? What the hell was he stressing over? They might never what? Date? Sleep together? Of course not. They met each other as kids and now it was years later so there was never anything really between them. Not at all.

Matt was glad she was so damn classy. She wouldn't tell him she found his career inhumane or any such thing.

"You aren't the first landlubber to be scared. If you ever change your mind and want to try it out, I promise to take you out there safely and give you, at a minimum, a completely new, extremely interesting experience." He grinned and set his hand on hers, squeezing it. She let him hold her small, cool hand in his. Matt found himself growing to like that and wished he could touch her in other places.

"I'm not ready quite yet. But I'll tell you what? I promise to work on it, and maybe even make plans to come back to do it. Okay?"

He nodded; his ribbon of hope flying high. Imagine if she came back. It sounded almost like she was already planning to do it. He wanted so much more from her. All of it. The connection. The warmth. The energy. The sexual chemistry. Her way of talking and her laugh. Her fascination with all things ordinary to him, that so surprised and intrigued her. The sex. That was a special commodity but one he wanted very much as well.

They spent the evening with Granddad and went to bed early. Lillian learned a new fact about chartering vessels: the boats went out before the light of dawn.

The excitement Matt experienced while showing her his hometown, his job, his passion and his love was almost embarrassing. What would she think of him? His doubts haunted him and kept his brain on fire as he lay in bed. He was blushing. Right. Crap. He rolled over and punched the pillow several times. She was a doctor and a vegetarian and all things amazing, while he was a lowly charter boat captain... How could he ever be enough for her?

Still, he couldn't wait to be with her again and hated the nights for keeping him away from her.

CHAPTER 8

*T*HE UTTER SURPRISE OF what Lillian found out this week about Matt wouldn't compute. How could the partner in her one and only one-night stand and subsequently, the father of her baby, be this guy? He was the jackpot of all guys. The decent, kind, hot boat captain with infinite patience and honesty? His eyes remained fixed on her. He was so warm and interested in her, she was almost overwhelmed. Lillian rarely ever embraced that kind of sexual need and energy from someone who found her so interesting and exotic with her wide knowledge and effervescent personality. She felt so ordinary, it was intoxicating when Matt treated her like she was so special.

Finally, on their last night together, he took her hand to share a new treat. Matt built a private, small fire on the beach under a blanket of stars. The ocean reflected a soft, trailing white glow of moonlight in the white foam. The vast expanse seemed to embrace her like a hug, and the dancing flames on the driftwood made a glimmering fire that smelled of clean, good things. She sat on a log and watched Matt, always the considerate planner, pull out a package of marshmallows,

Hershey bars and graham crackers from his backpack, along with a small fold-up roaster.

"S'mores!" Lillian exclaimed with unmasked delight.

He nodded. "I wasn't sure you'd like them. Or you might think it was kind of corny."

"I *love* s'mores. Me and B—" Oh, God! She clamped her teeth down and nearly bit her tongue. She almost said, *me and Benny love sharing s'mores over campfires.* All winter and summer long at their river beach they liked to make them. Their beach was so different from the ocean beach. But each was beautiful and enticing, the loveliest setting, if for completely different reasons. "Me and all the boys and girls at home, my cousins and all, love them."

"Me too. I don't often come down here at night to star-gaze next to a pretty woman and a fire. But s'mores make everything better."

"Pretty woman? There you go again with your pickup lines," she teased him with a snort and a soft smile. They had such an easy rapport now, and he smiled back.

Then Matt pulled out a bottle of sparkling wine and two plastic clear glasses. "Since this is your last night, I thought we could make a toast. This week has been nothing less than spectacular."

Lillian restrained the urge to clap her hands with glee. Instead, she replied with a soft, squishy smile. "It sure has. I didn't expect any of it when I barged in on you. But oh. It really has been wonderful."

They did not discuss her departure. Or their future. Or if they would even see each other again. Distance. Lifestyles. Commitment. Everything separated them. From the river to the Pacific Ocean, there was nothing to link them together, or possibly make it work.

Nothing except for their brief connection this week.

And their son, of course.

That thought kept bombarding her brain and searing her heart with guilt. She clutched the plastic glass and took too large a sip of the refreshing, soothing wine. She let it cool her burning, harsh thoughts and the remorse she harbored over keeping her secret. A secret that would change everything between them.

But not today. Not yet. She wanted to enjoy their last night. The soft breeze, warm fire, and squishy chocolate with gooey marshmallow between two graham crackers. She ate three, which was way more than she usually did, but they tasted so good. Sinfully better with the bubbly wine. She enjoyed way too much of both delights.

But mostly, she enjoyed way too much of Matt. His words. His conversation. His compassion. And his deep, appreciative laugh.

His joy with her was undeniable. He got so happy when he shared things with her and introduced her to new experiences. She appreciated this unexpected selfless trait.

He grabbed her hand, and she squeezed his back. "Lillian." His tone was serious all at once, and she doubted he planned to comment on the pretty night or magical atmosphere or each other. She knew there was so much they had yet to discuss. Never mind how to manage joint parenthood while being half a state apart and each pursuing two distinctly differing lifestyles.

Those inevitable conversations would start to arise. She knew they would. Decisions would have to be made at some point. The logistics of that event stirred up her fears, concerns, and even terror so she dared not let her thoughts dwell there long. What might that look like? What kind of pain and confusion might that entail for her and her son?

In her gut level, which she heeded for most of her life, she knew she could not deny her son an introduction to his father. This man was too good, decent, considerate, and knowledgeable. He could teach Benny things she could never begin to approach. He could engage him in ways that were simply unavailable to her. She always believed everything Benny required was already covered by her family. Her own father stepped in regularly as his primary male role model. But now Lillian realized Benny's real father had his own uniquely important set of traits to pass along to his son. If she kept that information from Benny, she worried that someday, Benny would seek Matt out on his own and never forgive her for denying him this man's identity. She was almost ready to release her heart to this man, yet he had no idea. She wasn't prepared to do it tonight, not at this moment. She was still working through her anxiety and fears.

The guilt of avoidance, however, grew far too strong to deny.

When Matt just muttered her name, all of her insides were strumming, and her heart began leaping. Turning suddenly and without any forethought, or even the realization of what she impulsively wanted to do, she set her lips on his.

Their kiss gave her a soft, warm sensation of skin-to-skin contact. Pulling back, their eyes met and they both stared for several long, torturous moments before she gulped and purposely moved closer, pressing her lips on his while slipping her hands around his neck. He sighed at first until his mouth opened and his soft, hot tongue outlined the seam of her lips and soon had her whimpering with lust. The small sensation gained magnitude as it jolted from his tongue all the way down her spine. She shuddered and shivered and—

And then, everything changed.

Their warm friendship burst into a total explosion of fireworks. Their lips met and mashed, tongues slipping and sliding in their eagerness to caress each other. Her hands grasped onto his shiny curls and she tugged his head even closer to hers, which was almost impossible to do.

He sat up and gripped her under her arms, pulling her towards him. She straddled him as he cupped her bottom with his warm hands, and she sighed gratefully. Kneading her flesh, he aroused her more until she closed the gap between them by planting her mouth on his. Their lips pressed together, and she sucked on his lower lip until he moaned into her mouth. In the next moment, she was the one moaning from his oral ministrations. His fingers squeezed her flesh as he lifted the round cheeks of her bottom.

She stood up and slipped off her shirt before tossing it. Simultaneously stripping off her leggings and underwear before she resumed her previous position, she was too excited and willing to take off her bra, and the lace barely spanned her nipples.

Matt groaned as he watched her seductive performance in the dying firelight. His eyes sparked with hot lust and appreciation, sliding down her half naked torso and watching the little dance she did, lifting one thigh and baring it before slowly repeating the move on the other. Hopping quickly back onto him, she settled in.

Filling his hands with her naked butt cheeks again, he planted his mouth on hers, plunging his tongue deep inside her mouth as she rocked rhythmically on his warm hands. He gripped and kneaded the soft flesh that filled his palms perfectly. Her small butt complemented her medium-sized boobs. She had a petite figure. Slipping his hand between her legs, he didn't press or rub her, but simply rested it there, letting her slick wetness moisten his fingers. She swung her hips and positioned herself over his hand and pressed down. Nearly overwhelmed by her lusty desire, the deep, gnawing need inside her was entirely new for Lillian. It took her by surprise in an unexpected way. How quickly it began to control her by offering her endless bliss. Wrapping her arms around his shoulders to stay upright, she pushed her tongue deeper into his mouth, and felt him smiling under the sudden onslaught of unbridled affection.

His finger touched her seam and she sighed with ecstasy even though he barely grazed her. The anticipation of what was about to happen in mere moments, *moments!* became her only thought. It made her calm down temporarily and remain still. Fighting the urge for instant gratification by sinking onto his fingers and riding them as hard and fast as her hips could manage crossed her mind more than once, but she relished the slow anticipation. It was crucial to her. The desire inside her grew until it felt tight, descending from her belly and swelling all of her capillaries as it engorged the lips of her sex. She was so ready for him.

He was *almost* tickling her when his touch became extra soft. She shut her eyes, trying to conceal her neediness. Oh, she was out of control already. Back his finger came, sliding along her slick flesh, heated and wet with the natural lubrication that promised their enjoyment and bliss. When another finger joined the first, a long moan of desire came from her mouth. Lillian kept her body still, but not for long. Ripping her mouth off his, she nearly wilted over his shoulder while burying her face in the crook of his neck and holding on. Her consciousness and all of her heart and soul were collectively focused on the one spot he touched, teased, and sometimes tickled.

"Oh." She gasped into his ear as he slid the two digits several more times inside and out of her. Her body welcomed his touch. Matt. The stranger. The friend. The father of her child.

But that was not important right now. All thoughts fled.

Slipping her head to the side, she put her tongue in his

ear and he groaned with pleasure. She swirled her tongue around the shell of his ear, and he tipped his head closer to her. She could feel him swelling and growing hot underneath her, separated only by his jeans. His relief would be coming shortly.

First, she needed him for something else. Craving his full attention, she pleaded, "Touch me… oh, oh!" With a loud moan and a sigh in his ear, she kissed and licked him in an effort to distract herself from his busy fingers that were now so well-rehearsed in providing her with sensuous delight.

His sliding, teasing fingers soon found the prize they sought: the hooded bead of her clit and that was where they stopped to play. She melted like lava onto his shoulder and let him hold her up. Her hips swayed and thrust at the clever, wonderful pressure of his fingertips. He strummed her like a banjo and played beautiful music that only his fingertips knew how to create. Sliding his fingers before sinking several of them inside her, she bucked, and her spine went straight, lifting her knees and pushing her hips back, zeroing in on him and pulling his fingers deeper inside her. Her entire body shook with unmitigated pleasure.

"Oh, yes… yes…" she moaned without restraint into his ear. She couldn't stop her bottom from swaying to the rhythm as he fingered her for a long time. It was so hard and perfect. He'd tease her until she was on the brink of orgasm and then release the pressure, lazily strumming her clit only to drift back and dip his fingers into the wetness he created so effortlessly. Swirling them inside her, she finally raised herself onto her knees and squeezed his fingers with her vaginal walls as tightly as she could. He grabbed her bra cup and pushed it down. Taking the strap, he used it to pull her forward until his mouth found the hard, distended and hypersensitive nub. She cried out, gripping his hair while moving her hips rhythmically. She rode his fingers back and forth and up and down until she was crazy, sloppy, incoherent and totally wild.

She jerked her nipple from him only to grab his head and put it back there. She moved and ground her hips until he eventually rewarded her heated body and all the sensations boiling in her gut to move in quick succession, spiraling into a crescendo. All her nerve endings, from the tips of her breasts to her fingertips, were heightened and anxious, waiting for the final culmination.

Muffling her cries of ecstasy, she wilted, and her bottom and her naked, wet slit rested on his jeans. He pushed inside her sensitive core and she groaned at the soft, but now, muted sensation. He cradled her against his chest and already, things once again began to stir. In addition to her fully satiated insides and genitals, her heart was satisfied too.

She lifted her eyes and rested her head on his chest. She found him staring at her with a kind, tender expression and eyes of adoration. Cow eyes that spoke volumes of affection and care for her. So much so that when he touched her cheek, he remarked, "You're bright pink."

"Everywhere," she muttered, licking her lips and giving him a dirty, little smile.

She moved her hips, and he lifted his thigh to support her. Closing her eyes, she ignored the abrasive material and let it soothe the aching tingles left by the orgasm. To her happy surprise, everything started to percolate all over again.

Moaning, she dropped her hands to his waist and stroked his thick erection. It felt hot even through the double layers of material. She undid the zipper, being somewhat clumsy and slow, and had to insist that her fingers cooperate. He lifted his hips to help her toss the pants away and create some space. She couldn't wait for him to take them off. Reaching into his boxers, she pulled out the red hot, swelling rod with her hand. He groaned. She smiled at him, licking her lips before she began a slow, torturous caress of long pushes and pulls on him. He closed his eyes, tipping backwards before catching himself with his hands.

"Do you have a condom?"

"It's in my wallet," he barely muttered. She searched around and found his wallet, which he dug into before popping up with a prophylactic.

"Put it on," she commanded in a husky voice.

"Here?"

"Yes, here. No one can see us between these logs unless they're sitting right on top of us. If that happens…" She smirked. "Then I guess they deserve a peek."

He shuffled around and reached towards her. "Lillian…" She sighed and slid down him. Once fully joined, she leaned forward to slip her hands around his neck. She pressed her naked breasts against his chest. Only after a long, soul-shattering moment of nearly sharing the same breath did she move. Slowly and with no hesitation, she went up and down as she rode him. They didn't speak, and only a series of soft sighs and moans escaped their lips, but they kept their gazes glued on each other. There wasn't one movement they didn't fully share and experience together, they were totally in sync and caught in the same moment.

Firelight flickered in shadows on their skin. The soft blanket provided a barrier from the sand. The darkness shielded them from the world. Like they fell off the earth into this perfect spot of warm, fresh air, and bright, shining stars with a roaring splash and a thunk! Lillian believed she might take flight with all the deep and fully satisfying sensations he created inside her.

Finally, he lay back, and she fell on top of him. Rolling both of them to the side, Matt positioned Lillian under him. He hovered over her. His hand came to her cheek and slid down it as he stared at her forehead, her eyes, her nose and then her mouth. His body pressed hers in the most intimate and delicious position. But it was the look in his eyes of adoration, disbelief, and amazement that he held her, right there, right now in his arms. His body moved inside hers and she let out a small, grateful sigh at the sensational friction. But it was the soft touch of his lips on hers that undid her heart. As if he were touching the most precious object in his life, Matt's lips kissed hers, with a long, languid surrender that enhanced the endless feelings.

As he kissed her, slipping their tongues together in combined sweetness that created a rampant, mutual hunger for each other, she opened her legs wider. He pressed her harder, using the lumpy sand to support his wild, wonderful coupling until she could no longer hold his gaze. Her eyes closed and she succumbed to his ministrations. Images of the endless sensations became dizzying colors and the burning satisfaction nearly consumed her. Their tongues tangoed, opening their mouths and devouring each other when Matt finally thrust himself fully into her and she cried out as he stiffened and shuddered when his own orgasm unfolded.

It took him several moments to finish. Finally, he fell to her side, his lower half releasing her, but his torso still half covering her. She opened her eyes to find him above her.

He stared down at her before lifting a hand and sweeping her bangs away. His expression was serious. No laugh. No sense of humor. The intensity that she missed before this was suddenly evident in his face.

Laying naked on a beach would have appalled her once. She'd never done such a thing until now. Yet she had no regrets. No hurry to get dressed or move away from him. No, she wanted this. So much. She wanted Matt to stay here with her. Under the stars, beyond the waves.

"I can't believe we just did this. Here."

She grinned. "I think I shocked you."

"You shocked me. I shocked me. Do you think I do this often?"

"Well, where do you usually do it?"

He smiled as he slipped out from her. Sitting up, he adjusted himself and removed the condom before putting it in the sand. She sat up and leaned towards him, kissing his shoulder.

"My boat."

"Really? Your business doubles as a love nest?"

"Yeah. Granddad is always at home, which kind of kills the mood. I need privacy. Easy alternative. Not so tacky as a motel. What about you?"

She smiled as she gazed at the now low flames of their little fire. "There hasn't been anyone in a long time. Holy shit. Poor you. That's why that happened. One hot kiss and I was done for."

"Just because of my kiss?"

She sighed. "No, Matt, something simply exists between us. No matter how old we get."

"No, you're right. It is something. I used to wonder how it happened. Like I am right now, wondering how this happened."

"Like rocket fuel and a lit match. Which is so not like me usually." She snorted.

"Me, neither. But I believe it's because of you."

"No. I don't get out of River's End very often, working with all the animals there. I have no new men in my love life, which is regularly few and far between."

Matt put his hand on hers. "I honestly can't believe that; much less, that you're still single. I'm just so glad you are."

Seeing lights coming down the beach, bobbing back and forth, they glanced at each other and grinned. "We could be cited for public indecency."

She turned until she found all of her clothes. Slipping her

shirt on, Lillian stood as she pulled her underwear up and Matt simply stopped dead so he could watch her. She gave him a little smile. "You're gawking."

"You're beautiful."

"That's almost another pickup line. Get dressed before we get caught."

He grinned as he reached over and pulled on his own shirt, boxers and jeans. He finally rose when he snapped and zipped his jeans. Now that they were both dressed, he reached for her and she easily collapsed into his arms. She loved the way he tucked her snugly into his chest and wrapped his arms tightly around her.

Her heart nearly melted when she felt him planting a kiss in her hair. "I meant to give you a private, romantic goodbye. I never dreamt we'd share this level of romance. But damn, Lillian…"

She tipped her head back. "I know. Damn. To us. And to each other."

They shared a profound, deep look and a smile. And then Matt held her. For so long. The ocean's rhythm matched that of her heart. Her damn heart got way too twisted up and heavy with all of these blissful feelings.

She did not want to leave. She loved this moment, this night, this evening, and all the trouble he went to in planning it. But most of all, she loved being in his arms.

But it grew late and much cooler. She shivered in the night air. "We should probably go."

They released each other and started gathering their things before extinguishing the smoldering fire. Waiting for her, he held out his hand and her heart plummeted into her stomach. Damn. She loved his polite manners. The way he always watched what she was doing so closely. He paid so much attention to her, he flustered her although she loved it. She never had so much attention before. They walked in warm, compatible silence. The words were left unsaid, but their emotions were very much expressed. It seemed impossible for her to dilute her reaction to the one man she didn't want to respond so obviously to.

Yet she wanted a good relationship. She wanted a decent, kind man and all the other things Matt personified. But not so much she was willing to lose her mind *and* her heart... Now what?

CHAPTER 9

*W*AKING UP, LILLIAN BLINKED at the grit and weariness she felt in her eyes. What had she done?

But how could she have avoided it?

The night, the atmosphere, and the ambiance created the spark, but when their lips touched, it was like gasoline and the spark they shared suddenly erupted into a blazing inferno.

Now? Everything crashed. Burnt. Torched.

She had sex with him. The father of her child who still didn't know he was. She not only complicated but also compounded a situation with plenty of built-in drama to begin with. Now she upset everything she was mentally prepared for to happen. What did she do? Shutting her eyes, she let the clearest images and snippets of their conversation filter through her.

Matt would hate her for not being crystal clear about why she went there. For withholding her greatest secret and doing what they did last night. Not to mention, the relationship they dallied at all week. They were well beyond being old friends even before last night. The chemistry, the private understanding, the *fun*, and the sparks supported a developing sexual desire and need. It remained dormant, unsaid and unacted upon. But instead of ignoring it now that she was a full adult and should have been capable of handling any situation, she completely betrayed herself, making it far worse and way more complicated.

Panic-stricken, she glanced over at Matt who still slept soundly. Sliding free of the bed, she quietly made way her to the bathroom. She showered and slipped into some loose, comfortable clothing before going into the kitchen. Opening cupboards until she found the coffee and started a pot, she waited as she stared at it with knots in her stomach and her clasped hands on the table.

What had she done?

More importantly, why?

Imagine what her parents would say… again. The first time, she was young and dumb and reckless. But a second time? With the same man? They might become a bit wary of her lame excuses.

The coffee finished brewing, so she poured herself a cup before sitting down again and contemplating her next move. The urge to flee like she did after her night of sex with Matt the first time naturally crossed her mind again. That morning, the shame and loathing of what happened and her fear of what others might think of her suffocated her like cruel hands on her throat, choking the life out of her, so naturally, she fled.

She obviously wasn't such a chicken shit anymore. Taking responsibility for one's actions had been hardwired into her and she was clearly to blame for this, never mind the bomb she still had to drop on Matt about Benny. Why did she do that before she told him? Nothing between them could survive after she told him the truth. It would turn ugly as soon as she revealed her secret. His opinion of her would change irreparably and she understood why clearly. But still, all of it disturbed her.

"I hope that look on your face isn't from remorse about last night or I've got some work to do."

She jerked up when Matt's voice startled her. He was far closer than she estimated as he walked nearer to her and set a kiss on the top of her swept back hair.

"It's not remorse from last night. That was…" Was she blushing? Yes. Heat filled her cheeks.

He gave her a sweet laugh and a shoulder squeeze. "It sure was."

He sauntered to the coffee pot in a relaxed, open, casual manner. He seemed totally at ease. And she might have been wrong, but he also seemed more at peace… and dare she say it? Happy. Was that because of her and what happened last night?

"I rolled over, and you were gone, so I got a slight case of PTSD from our first time and thought perhaps you ditched me again."

Her blush burned deeper. "That was rotten of me. I hope I'm substantially more mature than that now."

"I didn't hear anything out here, so the possibility really did occur to me… I didn't want you regretting anything that happened between us. Again. That's all."

He sat at the small table, very close to her in the corner where she sat. He set his coffee down and put his hand over hers. "You're okay about last night, this time, I hope."

"I was…" She gulped and the expression on his face crashed into a crestfallen wince. She quickly added, "I *am*. But there are things I should have told you and it's…"

"Okay, what things? I mean, it feels like we've known each other for the past six years in our conversations and the way we connect. But in reality, it's only been six days total. So, I can't know everything and vice versa. That takes time. That's what I wanted to ask you last night before you so vigorously and distractedly kissed me, thereby altering the entire course of my plans last night. Which did not include any attempts to seduce you. However, now that you seduced me, there are definitely no regrets on my end."

How could his calm decency make it so much worse for her?

"Is Granddad close to waking up yet? We need a few moments."

He frowned. "You woke up two hours before he usually rises. He shouldn't emerge from his bedroom until seven o'clock or so."

She nodded and slipped her hand free, bending over her coffee and inhaling it like a line of powdered cocaine. Here it went down so casually. Ordinary. At his kitchen table before the first light of dawn. Wearing casual, comfortable, slouchy clothes, everything seemed so common and ordinary. Their conversation should have taken place somewhere more dramatic to match the tone of it.

But here they were, in the old house with Granddad not even a corridor away so they kept their voices soft and low. She hoped he'd continue to accept her.

"Lillian? What is it? Don't you want to see me again?"

She blinked tears. "I do. Want to see you again, I mean. You might not want to see me again though. But you—you'll have to."

"What? Lillian, what is it?"

She cleared her throat and rubbed her eyelids while sitting up straighter. Wiggling around until she attained a stiff, grown-up posture, she said, "I should have told you sooner, but I wasn't sure how to admit that I lied."

"When and why?" His face watched her, staying somewhat blank but a weariness appeared around the corners of his eyes as he seemed to prepare himself.

"When you asked me if I had any kids. I didn't answer it. I should have told you yes. I do. I have one son."

Matt's entire posture sank. Then a slow smile filled his face. He reached forward and took her hand in his. Warm, gentle, and soft, he squeezed her hand like he always did to show her his care and concern.

"That's what has you sitting here so dejectedly, like you're waiting for the sky to fall on you? That's not a problem. Not for me. I mean, whatever we decide to do, that won't pose any problems. We can handle it if there is an *us,* however you see fit."

Her heart lurched with relief. She wanted to grab his face and shake it, demanding that he stop trying to make this so easy on her. Stop trying to be so good. The guilt only got worse.

She blinked and reeled her thoughts back in. Trying to stay steady, she searched for the words to tell him. Then he asked her, "What's his name?"

She lifted her face and stared into Matt's eyes. Studying the slope of his forehead, the dip of his nose, the flare of his nostrils, the arches of his dark eyebrows, the perfect O of his mouth and synchronized widening of his eyes. It was all familiar to her, the same as their son. "Benjamin Mathew Rydell. He's named for my father and—"

How could she say it? Her stomach roiled with ragged nerves. Here she goes. Stating the truth that could change everything. She gulped down the lump in her throat and held his gaze. Strong and sure, her voice barely wavering, she said, "—and his."

It took Matt a few moments to mull over the name and register what she said. He replied, "That's a strong name—" but stopped.

He shook his head, and looked at her, then away. His brain was cataloguing, shuffling through all of her comments until she knew he landed on the most important one, the one that could change everything.

"Didn't you think my name was Mathew?"

"Yeah. I always thought that was your name."

He shoved her hand away and sat back, his gaze clinging to hers now. His eyes widened into owl-like orbs and his mouth opened and shut before his jaw set in a grim line. Finally, in a low and measured voice, he asked. "How old is your son?"

"Six. He's six years old." She stared at him and added, "And he's *our* son... You are his father."

MATT STARED at Lillian's face in disbelief. In his mind's eye, her lovely, oval, tanned face with a dark swath of hair that swung freely around suddenly morphed into a fire-breathing dragon, spraying her hot, fiery, destructive breath all over him. Disfiguring him... and essentially his whole life.

Son. Six years old. Mathew. *Named after his father. I thought, all these years that your name was Mathew.*

He got up and left the table, suddenly unable to look at her. Her words did not compute or relate to him. But in his gut, he knew, despite how horrifying and destructive her words might be. They altered him forever. His whole life. His thoughts about himself. His opinions about Lillian. Of their relationship. The sex that was so perfect a few moments ago nearly prompted him to ask her to come up with a way they could keep seeing each other, despite all the conflicting factors, until she dropped this bomb on him.

He seethed with rage inside.

A son.

He. Had. A. Son.

The words were meaningless. He could not grasp the concept. He worried that the tight constriction in his chest was the first sign of a heart attack. Maybe he was having a panic attack? Perhaps both? It made him feel raw inside and more confused. Angry words were ready to spew from his lips and he could not look at her for fear of how angry his words could be. Never mind Granddad was right down the hallway and within hearing distance.

He tried to resist the urge to leave. Immediately. His lack of oxygen would soon have him fainting or dying of a heart attack. Either one suddenly felt plausible.

She could leave and pretend he didn't exist. But now he knew where she lived.

He'd have to hire a lawyer to find both of them. He'd never allow her to get away with twice disappearing from his life. This elusive woman who bewitched him before dropping atomic bombs on his emotions and future life. Hearing her claim she gave birth to his son nearly floored him.

She and he created a human being together.

A person.

She wasn't speaking of an abstract desire in the future. Something he might not want to know about. Something he might own up to or not. No, she was referring to a human being, their son, who already existed. Now. At this moment.

Matt simply turned and walked out of the house.

Let her leave. Run away again and disappear. She was pretty good at doing that.

He hopped into his truck and drove away.

~

LILLIAN WAS DUMBFOUNDED as she stared vacantly at the now slammed door. Horrified by her revelation, she wondered what to do. Leave again? No. She could not do that. But why should she stay? Obviously because she had plenty to discuss with Matt. Everything, in fact. But not with his anger and rage. Shit. What to do? Tears made her blink and she fought them. No. She refused to be victimized by any man. He was the victim in this situation. Her inability to locate him until now and her willingness to grasp her motherhood definitely gave her more say over their child. He would just have to find a way to accept it.

But that demanded more conversation.

That demanded more interaction.

"He'll go off to Sandcliff Beach."

She jumped at the unexpected comment.

Granddad stood in the hallway, wearing his flannel PJs and a light robe. A pair of slippers covered his feet.

"I'm sorry, what?"

"When Mattie gets upset, he goes down to a little-known beach to organize his thoughts. Especially now, being so early as it is."

Flames singed her throat and cheeks. "Should I go down there? I'm the one who made him so upset."

"I figured as much. I heard his truck tires squeal in his mad dash to flee. He doesn't often accelerate so fast and screech around like a jacked-up, cocky asshole."

She let out a small laugh with surprise at his words. "It's not his fault. It's all mine."

"Well, running away from a problem never solves it, huh?"

"I ran away from one originally and that's how we got into this mess."

Granddad shuffled forward. "I figured you had to have a pretty good reason for showing up here. No surprise when Mattie reacted with his nerves on display that first day. Had to assume you had a deeper connection than just friends. Old friends are visibly happy and casual, unable to conceal how glad they are to see each other again. That didn't happen between you two."

"I should let Matt tell you. It's his business now."

"Well, I'm well aware of how biology works and can make a pretty good guess as to what might have alarmed him to leave the way he did."

"You... knew?"

"No, but I suspected it. I hoped you'd tell him. I could see it obviously bugged you to keep it from him."

"Should I go to him now?"

"Yes. You ran away from him once and didn't like it. I'm sure he doesn't like himself right now for running away from you. So, don't let him get away with it."

She rose to her feet. "You're right. We're both adults now and it's time we acted like it. Especially considering what we have on the line. Even if he hates me, he'll still have to deal with me on some level."

Granddad nodded. "Dr. Lillian, my grandson definitely does not hate you." He spoke so softly and with care and conviction. Her heart lurched in her chest.

She paused before impulsively leaning forward and kissing Granddad's cheek. "Thank you, Granddad. You've been so kind to me from the moment I showed up on your doorstep."

"You don't get this old without knowing people. I still recognize a good egg when I meet one."

She blinked her sentimental tears away and replied, "That might be the best compliment I've ever received."

"Meh, I'm just an old fishing boat captain. Don't get

sappy. I'm no fancy, smart doctor like you." He gave her a wink and her heart lifted with joy.

After she exited, Lillian sat in her car and her heart sunk again. So begins round number two. She could only hope it would turn out better than number one.

CHAPTER 10

*L*ILLIAN FLOPPED DOWN BESIDE Matt right in the sand where she found him. He should have been startled, but maybe he guessed if she cared at all about him, she'd seek him out. Maybe it was a test. Maybe he didn't care either way.

But there she sat. Pulling her knees up and wrapping her small arms around them, she held them tightly next to her. She looked more like a small child than the educated doctor and practitioner he knew her to be.

And a mother.

She was a mother too.

That changed everything.

He turned and stared down at her as she lifted her eyes to look at him. They seemed to sense their connection without using spoken words.

She appeared so youthful and beautiful, it was hard for Matt to think of her as a mother and someone matronly. The contrast was impossible to imagine.

"We have to talk. About everything."

Her voice was soft, lilting, and calming. The huskiness

with feminine tones gave it a musical effect. He thought so the first time he ever spoke to her.

"How did you find me?"

"Granddad told me this is where you came when you were upset."

He snorted. "I'll bet Granddad didn't have a clue why."

"Actually… he did. He caught on early that there was something more than casual in our friendship."

"Well, glad to know at least someone suspected it, because I sure as fuck didn't."

She flinched. Matt rarely raised his voice and never swore in front of women. It was an old-fashioned habit insisted upon by none other than Granddad. Matt would have been swiftly cuffed if he ever swore around Grandma. Never. Ever. Not in front of a lady. Any lady. His opinion about her notwithstanding. Sounded so silly now. Women's demand for equality didn't matter and it was so important to Granddad that Matt simply adhered to it. Out of habit. So even he cringed when he swore at her in anger.

She tucked her chin to her knees and riveted her eyes on the breaking surf. The dim, soft dawn's sunlight edged the white foam with blue, looking so exquisite in the light pastels of the morning. Lillian continued her story of how their son came to be as if Matt didn't leave right in the middle of it. "I realized I was pregnant when I got home and had to tell my family. Imagine that fun conversation. I was a successful and motivated student of veterinary medicine. It was always my goal and dream ever since I was a little girl. Finally, I was on that path, and my good grades and bright future guaranteed my continued victory until I showed up pregnant. No boyfriend. No one in sight. Not even a face. Or a name, as it turned out. It was the worst thing I could think of happening to me. They were disappointed but everyone supported me. I looked for you, Matt, just like I told you. I looked everywhere for a year or more. But more urgently when I was pregnant. I was so scared and ashamed. It worried me that I didn't want a baby. But I was having it regardless and I would have given anything to share that burden with you."

Pregnant. She was pregnant with his child. And he never had a clue. All this time. She carried his seed inside her. He glanced down at her belly as if expecting to see some physical evidence of it.

"That would have been hard on me. But I would have done anything I could for you. Even back then."

"Maybe I knew that from our brief time together. I had to believe you were special or I could not have had sex with you on the first night. But I was searching for Mathew Griffin, not Mathias Griffin. I can't start to tell you how many Mathew Griffins there are in the world. A whole lot. After Benny came, I had to function again. You think you know what it's like to be busy? You don't have a clue until you have to care for a newborn. I had to learn it all while also trying to finish the classes for my degree. Luckily, I had my family to help with the money and give me moral support. Otherwise, I'd have to rely on waiting tables and government welfare. It was really hard. You can't ever overestimate the demands on a single parent."

He fisted his hands and released them. "I never wanted that for you. Even now."

"At first, I wanted to find you more than anything. But time marches on. With a child, it's even faster, here today and gone tomorrow. Everyday. I did that. I finally earned my degree and passed the state exam before I moved back home for good. We set up our house and my practice and we started living together. Benny and me. My father is a primary influence on him along with Grandpa Jack. He has plenty of aunts, uncles, cousins, and Grandma Erin who all contribute to his care. That's a lot of people. He isn't growing up all alone and he's never neglected." She shifted and fixed her gaze on the ocean waves. Then she licked her lips and said, "But he has grown up to the age he is, six, without knowing any father. And then one day, there you were."

"You chose not to tell me."

"There you were. A complete stranger with my son's face. He looks exactly like you. I even forgot how strong the resemblance was until I saw you. That's half the reason for my stunned response at our second meeting. That and sheer panic. I had to hide him from you. You'd know with one glance that he was your son and I feared you might try to take him from me."

"You were willing to let me go on without ever knowing I had a child."

"Maybe. Yes. I was fully prepared to do that. I came here to determine whether or not it was a good idea. Let me ask you something: did you expect me to be the type of mother who would hand over her son without first being sure you were strong and mature and not a terrible person? Like a pedophile, or a criminal, or a drug addict? What type of mother would blithely offer her son to anyone? The kind of mother who fails to make sure the people who influence him aren't monsters? Not I. I'm the kind who wants to care for him. He's small, weak and vulnerable and only I can provide for his safety and wellbeing. Think about it. In all your pain and suffering, think about what you're asking of me. You were and still are barely a stranger. But I'm letting you know about the existence of the most precious person in my life. Benny is my heart and soul and you're damn fucking right that you'd never know the first clue about him, if you were half the person you turned out to be. Along with your grand-dad. I would never give you access to Benny, despite your DNA connection, not if you drank or abused people or animals in any way, physically or verbally. Or if your granddad did that. I would never expose Benny to someone of such low caliber and I'm fucking proud of that. So, go ahead and hate me. Be mad at me for as long as you like. But it wasn't all intentional. You're goddamned right I kept him from you. You were on the biggest interview of your fucking life this week and you passed. You should be grateful that I trusted you enough to even give you that much. Benny is my son and no one, for any reason, is allowed to interact with him or to influence him if they aren't fully screened by me first."

She ran out of breath and he stared at her with a stunned expression. Her words rang true. His anger swiftly evaporated. Shoulders slumping, he sank forward to grip his knees and stared at the ocean. "I guess I just reacted without analyzing every factor. I can't believe that I… *we* have a son."

"I can't imagine how shocked that news must be to you either. I'm sorry to do that to you. But I didn't know how else to accomplish it. I had to observe you and test you out first. I had to decide if my son needed to know his father."

"You decided he did? I mean, I'm grateful to hear you say that. But did last night influence your decision?"

"No, a few days ago, I decided you were okay. Last night wasn't supposed to happen."

"And now that it did?"

She bit her lip. "I don't know. I don't know anything, now, not even how to do this. But then again, I haven't known what to do ever since the day I held my son for the first time. The only thing I knew with total certainty was that I would do everything I could to raise him with unconditional love and support."

"Everything you could do for him. Okay. I'm on board with that. I see your point. I need that baseline too."

She gave him a long, searching, and relieved look. "Yes. Exactly that. That's why I decided to tell you. Only because of that. You showed the same fierce love that I have for those you care for."

"Granddad. You based it on him and me."

"Yes. He was the best physical representation of someone who was close to you, and he filled the role of a father in raising you."

Matt shuddered as her words pelted him like gravel being showered on his bare skin. The father and child comment had a profound effect on him. What did he do with this new information? How to categorize and fulfill his new role in life? His new identity. A few words from Lillian managed to turn his life upside-down overnight. She changed it and him irrevocably. But such a rapid change left him not knowing exactly what to do next. Not this moment. Not at lunch. Not even tomorrow.

"I feared telling you. I cannot allow you to take my son from me and legally, I worry I won't be able to stop it. I had to make sure you weren't evil or vindictive in your heart. But I can't predict the future, and once you got upset and angry about it, the legal rights you have to my child could come into play. I had no idea what you would or could do with that knowledge. However, I owe Benny and you this morsel of truth. You will always have each other. I just don't know what that might look like or how I'll manage to handle it. But I will."

"Benny? You call him that?"

Her body seemed startled. "What? Yes. I mean, yes, we call him Benny. My dad is Ben, so my son became Benny."

"What... what is he like? What does our son like to do?" The words felt rusty on Matt's tongue and odd to say. He wasn't sure how to ask her about his son and what to do with the answer once he knew it.

But she was right about the changes he had to expect. He had to figure this out. Even as his brain spun in circles, his heart kept lurching with this new reality. He awoke to a wonderful woman with whom he wanted to expand their connection. Maybe see each other long distance and let it grow slowly as they began to explore the possibilities. Long distances often turned even the best relationships rancid so they had to proceed with the knowledge it probably wouldn't work out, but what if it did? He felt too strongly bound to her and she seemed to respond the same way. So, what harm could there be in a long-distance test?

No harm. None at all. Until she told him they were the parents of a damn child.

Not a baby, but a six-year-old child. A freaking... well, what grade *would* he be in?

"What grade is he in?"

"First grade. He'll have Mrs. Call, the same teacher I had. She's very capable, if a little brisk, but a compassionate lady who works hard to inspire her little students to love learning. I remember how she often encouraged us to be independent in our thinking."

"And he's six now?"

"Yes. Exactly six years, nine and a half months from the night we first had sex. I promise you, there was never anyone else. You are free to do a paternity test if you challenge it. But when you see him, well, I expect your doubts will vanish. He bears such an uncanny resemblance to you."

"When? Not if?"

She sucked in a breath and buried her right foot in the soft sand. "When I told you about him, I hoped you'd want to meet him; otherwise, you would have been relegated to being a heartless monster, undeserving of any introduction to my son. And in that case, I'd have no guilt to haunt me later. Nor any blame for denying my son the chance to meet his biological father."

Father. She kept throwing out that word.

"What... how..." Matt failed to voice his spinning thoughts. Taking in a slow, controlled breath, he slowly said, "So how do we go about arranging this introduction?"

"I don't know. I could bring him here. Or you could come there to visit."

"And what happens next? You'll just say *hey, Benny, this is your father that you never met all your life?*"

"No. That is just about the worst introduction I can think of. I'm far more creative than that. I was thinking maybe he could meet you and be allowed a few days to get used to it. That would give both of you some time to accept it without adding the pressure of an instant connection. I think time will show you and Benny the best way to approach it. The right time to tell him will be based on how things go."

His son was about to enter his life for the first time. Matt would soon get to see and visit and know his son. Two hours ago, he wasn't aware such a boy existed. Now he felt a rush, and even a panic to meet and get to know him. Matt had to process what that meant. How to be a father from three hundred miles away. What did that look like? What would they look like together?

He glanced down at Lillian's head and a pressing thought stabbed his brain. "We... we are parents together."

"Yes." She finally glanced up at him, and her shoulders stiffened but a smile formed on her lips. "I've been having the same overwhelming thought all week. How can we be parents without knowing each other's favorite color?"

Matt stared into her dark, smoky eyes. The perfection of her features still fascinated him as he muttered, "Red. My favorite color is red."

A small, chagrined smile tilted her lips higher. "Mine is purple. Lavender, really."

"See? Now we know something personal about each other."

"Do you think we can figure out parenthood without killing each other in the process? My greatest fear is to scar our son through us arguing and feeling hateful. Trudging through courts and expensive lawyers. I don't know if we can manage it, but—"

"By telling me, you are already taking that chance."

"Yes."

"I must thank you then for telling me the truth. I guess my shock at hearing it just sent me off the deep end. At first, I responded with anger. The biggest reason was because you didn't tell me all week. I have a son who is six. It seems so clichéd. So impossible that I could be the father of a kid I did not know about. It's not a familiar reality for me. I always wear a condom, without exception. We—"

"Used a condom too. Believe me. My own head exploded over that. I had to explain it to my family, so they knew I wasn't a complete idiot. Looking back now, I doubt they listened or believed me. But still. I knew. I never expected to come home from school pregnant without even knowing the father longer than one night. Parenthood has redefined my self-image and humbled me in ways nothing else ever could."

"Do you think…" he lifted his gaze from the crashing surf and looked into her eyes and face. "Do you think I'll learn how to be a good father?"

"Yes, of course, I do. It's nothing more than learning how to adjust. If you lacked something like a core decency, I wouldn't have told you about him."

"You hold a lot of power."

"I did before. Luckily, you didn't really know that."

"I guess… thank you again for telling me."

She grimaced and laughed. "A few hours ago, you had the opposite reaction. Seeing how far you swung in only a few hours to return to your reasonable self is part of why I decided I could tell you. It still scares me witless. And I am very uncomfortable about giving control of my son to anyone else. But here I go; I'm doing it. For Benny, in his best interest."

"We have to promise each other to work this out in a civil manner. Always putting Benny and his best interests first." Matt spoke with deep conviction and didn't seem to flinch at having to put his own needs on the back burner. He was suddenly filled with a ferocious desire and burning need to meet and know his son. She was right. Benny's needs were their first priority even if they didn't jive with Matt's desires and needs. Benny, his son, came first now.

"God, you can't know the relief that gives me."

"You have my word on it. My father never considered my needs. Only his own. Even when he showed up and pretended to be fun. Caring about me for a few weeks out of a year when he wanted or needed something; he just used me to get whatever it was. But it left me devastated and confused. I was so much better when he didn't show up. Enduring repeated abandonments each time he disappeared again, I began to internalize it and blamed myself when he left. I thought it was my fault he didn't want to stay longer. My fault he left. I swear to you I will never do anything to Benny that might make him feel that way. I will always put him first. Even if you and I disagree about what that might be, I swear I will do it without fail."

She put her hand out and he stared down at it. "It's a deal. I will too."

"You already took a risk to you and him by telling me the truth without knowing the possible results. It took guts to do that. And as always, I admire you for having the guts."

They shook hands and a small smile brightened her face. "My guilt for not telling you brought me here, not any altruistic desire."

"You still did it. You sought the best answer for your... for *our* son. I admire that. And well, as we figure out parenting together, it might be fun."

Her breath released in a long sigh. "I've never shared Benny with anyone before. I will be protective, bossy and probably bitchy too. So, I have to apologize in advance. I will try to be on my best behavior."

"I will too." Under the strangest circumstances and reality, they shared a smile.

They also shared a son. The critical revelation kept seeping through his brain. Overwhelming him. Such intrigue and interest. And also, fear. His newfound responsibility and status congealed in a way he wasn't sure how to process.

Sucking in a deep breath after watching several waves crash on the shore, he asked, "What... what do we do now?"

"How would you like to visit my family's ranch? Can you take some time off from the boat?"

He couldn't, of course. But he had to. There was no other way. He had to meet his son obviously, so he would take time off. He'd figure it all out.

His head started spinning. *How to make it work? How to overcome all the logistics?* He lived at the ocean as a freaking charter boat captain while she lived on a landlocked horse ranch with his son. How could that work? The magnitude of what it meant was only just starting to reveal itself. Would he need a lawyer? Yes. Sure. They would have to petition for shared custody Shit. Damn. All the legalities involved started to overwhelm him, spearing him with unanticipated panic.

"Matt?"

"Yes. Of course. I have day trips scheduled throughout the end of this month, but I'll try to find a relief captain for... let's see... some time in mid-August." Could he wait that long? His inner voice was impatiently demanding he seek out his son, Benny, now! Today! This very moment. But practically speaking, he could not upend his life so instantly as that. Even if he wanted to. Did he? Of course, he did. Desperately. But lacking the financial freedom she took for granted, he couldn't simply do that. There was nothing about his job that could easily be foisted onto others. It was a unique job that not just anyone could do.

"Whatever works for you. School won't start until the day after Labor Day so it could work out well."

"September seventh?"

"Yes."

"So… you'll go home?"

"Yes. I've never been away from Benny so long and I'm dying to get back to my work. It was a nice break for the first few days, and rather liberating to run around by myself and only having to worry and take care of me but now I'm sick and tired of it."

How the crap would Matt be able to care for a six-year-old child? He knew nothing, nada, about kids. His experiences with children were limited to the ones who boarded his boat, and they all came with their own babysitters in their dang parents, grandparents or whoever decided to bring them along. Benny would be his new responsibility?

Feeling slightly dizzy as his breathing sped up, Matt wondered how did one talk to a six-year-old? He had no idea. No way.

But he had a six-year-old son. Glancing at the woman beside him, he found her face and her presence too much to take. Like a punch in the gut, her physical being really got to him. It happened on the night he met her. That oh-so-typical night, that was anything but typical and its long-term effects so much beyond what he ever imagined. An energy, an aura around her was what drew him to her like hummingbirds seek bright colors. Now, she confessed to being the mother of his child?

Mother.

Child.

Father.

Dad.

All the words that connected them. His learning curve would be steep and sharp if he wanted to catch up to speed with Lillian.

"I was thinking I could let him meet you without explaining exactly who you are. Let him ease into it so he'll have a face when he hears the term *dad*. You know? I could say you were a family friend, and let you spend some time with him and then, when it's right, we decide exactly how and when to tell him."

"I have no idea when. I don't know anything about kids."

She smiled a small and knowing *motherly* smile. "I was like that at first. This is trial by fire. But it won't have to be that extreme for you. He's walking and talking and he thinks his own thoughts. A lot less physical, demanding care. More about figuring out what works for you two." She shook her hair and it fell from her shoulder. "I thought you might hate me, or resent me, or want to punish me, and would try to approach him by showing up and demanding to see him. If you're not still angry with me, perhaps we can work it out slowly and ease him into it in a healthy way that works best for him."

"You really thought I could take out my anger at you on him?"

"How could I predict anything? There was no test to determine how you'd take the news. But I had to tell you, so it was essentially a shot in the dark."

"Yet you accepted responsibility for taking that shot?"

"I did. He deserves only the best in life and if that means being exposed to more people, meeting you, I can't deny him that. Not if I think your presence would enhance his life. From what I've witnessed, that is what I think."

"What do you see for our future? Shared custody? Or what?"

Her head tilted downwards. Digging her toes in the sand, she watched the tiny granules slide down before replying, "I don't know. Anything could happen. I just had to take a chance and I hoped you wouldn't hate me for doing it. Or take it out on Benny."

"I guess you must be stressed over what I'll do?"

She slipped a weary look at him. "You can't imagine."

"Well, then it's better for you to go home. I'll come visit you on a later date and we'll start from there. I don't know how else to approach this. I have no idea what to do."

"No plan. No map. No clue. That's kind of been my blue-print for being a parent from the start. I try to make plans, but nothing really sticks. That's kind of how it goes."

"Sounds terrifying."

"Oh, yes. It can be. Constantly. But some moments mean everything. Exhilarating. Life-affirming moments when you realize nothing else matters. Nothing but him." Her eyes filled with a soft, misty, loving look and her face flushed. The gentle, small smile that formed on her lips showed an inner joy, a bliss he couldn't even imagine. But she seemed to love her—*their*—child and it was evident in her expression and the tone of her words.

"That sounds like something that grew and developed over a matter of years. How does one achieve it after six years in?"

She turned to him; her gaze aware of his drilling look. Nodding, she said, "It was pretty instantaneous for me when he was born. I can't say how all parents feel. But with time and trust, any relationship can grow. The start is insignifi-cant. I know it's too late for you to meet baby Benny. I'm sorry for that but it is what it is. Once the shock wears off, we just move forward and start building a foundation of love."

He nodded. Turning his gaze back to the ocean, he stared at the line of soft blue sky where it joined the dark blue ocean. Yes. All that was true. If he lived a few miles away in a neighborhood close to hers instead of the rural and almost desolate area where she lived, and they were not hundreds of miles away, time could allow him to see Benny more often. So, was he choosing how their relationship would evolve? Even if he didn't choose it, and it simply got dumped on him, now he was a father. A distant, absentee father? Who saw Benny when? And how?

The dizzying thoughts made him freeze again. No.

No. Not yet. No more panicking.

He needed to start with their first meeting and work from there.

"Okay. Obviously, you know better than me how to approach him."

Bitterness made his tongue taste sour. If he just told Lillian his name was Mathias that night, would all of these years turned out differently?

But that was a non-issue. The present was all they had. And a shared child. A deeper connection. Something that could last a lifetime. And yet she slept with him again. Last night. Why?

"What about last night?"

Her face heated with a deep blush and her gaze shifted instantly to the water. "I don't know. I didn't plan that. Not at all. It wasn't supposed to happen. Nothing I intended at all. But then—"

"Plans don't always work out?"

She gave him a small smile. "No. They don't. Especially when they concern you." Her tone softened as she added, "I don't honestly know, Matt. I—we probably shouldn't have as it complicates everything so much more than needs to be. I know that. And I should have told you about Benny before, so you could decide what to do. I just… it happened and all my thoughts, and the consequences, fled my brain—"

He knew. He knew exactly what she meant. It was simply them being caught in the moment. Nothing else mattered. He felt it as deeply and surely as she tried to articulate it.

But Matt wasn't aware of their relationship like she was. He didn't know that they shared a child. Flesh and blood and bone. The physical extension of their first connection didn't exist until now. Now that she inadvertently complicated it even more.

What did he want from her? To date? A long-distance relationship? It could never work. He could not leave Westport and she would never be happy living here. What reason could there be to outweigh that?

Except that freaking heat that invariably seemed to surround them. It never made sense and it still didn't. Yet here they were.

"I'm sorry. I shouldn't have let things go so long. Especially without telling you."

"Did you consider telling me before? Or was it then?"

"I decided before that. What I didn't plan to happen was last night."

"Which leaves us… where?"

Her head shook. "How about visiting us and we can take it one day at a time from there?"

Reasonable. Prudent. But Matt's guts screamed for more. More answers. More commitment. More words to explain it. More preparation. More to illustrate what the hell just happened?

Matt just nodded. "Okay. I'll start figuring out how to visit you."

CHAPTER 11

*W*HEN BENNY FILLED HER arms, Lillian curled him up against her body and sniffed his clean, silky hair. She brushed her lips through it, kissing his forehead and savoring the few moments of bliss before he grew restless, pulled back and said, "Grandpa is teaching me how to throw a football."

She let his words, smiles and innocent enthusiasm satiate her. Missing all of it, the excitement he had when he saw her, talked to her, and told her all about his latest events, meant the world to her. She loved this time that was so limited, only a few years before the preteen phase. But for now, Benny was all hers and he missed her as much as she did him.

Well, he was all hers for another two weeks. Until the arrival of his father.

She shuddered, wondering how to deal with the coming reality. The novelty of the role Matt might play in raising Benny was difficult to get used to. All the decisions she had to make until yesterday, were completely and totally within her control. She'd miss that now.

Fear knotted her guts when she tried to imagine where

this new reality would take her. Them. Would it turn out to be a blessed event they looked back on years from now, still thrilled that they managed to find each other? Or would it signal the end to the brief peace and happiness they had? Would it become relegated to legal fees and ceaseless fights? All this kept churning up her insides during the space of time that elapsed since Mathias suddenly popped back into her life.

Now that she told him the truth, the consequences had to follow no matter what. Having no control over that, she hoped to mitigate any negative factors and expand all the positives, of which there appeared many, and the reason why she took the risk.

That's what she kept thinking about and trying to convince herself on the long ride home alone. She replayed the entire week from her deepest doubts to the final reveal. And still she suffered from a crippling uncertainty. What if the night they spent together was the only thing that compelled her to tell him the truth? What if she allowed the second, incredible night they shared to skew her better judgment? What if she were painting rainbows for a man who didn't deserve it simply because she experienced another intoxicating night with him?

For that's exactly what happened. He once more got to her. Just as he did over six years ago. No one else could. Since that night, no other man came close to attracting Lillian long enough for a second date or even keeping her attention. Despite an active dating life, none of her dates ever inspired her with the sense of camaraderie and ease that she instantly received with Matt. It was undeniable. Never before had such a connection happened to her with a man. It had to mean something. Like her guts responded to him because they recognized the integrity and goodness in him. There was instinctually something upstanding about him.

Lillian trusted it so much, she staked her freaking son's life on it. Now, looking back, what if she were wrong? What could that mean?

What if Matt sued her for Benny's custody?

Her fears collaborated to twist and turn her guts. Like the tumbling mountain of water when the waves crashed on the shore, her thoughts plummeted and soared. When she was sure she made the right judgment call, her relentless fears re-emerged and scolded her for messing up. Being with a man on a romantic tryst was bound to change her perception of working as a parent with him and trying to raise a child.

Gripping Benny tightly now, she shut her eyes and prayed she detected Matt's true identity and her leap of faith would not be in error. That this would turn out to be a bridge for the breach in Benny's childhood and not a mistake she would later look back on and regret, realizing she created the entire problem for herself.

"How'd it go?" her mom asked when she came directly to them to see Benny. He stayed with them while she investigated his father. She still amazed herself by doing such a thing.

"It went." She shook her head.

Lillian checked in each day she was gone, but not on the last day. Her parents didn't yet know if she even told Matt about Benny.

"Did you...?" Her mom's voice trailed off.

"I did. I told him." Releasing Benny, who remained close to her, she distracted him with the toy boat she brought back from her "work vacation" that Benny believed was the reason she was gone.

"And?"

"He was furious at first and stormed out of the house. His granddad told me where he went and said I should go to him. I found him sitting on the beach and we had a long talk. I

135

pointed out the obvious reasons for my hesitation in telling him. I said I owed it to Benny to check him out first. Considering all the damage a bad father figure could do to my son, I had to be sure. If he were a detrimental influence on Benny, I would not have told him. He calmed down, and he understood my uncertainty."

"Then?"

"Then the full impact hit him. Hard. He had to repeat all of it more than once just to get his head around our connection. And the idea that he has a... well, you know."

Jocelyn nodded and set a hand on Lillian's shoulder. "If he is at least a decent human being, I think you did the right thing. Benny deserves it and maybe so does he."

"I think he is, or I'd never have told him. But it doesn't make it any easier on my frayed nerves when I imagine what he might do, the damage he could cause. These thoughts keep clashing in my head. It was the right thing... but what if he decides he wants shared custody? What if it turns into some lengthy, terrible fight in court?"

"You will always emerge the primary parent. Come on, Lillian. You're his mother. You've always stepped up and accepted Benny as your sole responsibility. He has an entirely secure and promising life here. No judge would allow him to be taken away from you and be replaced by a stranger in an unfamiliar life. Nothing beyond prescribed, judicially approved visits. Supervised visits, maybe even. But never to replace his life with you. I mean, really? The ocean?"

"I know. It's a nerve-wracking mess."

They finished talking and Lillian declined her mother's invitation for dinner. She was more than ready to go home with Benny and return to a familiar routine. She had to find a way to reassure herself she'd done the right thing, and Matt would only enrich their lives, not destroy them. Not alter them either. Or make hers more difficult. She also hoped

Matt would not advise her or comment on her parenting, which was strictly her domain. Her son belonged here, with her and the family, in the home and lifestyle he was already well accustomed to and happy with.

Matt was a good, decent man. Surely, he would see the logic of that and understand it. Though it might be hard, he would have to limit their contact due to the great distance that separated him from them. She'd welcome Matt to visit and become a part of Benny's life, but he could not ever take Benny away with him.

Later, as she tucked Benny in bed and kissed his smooth forehead, he turned on his side, closing his eyes in the complete safety and joy of a wonderful life he'd known since birth. Then Lillian prayed she wasn't rocking the boat.

MATT TOLD Granddad the real story behind Lillian and broke the news that Matt had a six-year-old son.

"Oh, Mathias. That is—" Overcome by his strong emotions, Granddad shook his head and his small smile revealed unmasked joy for Matt.

"Wonderful? Is it? The child is six years old and never knew the first thing about me. I don't know a thing about him either. I don't know a damn thing about kids, period. I can't learn the way Lillian did, I'll be abruptly thrown in with him and what do I even say?"

His granddad's jaw ticked, his eyes gleamed as he replied simply, "I don't know, maybe start with hello."

He gave Granddad a sharp look and rolled his eyes. "This is far more complicated than just a simple greeting."

"Doesn't have to be. Seems like a great place to start any relationship."

"I live halfway across the state. How can we sustain a relationship of any kind?"

"You can definitely have one. You *must* have one. Now that you know about him, don't be a deadbeat like your own father. You know the pain of being ignored by your father. Never even a thought or fleeting concern. Of not being the number one priority."

Matt's guts churned. Didn't he know that reality too well? How much it hurt to be irrelevant and no concern to one's parent? Yes, he knew that feeling. And his son didn't know he existed. Six years in. His worse nightmare horrified him. If anyone else had undergone this reality, he'd have sympathized and said the woman should not have hidden his son from him. But the simple reason why Lillian couldn't find him was oddly tragic and fully credible. She had his name wrong. Mathias Griffin is not as common as Mathew Griffin. She just assumed his nickname was an abbreviation for Mathew and he never said otherwise.

His heart clenched at the thought of Lillian Rydell. How to register all the developments during the last week? She upended his life in every way. This woman, the only one who could manage to capture his undivided attention, interest and attraction, lived so far away. The woman he looked forward to having a romantic farewell dinner with, if only to float the idea of seeing her again, suddenly launched him into an incredible night of wild sex. It impressed him so much he dared to voice his desire to be exclusive. She was that potent to him. Something he never desired before.

Then, she dropped the bomb. The words she said could have been landmines exploding at his feet as well as overhead. That's how confusing and volatile the ensuing conversation was. He went from wanting to see Lillian again, to hoping never to speak to her again. He wished she would disappear and take those awful words back. Those alarming, life-altering, mood-shattering words were a lie, and she could just swallow them whole. They could not be true.

He had a son? A son who never knew him?

Not exactly how he'd choose to start bonding with his offspring if he ever decided to have kids. In his heart, his guts, and his mind, fatherhood would always be a choice. His choice. Hence, the safe sex practices he so diligently followed.

But six years ago, his son was born.

Thankfully, he was being raised by a dynamic, interesting, fun, kind woman, at least so far as he knew her. The only woman who entranced him.

"Mathias?" His granddad's voice interrupted the mini-panic attack Matt succumbed to in the middle of their conversation. Lifting his gaze, he blinked and tuned back into the moment. "It's a good thing. Neither you nor Dr. Lillian intended to hurt each other or the child. Circumstances denied you three a chance to start together and be parents. But the gift, the blessing is: you know now. You get to know your son now. She chose to tell you because of the good person she saw that you are, Mathias. She was checking you out for your worthiness, as I commended her for doing. I give her more points for giving you the knowledge she didn't have to divulge. She had little to gain by doing so, it seems. She doesn't need your money or support, but she did it for him. For her son. The son you two conceived. That speaks volumes regarding the woman she is. The woman I believed I met, so this rings all true to me. So, you go there. You go and meet your son. If you start now, you can probably make up for the lost years. In the coming years, you'll laugh and say, *oh darn, we missed a little time, but look at all the years we've gotten to share together now.*"

"I don't live there. I can't just move my charter business to a small, rural town that's landlocked in the middle of the state."

"I realize that. But there are cars, trains and airplanes. Phones. Video chatting. There are endless ways you could find to connect. So what if it's second best? Far better than the six years of silence before. So, embrace whatever you can and try to be with him. And her too, if that's the path you two decide to go down."

His thoughts were flooded with doubts, facts and too many feelings. "I can't begin to worry about a romance now. It's all changed."

"Understandably. But go and meet him, your son. And then perhaps someday, I'll get to meet him. That would make me very happy. I look forward to that fine day."

His granddad could handle any news, be it huge and life-changing, and see something positive and constructive in it. He also knew how to navigate through it. Living a hard life, his chill attitude and thoughtful analysis of the situation started to percolate in Matt.

"You will meet him, Granddad. I swear it."

Granddad sighed. "Yes, but only if it doesn't become a battle between you and Dr. Lillian. She's his mother. Always was. Her time as the child's primary parent will continue and it'll take a long while before it is equitable. Fair or not, that's Benny's reality so it must come first. His emotional, physical and mental wellbeing are the goals here. So yes, I hope to meet him but only when Dr. Lillian feels the time is right for him to visit here. Only when Benny is good and ready. You must keep that focus in all your interactions with him. Do you hear me? That's how your grandma and I raised you. That's how we overcame your father's negligence. And look at the fine man you turned out to be."

Matt smiled gently at his elderly grandfather, realizing he was the sole reason Matt was worth a damn in the world.

Matt leaned forward and set a hand on his shoulder and gently squeezed it. "I swear to you, Granddad, I'll do right by my son."

Granddad patted his hand. "Then all will go well."

The next two weeks were spent making arrangements to leave his boat with a relief captain, who was injured earlier this summer, but claimed he was ready to go out with the help of his son. It cost Matt far more than he could spare, but there was no other way around it. Benny came first. Meeting him at all costs was just that. As Granddad said, Matt was a parent now and good parenting came with lots of sacrifices.

Matt and Lillian texted several times with details and questions. But they hadn't spoken again. Matt wondered why. Doubt and concern became his constant companions. He couldn't articulate why he hesitated in calling the woman he most wanted a relationship with. Someone he often contemplated speaking to, but being the mother of his child, he remained mute. Strangely enough. So, they texted. He did it first and she answered but no phone call ever followed.

Finally, the day to embark on his adventure arrived. Packing his truck with his belongings, he said goodbye to Granddad with a hug and an emotional hand wave. He worried a lot about leaving Granddad all alone, but Granddad scoffed at Matt's concern. "I live with you to keep you company, not for you to babysit me. Go and have fun. For God's sake, I'm not a child."

Matt grinned and accepted the chiding but asked a neighbor friend to check in on Granddad a few times during the week. Just in case.

The drive was long and tedious, but conveniently doable in a day. He left Westport mid-morning and sped through the highway toward River's End. His stomach roiled in nerves at seeing the exit sign for the small, quaint town. He briefly considered swinging off and turning onto the street where the infamous tavern was, the place where he over-heard the Rydell name on his first visit. And look what happened since that day... However, showing up with beer breath wasn't the best way to make a good impression when being introduced to one's own *son.*

So, he skipped the beer. The urge to turn his truck around and quickly start driving home when a sudden rush of nerves overcame him, came and went. His grip on the steering wheel got slick as his clammy hands and rising tension persisted. But then he spotted the offramp. Right there. He slowed the truck down as he passed the sign, *Rydell River Ranch and Resort* with a collage of pictures of horses, picnics, golf, and swimming.

His baby mama was kind of rich. Great. Not sure that excited or intimidated him.

Oh, and a doctor. Intelligent, super-educated, competent and real, she handled having a child alone for six years? Truly, what could he possibly offer to attract her? What could be needed from him?

Those harsh thoughts flooded his confidence.

Meeting Lillian was no indication she was anything other than classy and nice. She had an easy-going manner and personality, being pretty low-key about life in general. But she also cared about people and not like an afterthought. She was a serious person and important things mattered to her.

Finally, he emerged from the tall trees and the road opened up to reveal the Rydell River Valley in all of its glory. His son's home. He stopped the truck since there was no traffic behind him. Or anywhere nearby really.

Sending a quick text off to Lillian as agreed, he let her know he was within minutes of showing up. She had to prepare their son most likely. Or herself. Was she as nervous as he was? Confused. Uncertain of his trip, this day, and what the next few moments held. Would they be remembered always as something good or terrible? The beginning or the end?

The dirt road had no lane markings. If a car came from the other direction, one would have to drive to a pullout, which thankfully, there were many. The river was a winding, silvery ribbon, narrowing to a thin, blue trail. The land bordering each side of it featured varying hues of green, brown and beige. The lush green fields in various spots seemed to be pastures. They appeared to be the only oases in the hot, August, furnace-like air. Brown fields in the landscape offered a glimpse of what the entire valley would look like under the hot sun without any water to irrigate and transform it into verdant fields of grass and fruit orchards. The backside of River's End sat on a bank above the river. There, the river sloshed up steeply and some of the backyards of a few houses and businesses were barely discernible.

Further down river, the brown, bumpy mountains rose up high, seeming to cradle each other as they brushed the underside of the endless blue sky. Nestled on the left side of the river, beyond his view, lay the Rydell River Ranch and Resort. The family residences and their seemingly unlimited Rydell family holdings included the picturesque fields of horses, a tranquil addition to the fascinating landscape. White fencing hugged the road and soon became a wandering network of spiderweb-like enclosures. Closest to him was a huge indoor horse arena, surrounded by barns, paddocks, riding corrals and more fencing. The giant labyrinth had to be operated by someone who knew the property and all of its procedures very well. But wow, was it big and complicated.

Below that, the road continued like a curving ribbon, paved here and there, which ended near the small, quaint cabins. Standing like soldiers guarding the river, the resort cabins were dwarfed by a much bigger building that Matt believed was the Rydell River Inn. The grounds featured mature landscaping with a canopy of trees, lovely gardens, cobbled pathways and other popular amenities.

Based on Lillian's descriptions of the ranch and outbuildings, much further away and harder to view were the Rydell homes that followed the bends in the river, along with more barns and outbuildings. Again, someone had to manage a rather extensive enterprise.

Above him and across the road lay the freshly manicured green turf of the eighteen-hole golf course. Winding around and through the mountains, it greeted the viewer like a refuge in what would otherwise have been the barren, dusty, arid mountain tops.

Breathtaking scenery. All of it made him gasp.

The tiny river offered oceans of distractions. Matt doubted the water would be any deeper than his knees in most places. Where were the afternoon breezes? The cool air that never failed to arrive even on warm days at the coast? The sun felt brighter, hotter and more vibrant here, but also more apt to singe and burn him.

Suddenly, Matt felt very far from home.

His nerves climbed into his throat and lodged there as he slowly put his truck into gear and drove towards the second entrance, where a gigantic overhead sign read *The Rydell River Ranch.* That was the entrance Lillian told him to use before giving him the gate code. She expressly instructed him not to divulge the code to anyone else as it was strictly a family secret, known only to a few trustworthy friends. Lillian told him that her sort-of-cousin, Iris was assaulted on the ranch grounds before they installed more extensive security. Knowing that she trusted Matt with her private code was a true sign of goodwill. He had no complaints about Lillian Rydell. She was clearly trying to be as accommodating and open to him as possible. She viewed his role as the father of her child very seriously. He sensed that she respected him and appreciated his presence in their lives.

Tapping the code into the control pad, he waited as the gate slowly started to swing open. Matt proceeded through it before it just as slowly swung shut again behind him. He drove down the rural road, passing more horses and white fencing, along with dry grass pastures, and spots with green fields that had sprinklers watering them. A sign was posted that pointed out the various routes to the various destinations. Remembering which one Lillian told him to take, the furthest one on the left, Matt approached the residence where she lived with his son. The family compound seemed more like a monstrosity to Matt, but she lived here with Benny.

He nearly shuddered as he looked around. The situation was unprecedented to him. Showing up to meet his son, now aged six, without previously knowing him at all made Matt very uncomfortable. He estimated at least two dozen people lived here, all somehow connected to her family. They reminded Matt of a nineteenth-century dynasty, in which the Rydells were the lords and ladies of the manor. However, Lillian's personality was not like that at all. He felt odder, now that the time had arrived to face it, never mind all the potential witnesses to it. Ugh. God help him.

Pulling in front of the fourth house on the right, like Lillian told him to do, Matt parked his truck.

It was a modest, one-story house, very quaint and homey, but simple and small. He didn't expect that. All the land and buildings Matt glimpsed while driving there gave him much higher expectations. A basic design with a garage connected to the main part of house. The door that led to the garage featured a double entry and the large windows beyond that appeared to be bedroom windows.

Matt's sense of comfort was instantly bolstered when he

saw the charmingly simple but welcoming house. He recognized it. Someone closer to his income bracket lived there, instead of an extravagant, indulgent landowner.

Pine trees and thick vegetation dominated the land behind the house. A small, green lawn that was obviously irrigated followed the driveway and surrounded the pathway to the front door. A few small flower beds added a riot of colors to the scenery. The roof was a dark red metal with complementary siding. To his pleasant surprise, Lillian Rydell wasn't flashy. She didn't require huge amounts of her family's wealth to build the home she shared with Benny. It was pristine yet simple in taste and character.

Just like Lillian's personality, he marveled.

It warmed his heart when he imagined her living in this house.

His hand shaking, he began to press the doorbell. It chimed and in no time at all, footsteps were audible. A head popped up behind the small relite in the door. The double-paned glass distorted Lillian's face, but Matt had no doubt it was her. He felt sick as stomach acid boiled up into his throat.

Here he was.

The moment had arrived at last. Would Benny be at home? Or was he somewhere else? He should have clarified the plan with Lillian because he had no idea how this would go down. What did she decide was the best way to do it? It was the oddest goddamned situation he could ever imagine.

She grabbed the doorknob and swung the door wide open. No other noise came from behind her so Matt believed she was the only one at home.

Thank God. His relief washed over him. But maybe he shouldn't be so happy. Although he really was. He needed some time to psych himself up for this.

All at once, the full impact of seeing Lillian Rydell in the flesh hit him again. The snug way she fit beneath his collar-bone. The soft sway of thick, dark hair and the gleam in her eyes. Her coy smile, so genuine and shy, yet confident and welcoming. He sensed her confusion to the situation just as he felt the same. They stared at one another without moving or speaking. It lasted far too long to be a casual, easy greeting. Matt's eyes roamed down her body, taking in the black-ribbed tank top she wore over khaki shorts that stopped mid-thigh. Her smooth, firm legs were both shapely and well-toned. But Matt also saw the sparkle in her eyes. Her interest. Intelligence. Did he really see a flash of joy in them when she first saw him? He was sure of it. Lillian scanned him too, taking in his handsome exterior. His presence pleased her. An undeniable, mutual attraction and warmth brought them together long before they discussed it and no surprise, it continued to this moment. He never considered himself a particularly interesting or attractive guy, but with Lillian? Hell, whatever she saw in him he found in bucketfuls when he looked at her. Still, she was so far out of his league in her looks, her pedigree, her famous family, unlimited wealth and above-average smarts.

He was proud, actually, that he incited this usually care-ful, articulate woman to act outside of her normal behavior. Even at this moment, and both times they had sex, he never believed casual sex appealed to her.

Except with him.

After visibly swallowing, Lillian said, "Hi."

He stared at her solemnly and replied in a serious tone, "Hi."

That was followed by both of them plastering on strained, yet familiar grins. They were sharing this moment just as deeply as they so often did their other moments. Shaking her head, Lillian commented on the obvious. "This is so strange."

"Yeah. It's definitely that," he agreed.

She opened the door. "Please, come inside, out of the heat. And we'll..."

"Figure out how to be Benny's parents together?" he asked dryly as he passed her. She shut the door behind him.

"Yeah. I guess that's why I feel so uncomfortable right now."

"Most people would."

She gestured for him to leave the safety of the door and he turned and saw the small, tidy entryway that dropped into a sunken living room tastefully decorated in soft grays and blues. He scanned the room, saying, "What a great house."

She laughed. "I spent most of last week cleaning it. Obsessively. I also planted all of those flowers in front, trying to... I don't even know what. Improve the surroundings, I guess. As if having perfectly spotless floors would let me know how to approach this."

"I showered twice this morning."

She stared at him, her eyebrows jutting up with unmasked curiosity. "Really? Why?"

"I hoped it would calm my nerves and help me make some sense out of this. After the first time, I purposely didn't shave, trying to appear more casual and cool, but then I decided I looked lazy and careless. So, I undressed and took another shower, shaved, and started all over again."

Her eyes dilated with undisguised, (and he suspected), unintentional interest when he said he *undressed*. She covered her silly gaffe by lowering her head and releasing a little laugh. "Unfortunately, nothing seems to make this any easier."

"No. I guess we'll just have to muddle through it."

She exhaled a breath. "Yeah. I think so too. And... it's nice that you admit that... you own your uneasiness and confusion over what to do, and you're so honest about it. Puzzles me sometimes why that is, why we can be so honest."

"Always been like that between us. It puzzles me too."

And they went right back to being honest.

Their gazes glimmered as they stared appreciatively at the other. Matt was magnetically drawn to her, which was how they ended up in this situation.

"Well, I appreciate all the work you did, and it's a great house and garden."

"The best is this way." He followed her to a glassed-in sunroom. The space was expansive, airy, bright and wonderful. The sky was visible and huge pine trees spared the room from too much heat by providing dappled shade on the floor. But the view that overlooked the river was the real jewel. Flashing reflections through the red, wrinkled trees, the backdrop extending to the foothills, sounding like a loud, rushing fountain, it offered a soothing background and unparalleled serenity.

"Wow. This is fantastic."

"Yes, I purposely designed my house to be plain in the front so the entire back view would include the river and the forest while giving us a lot more privacy." She waved toward her patio wicker furniture that was covered in dark green cushions. "Please sit down. Let me get you a tall glass of lemonade."

He nodded with a smile and sat as she disappeared. When she returned, she carried a glass pitcher of lemonade with fresh lemon wedges and plenty of ice cubes. She filled two glasses and the ice cubes made a clinking sound. Matt sipped the cool, perfectly delightful concoction and Lillian sat down to enjoy hers. Matt was never so formally received by anyone before, and he was careful to remember his manners.

Finally, Lillian swallowed a gulp of lemonade and sighed, "Oh, fuck it."

"What?" Matt replied, somewhat startled.

"I've never made lemonade before. Nor do I often sip it

while sitting back here so formally. I don't even have a glass pitcher. I had to borrow this one from my grandmother. I'm not that type of person at all. I rarely entertain because I'm usually too busy and uninterested in socializing. Honestly, most of the time Benny's toys are scattered all over the living room and our shoes are usually in a pile by the door. Our two cats, which we adore, shed their hair all over the chair you're sitting in, and I had to spend an hour vacuuming most of it off there. I was trying to make a good impression on you, but I can't talk about it now. I feel unlike I ever have before."

He waited a beat and put the glass down as he started to laugh. "Do you have any beer? A can would be—"

"Great," she exclaimed loudly, and Matt finally heard her natural laugh. They happily abandoned their formal, picture-perfect pretense for two cans of beer, which they tapped together in a toast before taking generous gulps.

"So, how about starting over? What are your cats' names? By the way, it's damn nice to see you again," Matt said before swallowing the cold brew.

She tipped her head as a thank you and her cheeks began warming rapidly.

"It's nice to see you again too."

Their gazes collided, and they held each other captive. Why this incessant, irresistible draw? Matt sipped the beer to break the trance and cleared his throat.

He came there to begin a relationship with his son, not the woman who gave birth to him. The woman who had sex with him again, just a few weeks ago.

"So... um, Benny's not here?"

She sharpened her gaze on him and pressed her lips together. "No. I thought you'd appreciate having a few moments to collect yourself and allow us to connect first. Benny's at my parents' house, which is a short walk up the road. So, you won't have to wait too long. I just thought this was a better way." She shrugged. "I have no clue really what the best way to do this is. As you've already observed."

Matt drank faster when his nerves started feeling raw again. "Neither do I. That's good. I mean, we need a few moments between us if only to help us figure out exactly what to say."

"I told Benny a college friend of mine was coming here for a visit and wanted to stay for a few days on vacation. I hope that works. It takes all the pressure off you. You can talk and interact more naturally with him and just go with the flow. Eventually, when it's right, we'll tell him the unvarnished truth and explain ourselves then."

Matt's anxiety colored his logic, and he was nearly ready to fling the truth out and get it over with. Without any warning, he thought he should let the child know who he was. But this sounded much more sensible. Calmer, more rational and more child-friendly. Again, Benny came first. That had to be Matt's mantra from now on.

"Yes. That is a good way, I agree. So…"

"I didn't want to tell him by myself. Or toss it out there and confuse him or make him unsure how he should treat you. But perhaps a face, a voice and a personality will help Benny realize what *father* means when we clear everything up for him. And perhaps, it'll do the same for you. For us."

He nodded. "Because there is no other way to go, now that the truth is out."

"No. None. From the moment I realized I was pregnant by a man I didn't know, and had no way of finding, I considered what to say if Benny ever asked me about his father."

The stark reminder of what young Lillian endured for not knowing where Matt was and being forced to introduce him to his own child horrified him now. Learning that his life's path was suddenly irrevocably taking a new direction was a lot to handle. But Lillian's was much worse.

She cleared her throat. "So let me call my folks, and they'll bring Benny here. I think that would be better. That way, it's not like putting you under a microscope lens. Just give me a few minutes." She all but catapulted to her feet, eager for something to do, or so it seemed.

Matt rose to his feet too, and his stomach wrenched with cramps. Holy shit. Here it was. Finally. The big moment.

CHAPTER 12

*L*ILLIAN HELD HER PHONE and quickly texted her mom. Her fingers felt too large, and she fumbled when she pressed the small keys. It was Matt's presence. He was so potent to her senses. Yet, he wasn't really doing anything. Mostly quiet since entering her house, Matt barely moved, keeping his limbs close to his sides and calm. No nervous jiggling or toe-tapping like Lillian worried her whole body was doing. He spoke clearly and appeared sure, but when she suggested calling her parents, she didn't miss the streak of apprehension that filled his eyes. Thank God. He finally seemed to grasp the unique novelty and magnificence of this moment. How strange it would be to introduce a parent to their child for the first time. The blame would fall on the parent in most cases, who deserved their discomfort and any negative feelings that might have accompanied it. In this case, however, Matt and Lillian did nothing wrong deliberately. It was careless, perhaps. Whatever one thinks about one-night stands and casual sex with strangers was personal and beyond the judgment of others. Matt's failure to know his son wasn't his fault, nor was it hers. And now, here they were, surprisingly amiable still despite the ordeal that loomed before them. Matt obviously was more distressed and unsure about being a father.

One moment, he was single and childless and the next, he was the father of a growing child. Disconcerting? Ya think? Pretty unsettling for most guys.

And yet, Matt looked so good. Lillian's stomach fluttered with things unrelated to her son or their pivotal meeting. His dark brown hair curled and coiled around his head in adorable ringlets just like their son possessed. She was still allowed to twirl and twist Benny's hair and gawk over it, since Benny didn't mind. Lillian expected him to someday yank his head away with a sharp retort at her. But until then, she caressed the silky curls that danced all over his head and covered his ears and forehead when he went too long without a trim.

Matt's curls were the same. Adorable, framing a symmetrical face with deep brown eyes and a sharp, straight nose. He had a smooth forehead and high cheekbones. He seemed even more handsome right now in his tailored slacks and button-up shirt. He wanted to present himself in a well-groomed, respectable light, not the grungy clothes of his vocation. It didn't really matter what he wore because her insides began curling and stretching and longing to touch and caress him like always.

He was a sensuous man. A hot, single, intriguing man.

Matt was already far more than the biological father of her child. And co-parent. There was nothing to describe how she felt around him.

Lillian became an irresistible, pulsating, hungry, lusting woman whenever she encountered him. That never happened to Lillian before.

She bit her lip to distract her from her naughty thoughts as he stood up and stepped closer to her. She hated the way people towered over her, since many of her family members were tall but with Matt, she didn't mind being small at all. It made her hot when she imagined herself being so tiny and protected by him. A series of little bursts and urges ran through her entire body. His smile was a bit crooked, one-sided, and his nerves seemed to bring it out whenever he got distressed. Lillian loved how it sent little butterflies to flight inside her. Stop. She had to halt her fantasies and focus on reality.

Benny was what mattered now. This man was his *father.* He was the only person in the entire world with as much legal authority and claim to her son as she had. He was the only person who could challenge her in court over Benny. The power that no one else possessed, but she was fantasizing about his physically appealing wide shoulders instead of his reaction to meeting his son. At such a huge, poignant moment, she was lost in… what? Sexual fantasies? She hadn't had sex in eighteen months prior to her decisive night with Matt. Sexual gratification was never number one on her list of priorities, but a few weeks since being with Matt again, she was all but ready to grab him to relieve her from the swirling, hot images and passionate emotions.

Then came the knock. They were here. Matt tensed beside her, and she automatically reached out and set her hand on his arm above his wrist. "Do you prefer to wait here? I'll bring Benny in with me. It'll be okay," she added lamely, for lack of anything else to say. His mouth was suddenly bracketed with stress lines and he was unsmiling. She squeezed the flesh of his arm and quickly released him.

"That's fine. Yes. I'd prefer to wait here." His tone sounded strangled.

She withdrew her hand and turned to leave, adding over her shoulder, "Smile. You don't want to scare him."

He gave her a mock smile that made her giggle. "Not like that. That will definitely scare him."

"So… somewhere in between?"

"Yes. I'll go get him now."

He nodded since there was nothing more she could do to make this any easier for either of them.

Hurrying to the front door, she opened it and found her mom and Benny standing there with Benny's little hand in hers. Benny darted inside.

She and her mom exchanged long, heartfelt glances. "How's it going so far?"

Oh, fine. I want to jump his bones every time I meet his gaze was the first thought that crossed Lillian's mind, but she settled for a more polite response. "Good. I mean, when you think about the situation. He's very polite and he doesn't blame me. He's also unsure and nervous but that's probably to be expected."

"Yeah. That would be about right. I remember the moment your dad met you when you were only a few days old. So this must be… a lot more intense."

"It is. A lot more."

"Let me know how it goes."

Lillian nodded as she shut the door after her mom left. Turning, she grinned at her son. "Hey, Benny. Remember the friend I told you about? He's here now. Come and meet him."

"Okay." Benny's good-natured tone showed little reaction. Why would he? He didn't care about any of her other friends who came over. He might have reacted with more interest if the friend were his own age.

Benny took Lillian's hand when she offered it. She fought the urge to wrap him in her embrace and suffocate him with a bear hug against her chest. The compulsive need to shelter him and remind herself he was hers and that could never change made her squeeze his hand even harder.

But his father came a long way to meet him. She wished sometimes that Benny was younger so they could just include his dad without the need for explanation or worrying about the effects on Benny's psychological development. Other times, she wished Benny was older so she could just be honest. She felt bad too, like she was tricking him by calling Matt a friend since he eventually would learn Matt was his father. It was supposed to feel strange, she supposed. They knew the magnitude of this crucial meeting, but Benny didn't. How could he know what it meant? Even if she explained it to him, he wouldn't understand. He understood just enough to ignore it. She hoped she was doing the right thing.

With that, she pushed the door to the sunroom open and sucked in a deep breath to fortify her reserves. Here was the place where it finally would happen. After six years and countless hours of angst and worried concern, Benny was about to meet his father.

MATT TURNED when he heard them entering behind him. He was pretending to stare out at the landscape, watching the river, but he was actually hoping somehow to soothe his jittery nerves. Damn. This was so uncomfortable and difficult, he feared he could not breathe.

After turning around, he stared for a prolonged moment.

The child looked exactly like him. No one could doubt Matt was Benny's father if they saw them together. Holy shit.

Benny had the same deep chestnut ringlets, the same round eyes and the same eye color as Matt. Even his profile was identical to Matt's. Matt never suspected Lillian would lie, but after seeing Benny in person, he had absolutely no doubt. His mouth hung open for an extended moment and he failed to respond or even move. He was staring in disbelief at his son. That was all he could do. His own flesh and blood was staring back at him curiously but not nearly as amazed as Matt was. Clinging onto his mother's hand, Benny showed no sign of realization as he looked at the strange man with exactly the same face as his. *Exactly*. There was no flash of recognition on Benny's part. Matt's thoughts dipped. He dared to hope Benny would feel it instantaneously. Whatever "it" was. The sense of kinship a *father* feels for his child that usually occurs when his baby was born. A parent experiences that bonding instantaneously. Why not an older child? One who bore his freaking identical image?

But there was no immediate bond. The disturbing realization of knowing the kid looked exactly like him only further perplexed him. Matt had no idea what to do or say or feel. Benny was still a complete unknown to Matt, which made him feel even stranger about him. Matt's mouth opened and shut but he remained speechless. He blinked at his mini-me but felt nothing for him. No unconditional love suddenly emerged at the knowledge that this young boy was his son. There was no visceral link beyond sharing his flesh and blood. There was nothing. Nada. Not even a ripple of a bond. It was just like meeting any kid for Matt.

His disappointment nearly crushed him. Matt hoped and needed to make a connection, and he clung to that, expecting he would recognize the child as his own at once. His heart would sense his offspring and then he would just know what to do, and say, and feel.

Instead, Matt was just as awkward and unsure around kids as he was five minutes ago.

Lillian took a few steps forward. "Benny, this is my friend, Matt. Matt, meet my son, Benny."

The moment was so… deflated. Disappointing. Lame. His heart lamented with regret. He smiled, offhandedly trying to conceal his total ambivalence toward the child. Benny was her son. *Hers.* Not his. That was evident whenever the boy looked up at her with shining, warm eyes and a beaming smile. She nudged him towards Matt and only then did Benny glance up at him. "Say hello, honey."

Matt expected the kid to mimic Lillian and say, "Hello, honey." But thankfully, the kid was too young to respond with sarcasm at his mother's expense and he said, "Hello."

"Hello, Benny. It's… very nice to meet you." He glanced at Lillian for help. A lifeline. A link to his salvation. What did he say now? And it was not a big deal to meet him. It was fine. Like meeting the child of a woman he wanted to date. Sure. Part of the program for a single mom. Which Lillian was. But the part that threw him for a loop was: he was the single dad.

The kid was silent and so was Matt. They stood there awkwardly, and Matt shifted the weight on his feet nervously. The entire thing was so discouraging and disappointing, Matt really wished he could leave them and hide away at the River's End Tavern. This was what had him tied up in knots for the past few weeks? Since the moment she told him he had a son, Matt's vision, ideally and without any basis, had the two of them walking off into the sunset, holding the hand of *his son* in a proud manner. But there was nothing. Nada. No feelings. No pride or quite frankly, not even the slightest interest. The kid didn't seem interested in Matt either. In a word, their meeting was lackluster.

Turns out, thinking about a child, and being a father to that child, sounded better than it actually was.

Matt nearly recoiled at the devastating thought, and how awful he was for feeling that way, but that was the plain reality.

Lillian intervened on Matt's behalf. "Hey, Benny why don't we show Matt around? He's never been on a ranch before. I doubt he's ever seen or touched a horse either," she glanced up at Matt for confirmation. He nodded his agreement. "See? He's a tenderfoot. What do you say?" Her conspiratorial tone instantly drew the child's attention and he responded with an eager nod and quick grin, which Matt did not share. He appreciated Lillian's effort, but the glaring absence of any connection and warmth was too obvious to deny. It wasn't there. Something was notably absent. A connection. How to build something from absolutely nothing was a task indeed.

Benny failed to notice how inadequate Matt deemed their encounter and he happily nodded as he shuffled out with a giggle, entering the other room. Matt stared after the boy. Lillian took his arm. "It'll get easier in time. I know you must have so many expectations. Don't let this discourage you. Just give it more time and space. Be yourself and eventually, you'll understand."

What? What would he understand eventually? That he was six years too late? Too unaware. Too uncaring?

"Sure. Let's go pet the horses. That should be interesting." His smile was strained since he didn't give a crap about horses. Or farm animals in general. He liked the ocean and wide-open space. Sky and water meeting on distant horizons. That was the joy of Matt's life. Not this.

Whatever *this* was.

Following Benny, who chattered away without caring if anyone listened to him or not, Matt silently watched Lillian. She was obviously trying to gauge his reaction and he slipped her a small smile, hoping to convey his anxiety without disappointment.

Going outside, they started up the dusty, single lane road to the small cluster of houses. Lillian started pointing out all the homes of her family members. Grandparents lived there, aunt and uncle there, cousin there, and on it went. There were quite a few Rydells with similarly charming houses.

Some were much bigger and more elaborate, and some were small and quaint like Lillian's. They were very neat and tidy and Matt was reminded of the neighborhood in *The Stepford Wives*. He wondered how crazy it might be to have your family members always surrounding you. How could you ever have any privacy? Good lord. He thought it was crowded with one granddad, imagine a dozen or more people of varying ages and relationships?

Then he wondered if any were lurking about and judging him. Everyone had to be eager to see how Benny's newly located father acted, looked and interacted with them and Benny.

But Matt kept all of his thoughts to himself, smiling when conversation came his way and interacting accordingly. They walked past the private housing, which he learned was only available to Rydell family members. The land was essentially free except for property taxes and insurance, and long ago, they split it up into smaller holdings.

The plans for more such lots to accommodate not only the current but also the future family members would only continue to grow to meet the needs of successive generations.

Then they came across another set of barns that were separate and at the other end of the ranch, above the resort. Lillian told Matt all about Grandpa Jack and invited him inside one of the barns to meet her grandfather. That was where she did most of her more specialized work. Benny ran ahead, eagerly entering the barn, and running into a whole bunch of Rydells. Jack, of course, and someone named Finn, and a chatty woman named Brianna, and later, someone named Charlie and his wife, Cami, strolled by. They became a blur in Matt's mind of heat, horses and strangers.

Then they passed the barns where Lillian's dad worked. He managed the boarding, breeding and husbandry to keep the ranch's stock healthy along with all the horses they boarded and trained. The vastness of their enterprise appeared unlimited, and Matt tried to imagine how much time and money it had to consume.

"This is my dad, Ben Rydell. Dad, this is Matt."

In seconds, Matt was aware that Lillian's dad knew who he was, being the father of his grandson, and he instantly sensed her dad didn't like that. Upon entering the space, Benny ran up to Ben and the tall man happily scooped him up in his arms, swinging him around in a circle. Giggles of glee came from both of them.

Ben played the primary role as Benny's father figure. Ben also acted more like a dad even though Benny called him Grandpa Ben. Seeing a flash of anger on Ben's face that quickly, followed by a cold scowl was enough for Matt to know he was not welcome as far as Ben Rydell was concerned.

Holding onto Benny for a moment, Ben set him back on the ground and Benny scooted off to feed a carrot to one of the horses. Ben glanced over at Matt and studied him for a moment before he said, "So you're…"

"Yeah." Matt answered him before he finished his question. Coming from this guy's mouth, whose lips twisted into a wry expression, and the gleam of distrust Matt glimpsed in his eyes, Matt considered Ben's comment more of an accusation than anything else.

Ben didn't lean forward to shake hands and neither did Matt.

"Dad…" Lillian's tone was a warning that drew her father's attention. Her imminent alert remained unspoken. Ben's mouth tightened but he nodded at her and forced a small smile towards Matt.

"Well, it's good to finally meet you."

Matt nearly choked at the odd greeting, which was so unexpected. He wondered if Ben were being sarcastic.

Several more awkward moments occurred between the three adults, but Benny eased the discomfort with his prattling and incessant jabber. He was more than excited to show Matt everything he could find or think of. Matt followed behind him, learning the names of the horse tack in the barn, from the obvious, like saddles, to items he'd never seen before. There was one handtool Benny called a "hoof pick." Benny beamed with pride when he shared the specialized knowledge that evidently came from his grandfather and great-grandfather. He ran past all of the stalls and hollered over his shoulder the names of the horses. One was called Saturn, and another was Sun Flower and Benny identified every single one. Matt learned which one was Benny's favorite and which one he was never allowed to ride. Benny hung by his knees like a bat on the low walls of the stalls and bounced around them with obvious comfort and ease. He had to spend a lot of time in there.

"What's the difference between this barn and the one your grandfather works in?" Matt asked Lillian when Benny paused for a breath.

"Grandpa Jack heads the horse rescue. He saves beaten, neglected, sick, and injured horses and nurses them back to health. Many of the abused horses don't trust humans anymore and need psychological healing. Grandpa Jack knows all kinds of ways to treat them and rehabilitate them. Dad? Why don't you explain the differences in your job and Grandpa's?" Lillian's obvious nudge to force her father to acknowledge Matt was neither subtle nor appreciated.

From pictures Matt had seen in Lillian's house Ben Rydell was obviously Jack's son. Ben's rusty-red hair was how Jack's looked before it turned white and they shared the same face structure, along with similar builds and smiles. But Jack was quite friendly and welcoming, while Ben kept scowling and glaring at Matt with an unpleasant frown. Ben leaned against an old, wooden sawhorse, crossing his arms tightly around his chest, and crossing his legs at the ankles. The narrow-eyed stare he shot at Lillian was all but furious. His mouth refused to change the rude scowl. Lillian didn't back down. "Dad?" Again, her tone was another unspoken warning.

Without softening his facial expression, Ben finally replied, "I run the commercial end of our business. This barn is reserved for the horses we board, train, or do both with. We were lucky to expand the facility during the last decade and now we have half a dozen trainers on staff to work with the horses in their various stages of training. We also have a crew that handles twenty-four-hour mainte-nance and care. They provide for the daily needs of the horses: feeding, mucking the stalls, regular check-ups, and things like that."

"I see, and that's where you enter the picture?" Matt replied with a respected look at Lillian.

She nodded. "Yes. That's where my part comes in. I've only been in practice for three years. I'm so glad they can use me." She gave her dad a little smile and he couldn't resist her.

Ben grunted and smiled back at her fondly. "Your skills are those of someone with decades of practice. You grew up here, which is also a factor in heightening your proficiency."

"Thank you, Dad," Lillian replied with an eye-roll but a sincere smile.

"So, you run the arena events and all of that show stuff?"

"No. That falls on my Uncle Ian and Aunt Kailynn. They're like the general managers who oversee everything. Dad and I share two different businesses. And my Uncle Joey and Aunt Haley operate the resort and its facilities. That's the bare bones of it in a nutshell. The rest of the staff and family members fit in with whatever skills are required."

Matt shuddered. This place was *weird*. He never imagined such a strange environment.

Suddenly, a body rushed through the barn doors.

"Hey."

Turning, Matt saw an unusually tall girl. Maybe in her late teens. She had long, brown hair, an athletic build, and toned, hard muscles on her shoulders and arms. She had big feet and almost met him eye-to-eye. "Jade. Hey, come meet a friend of mine," Lillian said.

Jade obviously knew Matt was Benny's baby-daddy and she was already eyeing him up.

"Matt, this is my little sister, Jade. Jade, this is Matt."

Matt put his hand out and repeated the whole introduction protocol for the sixth time that day. Jade was grinning at him. She stretched her neck and spotted Benny far down the aisle of stalls in the huge barn. Then her voice dropped, and she said, "So you're Benny's dad. I've always wondered what you were like. I can't believe I finally get to meet you. I always tried to imagine the man who convinced my strait-laced, goal-driven sister not only to commit an imperfect act, but to turn it into the epically most shocking thing of her entire life."

"Jade," Lillian hissed crossly.

Ben turned away as if he was too stressed to be there and muttered, "I'm going to check on Benny."

"Well, you can't blame me. C'mon, Dr. Lillian? Raising a baby without knowing who the dad was. I mean…" She flashed another grin.

Matt shrugged and asked her, "Well, what do you think of her greatest mistake? Am I hot enough for you to accept how it happened?"

Her mouth made a little "O" and she let out a surprised laugh.

"Well, isn't that why you really wanted to check me out?"

Jade nodded with a huge laugh before her head dropped back and forward like a bobble head. "I like you. Damn right, that's true. I did always wonder. I mean, Lillian doesn't even date. How did you manage to get her pregnant in one night?"

"Biology 101. You should probably know that by now."

Jade laughed again, harder. "You are so awesome. Okay, good personality and super hot. I'm getting it now." She turned and high-fived her sister but Lillian didn't respond. Her hand was limp, her cheeks were pink, and she was all but growling at her little sister.

"Leave, Jade! Before Benny hears you."

Jade's expression immediately dropped into a fierce scowl. "I would *never* let that happen."

Lillian's annoyance softened. "I realize that. But please stop embarrassing me."

"It's just so rare to see you with a guy."

"Well, maybe you could try not to get so much enjoyment from it."

"Okay, okay." She turned towards Matt. "We'll hang out soon. I have so many questions for you."

She ran away before her sister could reach her. Lillian was shrieking and prepared to run after her, but Jade was too fast. A huge grin at her sister from over her shoulder was Matt's last sight of her.

Lillian stopped at the barn door as if she just shooed out an unwanted critter. She slammed the door for more effect.

"That was my obnoxious, little sister. I can't believe her."

Matt walked closer to her. "She was great."

"She was awful. Such an embarrassing brat. How could you think she was great?"

He shrugged, his shoulders loosening. "Because she was real. She interacted with me and I liked her sense of humor. Unlike your dad, who detests me, she seemed willing to meet me on my own terms. And of course, Lillian, she's so jealous of you, she can barely stand it, but she also seems to care very much about you. So, try to imagine her viewpoint."

She shut her eyes and wilted. "Don't be so damn decent. Yeah. We do like each other. But we're so different. I don't know why she's jealous of me."

"Dr. Lillian?" He quirked an eyebrow.

"Jade is only twenty. She can still grow up to be whatever she wants."

They glanced back when Benny and Ben crowded over something and seemed intent on watching it together. Lillian sighed and motioned for Matt to follow her outside. "Okay, yeah, my father is definitely struggling with your presence. He's the only dad Benny knows. He adores Benny. He's definitely jealous of you. He's worried..."

"That I'll be a grifting, opportunistic asshole? Or violent and harmful? Or flaky and stupid? I'm sure you took a big risk by bringing me here. I don't blame anyone for their hesitation. Hell, I'm hesitant even. Maybe that's why your sister's reaction was so refreshing. It was honest."

"True. She's always that." They easily fell into step together. "If you could see pictures of my Grandma Lily, Grandpa Jack's first wife, you'd be amazed at the resemblance. Jade is an exact replica to her. They could be freaking twins, separated by two generations. It's insane. Jade is athletic, smart as a whip, awesome on horseback, and an ace with all sports. I was the polar opposite: poor in athletics, scrawny, but unafraid of horses so I decided to study them. We are so different. Jade is bold and real. I'm timid and a people-pleaser. So maybe you're right. I'm annoyed when she says things that I dare not speak."

"Like what?"

"What do you mean?"

"What would you like to say to me but won't because you're too timid to say it? What are you not ready to be honest about? We share a child, so we might as well get real and be honest to each other and really fast."

"I worry about the same things my dad does. He takes it too far. But honestly, I don't think you like it here."

"How would you prefer me to be?"

"What do you mean?"

"Polite and formal? Or real and honest?"

"The second way."

He grunted. "You asked for it. No, I don't really like it here. The horses and the smell for one thing. It's too damn hot. Sweltering. I detest that. Not much of a fan of the mountains. Prefer the cool ocean breeze and dune grasses and lush forests of trees."

"So, you don't like the ranch. What about my family?"

"For a first impression, I liked your dad and your grandpa. I definitely liked Grandma Erin. But—" He rubbed his neck.

"But? You can go there. Say it. You're right. Get real and do it fast, we have to figure out how we plan to be. We have to cover years in a matter of days."

"I find it rather odd that you're all just... together here. Together on the same compound and living next to your extended family members. It's like a damn town... or a cult. It scares me if it's the latter. As you show me more, I'm believing that it's not, but honestly? I wasn't sure at first."

Thank God, she was cool. Lillian burst out laughing. "I've never been accused of being a member of the Rydell Family cult. I love it. No, we're not a cult. You can leave if you don't like us. We can leave if we don't like it here. I get what you're saying. And I can't imagine how overwhelming this appears to you, with all of us right here. But it was a blessing for me. Alone at age twenty-four with a newborn and trying to pursue veterinary school was a huge feat for me. They had my back, and Benny's. They provided all the childcare, financial assistance, and emotional support I required at the time. So, it might be weird for you, but for Benny and me, they were the nurturing factors that allowed it all to work."

Feeling ashamed for not considering her circumstances again, Matt stared at her. Then he shook his head, pressing a hand on his neck. "Damn, Lillian. I'm sorry. I didn't fully think it out."

"I know you didn't. That's why I'm explaining my reasons for why I still live here. I need them now. All of them still support me in different ways."

"And your dad needs both of you too."

She nodded. Her gaze skittered off as her shoulders wilted. "Yes. I think that's what I mostly mean. Why I pressed you about what you really thought."

He waited a long moment before reaching forward to rest his hand on her shoulder. "I don't have to fall in love with it right off. It's new and so different from what I'm used to and normally prefer."

"I loved the ocean and your boat and all the unusual scenery when I witnessed it."

He let out half a grunt and half a laugh. "Okay, you're much more well-rounded than I." She eyed him wearily. "But that doesn't blind me. I can see how important and vital this place and all these people have been to you and your son. I admit he's mine and I'm trying to devise a way to make me feel like his father. But until now, he's so obviously your son. And I couldn't respect you more for that. The child you've raised is a total success and if this place and your people helped sustain and foster that, then it's got to be the best place and the best people on earth."

"Y—you do see it then?"

"That Benny can't be taken away from here or from them?" Matt's heart sank and he understood the source of her panic at that moment. "Yeah. I see that," he admitted with complete honesty. "I have no intention of taking your son away from you, from here or from your family. I promise you that. We'll just have to figure out a visitation schedule and go from there. But I promise you, his wellbeing will always come first."

Lillian slowly released the breath she was holding. "I believe that. For some reason, I know your integrity is real. I feel it coming from you, Matt. That's why I told you about our son. But I feared you wouldn't see the true value and necessity of this place and my family in Benny's life."

"I see it clearly."

She nodded and looked over at Benny who came bounding out of the barn. "Is this different from what you pictured?"

"Yes," Matt replied. "I wasn't sure what to expect. It's so hard. I know intellectually he's my son. My God, he's like a tiny twin. There's no doubt. But he's also still a stranger. We are unknown to each other so it's hard for either of us to know how to feel or act. The pressure and panic on me to be his father is relentless, but I have no idea how to be that or what to do... I have no clue how it feels."

Lillian touched his hand with her own and Matt gripped her cool, soft fingers. No problem connecting with her. Never. The comfort between them was a given. "I think it's just hard at first, but in time, I'm sure it will come."

"He's smart, funny, and so handsome." Matt gave her a little wink and smirked after calling Benny his twin and as usual, Lillian got it and responded with an eye-roll of amusement. "He obviously knows this is his home and his sense of self comes from you and your family. The joy and warmth he exudes comes directly from you."

"I'm glad you see him like that. It's a good start. But it's just that, Matt. A start. This is new and strange for all of us."

"Do you think eventually we'll figure it out?"

She smiled with a knowing expression that reassured him. "Yeah, I do. Seeing that you're the guy I believed you to be, I think we'll come up with a functional plan."

He hoped she was right. But his doubts still swirled in his brain. He adored this woman, but not this place. Benny was a great kid. But Matt still longed for a deep, emotional connection between them. There could still be fun in the meantime.

Possibilities were abundant. Maybe Lillian was right that they needed some time to bond and create memories. Something had to exist besides the DNA connection.

"Come on, let's go home now and get some dinner."

What bothered Matt the most now was how much he liked it when Lillian included him in their plans. That appealed to him more than almost everything else.

CHAPTER 13

*M*ATT GLANCED DOWN FOR the dozenth time at the oddly jarring sight of seeing his own face on a much smaller body. It still floored him when he realized how much they looked alike. This little person with a face, a voice, and his own mannerisms jolted Matt out of the fantasy that occupied his brain ever since Lillian told him he was a father. Now his son had become reality and that reality had a name and an identity. A voice with opinions. But still, Matt didn't know him at all.

Benny's entire life was centered here. There were no doubts of that. He'd been well cared for by his grandfather, great-grandfather, grandma, great-grandma, countless uncles and aunts and great-uncles and aunts and cousins galore. Some were first cousins, some were once removed or hell, even twice removed. It was like a tribe on some creepy island where only Rydell people were allowed to live.

Matt booked a room at the inn for the night. They even had onsite accommodations. It was bat-shit crazy to him. He never encountered a family with so much land and so many diverse and unrelated operations that all blended together and functioned like a huge, self-propelling town. He found it disconcerting as an ordinary Joe-Shmo and couldn't imagine things like built-in jobs and an infinite, steady source of financial support. Lillian told him being a single mother was hard, but not really. Not with the abundance of resources available to her, not to mention an endless supply of willing and able Rydell babysitters. They were everywhere. They all knew Benny and fawned over him whenever they came near him. No doubt, the child was loved and nurtured by all while Lillian pursued her DVM and thereafter. Even she admitted she didn't have to endure the typical struggles and sacrifices other single mothers did. Lillian was fortunate it was so doable, despite being totally unexpected.

In the back of Matt's mind loomed the burning question: what did Benny need from him? He should have gone home, letting the Rydells go on. Letting them continue to fawn over Benny. Matt predicted as Benny grew older, they would ask him what type of job, nay, career would he like to begin in any of their vast enterprises? If they didn't have a need for his preference, Matt guessed one of the Rydells would manufacture a reason to invest in it. Create it from nothing.

There wasn't much the Rydells didn't already have covered. So, what could this child whose most formative years were already behind him, possibly need from Matt?

Feeling churlish, alienated and discontent, Matt woke up, like usual before the sunrise. He tried to enjoy the fantastic view of the sunrise from his hotel room, while reviewing everything that went wrong yesterday. The rushing, clear river meandered through the angular mountains that stacked, hugged and twisted beneath the underside of the blue, cloudless sky. Each view he saw was more beautiful than the last.

But the heat was unbearable.

Even at night it never completely disappeared. Their

nighttime lows were the summertime highs where he was from. He found it hard to breathe in the oppressive, furnace-like, dry inferno that made his skin so hot all day yesterday.

Walking the grounds yesterday his energy levels quickly faded. It felt too hot to even put one foot in front of the other. Yet Benny buzzed around like a bumble bee, fully energized and so excited as if it weren't hot at all. He was so happy to show off the barns, the people he loved the most and the horses. He was not scared of them, but rather, totally thrilled.

Horses?

They smelled to Matt. They were huge, unpredictable, and dangerous. When they looked Matt in the eye, he got a creepy sense that they knew he feared them. They snorted and stomped in a threatening manner. That was the totality of his experience with them. He didn't like them at all. Nothing could possibly redeem them in his opinion. They were too expensive to feed, pooped all the time, and occupied too much land. Matt failed to see the point of owning one. The former role horses had in society was obsolete now in Matt's opinion. The huge ranch was crawling with them; there were more horses than Matt ever saw before.

And his son loved and knew every one of them. While exploring the ranch grounds, Benny was a constant stream of questions.

"Do you like horses?"

"No."

"Do you ride?"

"No."

"Do you want to learn to ride?"

"No."

"Have you ever even gone riding before?"

"No."

"Do you golf?"

Snort. As if he could afford to golf. "No."

"Do you like to swim?"

"No."

"Do you like to river raft?"

"No."

"Do you like kayaking?"

"No."

"How about paddle boarding?"

"No."

"Do you like hiking?"

"No."

"Do you—"

That summed up their afternoon together. Everywhere they went, the kid sprinted, skipped and frolicked. They toured the huge compound, especially the barns, and Matt got to see all the different therapies and operations for rescuing horses. One was dedicated to the injured, deformed, neglected and more challenged horses. Great-Grandpa Jack ran that. The other side was where the money to rescue the horses came from. That included the breeding, selling, showing, boarding and any other special events associated with them. Matt wondered about the astronomical food bill incurred by the ones they boarded and trained there. Grandpa Ben, Great-Uncle Ian and Great-Aunt Kailynn took care of ordering the necessary supplies.

Lillian had an honorable place in the family dynasty being their personal big-animal vet.

Yep, everything was so tidy. All of it. So once again, what did Matt have to offer Benny?

As they toured the ranch, Benny's constant monologue made it harder for Matt to follow his thoughts with so many distractions. Flowing without any pause from one subject, observation or question to the next, Benny could do it with the speed of a super-sonic jet. He fired his inquiries like missiles, without caring if anyone answered them. His mother, family members, Matt… all were fair game. But the questions Benny asked Matt involved things Matt had no experience with. They were all the same. And all the answers were *no*.

Matt was smart enough to refrain from answering no each and every time, however. He hemmed and hawed, making up excuses for not answering and responding with pleasantries like, *no, but I'd sure like to try it sometime*. Mostly, Matt reserved the polite responses to all of Benny's horse questions. He fought the urge to plug his nose and say *never in a million years* to Benny's innocent questions. At least he tried to connect with the kid on some level. But nothing came of it.

That didn't matter. Matt had to care about the kid because he was Matt's son. There was no litmus test Benny had to pass in order to please Matt. Didn't he know that game inside out!? Remembering his own father, and the few times he bothered to visit, Matt assumed his father did not like him. Not at all. Matt loved to fish. He was all things fishing, all the time. He loved the ocean, and anything related to it. Benny was into all things horses, all the time. Matt's father abhorred fishing and being on the ocean. He called his family "failures" and Matt loved the things his father despised, so he was also a huge disappointment to his father, who never accomplished anything in life. Always broke and grifting, his nefarious father still believed he was better than his family.

So, of course, Matt wanted to encourage his son to be exactly who he was. Matt struggled with the unfamiliar thoughts and emotions he now experienced. How disconnected he felt with the little person who spoke so freely and excitedly to him. Matt supposed any kid would act like Benny if a person followed him around and appeared interested in what he was saying. Benny was too young to detect the changes in tone and body language when Matt's words did not match up.

But, of course, Lillian knew. She could read Matt. She frowned at him in puzzlement many times. Matt mostly regretted that. He really wanted her to like him. The spontaneous connection he felt with her happened in an instant. He erroneously assumed it would extend to *their* child.

They walked all over the ranch, and met what Matt assumed *must* have been everyone. The conversation mainly centered on the amenities at the ranch and resort. The huge expanses took a long time to cover. Especially in the withering, melting heat. Lillian didn't break a sweat, but Matt's shirt was soaked through and through. It was unbearable.

Finally, they retreated to her air-conditioned house. She planned a dinner of fettucine with vegetables and parmesan and a green salad. She remembered it from their first date.

Matt gratefully returned to his room at the inn. The little mini-cabins on the river were self-contained with all the necessary equipment. Since Matt didn't want to buy groceries or cook, he chose a plain hotel room at the inn. It had a small café just outside in the same building where the resort check-in and gift shop were located. There was sign ups for the recreational opportunities they provided. Guided kayaking, river-rafting trips, horseback riding, for beginners and intermediates, hiking on advanced trails, horseback-riding lessons, again, for all levels and golfing, of course. A veritable smorgasbord of outdoor activities and all the guides and coaches required for all were available to any guest.

Yeah, like all families should have such things. Oh. Beyond the café was a full grill that overlooked the giant horse arena. Lillian's mother ran that, and everyone knew it was hers.

They had plenty of attractions for almost everyone's taste.

Except Matt.

Matt lived for a day on the sea. He loved to venture down unknown waterways that he could not see the ends of. Never happy or relaxed unless a boat was rocking under his feet, he only kept the house he had in town for his granddad's comfort. If the awful day arrived when Granddad was no longer in this world, Matt planned to move onto his boat permanently.

For now, it served many purposes: business, recreation and yeah, the best place for a tryst when a rare date agreed to indulge in sex. Lillian was the only woman Matt ever had stay with him at his house to be around his granddad. She was the only one he *ever* considered wanting something more with. But here at the ranch? He wasn't sure how that translated.

MATT DIDN'T KNOW what to do when he was with Benny. He hated the ranch, the resort and the whole area. That became startlingly clear to Lillian as the day wore on. Damn. The heat was his constant complaint. Sure, it was hot, but Lillian never felt so bothered as he was by it. The sweat beaded on his forehead and he gasped for air, growing tired far more quickly than she, and only from a short walk around the arena.

All the questions Benny asked Matt were answered with polite, ambiguous replies and most of the responses were negative, even if Benny failed to realize how often.

They shared nothing in common but their looks.

Lillian's stomach started to knot as the day progressed. Nothing felt right. From the first moment Matt met Benny, no instant recognition or bond manifested. She bonded instantly with baby Benny. Why not Matt? She scolded herself when she started to lose respect and interest in Matt because he did not feel a link to his son instantaneously. Benny was the most wonderful child in the world. Bright, inquisitive, funny. So funny. Why couldn't this asshole see that? Feel it? Know it? Benny was his son with the same face and hair, and yet… Meh.

That was how Lillian felt after the day they spent together. Panic gripped her and she wondered what she'd done? What kind of a man had she brought into their lives? A dull, whining dud who didn't instantly love the best kid in the world? Matt seemed critical about everything in their lives.

Such an unusual reaction. All her life, Lillian was told how lucky she was to be one of the Rydells. Her neighbors and classmates and people she met at college never failed to admire her home and family when she showed them the website for their resort and holdings. It was impressive. Awesomely so.

But hell, not to Matt, apparently. His anger percolated, becoming intense, deep and annoying until she almost told him to go home and forget he ever knew about Benny. Or her. She didn't need his negativity. His son was a precious gift. Benny Rydell. Having so many male role models in his life, who were healthy, wonderful men that loved and adored him, he didn't need another father figure. Not in the traditional sense, as some single-parented boys might need to supplement for a single mother. Nah. Benny had no shortage of healthy male influence and on a daily basis.

She and Benny didn't need Matt Griffin.

But Matt only came there at her invitation. That quickly, she was living to regret it but not for the reasons she anticipated. Matt didn't fit into their world, or the home they made here. He didn't get it, which offended her. She wholeheartedly embraced the life she experienced and wanted to pass it on to Benny.

FINALLY AT NINE o'clock that morning he tromped down the securely protected road, the Rydells' private property, he held the coffee he purchased at the café, and crossed their land. Strolling past the auto shop, he thought if his truck ever broke down, he could fix it right there. The gift shop had all the basics, including groceries, although they were exorbitantly priced. Matt tried to imagine what it might be like to live on their land, having most his basic needs and obligations met. Hell, all they needed was a medical clinic and a hardware store and they'd be there. He recalled the endless clusters of outbuildings and barns, so maybe a hardware store wasn't required. They probably owned every type of tool and tractor equipment already.

So, a doctor was all they needed. Yeah, so normal.

Knocking on her door, he was invited into Lillian's house. Benny was wearing shorts with a t-shirt and munching on what looked like a homemade granola bar. He guessed they manufactured those somewhere nearby too.

Matt greeted Lillian and she made some small talk, asking how he slept, so he decided not to mention how strange her family and their entire mini-empire, located in the desert they called their home, appeared to him.

Then Benny started asking questions.

"Do you like this cartoon show?"

"No."

"Do you like Lucky Spoons cereal?"

"No."

"Do you like to play video games?"

"No."

"Do you like dogs?"

"No."

"Cats?"

"No."

Matt said it diplomatically and explained he just wasn't home often enough to care for them, but in essence, *no*.

The questions continued until he was half answering when suddenly he asked one that wasn't answered by *no*. Or an ambiguous reply. Benny asked Matt something that actually applied to him. Finally.

"Do you know how to fish?"

He stared at his son's big, inquiring eyes that blinked with innocent curiosity, and looked just like his eyes staring back at him. Like he was looking into a mirror. At last, Matt could answer with, "Yeah, I sure do know how to fish."

"Me too." Benny said with a grin. "My Grandpa B and I go fishing *all* the time. We catch *huge* fish."

"Yeah? Me too."

Lillian heard them and reached over to ruffle Benny's curls. "Matt is a fishing boat captain and guide. People pay him to show them how to fish and where to go to catch them. That's how much he knows about it."

For the first time, Benny looked at Matt as if he finally knew they shared something, and he wasn't being completely off the wall. To date, everything Benny discussed was unfamiliar to Matt who either didn't do it or knew nothing about it.

But, of course, Benny went fishing all the time with Grandpa Ben. This was the only thread that linked them, and Matt clung to it. He feared if he tugged too hard, it might unravel into a disaster. But if he were gentle, it could be something he might be able to share with the child.

His head tilted. "You actually catch fish on a boat?"

"Yep. All the time. All kinds of fish."

"Big ones?"

"Huge ones."

"Trout? You ever catch trout? 'Cause that's what we catch. We're expert pros. There're suckerfish and pike minnows, but we don't like catching those. Trout are the best. Those are gold."

Matt put his tongue in his cheek to keep from smiling. He believed those words came straight from Grandpa Ben. Naturally, the little guy idolized the man. And assumed he was his father. Not just a father figure. Matt felt sure that neither Grandpa Ben nor young Benny saw any reason to change that. Matt was obviously lacking any skills that could be of use to them in their lives on the ranch.

But fishing? That was his divine calling. Fuck yeah. He could and would beat Grandpa Ben in any fishing competition.

Matt didn't usually go trout fishing. Lake trout and river trout were nuisances to him, but he'd done it before, and he could and would. He'd show Benny he did have something of value to share with him.

More than Grandpa Ben, at least where fish were concerned.

"I catch trout sometimes. So… what do you say?"

"I say yeah!" Benny jumped up and ran to the door that led to their garage. Moments later, he was hauling a tackle box and two trout rods. The kid wasn't kidding and as always, very enthusiastic.

He glanced at Lillian. "Do you mind?"

"No. Just be careful along the river's edge." She directed the warning to Benny.

"Life jacket in the rapids?"

"Duh!" Benny replied with sarcasm at his mother for pointing it out to him. She gave him an evil-eye and he turned away with a little grin and a quick, "Sorry."

For being rude? Matt guessed so. He winced at the conversation since it never occurred to him that the kid had to wear a life jacket. The river was no more of a threat than a newborn kitten to him. It was not even a real body of water. From driving along it he'd noted it was knee-deep in most places, and the rapids were even shallower with endless rocks jutting out like speedbumps as the flowing water splashed all around.

Matt was used to huge swells and rogue waves, fishing in depths of hundreds of feet. So, life jackets were naturally a necessary requirement.

But on the river, he could always see the bottom, and that kind of waterway couldn't culminate in visions of drowning or any other danger to him. But to a kid? Sure. Duh, as Benny said. How many other things did he not know? What they considered common sense might never occur to him. Swimming in doubt and an overwhelming sense of ineptitude, Matt regretted his admission to knowing how to fish. In meeting the undeclared challenge of Grandpa Ben, it pitched him and Benny alone. All alone together. And Matt would be solely in charge of Benny.

And his life.

Shit. What did he know of keeping a child safely alive? What pitfalls and dangers awaited that he might not foresee or realize? Matt didn't know. It would not be malicious or intentional, but that wouldn't change the outcome if he were wrong.

Shit.

"Um... are you sure? Perhaps you'd like to come?" He threw out the lifeline to Lillian, hoping and praying her common sense and keen intuition would make her realize he was not a trustworthy person who was ready to be put in charge of her precious son. He was, in fact, unaware of looming mishaps. He thought some people were neurotic at times regarding possible dangers or pitfalls. He saw plenty of kids running on the docks of the marina without a worry, only to hear their concerned parents screaming to *stop and put a life jacket on!* Only then did it occur to him how dangerous it could be. They could trip and fall right off the dock. The deep water was only one of many hazards. A kid might get trapped under the dock or a moored boat or something equally as ominous. But until he witnessed it, the thought of safety precautions for kids never occurred to him. Where did one draw the line? After witnessing one fall, Matt was careful to caution a young teen about the same thing. He laughed in Matt's face and his parents also smiled saying, it was fine, since he was fourteen. No worries.

So, when did one have a valid reason to worry?

Apparently, at age six.

Matt was swamped by the profundity of his inadequacies and what else he didn't know.

Benny had his life jacket on his arm, and he nodded at the ground. Matt realized he was supposed to carry the rest of the stuff. Sure. Duh. Made sense. He grabbed it all.

"So, where's the hot spot?" he asked as the door shut behind them and he was suddenly all alone with this young child. His child. This stranger that he was solely responsible for now. He had to converse with him and keep him alive? Did he have to feed him too? How long could a six-year-old kid go without food? Or water? How long before dehydration became a life-or-death factor? In this heat, all the moisture in Matt's body seemed to drain, leaving him a withered shell.

"Over this way. Come on. It's a long walk, but it's worth it." Benny's high voice rose even higher when he said *worth it*. The rapidly rising temperature was beyond seventy and must have been closer to seventy-five when they started walking along the sandy trail. It was peppered with round river rocks. Matt had to watch his step to avoid twisting an ankle, but Benny never even looked down. He all but glided over the trail and his little feet ran and skittered, even stumbling at times, which contributed to the magic of the moment. Benny seemed to float above the trail. The river's noise in the background continued as always, and they walked farther, dropping below a steep bank. Matt saw the backside of some of the barns he toured yesterday, and they came to a flatter section where the willows and cottonwoods grew haphazardly. The water appeared to be from knee to chest height. As the river gushed over the rocks, it sounded louder, like a stereo, so they had to yell to each other.

Benny stopped and put on his life-jacket, clicking it as he nodded down. "We can leave the tackle box here, and just take a few flies with us."

"Okay, Captain," Matt teased, immediately regretting the snarky moniker. Yeah, Matt was a boat captain and used to it, so taking orders, especially from a six-year-old, was ironic and funny, but would the kid get that?

Benny took his pole and eyed Matt closer. "You really a boat captain?"

"Yeah, really. Why? Is that stupid or cool?" He couldn't tell by the kid's voice.

Benny nodded. "I think it's cool. Like Captain Phillips? From the movie?"

He laughed. "Well, he was cool. But my little boat would probably fit on the bow of his." Thinking about the story of the captain who faced down Somali pirates when they took over his ship, Matt remembered the movie starred Tom Hanks. It was all about heroism and yeah, any kid would call that captain a hero. Matt's version? Much more domestic and small... who knew?

"Well, we'll see how being a boat captain on the ocean

works when you fish for trout." Matt smiled. Damn, the kid knew how to throw shade! Grandpa Ben teach him that too?

"We'll see..." Matt nodded, accepting the challenge, but why was he stressing now? Having a freaking fishing match with a six-year-old? When did his life come to this? It felt like he had to prove his value and worth, as a person, and a freaking man, and a boat captain and a fisherman, by competing in this little section of water for a freaking trout. They were so small and light compared to the fish he usually caught, Matt didn't really think of trout as fish. They were more like bait for him. He used bait that were lots bigger than these. And yet, he had to earn his worth in the eyes of this small boy, his son, even if it were based on catching one of these stupid creatures?

Still, trout were fish. And Matt knew fish.

The roar of the water grew louder as they stepped out of the bushes and waded to the other end of the long, white-capped, gurgling mass of river.

"We fish here to avoid the suckerfish. They don't bite or hang out in the rapids, just the trout," Benny explained over the noise while looking up at Matt with the eyes of a teacher. He was freaking teaching Matt how to fish!? Fishing was Matt's reason for living. No doubt, he was merely reciting all of Ben Rydell's words of wisdom. Fuck that. Who knew if they were true?

In all honesty, Matt never fished white-water rivers, so he didn't really know. The rivers he fished in back home were calm, smooth, placid, not rushing water like this.

Damn it. He was a fishing boat captain. Not a horse rancher. No. This was a test of his manhood.

All the inadequacy he felt when he was around Dr. Lillian Rydell, including her glamorous, admirable career, her wealth, her class and her family backing was being exploited. He knew he wasn't good enough for her. He was seeing it in live-action footage. The huge, monstrosity of a compound and the empire founded by her family where she lived. There was no competing with that. All he had was a miserly, fairly small, fishing boat. A smelly, functional, simple vessel. His legacy.

Until Lillian re-entered his life, Matt was proud of his family business, Griffin Family Charters. It belonged to him and his granddad. It provided a solid, middle-class income for his grandparents and met most of their needs. In Westport, Matt fit right in as one of them, albeit luckier than many others in owning his boat free and clear. Thanks to his granddad's hard work, which included swabbing the decks, scrubbing off the barnacles, cleaning the fish, baiting the hooks, along with many other odd jobs, and Matt's many years of learning the trade which he did with pride and care.

On the ranch, none of the life skills Matt picked up from Granddad applied in the least. Just like the skills required to run the ranch did not apply where he was from. Any veterinarian practice in Westport most likely centered on family pets and perhaps a few pleasure farm animals like goats, horses, chickens and cows. But nothing to compare with the magnitude of this. As he stared out at about a hundred horses, Matt realized Lillian was the sole vet responsible for all of them. Right here.

But Benny didn't know anything about the ocean or salt-water fishing or what a boat captain had to do. He only observed that Matt was totally unfamiliar with everything at the ranch. From the dry heat to the smell of the horses. To Benny's eyes, Matt seemed a little incompetent and rather uninteresting so far.

This was the moment of truth and Matt felt the weight of it. His test. The measure of the man, and his worth as seen through Benny's eyes. Even if the kid wasn't aware of the significance, Matt was thoroughly conscious of it.

Walking up to the splashing water's edge, Matt stared at the bubbling, foamy mess and wondered how he'd cast a line without hooking every freaking rock, big and small, in its path? He decided to make it a reconnaissance mission and started by asking, "So, Benny why don't you show me the best way to do this?"

Matt was pleased Benny failed to realize he was studying everything he did, from his short arms and tiny hands to the way his body relaxed as he released the line. Matt was surprised at how far the small fly flew and more precisely, the speed at which Benny reeled the line back in from across the rocky waters and natural obstacles. He was fast. Okay. Speed was the goal in this sport. No allowance of time for the small spoon to sink and catch on anything. Duh. He smiled. Benny's technique made sense and Matt saw why he tried to be so fast as he skimmed the top of the water, careful not to jerk too hard lest he fling the spoon off the water and wrap it around his head or somewhere behind him. It definitely required some finesse.

But if a six-year-old could do it, so could he.

Taking the small, lightweight fishing pole, Matt pressed the release on the reel as he swung it back and flung it, releasing the line when it passed his shoulder. The spoon flew across the water with ease in an arc, landing behind a large rock with a mini-waterfall above it.

Matt immediately started a steady, but speedy reel-in, letting the spoon sink barely inches into the impossibly clear water before bringing it back towards him. The idea was to allow the quick, darting trout to see a second flash of the spoon, which instinctually attracted them, and then hook one.

Nothing was biting for either of them. But when Benny gave him a nod, Matt wondered was he nodding his approval of Matt's cast? Yeah. Apparently, the kid liked it. Matt supposed his success in not getting the line stuck was an instant win.

"Let it sink for a moment so they can see it," Benny advised him. "They sit behind those big rocks to rest. The current there is calmer because the rock blocks the water from coming down too fast."

Duh.

Sure. Benny made perfect sense. Even if he didn't know it.

But they were merely trout fishing.

Matt fished for trout before but only from a lake. In that situation, a slower reeling in of the spoon was the best method since there was nothing to catch the lure on.

The river was fraught with endless hazards. And yet his son cast every line without getting snagged and reeled them in with practiced regularity.

Something weird bubbled up in Matt. Pride? He was definitely impressed and deduced that Benny's competence with the rod and reel came directly from Grandpa Ben. He had to give him credit for so obviously teaching the kid the right way to do it.

After four more casts, Benny shouted, "Move up. They aren't here or they would have bit already." So, they waded up a few steps and started the procedure all over again.

Suddenly, Matt's line got a bite and a small, shiny fish danced and flopped in the rushing water. It twisted and jumped clean out of the riverbed. It was not very long, less than his hand, and weighed only a few ounces but the little guy put up the fight of his life, throwing his whole body into it. Matt dragged the little fish across the foaming pools of water until he finally landed it at his feet. The fish was still protesting the hook in its mouth by flipping and flopping, but not giving up. It took several moments before Matt could contain the wiggling little body and stop it from frantically bending back and forth. When it finally stilled, Matt removed the hook from its mouth and set the little body back into the water. It lay there a moment, then darted off, instantly lost in the shadows and dappled sunlight on the river. The trout's body was a bright, beautiful silver with a rainbow of pinks topped with browns and beiges. The crystal-clear water spotlighted them, yet they were impossible to see unless you knew exactly where to look. Even then, you needed good vision to keep them in sight.

Benny squealed with delight. "You caught it. That was so awesome! I told you. I'm sure that was a rainbow. It was so huge!"

Matt reacted with a warm feeling that swiftly spread all through him. Was it pleasure? Benny was beaming with his approval for Matt's skill in wrangling the small fish and releasing it. Was it really huge? Judging by Benny's reaction, Matt assumed it had to be.

Matt's chest expanded and his spine straightened at Benny's unexpected approval. Matt was so glad to know that maybe he proved he had something of worth to offer little Benny? What if he wasn't completely useless? A huge smile beamed on his face when he saw Benny's happy grin. Benny leaned forward with his hand out and Matt's heart twisted in response. Benny gave Matt a high-five.

His son was so excited and thrilled and proud, he actually gave Matt a high-five. Matt was instantly choked up and the urge to lean forward and wrap his hand around Benny's to touch it and feel the smallness of his little hands in Matt's huge mitt-like hands nearly overwhelmed him. Nothing like that ever happened with any other kid before. For the first time, Matt studied the boy's face as he thought, *this is my son.*

CHAPTER 14

*M*ATT CAUGHT TWELVE MORE trout as they proceeded higher up the rapids during the next twenty minutes. But Benny didn't catch any. All his previous bluster eroded away as each cast brought nothing back on the line. A few times, he even got snagged, and had to cut the line twice to get it free. Perhaps Grandpa Ben was the one who caught most of the fish in this river.

Benny's little face looked down and he bit his lower lip. Tears filled his eyes on the last snag before Matt made his next catch. Matt only realized his grave mistake then. The contest between them had gone way too far for a six-year-old boy. Benny refused to cry because Matt caught more fish than he did, but the boy's frustration grew. His casts became sloppier, and he got his line stuck more often.

Oops. Crap. Matt just learned lesson number one: don't make the child cry.

Another trout grabbed his line and Matt quickly pretended to trip. "Benny! Can you grab my pole?" He stuck the pole out as far as he could before taking the fall and allowing the rushing water to wash all over him. Benny grabbed the rod and started reeling the line in. Matt slowly rose to his feet just as Benny landed the fish on the shore.

"You did it, Benny! Look at that monster." Matt cheered and threw a fist in the air.

Benny stared down and grabbed the slippery, wiggling fish. "It is a nice one."

"Biggest yet, I'm sure of it. That's why I got so excited I slipped."

Benny nodded. "It really is big." He grinned down and tried to work the hook out. Fearing the fish would soon perish, Matt gently pushed Benny's hand away and quickly released the fish. It bobbed below them for a few moments without moving. Then the eyes rolled up, a sure sign it was already done for. "Uh oh, guess the fight might have been too much for him."

Regretfully, Matt picked up the fish and said, "We could eat it for lunch?"

Benny glanced around. "We can't keep it."

"It's not coming back to life, Benny. Rather than wasting its life, we should eat it. Something I learned from Granddad when I was your age, we don't waste anything. I know it's sad. That's the hazard of fishing, even with catch and release. Some inevitably die. It's okay. I'll take responsibility for killing it." He winked and added, "Besides, this way you can show off the catch of the day, making you the winner, Benny."

Benny brightened and his entire face glowed with pride. "It is huge."

"Humongous. It'll feed both of us and then some. A real prize you got there."

Benny smiled as if it were gold medal he held in his little hands. Something swelled in Matt's chest when he saw his little face beaming down at the fish and then back up at him.

"I guess being a fisherman every day makes you really good at it. So, if I can beat you sometimes, then…"

"Then you must be pretty amazing at it too." He gently set a hand on the boy's shoulder, analyzing his logic and sensibility. Were they extra special for his age? Matt had no clue what was considered typical, but he would not have been the least bit surprised to learn the kid was gifted. Or maybe Benny was just wise beyond his years. And that odd thing that kept thumping in his chest was pure pride.

Pride in his son.

Matt shut his eyes. Maybe something *was* there. That thing he expected to pop up the moment he laid eyes on the boy. Or at least when he spoke or moved or interacted with him. But it never happened until now. For the first time, Matt believed something intangible was cementing them together.

Matt ruffled Benny's hair and said, "Let's go show your mom."

Benny beamed as he started hopping down the rocks, and Matt followed, using much more care and caution. Still wet from his staged spill, the warm temperatures would dry his clothes in no time. Besides, it was well worth getting wet to see Benny's immediate mood reversal and the sudden interest he now displayed when he spoke to Matt.

They hurried back to the house and Lillian stepped out to her back patio when she spotted them. Before they got within hearing distance, Benny started running, grasping the mangled fish in his hand and yelling. "Mama! Mama! Look what I caught! Matt fell on the rocks, so I saved it, but it died so we get to eat it. Look how huge it is. Bigger than huge."

Benny repeated his news four more times as his little legs ran closer to her. Finally, gasping and out of breath, Benny stopped and began to repeat it all again. Matt finally joined them to hear the *huge* description one more time.

Lillian wrinkled her nose. "Trout are gross."

"Not my favorite either, but it died so we couldn't waste it. Come on, Benny, let's go clean it."

Benny shook his head and replied, "I'm not allowed to touch gutting knives, you know."

Right, *duh!* Matt had to know that; he just didn't think of it. Made sense so he cringed. How many more times would Benny have to point out the obvious? The constant pitfalls made Matt freeze with self-doubt. So many things to worry about, things even Benny recognized.

"Can you watch me do it? Wouldn't you like to learn? As you get older, you have to clean your own catch. Granddad always said: don't kill anything you can't clean and eat. Always. Otherwise, it's a cruel and unnecessary waste of a valuable resource. Killing for sport or just 'cause is never okay."

Benny eyed him closely and so did Lillian. Matt glanced at her, looking puzzled. "Is that okay to tell him?"

She nodded and her eyes softened. "Yes, Granddad is a wise man. I never thought of it like that. I just didn't want him getting cut because of how sharp the fillet knives are."

Benny was holding Lillian's hand. "And because Mommy thinks it's gross. She hates to see any animals get hurt."

"Right. The vegetarian veterinarian."

"I try to save, comfort and nurture injured and sick animals. I can't stand the idea of killing them instead of allowing them to live out their lives as happily as we would like."

"Yet you let Benny fish with his grandpa."

She sighed. "Yes, I do. I never encourage it. But he's been following my dad around since he began toddling. Both of my grandpas and also my uncles like to hunt for sport. Besides fishing, they go duck and quail hunting in the fall.

Benny took to it instantly, despite my efforts to discourage it."

Matt slipped the fish from Benny's hand and tilted his head as he watched the small, lovely woman before him. She was holding his son's hand. His heart seemed to speed up and swell in his chest. What was that strange feeling? Pride? Again? For what? A woman he barely knew holding her son's hand and trying to do the best for him? He had no say in their relationship, which had nothing to do with his presence and yet, he felt pride. Possessive even. It was insane. How like a caveman for him to feel.

He tilted his head with a smile and said, "You're not much of a ranch girl, you know. Being raised on one, you don't eat farm animals, which are intended to be eaten, and you refuse to consume any wildlife for dinner."

"Exactly. And I grew up on a *horse ranch*. None of the horses were killed for food. I never liked any sports that involved fishing and hunting or the killing of animals."

"So, all animals should be pets or sources of pleasure and companionship?"

She rolled her eyes. "Of course not. I obviously understand the reality of the world. I provide care for both domestic *and* farm animals. So don't even lecture me." She smiled, more than aware they had clashing opinions on some subjects.

But still Lillian let Benny do the things she disdained in order to spend time with her dad. All for Benny's benefit. Interesting.

"Does your grandfather keep a fillet knife somewhere around here?"

"Here it is." Lillian sighed as she came back with a sheathed fillet knife. "He does it over there." She pointed towards a hose bib and a slab of concrete beneath it. He nodded and grabbed the bucket he saw nearby. "Come here, Benny, and I'll show you."

Benny leaned over Matt as he demonstrated the way to clean a fish. Setting the fish on the ground, he held one end, piercing the sharp tip of the knife just below the gills on the underbelly. He made a slit and the guts started slipping out. Benny squealed with joy as Lillian, looked on, wrinkling her nose. Matt glanced up at her, meeting her gaze. Her quirky contradictions fascinated, amused and intrigued him. They only added to his intense attraction to her. His goddamn enjoyment with her. She was so damn cute. Raising his eyebrows at her unpleasant reaction, he asked, "Don't you do surgery on the animals sometimes? Cutting open their bellies to spay them? I mean, Lillian, come on! Are you really grossed out by a little trout being disemboweled? Come on. You can't be that squeamish."

"I'm not squeamish. I do perform surgeries on animals. Yes. Duh. But only in order to help them. Not to prepare them for cooking." Her nose wrinkled again.

Yet she continued to observe as he set the knife down. "Okay, Benny, you grab here and yank." He showed him how to pull the intestines out.

"Wanna do it?" Benny asked his mom, who sighed and waved him on. Benny grabbed some guts and pulled and squeezed, throwing them into the bucket. He was grinning wildly and obviously loving it. Matt suddenly was too. He washed off the blood and left only the bony, white meat. The skin was still on the headless creature although he left the tail. "Got any foil?"

Benny ran off and came back with a roll. Matt wrapped the fish neatly in it. "Ever bake fresh fish over an open fire?"

"There's a burn ban on."

He grinned at Lillian's warning. "Okay, what about barbecuing over the propane flame?"

"No. Never," Benny said excitedly. His anticipation was already growing.

"Don't you put anything on it?" Lillian frowned with distaste.

"Got any salt and pepper?" She sighed and disappeared but came back looking annoyed at preparing the unfortunate dead fish as a meal. "Here."

He flashed her a grin and a wink and she blushed in response. Surprised by his effect on her, he hung onto her gaze for a long, intense moment.

"Let's grill it then!" Benny's loud words interrupted the heated look. He turned and started her oven, putting the fish on low to bake.

"That's it. But someday we'll have to cook it over an open fire. You stoke it down to hot coals and let the fish simmer in the foil. It blackens the outside and the inside just falls apart with culinary perfection."

Lillian crossed her eyes and said, "Sounds as gross as this looks."

He leaned over to Benny with a fake, conspiratorial voice and said, "Your mom doesn't understand the need for meat, does she? Sometimes, a guy's just gotta have it."

He put his fist out and Benny fist-bumped him, grinning and laughing with unmasked glee. Matt stole a look at his mom to gauge her reaction. She rolled her eyes, huffing with a sharp, "Oh, spare me the caveman shit," she said under her breath.

The fish was cooked, and Matt and Benny ate it right from the foil, picking all the soft, white meat off and spitting out the small bones. Not Matt's favorite fish by any means, but still, it reminded him more of home than anything else he came across there.

Lillian invited them in. "Time for some real lunch now." Weary of her vegan ways, Matt was surprised at her comment. The menu she provided thus far was fine and surprisingly filling. Leaning back, he patted his stomach like he was stuffed and full.

Her gaze lingered on his stomach, which was in fact, a well-defined six-pack from his years of hard work on the boat as well as onshore. He didn't have to work out in a gym because his life required strong muscles to physically accomplish it. But right now, he was stuffed and felt lazy from her food.

Plus, the wonderful invention of air conditioning made the house so inviting compared to the incessantly climbing heat outside. As far as Matt was concerned, they could do anything at all, as long as it was inside the house.

Benny came bounding out of the bathroom. "Let's go swimming now."

Matt never swam for pleasure. It was so rarely warm enough in Westport and the Pacific Ocean was always frigid even in August. So, no, thank you. But Matt didn't miss the eager expression on Benny's face.

Being included was a minor breakthrough. The way Benny turned to him and *assumed* Matt would go. After the false start yesterday, frustration and being the odd man out of everything, all it took was one successful fishing trip that barely lasted an hour. He showed Benny how to clean a fish, and Benny was instantly Matt's friend.

They made huge progress.

Matt had to learn to get over his stubborn ways. It was all glaringly apparent to him now. Raised by his granddad mostly, there was not much female influence on Matt. He and Granddad stayed on their boat for days at a time, eating whatever they wanted, and doing whatever they chose. As Matt entered adulthood, he and Granddad became more like old friends than they were when he was much younger. Matt never had to worry about anyone else, and Granddad and

RIVER TO THE OCEAN

Matt were in unspoken agreement about most of the issues that arose in their lives. It was new for Matt to be responsible for a woman and a boy. They might not like to do what he wanted to do and when he wanted to do it. The child especially. If he wanted to go, you had to go now. Resting in the cool house failed to interest Benny. It was hard and unusual for Matt to force himself to do something he wasn't planning or even wanting to do that day.

Having a relationship with a woman that took him away from his schedule was a brand-new experience for Matt. No one ever interrupted what he wanted to do. Matt was finding that harder to adjust to than most other things. It made him suddenly aware of how set in his ways he was.

Perhaps that was a negative factor. He didn't realize how often he did what he wanted with little thought to anyone else's needs or wants. Maybe that wasn't healthy. Maybe he was far too young to be acting so crusty and crotchety as an old crab. No wonder Benny struggled so hard to relate to him at first.

And the only thing that linked them was fishing. A fish. His thing. His hobby. His freaking sphere of being. It was his comfortable zone, so he opened up and became fun. Approachable. The boy had no idea Matt was his father. This "friend" was moody, annoyed, and very critical of what they did and how they lived. Matt was sure Benny picked up on all that. He was not used to hiding such things because he so rarely stepped out of his comfort zone. His sphere.

He owed the child more time, doing things the boy chose to do. Not how Matt preferred. The sinking feeling that a truly selfless, involved *parent* would put their child's desires, likes, needs and wants before their own, without getting annoyed at the child, haunted Matt after it happened several times. Matt was gritting his teeth to hide his emotions.

The boy knew, of course, he knew. But with fishing, Matt

regained his confidence and interest and pride. He was happy to show the child how to do something. He interacted and was pleased how well and fast Benny blossomed. He never expected how good it felt.

What a fucking far journey he had ahead of him in learning how to be a parent. A father. It wasn't a natural state of being, obviously. Not for him, at least. Maybe every other man alive, but not him. He believed their simple act of meeting would be like a rainbow above them, transferring instant love, bonding and intimacy between them.

Lillian eventually thawed over the fish infractions. However, she seemed to detest the stains from the dead fish being cleaned on her patio. Teaching her son to kill, clean and properly cook them was thoroughly distasteful to her, and went against her beliefs. But she let her son, *their son*, experience it with Matt. Lillian put Benny's needs and wants first.

She was a good parent. How could Matt learn how to be? How could he catch up with her? How could he stop doing everything wrong?

Matt cleared his throat. "I'd… love to go swimming. You don't mind me tagging along?"

Benny grinned. "Nah. We got tons of floaties. There's plenty for all of us."

Floaties? What the hell were those? He cast a glance at Lillian, who tilted her head with amusement that he didn't know. At his curious expression, Lillian said, "Inner tubes, inflatables, air mattresses, plastic air-filled alligators and unicorns? You know, floaties? What are you, a newbie?" she teased with a smile and an eye-roll.

Oh, yeah. Floaties. Water toys. Hanging around the water just because. That also seemed strange to him. Lacking a boat and a fishing pole, the water wasn't very interesting to Matt. Benny liked hanging out on the plastic, inflated creatures and

RIVER TO THE OCEAN

it seemed to be a thing around there. Matt lumbered to his feet with a glance of approval from Lillian. Damn, he liked it when he pleased her and Benny.

How could they manage to become so important to him after knowing them for only a matter of days?

CHAPTER 15

*M*ATT SLIPPED HIS SWIM trunks on and ditched his shirt and socks. He stepped out of the bathroom with a beach towel draped over his shoulder.

Lillian came out of her bedroom at the exact same moment, and they stared at each other in the hallway. Benny must have been outside because the house was quiet. Whenever Benny was inside the house, he was never quiet. Unless he were sleeping, *maybe*.

Her gaze held his for a long time, but she was unsmiling. Her eyes flashed with heat. Then she looked down and Matt assumed she was checking him out. A smile spread on his face. His muscles were well-defined from the work he did, but his skin was white as sand since he never sunbathed. His only concession to hot temperatures was a short-sleeved shirt. Matt's tan ended halfway up his biceps, going from a dark brown to all white.

"Nice tan line," she said softly to let him know his tan wasn't his most interesting feature to her. Her eyes were heavy-lidded, the same as when he kissed her on the beach next to the ocean. His beach. That was before he knew all the details and complications she brought with her that were now his details and complications. It was hard to get their new reality through his head. He too was a single parent with a young child to care for until adulthood. That was the new fact in his life that he would have to convey to whomever, whenever he started dating again.

Would he be dating someone other than the mother of his child? Was he really dating Lillian? Did he ever actually take her on a date? No.

But goddamn it, he sure wanted to right now.

His gaze slid down her body and he imagined his hand on her breast, then her hip, then her waist, and finally, her soft, round ass. She was as gorgeous as she was smart, funny and captivating. He liked seeing it all displayed in her two-piece swimsuit.

But the real reason why he was there kept popping up in his head. "I'm not very good at this."

"It's a lot for anyone to be thrown into without warning." Her gaze darted to the wall over his shoulder, and she added, "I'm still sorry about that."

"No, don't be. We got through that; so onward and forward we must march. I just really suck at it. I thought—"

"You'd magically know how to be a parent?"

"Yeah," he admitted with a huge sigh of disappointment— mostly in himself. "I thought it would simply happen. And I'd know exactly how to approach him."

"I think you made a breakthrough today."

"Only because we were *fishing*." Shaking his head, he wondered if he dared to admit his failures to the one person he should have been hiding them from. What if she used it later to keep Benny from seeing him? What if she sued him for full custody so he couldn't see Benny again? Matt didn't want that. Not at all. Not even if he were drowning. "Fishing is my thing. The thing I'm most comfortable with and like to do." He flapped his arms around. "Everything here is new and strange, and I don't usually want to do it… but I didn't realize how selfish and set in my ways that I was."

She set her hand on his arm. "Your awareness of it suggests that you're not. Yes, you are obviously not in your element and we all still have some compromises to figure out, but you are definitely starting to get it. You agreed to go swimming."

He shook his head and appeared defeated. "You should hate me. He's your son."

"He means the world to me. But I'd rather have you stay honest and try to have a relationship with him than acting all fake and smarmy. We both know you're struggling and yet you keep trying. That gives me hope. And faith. I always thought you were honest. The person I see and know before me is the real thing. As long as we remain straight with each other, I know we can make it work out."

"What if you have more faith in me than I do? Giving me more credit than I deserve? How can you *know*? How can *I know?*"

She let out a soft, husky laugh that was both seductive and sweet. He was seeking her maternal advice, but her laugh brought images of warm honey sliding all over his skin. Or maybe it was her skin. Was it wrong to be so attracted to the woman he already had a child with? His obvious struggle to be a parent to their child had to come across negatively and appear distinctly *unattractive* to her. She clearly adored their son and acted like a saint in her selflessness. Matt intended to make sure he thanked her for that. He was glad and felt very lucky she was the woman he unintentionally and unknowingly knocked up all those years ago. But still, the skills of a natural father eluded Matt and nothing could have been less attractive than watching him muddle through his encounters with Benny despite his most sincere and earnest effort.

"If you thought you'd have some kind of epiphany when you saw him and suddenly know how to act and feel, you must be sorely disappointed. Honestly, I think the uncertainty and hesitation are much more natural. You're trying to pick up an acquired skill way too quickly. But that's what impresses me."

"What if…" Matt shook his head, wondering if he dared to admit this to the boy's mother? But Lillian was so easy to talk to, he took a chance. "What if I inadvertently mess him up and make a fatal error without realizing it? What if I cause Benny irreparable harm without even knowing it?"

Lillian's eyes widened and her mouth made an "O." She gazed into his eyes for a long moment and then shook her head. "Is that what's stressing you out now?"

"Obviously."

She couldn't help smiling at his answer. Yes, he expected to see her crack a grin and release her mirth. "Not *obviously*, and it's rather sweet your worries extend that far. First, your access to Benny is limited, and strictly by my design and permission. I'm right here, Matt. All the time, just as I've been here all along, right? No, you could never do irreparable harm to Benny no matter who you are to him or how much I like you. So, you can shelve that concern for now. You aren't doing damage to him. He thinks you're a family friend who doesn't like excessive heat or horses. That certainly can't scar him. It might scar you, but not him. And in trying so hard, because you're so painfully aware of how big this occasion is for him, even though he doesn't know it, your doubts replace your logic. Don't worry so much. Honestly, it's going to be fine. And the fishing expedition today seemed to be the first real chink in your armor."

"My armor?"

"Yes, you seem very stiff and formal, even with me. I think Benny can read that, without knowing why. So, just try to relax and be yourself. Most kids don't examine or analyze an adult's personality as long as they show some interest and are nice to them."

"I do feel awkward at times."

She bit her lip, nodding. "It shows."

All the things Lillian said swirled inside his brain. Did she like him? His ears and another not so noble part of him perked up at that remark. *No. Down, boy.* Even if she were standing half naked before him. But back to her words, from a mother speaking about her child. Focus on those. He was too self-conscious and appeared stressed. Of course, Benny would pick up on that. She was right. But she was also monitoring him. He wondered if he could trust her to tell him if and when he was inflicting irreparable damage.

"So—you'll tell me then? When I do anything wrong? And help me fix it?"

"Of course, I'll tell you if it will make you relax. I've had six years to learn all about parenting. Benny and I learned it together. I can't imagine how awkward you must feel at being simply dropped into his life so unexpectedly."

His head shook and he smiled. "You, Lillian, are so unlike almost any other woman."

"Why would you say that?"

"You could have been shit-stormed angry at me for knocking you up and leaving you single and pregnant. For not being around during the past six years. For not sharing the full financial, physical and emotional burden that two parents usually provide for a child. For making you finish your doctorate with a newborn baby to care for. And for creating the safe, happy, home Benny has and is so obviously thriving in. And then I plop into it out of nowhere, and start whining and saying how hard I find it. You must want to kick my ass."

"No. Actually, it's just the opposite. I'm relieved you aren't telling me what to do. Or acting like I did anything wrong. Or didn't do it the way you would have done it. I'm glad you're so grateful for my parenting skills thus far, but mostly, I'm so glad that I had Benny. And kept him. When I saw you again, I knew I could finally trust you with the news. Seeing that you're here now and how hard you *are* trying means a lot to me."

"What if my efforts are always so pathetic though?"

She laughed and stepped forward to touch his arm. "Any efforts are appreciated and that's also when you become the sexiest to me."

Puzzled, he couldn't comprehend how an awkward, confused, unsure mess could appear sexy to this or any other woman. "I've been so misled. Don't women want confident, alpha, capable men who rush to any dangerous situation and prove themselves? I'm more like a complete idiot. Someone who needs a child to tell me to put a life jacket on him in the middle of river rapids, because I failed to realize the danger. The water wasn't deep to me, so it didn't occur to me how a small boy would find it. What else have I failed to observe or notice? Don't you see? I could be a serious detriment to Benny. An avenue heading toward irreparable disaster for him."

Lillian suddenly stepped right up to him and pressed her hand on his chest as his heart skittered in a rush of blood. Her hands felt cool and silky as she slipped them around his neck and her body fit his so nicely, like a hand inside a glove. She was so comfortable in his arms. Right there. He stared down at her, puzzled after finishing his unmanly and self-deprecating tirade. How could she find him attractive after that?

To his relief, she still did. Despite his honest revelations for coming here and how freaking hard it made him feel and so uncomfortable, she didn't mind.

She remained nestled in his arms. Rising on her tiptoes, she planted her lips on his. His eyelids closed and all the passion from before slammed through him again. The strange sensation and familiarity made Matt feel like he'd kissed her all his life, and he was coming home; but it was also a new, exciting experience like fireworks blasting off behind his eyelids. She was all of that for him. His hands slid to her waist, all bare and smooth, and he groaned at the contact. The contours of her petite body under his hands were irresistibly sexy. Everything about this woman, from her voice and quirky contradictions to her shape, was exactly the way he liked.

She pressed harder against him and her breasts smashed on his bare chest. The thin fabric of her bikini top was the only barrier to soften the sharp nubs of her nipples. They were there and then not. He shifted his attention from them to her lips, and her tongue in his mouth, sliding with his in a perfect dance, punctuated by soft moans. She thrust her hips toward him and although their height difference prevented all their hot parts from aligning, Matt liked it when her hips began moving against him. He positioned his thigh between her legs, and she blew his mind when she sat down on it and pushed against it. Her efforts to relieve her ache became his efforts now. He started to slip his hand downwards, tracing the outside of her swimsuit, and going back up when his eyes opened and he noticed Benny's toys... Oh, wow. No. No. This wasn't okay.

He pushed her back and held her at arm's distance while gulping great lungfuls of air into his overly stimulated body. Too hot in his brain. And lips. Mostly his dick. She nearly made him lose his mind.

"We are standing in your hallway, Lillian. And your son, *our child*, is outside *waiting* for us."

When he glanced at her face, he was startled by her laughing gaze on him. Her eyes shone with mirth and her lower lip trembled in her feeble endeavor to conceal her grin.

"What? You get that, right?" Matt grumbled as he realized she was having fun with this.

Why?

"You're right, of course. But it's kind of amusing to see you in the role of the adorable but stern, controlling father." She gave him wink. A freaking wink as she sauntered past him. Looking over her shoulder with a seductive, little grin, she sighed and added, "I didn't know what a turn-on that could be. You better watch yourself. All your attempts to spare our son from irreparable harm might have me attacking you when you least expect it."

She was teasing, of course. But still interested in him and sex. Obviously. Matt didn't know until that moment. He wasn't concerned about it since learning THE NEWS of his child's existence. Their child.

She seemed to be enjoying it all as he rushed after her and caught her arm. Now they were in the living room and Benny was out on the patio. What on earth was he doing? Lying on his stomach with his arms flailing about. Was he pretending to swim? Yes, yeah. Who knew? Okay. Matt had lots to learn.

"Everything I just told you should make you wary and even angry at me."

She stopped and gave him her most sincere, listening face. The flirting and fun were all gone. "I heard you, Matt. I did. This entire situation is hard for me too. On the first night, I almost asked you to leave. Seeing how much you hated it here made me mad. Then I realized, it was all because you were stressed out. Trying so hard to be the perfect dad that day. That moment was when I realized all the weirdness between us was because you were trying so hard. That went above and beyond anything I could hope for."

He still didn't understand. "But I keep bungling it."

"You never stop trying. That's what matters. It shows that you care so much. Overcompensation and being overly insecure, which you've been, tells me you're here to stay. For Benny. I have every confidence now you'll figure it out because of that exact reason, you'll never stop trying. And that, Matt, is what being a parent is all about. There is no special formula. When one parent remembers to put the kid's life jacket, and another forgets, it doesn't mean the one who forgot is neglectful. You also have to experience this life-changing event and learn to trust your self-reliance by making mistakes. Which method is right? Depends on whom you ask. I don't believe there is any way to be exactly right. You're still learning that. It's been only a matter of days. This is a lifetime gig. So, the level of expectations you demand from yourself for my son, sorry," she said with a small smile, "*our son*, lets me know you're not going to give up. Or quit trying. You'll just keep doing whatever you need to do until you figure it out. Like using the floaties on the river. That's something you don't like, and I know how much you detest the heat. But still, you are willing to do it."

"You think... maybe there's hope for me? For us?" He wasn't sure which *us* he meant. Him and Benny? Duh. That was what he meant. But now that he thought longer on it, maybe he was referring to him and Lillian? Yes. That kiss. Yes. Maybe he meant the three of them?

He shied away from that thought. Too premature. The idea of having an instant family? It couldn't work that way successfully. It couldn't be that easy.

"Hope springs eternal," she said with a smile he couldn't

read or interpret. It was small and secretive, but sweet. Then she set her hand out and ruined the moment by saying a snarky, "Shall we go now and watch you scrabble with the floaties?"

She instantly released any tension with her sarcasm by lowering her expectations. Matt fought the urge to pull her toward him and kiss her again, and grinned. For real. There was no more stress or insecurity. He said over his shoulder, "Try and keep up with me, Mama. I'll be the best, the brightest, and the most fantastic… What is it? Floatie rider." He puffed out his chest like a superhero on steroids. "Scratch that… floatie *tamer*, and my parenting skills will become so refined, you won't be able to keep your sarcastic, mean hands off me."

With a huge grin, he finally allowed his confidence to emerge. When he stepped outside her house, the heat literally made him gasp to catch his breath, and he almost wilted that fast. But Matt surprised Lillian when he sucked in the unbearably hot air and said, "Race you to the beach. Last one in the river is a rotten egg…" before sprinting off the deck.

Benny squealed and protested, "No fair!" as his little legs fled past Matt. Lillian was spot on about one thing: Matt was willing to learn. From the fishing trip, he already knew how to let the kid win. Without being obvious. Matt struggled to walk in the deep, blistering sand. Benny hit the waterline first, but Matt wasn't totally letting the kid win that easily. Benny squealed with delight as he dived in, saying, "Ha! Beat you!" before sinking under the water.

Luckily, there was no one else at the beach. If any other Rydells were there, Matt feared he'd have to stop dead. Witnesses were too much to factor in as he struggled to figure out his new role. They made him too self-conscious. Alone? He thought he could muddle through somehow. He actually felt a little better about it now, after Lillian confessed her faith in him and gave him a well-needed and much-appreciated pep talk.

As Benny ran up, Matt eyed a large boulder at the side of the beach. Sucking in a huge breath while running full speed toward it, Matt jumped up onto it and glanced down. The green water was deep enough that he guessed he couldn't get hurt. With a loud yell, Matt jumped as high and far as he could, launching himself across the water surface and landing with an explosion like a cannonball. He splashed Benny who giggled and squealed with unbridled glee.

And that was how you had fun in the water. Matt realized it wasn't as hard as his brain kept making it out to be. The key was no big shocker: just relax. Quit overthinking every single minute.

By trying to have fun, Matt made it more fun. He was not so strangely awkward and formal. Benny's laughter was his reward and Matt believed he was succeeding. Yeah, the air was way too hot, the water way too cold, and several of the Rydells were walking down the beach. Lillian's cousins? Yeah, he believed he spotted Lillian's cousin once removed. Lillian's more distant cousins were closer to her age than her first cousins who were younger by a decade or more. Matt often felt confused as to which cousins he could identify. No, maybe that was Iris and the rich billionaire she married? No? Sigh. It didn't matter. He turned back to Benny when the kid splashed him before swiftly lifting him up and throwing him into the deeper part. Lillian finally caught up to them. Her head was bobbing along the trail behind her cousins once removed.

The grin of approval on her face warmed his heart and everywhere else in his body.

THAT DAY, when they swam with the floaties, caught and cleaned the fish, and Matt kissed Lillian in her hallway seemed like a turning point for all three of them. Benny warmed to Matt far faster and damn! so did Lillian. Even more than she did at his house. There was something so endearing about Matt's earnest desire to do it right. His serious approach never failed to amaze her. Of course, that's what she wanted, but Matt had to learn that acting warm and fuzzy with the six-year-old was a lot more fun than being formal and stiff with him. Once he discovered that, which he did all on his own, the change in Matt was astounding. Lillian found it heart-warming as Benny's mother but also, panties-dropping as someone who could not deny her attraction to him.

The rapport between Matt and Benny grew substantially from that day to the rest of his stay there. Matt hung outdoors with them in the stifling heat. Most mornings began with them fishing along the river. Like magic, Benny started catching more fish than Matt after he learned to let the kid win sometimes. He showed Benny a few tricks that helped Benny hone his skills. They spent most of their spare time on the river because it was that hot in August and Benny said it was what he wanted to do. So, Matt did it. Matt still found her abundant family members both overwhelming and strange. Strange that they all lived there. His comments became predictable. Saying things like, "How compatibly they share their community." Or "All you need is a doctor to cover most the major industries as far as jobs go, huh?" Or "This is like your own town, huh? Should have been called Rydell's End, considering how the river and the valley were practically founded by you guys…"

Lillian became a little annoyed with his incessant comments about the family. She'd never heard anyone sound so disdainful about it. Maybe people got jealous, and some were surprised. But no one downright disliked it or called it "weird." Most of their friends thought it was neat to stay so close and be able to look out for their own. Yes, the Rydells were successful, and most people considered that an admirable thing… but not Matt Griffin.

He thought they were weird.

The only ones who really didn't get along were Lillian's father and Matt. They were constantly in a pissing match. Lillian never addressed the subject with either of them. She was more than tired of their incessant slurs, which were poorly disguised and rarely subtle. They were a thorn in her side. Her dad was overly suspicious of Matt and refused to relinquish his control and time with Benny to him. Ben didn't trust Matt at all, which Lillian resented. As Benny's mother, she had more to lose than anyone else if she were wrong. But her dad wouldn't give her that credit.

Unfortunately, they also couldn't avoid seeing each other. Both Grandpa Ben and Matt became Benny's favorites to hang around with. They fished together, hung out at the beach together, and even ate dinners together, all at Benny's insistence. He loved it when the people he valued most were all together.

Lord help her if Lillian didn't enjoy it too. Matt's critical attitude toward the multi-tiered family members having jobs and living in so close an area simmered without comments, but Lillian knew the extent of his alienation. She had to forgive him since he withheld his true feelings from Benny and to her surprise and delight, indulged Benny at every opportunity. From tromping out to the barns to visiting a grandparent or another, to trudging through the fields to find his three favorite horses. Two were being boarded at the ranch and were not theirs.

Matt failed to comprehend the pros about ranch and rural life in a landlocked setting like this. He never got used to the hot, dry weather, but he was pretty amazing in his willingness to spend most of his time with Benny outside.

And Lillian.

That did a lot for her. How often (okay, never,) did any man spend time with her like this? Treating her like she mattered? Trying to provide for her wants, desires, and needs? He listened to her, and he indulged her. He was fun too. Even if he had misgivings regarding why they were doing something.

And damn! All that attention started to spoil her. Solely self-reliant as an adult and in her views of how to raise Benny, Lillian was oddly comforted by simply having someone there who was legitimately involved and so eager to be part of it. Not only her son's life but also hers.

"So, Dr. Lillian, where do you hide your office? I haven't seen it yet. Where did you tuck it away on the compound?" Matt's eyes twinkled and his mouth smirked, which looked both warm and mocking.

"My clinic office isn't on the compound, as you call it. And it's a ranch, not a compound." She gave him an evil-eye but smiled.

"Where is it then?"

She sighed and gestured across the river. "Securely tucked away over there."

He let out a laugh. "Wow, so far from the family com—"

"Ranch!" she snapped with a glare.

"Ranch," he repeated with a raised eyebrow. "I'd really like to see it. Why isn't it located here?"

"Because the ranch animals are not my sole clients. Being closer to town makes more sense."

215

"But if you relocated it here you could save all the office costs."

She squinted her eye at him. "Inside the cult you call my family?"

He beamed and replied, "Exactly." Then he shook his head and his expression returned to neutral. "Would you take me there to see it? That is, if you don't mind."

"I don't mind at all." She had to refrain from setting her hand on her chest to calm her beating heart. Every little thing this man did was so considerate and carefully thought out. It made her heart palpitate inside her chest. Lots of people did nice things for her but when Matt did them? He made her knees wobble and her heart race.

Benny loved going to his mom's office, so they left and drove there in a few minutes. They entered a small reception area, separated by a desk where a part-time worker answered the phones, emails and greeted the walk-ins. The office hours lasted most mornings from nine to noon, and her afternoons usually found Lillian on the road, stopping at the various ranches and small farms to examine their livestock. A lot of time was dedicated to her family ranch, of course. She also personally answered calls and texts on her cell phone if anyone called the office and failed to get an answer.

As she showed Matt the clinic, she explained, "There's no predictability from day to day for me. I spend most of my time here or in surgery; or being on the road to answer a call, which takes me all kinds of places."

"You work as a large-animal vet, right? I didn't realize you also worked with people's pets."

"Yes. I'm a mixed-animal vet. I treat any kind of domestic animal. Most mixed-vets spend two-thirds of their time treating large animals, but two-thirds of their income comes directly from the small ones. That's how it works for me most of the time, excluding my family's ranch, of course."

"Yes, of course."

She gave him a mock punch in the arm but considered making it a real one. He laughed, and took her hand for a long moment, squeezing it as his eyes sparked with humor and lust. "Just kidding. Really. So you don't mind working with big animals? I bet you must shock some people when you show up to do what you do…" He cleared his throat. "I don't say it in a sexist way, I wouldn't think of doing that, I meant, when you show up to work your magic. But I expect there is still way too much of that kind of chauvinistic thinking."

She gave him a quick smile. "True that. I show up at half their height with my long ponytail and I'll admit, mostly the cattle producers give me the stink eye. After I jump through a few hoops and roll up my sleeves and get to work, they usually get over their distrust. *Usually.* Did you know female big-animal vets outnumber male vets right now? More women than men are enrolled in vet schools too and more female vets graduate than males."

"Truly?"

"For real."

"I had no idea. That's actually kind of cool." He glanced around and saw Benny playing in the waiting area with some horse statues. They were mainly used as decorations, but Benny always played with them and his creative imagination devised all kinds of adventures. "But I can totally see how intimidating you could be as soon as you rolled up your sleeves to work, then they better watch the fuck out."

She beamed at him. "Yeah, actually you're absolutely right. It is like that for me."

"Such a mighty mite."

"I'm not a mite."

"No, you're a *mighty* mite. Not an insult or compliment, just a fact."

Beyond the waiting area were two exam rooms. Each had a long bench for seating and a table for small pets. The sink and cabinets were pretty generic. In the back was her surgery area, supply room and a few kennels to hold the larger animals she had to treat. At the moment there were none. The clinic was no more than a small office, so the tour was over in a flash. Matt looked around, asking her questions, demanding more specifics on the way she ran her practice.

"What's the worst part of your job? Euthanasia?"

"It's pretty tough sometimes. Yes. But I wouldn't call it the worst part. Sometimes it's a matter of giving relief, which is comforting for the owners to know their beloved family member does not have to suffer anymore. When a dog or cat comes in with terminal cancer and their quality of life is rapidly diminishing, it's more humane and a huge relief for all to give them peace. It's sometimes the best thing to do. But it's never easy. And almost always sad. Worst cases for me come from abuse. Happens a lot. Not all are physically beaten up or injured but suffering from neglect or unsanitary living conditions is almost worse."

"What is the worst you can imagine?"

"Being unable to treat a curable animal."

"What do you mean?"

"When the family can't afford the treatment. I do some pro bono work, but you'd be surprised how much it costs to run a tiny clinic like this. I'm not a charity and I can't afford to fix every animal for free or even at cost. I hate to see perfectly treatable, curable animals leaving without treatment or having to be put down because the owner can't afford it. That's by far the worst cases for me. It causes so many sleepless nights and sorrow. I hate life-or-death cases that just boil down to having enough money to afford the treatment."

Matt froze as she spoke and shook his head. "I never once

considered that perspective. Damn, Lillian, you're both tough and compassionate. I can't—"

"You can't, what?"

He smiled softly. "I can't imagine how a woman, an amazing person like you, could manage to find me attractive."

"*Manage* to find you?" Raising her eyebrows, she set her hands on her hips, jutting her elbows out, and her tone challenged his comment. "I didn't *manage* to find anything. You *are* attractive to me."

He swallowed and the ghost of a smile curled up his mouth. "You can't imagine how good that makes me feel. And thank you for showing me where you work. But most of all, for showing me who you are."

She nodded and smiled. "You not only asked, but you're also interested, and you get it, which just about validates all my feelings toward you." She stepped closer to him, reaching out to close the few inches between them with her fingers on his hand, which he dangled at his side. He clasped her hand as tightly as she did his. "Including how I feel now."

He breathed heavily and her heart sped up. "Lillian, someday when we're alone again, I plan to show you every blessed sensational feeling you could ask for."

His smile was the perfect combination of being hot and tender and caring. She could feel his freaking respect for her oozing from him. Hers was growing just as deep, and just as fast.

Suddenly, Benny's voice rang out. "When you gonna have a doggy back here? Soon?"

Matt and Lillian instantly separated and exchanged their guilty, hot glances before Matt turned to Benny and asked, "You like dogs, Benny?"

"I love dogs. But all we have are kitties."

"He's right. We have three here and two at home. And the

ranch has several barn cats to control the rodent population. I keep collecting the strays and neutering them. It allows me to let them live in a safe place as well as helping out the ranch."

Benny stared up at him. "Do you have a dog?"

"No, I don't. I guess being on the water all day isn't enough time to justify having one. But maybe…" His voice drifted off as he gave Lillian a look. "Maybe I should rethink that."

"Really? Awesome. Could I meet him?"

Matt laughed as he ran his hand through Benny's twisting curls. "Of course, you can. If and only if I get one."

"Well, talk to my mom first, 'cause she can hook you up. Lots of people ask her to take them."

She nodded. "True story. I come home ranting about irresponsible owners pretty often."

Benny shook his head, looking big-eyed. "People should never get a pet unless they can take care of it. Pets need food and water and exercise. And a house to protect them from the weather if it's hot or cold. If people lose their jobs, they have to give up their pets sometimes. But that's the only reason my mom understands because pets and kids are part of the family and they should always get all their love and respect."

Lillian shrugged. "He listens to me, huh? But everything he just said is true. I feel passionately about animal rights."

"Hence your vegetarian diet and choice to be a vet. If only all vets were just like you."

"How's that?"

"Tough, strong, tender and compassionate. One hell of a sexy combination, Dr. Lillian."

Her freaking heart twisted at his kind words and his deep look of reverence and affection with a glimmer of heat that smouldered in the depths of his chocolate gaze was irresistible. Oh, damn. Lillian was quickly becoming smitten.

Too quickly.

She swallowed the lump of emotion that lodged in her throat and turned away in her effort to keep cool. "Well, if you decide to get a dog, just let me know and I'll hook you up."

His hand gripped her arm, and his smile was small but real. "Oh, you'll be the only call I'll make. I'd never consider having a pet if you aren't involved."

She gulped. She wasn't sure exactly what he meant. Did he expect her to remain involved? How much? And in what manner? As his veterinarian? No, she believed it went far beyond being a pet owner with him.

But how could that reality ever develop when they lived halfway across the state from one another and neither of their jobs allowed them to relocate? Or even be away for too long. Damn. There was no solution.

They shared a son. And a mutual attraction that mystified Lillian.

CHAPTER 16

*I*T WAS GETTING CLOSE to the day Matt planned to leave. He had to go back to his home, his job and his way of life. It was almost dinner time and Lillian started to prepare it. Matt was cutting up the vegetables per her request. He felt far healthier than he did when he arrived since they constantly ate green, leafy foods. Everything was green. He thought he'd hate eating vegetarian food, but in all honesty, it wasn't as bad as he expected, although not a life choice for him. Benny was visiting his aunt and grandparents, so it was the perfect time to discuss their next step.

"When do you think we should tell him? I mean, we definitely *are* telling him, right? I mean, yes, of course we are. But when? Before I go? And how do we?" Lost as usual, Matt relied on the primary parent of their son for all of his answers.

Lillian's head bobbed and her long hair bounced over her shoulder. "I think we should tell him before you go home. That way, he can adjust to it slowly. Do you foresee any visits in the coming months?"

"Yes." Matt could hear the wavering in his voice and hated having doubts. Why couldn't he just say *yes* with confidence, affection and ease? But the thought of Benny being all alone with him, solely under his supervision, terrified him. What if he missed something? Real, serious consequences could result if he lacked the sense to ensure Benny's safety and health in all events and circumstances. Matt wasn't willing to risk Benny's wellbeing just to have what he wanted most now, which was filling his role as a father. He still had no damn clue if he were on the path of success. "If you agree to them."

"I certainly do. Benny might be more comfortable if I came the first time. But once he knows he's safe with you, I'm sure he can visit more often…"

Matt nodded. So many questions and unknowns still concerned Lillian and yet she never tried to fully shut him down.

"Then I think we should go ahead and tell him."

"How?"

"Explain that you didn't know about him but now that you do, you would like to see him more often. Make him understand it was no one's fault, and no one made a mistake. We don't need to be too detailed. He's young enough to accept any answers from us without asking too many questions. Maybe later on, he will require more details, which honestly, sounds terrifying."

"It really does. But I'm ready to tell him now. If you are."

Lillian hesitated before a small, soft smile appeared on her lips. "Matt, you must realize as his father, you can decide to tell him anytime you choose."

Matt shook his head. "I would never do that on my own. Never. I respect you as his primary parent. I've observed enough to know your first priority is and always will be Benny's wellbeing, whatever form that takes, I have no doubt it will always come first. You aren't a vindictive person. You don't want to fight me for Benny's custody. Hell, you invited me here, which already gave me a slight advantage, for lack of a better word. I won't turn it into a fight. No matter what happens, I vow to honor you as Benny's primary parent, because I know you will insist on it too."

Her entire posture seemed to melt into a puddle on the floor. "You can't know what that means to me. I did bring you here and I was so afraid at the time. But I also knew that it was the right thing to do if you were even half the man I observed and believed you were."

"Thank you. I like to think I'm at least that decent. I'll try to set my ego aside, and like you, always put Benny first." He rolled his shoulders to relieve the tension from thinking about his imminent mission. *Benny, I am your father.* He couldn't stop visualizing Darth Vader from *The Empire Strikes Back* telling Luke Skywalker the truth. Even the damn voice kept echoing in his head. Not helpful. Why couldn't he be half as confident and mature as Lillian seemed? Would that also come with time? Maybe becoming a parent just automatically made one wiser.

Crap. What should they do? Blurt out the shocking news to the child like a foghorn?

"Then if you agree, I think we should gently break the news to him together."

"I agree, but I think you should tell him. He trusts and knows you better. In his eyes, I'm still just a family friend visiting."

Lillian unexpectedly launched herself at him. Startled, Matt was bracing his legs to try to anchor himself before receiving the minor impact of her momentum and her weight. Her arms wound around his shoulders and her hands gripped his upper back. Smashing her face against his neck, her entire body collapsed into the most comfortable burden he could ever imagine holding. He was stepping forward and preparing to kiss her when she wrapped her legs around his waist and patted his back as if she were consoling him. What was she doing? Unsure, he waited.

"I'm not sure what I did to evoke that kind of a response."

She leaned back and he saw tears glistening in her eyes. She wiped them with the back of her hand. "You are just so decent. That's what. The best gift I could imagine giving Benny is two parents. Finding out you don't blame me for the six-year gap, or want to punish Benny for the circumstances leading up to his birth, and you aren't threatening either of us, is wonderful enough, but now? The risk I took panned out to be not only fine or okay, but a truly positive, wonderful thing for all of us. I never dared to hope for that. So, yeah, Matt, you deserve a giant hug."

His hands drifted to her waist and he tugged her slightly forward before resting his forehead on hers. She stared up at him and their breathing seemed to synchronize. He touched the side of her face. Her cheek felt so soft and warm in his palm. "What if I want far more than a hug from you?"

Her breath hitched. "What if?" Her voice sounded sultry, deep and husky all at once.

"Lillian…" Matt's brain twisted in half; he was trying so hard to keep the thread of conversation going. Discussing the right moment to tell their son his true identity. Like always, his connection with Lillian was mental, physical, sexual, and hot, but it also contained an abundance of compassion. Their personalities just seemed to click without any explanation.

"Matt…" her voice mimicked his tone.

"I know we were having a real discussion but now I don't feel like talking very much."

"I don't either." Her tone was breathless. *Because of him?* It felt surreal to believe he had that kind of effect on this woman. She was exquisite in her looks, poise, intelligence, and personality. He was... nice. Just a nice, decent guy was how most women who met him would describe him. Women liked his looks. But not once was he something special to anyone. Never an irresistible heartthrob. He was usually portrayed as the nice guy next door. Not the hot stud women couldn't resist who exceeded all of their standards.

"But we have to. I mean..."

"We have to." Lillian's lips moved closer to his mouth. Their breaths mingled and their lips touched. It was a soft kiss that sparked more warmth. Pulling free of each other until their lips were bare millimeters apart, he leaned forward and gently took her lower lip between his teeth before he licked it. She groaned and her tongue met his. They almost consumed each other, opening their mouths and turning their heads to get closer and deeper inside each other. Her hands strummed through his hair, tugging his curls while his hands caressed her back and moved higher to her head. She moaned when his hands slid along her scalp.

So easily they could have slipped into her bedroom. That's all he wanted to do. But there was so much more at stake now than a simple date. Long-distance relationships. A son to share. A son who didn't know who he was. Not yet. What did it mean to be co-parents?

So much he had to learn.

He retreated just a hair's breadth and her lips followed his. He was instantly drawn back to the warm, wonderful feel of her mouth and pulled her tightly against him. Seeing her mouth automatically made him want to kiss it again.

Breathing frantically, he tried to gulp in more air.

"We... should... figure... out... some... things," Matt gasped. "But all I want to do right now is kiss you. But we should—"

Her head bobbed against his chest. "Yes, we should. You're right. But oh, my God, I want to keep doing this."

"Me too." Eventually, they both released each other with small, almost sheepish smiles as they moved apart. Lillian went over to the small kitchen island. Maybe putting the kitchen appliances between them could dissipate the heat they created.

Shaking her head, she leaned forward, resting her elbows on the bar. "I can't believe how fast that happens between us."

"It's like lightning striking without any warning. I don't want to stop. But considering..." His head shook.

"Considering we were discussing when to tell your son about you, perhaps not the best time."

"I wish it were less complicated."

"It isn't though."

"No," he agreed, his tone softer. She smiled.

"We should tell him tonight."

"Tonight?"

"Yes. Being so unsure and dreading it will just increase the enormity of it. There is no easy way to do this."

"Okay." Matt really wanted to know what she thought of kissing him and what they were going to be? How could they co-parent without this happening each time? Matt wanted it to happen, so he was reluctant to shut it down. Was it for the greater good? Or his fear of things turning sour? If so, their co-parenting skills and all the goodwill they exchanged, despite the contentious circumstances, would be for nothing.

He gripped the edge of the counter and leaned his weight on it. Staring down at her, he said, "I think we have to be careful with whatever exists between us. Mostly because I live far away, not here and we are only connected by our child. He is fully familiar with you and I want to develop a similar connection with him. If things go bad—"

Her hand shot out across the counter before she stopped

and withdrew it, smiling as she shook her head. "I find it far too easy to touch you. I know what you're saying. Of course, you're right. We can't do this. Not now. Maybe not ever. We have to be parents first. We have to make sure we can work that out."

"Yes." He lifted his eyes to study her. His heart swelled until it pinched inside. Damn, he wanted this woman. As a woman and a friend and a freaking parent-partner. He tried to resist the urge to take her in his arms. He could not continue to need or want her like this. Way too soon and way too much pressure. They were still too far from devising anything that might work out.

"Then you can't..." She swallowed visibly as she held his stare with a deep, long look. "Then you can't look at me that way anymore."

"I don't even know when I do it."

"Benny comes first."

"Yes. Benny always comes first."

They agreed on the same plan, to put their child first, in every decision. But underneath the words, something was simmering, something so explosive, both of them worried they might make some terrible choices. Neither of them could predict the future, or foresee a problem yet, but what if their choices ended up becoming major mistakes?

What if their chemistry sizzled and burned out? What if their mutual attraction simply fizzled out or eroded into a deep hatred? What would happen to all the years they still had to navigate around each other for their son? Being friends was far easier on all parties and less volatile than being enemies. But what if they dated and found it was everything they both ever truly wanted?

No. He had no clue what might happen in their futures.

So there had to be a pause.

Lillian turned away and Matt realized he could only

breathe regularly and think clearly when he was not staring at her. Making eye contact and touching her were far too distracting.

Ugh. Stop. Cut the damn vegetables and adhere to her diet plan and her refusal to kill things like fish for food. That would get so annoying in the long term. He could totally let that go. Her job required her to cut into animals, maybe not all the time, but she did it. And yet, watching Matt clean a little, tiny trout made her hold her nose. That would get annoying too. Especially since he ran fishing charters. And caught big fish. He had killed and cleaned so many fish in his career on the sea, he couldn't imagine how many there were. Would he have to justify his freaking living to her now? No.

No, it would never work.

Chop, chop, chop. His knife smacked the cutting board. Lillian was facing the stove, boiling a big pot of pasta and stirring the sauce. She made a tasty sauce. But Matt could only imagine if she added some chunks of any kind of meat: turkey, beef, deer, elk, or moose; any one of those would have made it even more excellent.

The vegetarian veterinarian who belonged to a cult and lived in a desert with horses offered nothing to him. It was ridiculous—

Matt turned when Benny's bare feet suddenly slapped the foyer as he squealed while opening the door and smacking it shut. "Mom! Matt! Guess what?! Guess what?!"

But all Matt could do was stare in wonder as a new, hot sensation filled his chest.

Home. This was home to him.

Fuck. Matt blinked with alarm. It was way too intense for the situation.

The woman he wanted to take to her bedroom and fuck until she was wrenched out of his system, became a lost image. His heart now swelled when she turned from the stove and knelt down with her arms open. Benny never lost a step or slowed his momentum but smashed into her with total abandon. Lillian always caught him, both literally and metaphorically.

Matt was so much more than attracted to her. But it could never be. His lifestyle didn't fit here, and it was way too soon to contemplate the logistics in trying to make such a proposition work. Besides, the child didn't even know yet.

Matt was trying to tune back into Benny's excitement. "I found an ant hill."

"Benny, stay away from it!" Lillian exclaimed.

"I know that, Mom. Grandpa Ben was with me. But we watched them go skittering everywhere. It was so great."

Of course, Lillian offered him just the right amount of interest and validation. She rose with Benny's hand in hers and said, "Okay, go wash up now. I'll get dinner on the table. You hungry?"

"Yes. I'm star-r-r-rving. Aunt Jade tried to make me eat asparagus and it was so gross."

Matt was smiling and his heart hurt with seeing how much he liked Benny's presence and sharing the entire evening with Lillian by making dinner, having a knock-your-rocks-off kiss, and the sweetest sense of contentment and fulfillment.

They shared timid glances above Benny's head and Lillian blinked nervously, seeming to be as affected as he was. She turned to finish preparing the dinner. She added all the vegetables Matt so diligently cut up.

She served the plates with fresh bread, pasta and vegetables, and a green salad with homemade dressing. Benny blathered on with his description of the amazing ant hill.

After dinner, Matt helped Lillian with the dishes and shared another easy conversation. All the heat between them dissipated as life's ordinary tasks and chores occupied them.

But damn! Matt was just as content doing chores with her as kissing her. No, maybe not that content.

He shifted his weight from one foot to the other as he studied her. He was always interested in the things that involved Dr. Lillian Rydell.

She tilted her head and he realized she'd been talking to him. "Sorry, what?"

"You seem miles away."

I was just imagining this being my home and sharing a life with you and Benny, Matt thought and it would have been the honest answer. Instead, he said, "Just grappling with my nerves."

She didn't recite any platitudes but reached out and set her hand on his arm, squeezing it, and smiling with reassurance before turning to finish washing the dishes.

Afterwards, she asked, "Now?"

"Now is as good as ever, huh?"

"That's what I would say."

They turned together and walked out towards the living room. Benny was crawling into the fort he made days ago using couch cushions and blankets. It was now filled with multiple toys, books and blankets. He often retreated and hid in there, leaving only two cushions on the couch to actually sit on.

"Benny, come out. I have something exciting I want to talk to you about."

Matt's stomach dropped when she referred to their task as *something exciting*. What if Benny saw the anxiety he and Lillian shared over telling him this? What if Benny thought it was terrible news and wrinkled his nose in disgust? What if he didn't want Matt for his dad? What if he got angry and blamed Matt for not telling him sooner? What if he felt suckered into spending so much time with him and resented that?

Benny's head popped out of the fort and he had to crawl carefully through the small opening lest it topple into a heap. It was quite a feat of engineering, Matt had to give Benny that. He flopped on the floor once he emerged. "What?"

They glanced at each other and Lillian sat on the floor near Benny's head. Matt did the same but closer to his feet.

"Well, you know how you and I have never known where your dad lived, right?" Benny kept throwing a small ball over his head and catching it. He paused at the word "dad" but showed no reaction. She continued. "Well, I found your dad recently."

Benny flipped over.

Matt sat up. She sure went there quickly.

"You did?" Benny replied.

He didn't even glance at Matt. That was a revelation to Matt, and he thought how different a child thinks than an adult does. His heart squeezed with pride at seeing something new about Benny. He was so innocent and guileless. So eager to hear Lillian's life-changing news, without any prejudice or anger.

"I did." She smiled and her hand inched forward to sweep the curls off Benny's forehead. "You have to understand that he never knew anything about you. I… we just lost contact and had no way of finding each other. It was no one's fault. If he had known about you sooner, like when you were born, he would have gone there to meet you. Okay? He's so glad I told him all about you. And you know how much I love you."

Benny nodded over and over, now on his knees. "Who is it? Where is he? How did he get lost?"

Matt's stomach cramped. Shit. How *did* he get lost? Matt was so lost his son wasn't introduced to him for six years.

But Matt was there now. That's all he had to offer. His own father was still alive—Matt assumed—somewhere, even though he hadn't seen him for years. Matt doubted he'd even know him if he saw him. But Benny knew Matt. Whatever it took. He fisted his hand and Benny stared in avid wonder at his mother. He was very interested now, and his big eyes were clueless that his father was sitting right beside him. Benny really didn't know.

"He's actually Matt. He came here to meet you because we wanted to tell you together. We just wanted you to have a chance to get to know him first. We—"

Benny swung his head around and stared at Matt. He looked startled. It was obvious he could not grasp her words for a moment, and they didn't fully register. "Matt?" Benny repeated.

Lillian glanced at Matt and he at her and she nodded. "Yes, honey. Matt is actually your father. He… now he really wants to be. And he already is. I mean…" She licked her lips. Her nerves reducing her to babbling. Matt's nerves were playing with his sanity too. His leg jiggled up and down and his eye started twitching. What did Benny think?

Maybe Lillian was wrong and completely failed to predict how Benny would feel and react. Maybe telling him was far worse than they assumed.

"You're my dad?" Benny said the words and Matt felt like he got sucker-punched in his gut. He held Benny's wide-eyed stare.

Slowly nodding his head, Matt said as clearly and simply as he could, "Yes."

Benny stared at him longer. Then his gaze fastened on Lillian. She had a small, hopeful and encouraging smile on her face. Softly, she said, "Benny? What? Are you okay?"

Matt's stomach twisted on itself.

Again, Benny looked at Matt. "Where do you live?"

"By… by the ocean."

"Why don't you live here? If you're my dad, how come you live so far away?"

His use of simple logic wasn't what either of them expected. Matt was startled and he exchanged a puzzled glance with Lillian over Benny's head. She shrugged as she lifted her eyebrows and waited for Matt to reply.

"Um… we didn't realize… *I* didn't realize… that I had a son. As soon as I knew I did, I came to meet you."

"Why didn't you know?"

"Because we…" Matt wondered if Benny knew where babies came from? How could he honestly answer that? Say they had sex without knowing each other's names or contact information? That was a little too much. Wasn't it? For a child this young? Matt had to consider saying something age appropriate.

"We had a misunderstanding. He didn't have a way to know. And I didn't know how to tell him. I swear, honey, Matt *wants* to be your dad."

Benny's face scrunched up. "What's a mis-misunderstanding?"

"It's when two people don't hear the same thing. Not on purpose. When something happens and one of the persons it happens to doesn't know it did, it isn't anyone's fault. No one can be blamed for not knowing something. Does that make any sense?"

Benny nodded. Matt gave Lillian a look that said *respect*. Damn. Matt found it totally impossible for him to respond to that question.

"So, it wasn't bad that Matt didn't know he was my dad. And you guys didn't want it to be like that?"

"Yes." Lillian's smile was huge and tender. "Yes." She reached forward and acted like she wanted to hug Benny who didn't relax into her embrace but held himself back now as he stared at Matt.

"Do I call you *Dad*?"

"You can, sure, or you can call me anything else you'd

rather call me. Whenever it feels right, you can decide what you prefer. I want you to call me *Dad*, of course." Matt cringed at his rush of words. He had no idea what to answer.

"Will you live here?"

"I'm afraid I can't. I'm a fishing boat captain, remember? I need an ocean to work."

Benny nodded. Was he remembering Matt needed the ocean? And was he okay with that? Or was he already mad at Matt? Maybe he should have been. Why should Benny accept their misunderstanding because it put him in this situation? How was he supposed to take it? Did he suddenly welcome Matt as his father?

"So, you came here to be my dad?"

"I did." He glanced at Lillian, who nodded. Was it a good sign that Benny asked? He wasn't sure. "And to give you a chance to meet me."

Lillian scooted forward and set her arm around him. "Benny, it's okay to be confused and unsure. This is a lot to hear all at once. You don't have to do anything differently now. You and Matt get along, right? You can just keep doing that."

Benny tilted against her, pressing his weight on her. Lillian just knew the right way to take care of him no matter what the situation. The perfect hug. The tender touch to reassure him. The right words to clear his confusion. Nothing was demanded or expected of him.

"Yeah, Benny, your mom is right. I hope we can still be friends. I felt like we were getting there during the past few days. We can just do that some more. If you want. This is hard, but we can just go on the way we have been."

"Is that what dads and kids do? Act like friends?"

Matt darted a big-eyed look at Lillian for help, unsure of how to answer that.

"Oh, Benny. A dad is a lot like how Grandpa is with you.

235

There is no one way to be. Just doing whatever feels right. Yes. Acting like friends is a great place to start."

"So, I really do have my own dad? Corey made fun of me last year because he said I didn't have a dad. But I never knew I had one. He said everybody has to have one. I thought he was lying. I just didn't get it."

"I'm sure that must have confused you. But it takes a mom and a dad to have a baby. Sometimes they don't stay together, and many kids don't live with both of their parents. The difference is Matt wants to be your father, he just didn't know how to find me and you." She rolled her eyes and winced at Matt again over Benny's head. He gave her a sympathetic, small smile. She was so adept at explaining complicated things to a child.

"We just wanted you to know who Matt is, Benny. There is nothing you need to do or say. If you have any questions, go ahead and ask. We want you to but only if you want to."

Benny was solemn as he glanced at Matt from under his mom's arm. "Are you glad I'm your son?"

Can a heart simply freeze and break, shattering into a thousand pieces? Can it hurt so bad while also bringing forth such joy? Matt felt it all. This child, his son, was so sweet. Confused. Benny was quiet and seeking comfort from the one constant in his life, his mother. But when he asked was Matt glad Benny was his son? Matt's throat was raw as he tried to swallow a lump lodged in it. Was it tears? Raw emotions? Regret? Or tenderness for this child? All of the above. "I was never so glad of anything in my entire life as when I knew you were my son."

He nodded. "So, the misunder-thing is what made you mad?"

"Not mad. Your mom and I were just sad it took us so long to figure out."

"How did you figure it out?"

236

"I actually heard about this place, your home and I came to see her."

"And she told you about me? About your son?" His voice sounded so bright and peppy.

Matt smiled with inner amusement. "Well, we didn't know about the misunderstanding. But she came to visit me and told me about you."

"At the ocean? When?"

"That short trip I took? Remember? I went where Matt lived and told him. We both figured out the misunderstanding and he was really excited to get to meet you. Benny? What do you think?"

He glanced up at his mother. "Okay. I think it's okay I have a dad. And he's nice. So, we can be friends."

"Yes." Matt wanted so much more than just to be friends. Two weeks ago, he was disappointed when he failed to feel an instant connection. But in their recent interactions he saw the beginnings of what could be, and his opportunity to be a real father started to take root. Now? It all gushed forth and Matt wanted it more than anything.

Most of all, Matt was grateful that Benny did not seem angry or utterly confused or upset about discovering his dad. He was relieved when Benny agreed they were friends.

Lillian and Matt all but exchanged deep sighs as Benny hopped to his feet. "Can we have dessert now? To celebrate?"

Lillian nodded and her smile got huge. "I think celebrating our news with dessert would be the best thing to do. How about we make a bowl of chocolate pudding?"

"My favorite."

"Duh," she said with a mock eye-roll. "And we'll teach Matt how to make it just right, okay?"

Matt rose, waiting for Benny's reaction. Benny nodded. "Sure. It's the best ever, he'll find out."

They smiled and Matt was so relieved, he almost wiped

his brow. Wow. It was over. They'd done the awful task without any scarring or permanent damage. This would most likely be the first of many conversations. When Benny got older and connected all the dots, as well as learned the facts of life, he'd no doubt have more questions. Or at least, comments. Matt committed himself to remaining open, honest and real. As transparent as he possibly could be. But for now, he was just grateful to stand in the kitchen and take orders from someone half his size who looked just like him.

CHAPTER 17

*B*ENNY DIDN'T FLIP OVER the news that Matt was his dad. Or act like Matt was part of the family he considered Lillian, her parents, and her siblings. Benny remained cautious, but friendly. His read of the situation was more mature than Lillian ever predicted. Seeing his reaction actually filled her with pride and watching his handling of the news all but made her burst with love. Her relief in Matt Griffin's response also thrilled her.

Matt held both her life and her son's life in his hands in some ways. She was anxious until he promised only to do what was best for Benny always. Their son had to come first, and Matt already accepted it and deferred to her. He basically dispatched all her deepest fears. However, he failed to see that his kindness was the greatest aphrodisiac for a woman he could offer. Basically, his respect and admiration for Lillian as a mother exceeded all expectations and he could never think of taking Benny away from her. She was best for Benny and he was best for her. But Matt was also more than aware of the way Benny looked at her. And relied on her. That also managed to cement them together.

At long last, they both abandoned all the problems they previously imagined encountering. Since they never happened, they could finally stop worrying about them. Her attraction to the man only grew deeper as she watched him interacting with their son. It made him even hotter and more appealing to her.

Benny settled into calling him Matt, and Lillian often caught Benny eyeing him. Matt saw it too. Her heart melted every time she noticed how sincerely Matt talked to him, squatting down to Benny's eye-level to listen more closely to him. Matt tried to be Benny's best friend, without confusing the child. Benny was more than willing to reach out and hang with Matt, but he wasn't ready to call him *Dad*. Lillian suspected that might happen, but Benny's persistent caution was instantaneous and lasting, which surprised her.

And as for Matt's reaction, did he get offended or annoyed? No. On the contrary, he tried even harder to do whatever Benny wanted. Matt always listened. He never watered it down by being present physically without really listening or giving Benny his full attention. Like many six-years-olds, Benny talked incessantly and repeated his questions frequently; yet Matt never failed to respond to them as if Benny were asking for the first time.

But the two weeks Matt allotted for his vacation was coming to a close. It was approaching the time for him to go home and resume his life and career. His responsibilities were waiting in Westport. Lillian had no idea what that meant for the three of them. Of course, her heart was heavy when she imagined him leaving, although she expected the opposite to happen. She thought she'd be glad to see him go home. If only to let her regain full control of Benny. But much to her surprise, she harbored no resentment in sharing Benny with Matt. It was an invigorating experience for all.

Then the morning of Matt's departure arrived. Lillian and

Matt didn't touch on "them" as a couple again. Not yet. Both of them understood they would continue seeing each other for Benny and maybe... what then? She wondered and hoped. Maybe time would work it all out. God, she found herself wishing for that to happen. It would make it so much easier. She wished she liked Matt in a friendlier, more platonic way. Non-sexual. Unlike now, when her body reacted to his physically and her emotions grew overwhelmingly enormous. Lillian wanted it to be casual and nice, not amazing, mind-blowing, heart-wrenching and filled with eager anticipation. His mere greeting, "Good morning, Lillian," made her body shiver with lust.

She was far beyond having just a crush on him.

It was dangerous and irresponsible to allow that to happen, considering the long-term consequences of their *child's* reaction if anything went wrong.

But the time had come for Matt to go and Lillian's heart reacted much more dramatically than she expected. It failed to correlate to the small amount of time he spent there. But she could not deny how colossal his departure was to her.

Setting his bag in his truck cab, he shut the door on the passenger seat before walking around. He gave Lillian a pensive look while kneeling down next to Benny. "So, Benny, I've gotta get back home and catch some fish. Big ones, I hope. I'll send you pictures of them, okay?"

Benny nodded without any words. His cheeks were pink. Was he upset? Glad? What? Lillian even wondered, which was a first for her.

"And you'll send me any pictures of the trout you and Grandpa Ben catch, right?"

"Right."

"Promise? Don't forget. I really want to see the pretty trout you guys catch."

"I won't forget."

He swallowed and squeezed Benny's arm gently with his hand. "Okay, then, I'll look forward to getting those."

Matt started to rise, and his gaze sought Lillian's. As always, the hot spark in his eyes gently softened, becoming more like molten hot chocolate. Matt was so expressive, which was like kryptonite to her. She never managed to affect any man to that extent.

"I'll stay in contact." He glanced away. "Maybe, once Benny is settled in school, you two could come out for a weekend to visit me."

"Yes," Lillian all but jumped at the opportunity. Then she had to tone it down. Why was she so excited and giddy about his invite? Was it for Benny? Or herself? The probability it could be herself made her feel horrible.

"Do you think you'd like to visit me, Benny? You could see my boat."

He nodded. "Yeah. I'd like to go out on your big boat."

Matt exhaled a sigh of relief. "Oh, boy! I'd love for us to do that. More than anything else I can think of."

Benny didn't approach him for a hug. Hugs were something Benny generously gave to almost everyone he met. There was something much more serious in the way Benny reacted to Matt. It surprised both Matt and Lillian. They gauged their own responses according to Benny's reactions.

Slow and steady seemed to be the key.

Matt touched Lillian's arm, leaning forward and grazing the side of her cheek with his lips. It was a cool, quick, soft peck but her entire body broke out in goosebumps. "Lillian, thank you very much for all of your generous hospitality. These two weeks have flown by and thanks to you, they turned out to be much better than I could have wished for."

How could she not fall for this man?

Lillian didn't dare say that. She settled for, "Let me know when you safely get home, and we'll talk again."

He let her go. Was it disappointment or regret that flashed in his eyes and extended across his face? "Goodbye."

"Bye, Matt," Lillian replied.

He got into his truck, giving them each a long last look and a wave before he pulled out and drove away. His taillights disappeared and Lillian's heart sunk. She felt as sad as if she'd lost someone dear to her. Such a stupid overreaction. He was only there for a two-week vacation. For her. Now it felt like even that was way too much.

Lillian and Benny had to resume their lives on the ranch, including their family obligations and work.

"Well, should we go find Grandpa? Maybe we could take a quick evening ride before dinner?" She hoped that might distract her from the sinking sensation in her chest and stomach.

Lillian could not judge Benny's mood. He nodded obediently, slipping his hand into hers and walking quietly towards the barns. None of his usual talking and gabbing. Was he confused? Wondering if Matt would contact him again? Distrustful? Whatever Benny felt belonged to him, so Lillian let him be as she retreated into her own silent world.

MATT WAS glad to see Granddad and had missed him. He told Granddad all about the past two weeks in an uninterrupted monologue. There was so much to remember. Granddad was unfamiliar with using smart phones, so they hadn't really spoken to each other than to make sure they were both okay.

"It sounds like you really like both of them and not because you have to," Granddad remarked.

"No, it's not at all because I have to. They are both amazing. I mean, you would say the same thing. They are so—"

"Mattie, when will they visit here?"

"As soon as I can convince them to."

"I think you should sooner than later. Sounds like Benny is a little confused and might appreciate your quick response. It also shows real interest on your end."

"I think so too. But Granddad, the thing is: I want him out here. I want to show him the boat and watch him catch a real big fish, not the dinky trout he calls *big*. I can't wait to show him..."

Granddad set a hand on Matt's shoulder. "I'm very proud of you."

"For what?"

"For stepping up to the plate and being the father you never had."

Matt snorted. "Yeah, for a total of two weeks, Granddad."

"Yes, but you and Lillian already made plans, and I can see the excitement in your eyes, and all of that was absent in your own life. So, seeing it now is just astounding." His old eyes shone with affection and his chest swelled with button-popping pride.

Matt's heart was full too. "I really do like Benny."

"Both of them. You really like Dr. Lillian just as much, I think."

"She's..."

"She sure is," Granddad interrupted with a smile. "She really is that."

Matt waited a month for Lillian and Benny to visit. They exchanged phone calls and sent photos in the promised texts often. Lillian took pictures of things Benny made, from coloring pictures to building forts as well as his outside adventures. Matt looked forward to all of the things he received and considered it a chronicle of *his son's* active imagination and playtime.

"Benny has next Friday off school for a teacher conference day."

"Really? Come here then. We could have a three-day weekend."

"I was hoping you'd ask. I was thinking that too."

Matt's eyes closed. "I really want to see you… *both of you*," he clarified.

"*We* both want to see you too."

Her husky voice promised unlimited pleasure and undiscovered thrills. Matt wanted that so badly but in reality, it was impossible to sustain. There was no way he could manage it all. So much had changed in both of their lives during the short amount of time they spent together. And now, Matt wanted so much more. With Lillian and with Benny.

He had to ignore his desires for now. Go slowly and let things happen naturally. Forcing things to happen never worked anyway.

His relief at hearing they were planning to come see him felt like a fresh bucket of water being poured over his overheated body.

In such a short time, they mattered more to him than anything else.

They finally got there at the end of the month. Matt waited six weeks since leaving River's End and it felt like six months. He missed them like he never missed anyone before. A woman and a child. He'd been answering to Granddad all his life, but this was far different. Granddad was more like a roommate who rarely needed Matt's help. He wasn't a feeble, old man in need of a family member to take care of him. They continued living together as family and companions because neither had anyone else and there was no reason not to. After Grandma died, their mutual lifestyle suited both of them. Matt never considered changing that arrangement until a dark-haired vegetarian came up to stay with him.

But now? It had morphed into so much more than anyone expected.

His son and his son's mother complicated things. Being so far away, they were still half strangers. It was odd to feel so connected while longing to be with two people he still had so far to go before he could fully know them. The strangest part was all he wanted to do was spend more of his damn time getting to know them better.

The distance factor really hampered their plans.

Matt called Benny previous to their visit and learned all about first grade with Mrs. Call. She promised to bring her pet snake into school one day for show 'n' tell. Wasn't that cool his teacher had a pet snake? Their daily conversations included many texts and pictures that went back and forth. Granddad was right when he said there were many ways to reduce the distance and spend more time together. Getting to know both of them increased with every form of communication.

And now they were coming here.

The days couldn't pass fast enough for Matt. When Lillian and Benny finally arrived after their long drive to get there, Matt was giddy and had to calm down before running out to meet them as soon as Lillian's car pulled in.

Matt couldn't play it too cool. He flung the front door open and rushed towards her car as they both got out. Benny skipped forward, stopping dead before Matt without touching him. Matt's heart hurt and felt like it bumped against his chest.

A huge grin all but split Matt's face in half. He had to keep his hands tucked into his pockets. "Hey, Benny. How was the long drive?"

"It was okay. Mom let me play this most of the way." He held up a video game attachment. Matt had no clue what kind it was. He had a lot to learn from Benny.

"Mom doesn't usually let him play video games for so long," Lillian clarified as she came up behind him. Her eyes glowed and so did Matt's. They stared at each other for too long and his gaze nearly consumed her. He stared at the thick bangs, and the long strands of hair over her shoulder that dropped below her elbow. Her hair was so exquisite and healthy. She was gorgeous.

"Hey," he said softly.

She smiled at his huge grin and eye lock. "Hey."

They gave each other bigger smiles. Then Benny shuffled below them.

"What are you doing?" Benny asked.

Matt glanced down to find Benny staring up at him, his glance alternating between the two of them. "I forgot how pretty your mother is. Just had to remind myself." Matt stepped forward, setting his hand on her lower arm and swiftly kissing the side of her mouth.

She gave him the same type of friendly kiss. But a pause drew their gazes back to each other and it was instantaneous fireworks. Right there. Matt had to fight the urge to grab her, lift her up and drag her into his bedroom and—

No way. Not with Benny and his grandfather right there.

Matt turned and swept his hand towards Granddad, who stood in the front doorway. "Benny, this is my grandfather, Jefferson Griffin."

"So, he's my great-grandfather, right? My mom told me. Like my great-grandpa Jack."

"That's right," Granddad said while chuckling. "And you can call me Granddad or Jefferson, whichever you like."

"Can you ride a horse? My great-grandpa Jack can. Grandpa Ben says he's one of the best horsemen still alive."

"No, I can't. But I can steer a boat into any dock. I'll bet Great-Grandpa Jack can't do that."

Benny's face scrunched up in thought as he replied, "I'm not sure. But I don't think he can."

"No. Grandpa Jack can't steer a boat into a dock. I doubt he's ever been on a boat, let alone, driven one," Lillian said, biting her lip to keep her mouth from stretching into a huge grin.

Benny tilted his head and squinted his eyes. "Can you really steer a ship?"

"I can steer a boat. Yes. And we'll prove it to you, huh, Mattie?" Granddad said as he raised his eyebrows towards Matt.

"Yes, but first maybe they could come inside our house and eat some dinner?"

Granddad chuckled as he stepped aside. Benny leapt through the front door ecstatically and Lillian followed, being far more sedate and slower. She gave Granddad a warm hello and a hug. He showed them to the room Lillian previously used. It was the only guest room in the small house. Benny and Lillian had to share the bed.

A hearty dinner of fresh salmon for them and a Caesar salad for Lillian was followed by a long, casual conversation around the dinner table that spilled into the small den. Benny quickly got along with Granddad and the strangeness between Benny and Matt eased up. Benny called him Granddad and Matt tried not to let it bother him that his son still didn't refer to Matt as "Dad" or anything but Matt. Matt totally understood Benny's hesitation, but it puzzled him that Benny was so much more comfortable with Granddad. Jefferson Griffin was warm, direct, and honest, the what-you-see-is-what-you-get, no-nonsense type of man. He had no qualms regarding Benny. No hesitancy or awkwardness like Matt radiated. Benny must have immediately realized the difference.

But in his defense, Granddad was introduced to Benny as

the man he truly was. Matt was introduced to Benny as a family friend who became his father before he left him again. Poor Benny had to figure it out. But for now, Matt was just grateful that Lillian and Benny were finally there.

Meanwhile, talking to Lillian picked up easily where they left off and fast. Like they were always communicating. In such a little amount of time, their souls seemed to recognize each other as lifetime lovers.

Benny and Granddad went to bed, so Matt and Lillian sat together on the front stoop. They watched the moon rise and listened to the waves in the quiet neighborhood. Tall trees obscured the view of the sky as well as the neighbors.

"What are you thinking?" Matt asked.

"About fishing. It's always been my dream." She gave him a teasing shoulder push. Then she slipped her arm through his elbow. "I think we should definitely go out on your boat. And I won't fish. But I know Benny will, of course."

"I honestly can't believe you're here now with him."

She breathed a long sigh. "After the first time I came, I wasn't sure we'd ever get to this point. But here we are."

Their gazes met and became riveted on each other. He leaned forward and his lips touched hers. At first it was an easy, soft kiss of how glad he was to see her. The chance to finally be near each other again. Her tongue slipped into his mouth and his hands grabbed the back of her head, which exploded into a tongue-to-tongue, mouth-sucking, body-slamming, heart-throbbing kiss. They scooted closer together on the steps and smashed their knees together. She moaned into his mouth and turned to unceremoniously swing her legs on either side of him. Straddling his thighs, she smiled without any shyness, and the strength he saw drew him even more to this woman. She licked her lips and gave him a suggestive eyebrow waggle.

He pulled her closer and their kiss was as hot and heavy

as before. She scooted forward with a groan, snugly placing her crotch against him and he sighed at the contact.

They kissed like that, on and on. His hand moved up her shirt and he pushed her bra out of the way to take her breast in his hand. His thumb rubbed back and forth, and her nipple got instantly hard and taut at his touch. She groaned, deepening their kiss before she leaned over him and held his face. She plunged her tongue deeply and hard into his mouth and he groaned at her rough handling, literally lapping it up.

She moved her hips over him, and he nearly lost his mind at the contact. He gripped her hips with his hands to stop her and pulled his mouth free. Breathing hard, he rested his forehead on her chest. "Why are we always outside when this happens?"

"Granddad and now Benny, and paper-thin walls in small houses."

"We should try doing it somewhere more…"

"Respectable? Decent? My entire life is that. I'm the responsible, sensible, conscientious one. The only times I haven't been those things happened with you. And I guess it would have been horrifying years ago. But now? It's the single time I don't feel like being a responsible, bill-paying, frugal mother who is always doing the right things for her family, friends and jobs. With you…"

"You're not any of those things? Those things are great things to strive for, Lillian." Lifting his head off her chest, he met her hot gaze. He couldn't restrain a short laugh of disbelief at her cavalier summation of them.

She smiled at his interruption. "I know. For being a doctor and a mother. But sometimes… well, as it turns out, only with you, I feel like being a woman. A young, wild, fun, beautiful and sensuous woman. Don't you see? I'm never those things. I've never been them before. Except when I'm with you. And I had to do some serious thinking on the subject. Do you know why I think it's you?"

"No. I'm not amazing or exceptional. I'm just kind of ordinary."

She gripped his face in her hands and her gaze drilled into his before studying his face and chest. "Matt Griffin, you are not ordinary. First of all, you're super hot. So hot you make me forget everything when I'm around you. Second, you're funny, kind and smart. You're also interesting and unique and you think differently than I do. And that makes you sexy as hell. But there was something else I realized: for some reason, I just trust you. You've had my trust from almost the start. Gut-level confidence. And so far, you haven't proved me wrong. The more I get to know you and see you dealing with our son, the more I see an amazing man who becomes more sincere and more trustworthy to me as time goes on. Trust is the most important gift I could offer anyone."

"I don't know if I deserve your accolades. I was clumsy and unsure with Benny. I'm still learning and trying but—"

Her mouth covered his and she aggressively kissed him for a long moment. When she finally leaned back, he looked half dazed as he moved towards her heat. She held his face. "Don't you see? You're the only one to stimulate me. My need to have and want sex. It's because I trust you. With myself. And with Benny. If you don't think your reaction to him isn't the sexiest, most seductive thing I've ever witnessed, well, it is."

Her lips took his again and he moaned into her mouth. She spoke as they kissed. "I want you. Right here. Now. I can't wait."

"Lillian, we're on the front porch step…" Grasping at straws for logic, Matt struggled for words as she sat on his lap and covered his mouth with hers.

"It's too dark. No lights are on. Everyone is asleep. No one will see us. And…"

He smiled under her lips as she kissed his mouth, his cheeks, his chin and took his hand to slide around her waist. "And you like that."

"Only when I'm with you," she mumbled as she tilted her pelvis forward. He sighed at the contact.

"This could be risky."

She kissed his chin and licked it. "Or so hot you'll never look at your porch again without getting turned on."

"I already won't." He gasped when her hot tongue entered his mouth again.

Smiling with glee, Lillian slowly slid back and dropped her hands near his sweatpants. He almost whispered a prayer of gratitude for putting on casual pants before bedtime. He never imagined their easy access would be more than appreciated after this. It blew his mind that the ever conservative and responsible Dr. Lillian Rydell was begging to have sex on his porch because she couldn't wait to go… where? He now agreed going inside was much riskier. The walls were extra thin. But the chances of anyone coming to the front door at this hour were slim.

But not entirely impossible.

Too late, she stood up and slipped her freaking panties down her shapely legs before stepping out of them. He stood and took her hand. "Come on, let's go someplace where we can't be so easily spotted."

She let out a squeak and a laugh as she dipped down to grab her discarded panties. She gripped his hand as he took her around the side of the house into the back yard. It was a lot more discreet, and the trees and a wooden fence made it more secluded. No access by door or through a window in case his son or grandfather decided to wander or peek out.

Oh, damn. Lillian's underwear was gone and now she was begging him.

He spun her around and pushed her back towards the side of his house. "You sure you want this?"

She all but attacked him with a bite to his lip. "So sure." She was nearly breathless.

His hands slipped over her bare ass. Groaning, he filled his hands up with her soft, round cheeks in each palm and pressed her towards his erection. He could feel her heat through the material of his tented pants. Moaning and laughing with glee, Lillian tossed her head with what appeared to be ecstasy and her hair fell in a long cascade of unbound glory.

He pressed his hips forward and used his hands to push her against him. She gasped and his mouth dipped down to kiss her nipple over the material of her shirt. She rubbed his head. "Someday, I'll slowly make love to you in a bed that will last for the entire night," he whispered as his mouth went up her collarbone and her neck.

She smiled but only cared about right now. "Someday. Sure. But this is... so hot. What I need. Please... Matt. Fuck me..."

Wow. Damn. She was *everything.* Smart. Hot. Beautiful. Tender. Sweet. Educated. Caring. All the things he admired. But now she wanted him to fuck her in the darkest corner of his back yard against his house. He surprised her and set her on the sawhorse he kept beside the house. Never before had it been used as a prop for sex. But he set her on it and pushed her skirt up higher. The light was faint, but the silvery moon-light shone on her. He could make out her dark curls and pink center. He groaned and she moaned his name. First, he gripped her shirt and pulled it free, then he bunched up her skirt. He held one breast and tilted it upwards, bathing her dark red nipple in the scarce nighttime light. It had to be the hottest moment of his entire life.

He stepped forward, joining their mouths and dipping his fingers into the exposed, glorious skin. It was wet and warm, and she gasped at the contact. He started to sweat at hearing the sounds she made. She pulled his shoulders closer and lifted her mouth to his. He held her against him and finger-banged her. In and out, hard and unrelenting, he almost made her cry out before using his mouth to muffle her when she screamed. Her body dripped over his hand as he pushed his palm up against her clit and center.

"Oh, God…" She wilted and her head dropped back. "So… good… so… good."

A moment later, she slipped off the sawhorse and grabbed his waistband. In seconds, she freed his erection and began pushing him towards the house so he could rest against it. Then she dropped down to his hips with her mouth, all hot and tight, and launched Matt into the throes of ecstasy. She licked and kissed and sucked him in her mouth. Deep. Matt worried for a nanosecond about the gravel scraping her knees, but when her head kept moving up and down on him, all worries about her comfort evaporated. Matt was lost. His entire existence centered on the warm, moist hole of her mouth. That was all that mattered. Happy sounds escaped from him. He stared down at her bobbing, moving head, her hair swinging and that's all it took for him to explode inside her. She swallowed him whole.

Startled and shocked, she slipped away from him, wiping her mouth as she rose to her feet.

Matt, utterly weak and humbled, was still recuperating from his orgasm that was shockingly fast and totally unexpected. "Lillian…"

She didn't answer as she grabbed his head and pulled him towards her. "Now, Matt."

Those words made him grow hard again. He nodded, grabbing her and sliding his hands over the front of her. Clasping her pert, bobbing nipples in his hands, he twisted each one sort of hard. It was a commanding gesture. "Turn around, bend over and grab that," he said authoritatively, pushing her towards the sawhorse. She obeyed his instructions with a gasp of excitement that made his dick twitch.

She leaned over, sliding her skirt all the way up to frame her slit for his full amusement. She grabbed the sawhorse, something he never considered using like this, but he enjoyed improvising and fucking.

As his lady demanded.

God damn. She was so amazing.

He slid his hands to her bare ass, and she wiggled it towards him. She definitely liked it and she moaned, which told him even more when he kissed it. Sliding his tongue along her bare ass cheek, he was moving toward her center. Wetness dripped and she instantly parted her legs to give him more access. His tongue dipped into her from behind and she whimpered for more. Her legs nearly buckled. He licked her and his fingers explored her. Eating her out as she shivered and moaned, Matt realized she was trying to hold herself up. He grabbed her hips to hold her still and aimed for his next onslaught. Then he stopped and she almost protested before her butt pushed back for more.

He rubbed her, his fingers examining the wetness that her body made. "Oh, you'll get more. Just a moment."

"Tell me you brought a condom."

"I did. Luckily, I still have my wallet with me." He dived for his pants and found the precious prophylactic. After rolling it on, Matt returned to where he left her. She was still bent over, her delicious ass facing him. He loved the view and rubbed his hands over her bare butt, going up her back as she shivered and all but purred. He dipped his arm around her to grab a breast and began playing with it again, something he could imagine spending hours doing. Lifting her bottom higher and towards him, she gasped when she felt his dick.

"Oh... oh...." Her moans increased as he slid into her. Hard. She pushed back to receive all of him and braced her legs. Fully thrusting into her, he went still for a moment, savoring her intense heat and the pressure from her responding to him. The anticipation he had for her made his heart hammer and his entire body was throbbing just for her.

He lifted up and pulled her torso against him. Placing his tongue on the shell of her ear, he was thrilled when she shivered. Her body was pressing back against his. "Now... oh, now..."

Matt pushed and pressed harder as he held her closer to him. He rubbed her breasts, pulling on her nipples as she braced herself. "Hold on."

"Yes... oh! God... yes." Lillian groaned when Matt slammed their bodies together over and over in rapid succession. He had to hold her ass to keep them from becoming disconnected. His hips were the pistons and her body was the engine. A whirlwind of heat, sweat, breathless gasping and moans. Lillian's body shook even when he held her with his arms as still and solidly as he could. She came right before he plunged his last thrust into her and also came.

Ever so slowly, time and space returned to him. They were still joined together. He pressed his forehead against her back. Then he released her and pulled out before standing up and lifting her with him. She seemed boneless. He turned her half naked body and held her close to him.

"Lillian?"

"Oh, God, every part of me is rubbed and licked and fucked. I thought my head would spin off my neck. That was so... oh, God."

Matt chuckled as he bent down to rest his head on hers. Sweaty bangs lay under his chin. "Good. I feared it was too hard. Being outside, against my house… and not…"

"It was hot and wild and excellent. Everything I asked for."

"I've never done it like that. I was pretty unimaginative before you."

She smiled and lifted her face. "Well, there was nothing unimaginative about that. And fuck any other woman before me."

"After you. You were one of my first."

"Okay, fuck 'em before and after me." She grinned with a new smile that was so different from her usual look.

Her hands were rubbing his back and waist, exploring his ass and moving around to the front and oh, damn… "I… we…"

"What?" she asked innocently, licking her lips and staring up at him with big, puppy-dog eyes.

"You can't mean to…"

She smiled with a wicked gleam in her eyes. "Oh, but I do mean to, Captain…"

"How?"

"In your bed. And I swear I'll be quiet."

He gave her a stern stare, his dick jerking with instinctual interest towards her hand. "You promise?"

"Tell you what, you can tie me up and make me behave."

His heart leapt at the thought. "Lillian, you're not serious?"

"With you? Now? I think I am."

His heart jerked to attention like his body did. "You are the most perfect woman ever created."

She laughed, but he really meant it. Matt grabbed his pants and pulled them on temporarily, while Lillian let her skirt fall back down and put on her shirt. Then they held hands like wayward teens sneaking out. But instead, they were sneaking in. Trying their best to be quiet, they somehow stumbled into his bedroom, falling onto his bed, while their clothes landed somewhere behind them.

She grabbed his sweatpants. "I think these would work to tie me up. What do you think, Captain?"

Matt's mouth hung open as he stared at her on his bed, proposing that he tie her up with his sweatpants. He nodded, speechless, and the blood was rushing like hot lava in his veins. He grabbed the garment, and she politely crossed her hands at her wrists for him. Gently, he rubbed her pulse that throbbed. "I've never done this before."

She giggled and his heart swelled. He not only loved all the things they did but also how she laughed when he was trying to tie her up for sex play. "Neither have I," Lillian replied, pressing the back of her hand to her mouth to drown out the laughs that shook her.

Then the mood changed. Matt was crawling into the bed and laughing with her. Trying to contain his gut-clenching laughter with the pillows, they were helpless. The more they laughed or caught glimpses of the other laughing, the harder it was to contain. It was thrilling fun and so awesome to experience. God damn. Lillian was the best woman in the entire world.

They must have laughed for fifteen minutes over their failed attempt at kinky sex.

Finally, their cackling started to die down. Lying beside each other, he leaned forward, grabbing a length of her long hair and dragging it out of her face before tucking it behind her ear. "I guess we'll have to get some better ties."

"I don't care. As long as whatever we do is together. It's all great. Even this."

"What? Trying to contain our laughter over something that should have been hot and sexy?"

"Especially this." He took her hands together and instead of tying them, he leaned forward to kiss them. "These hands…"

"You have a hand fetish?" She was smiling without giggles now.

"No. I just like to think about all they do. Caring for my son, which you do so perfectly. Caring for all the animals of your family's ranch and in the valley and now, caring enough to come here and be with me."

"I thought you might say *caring for your dick*…"

He gave her a look. "I was trying to be romantic and that's kinda crude, Dr. Rydell. Trying to seduce a guy who's trying to woo you."

She leaned forward to kiss his mouth. "You don't have to woo me. You breathe and seduce me. I love the wooing though, to be honest. You think I'm so amazing when really I'm usually dropping all kinds of balls…" She held up a hand. "And there is no sexual innuendo there. Even if I might have slid it in perfectly."

A strange laugh exploded from him. She made him so happy inside. She was so easy to be with. She provided everything his life previously lacked. He was content, even invigorated with this new life. No woman could add as much fun and dynamic power to the sexy friendship they shared, and which made him hot as hell. And yeah, he was no longer so damn lonely.

"You're such a dork," Matt said as he tucked the side of his face into her hand. "And also, brilliant. Funny… And just…"

Her laughter faded and her eyes lost their sparkle. She touched his face too. "Yeah, you're just too good to be true…" Lillian started to sing, and he laughed.

They held each other and the quiet replaced all the kidding and fun and sex. "It's dangerous to flirt with this, considering the problems if it went wrong. And we have to remain civil because we are parents together."

"It's pretty unbelievable to me. But it feels so damn right. I can't explain it."

His breath released. "I can't believe you feel the same thing I do."

She brought his hand to her face and kissed the back of it. His heart flipped at the sweet gesture, which he considered silly when it involved other people.

"I do. Every moment."

They became quiet, holding hands and facing each other until their eyes grew too heavy.

Lillian barely moved when Matt lifted her from his bed at two in the morning and slipped her next to Benny. He wanted his son to know she was there in case he woke up. He kissed both their foreheads and feared his heart would explode from pure joy. How wonderful to have the two of them right there.

CHAPTER 18

ILLIAN ROLLED OVER WITH a soft moan of protest when her phone alarm woke her at four o'clock. Blinking with confusion, it took her a moment to orient herself: why was her alarm blaring while it was still dark out? *Ocean. Matt. Boat.*

He must have carried her back to her bed last night. Warmth flooded her body when she remembered all the things they did and how she felt. She not only initiated most of them, but she also demanded them from Matt. Wow. How unlike her. She started to blush as she lay there staring up at the ceiling.

Flipping the covers off, she sat up and rubbed her eyes. There was no animal needing her help or attention, no, not today. But Lillian would have to witness fish being killed for sport. She cringed reflexively at the very concept, until she remembered how considerate Matt was when it came to her preferences and differences in lifestyle. That took a lot of maturity and empathy. She could extend him the same favor.

She actually wanted to go on the boat. Not only did she respect Matt, but Benny was so thrilled to go out on a boat

261

for his first time, she had to brave it. Running a brush through her thick snarls of hair, she stuck most of it under a baseball cap, pulling the rest into a thick tail that trailed down her back. She had fun remembering how her hair got so thrashed, and she did not pretend to be upset and even grinned when she recalled the images of her unbridled hedonism.

She begged Matt for sex. Outside in the back yard, pressed against the house. How appalling. And unusual for her. But it was also blazing hot. So hot she came three times, leaving her body more refreshed and sated than it had been in years. She didn't even know how much she missed and deserved it but quickly realized she wanted it to remain an integral part of her life from now on. Like a magician, Matt created that hunger inside her.

Last night was pure magic. Enhancing their sex was all their laughter. Hotness and tenderness made a great combination. Love and friendship. He provided it all and she never imagined one man doing so much for her.

She wore her oldest hoodie, which she brought to sleep in, and black leggings. The forecast was mild winds, high tides and sunny skies. Matt mentioned "going over the bar" and she guessed a good weather forecast was golden. She would have never agreed to do it or trusted anyone else except Matt. He was careful, cautious and never too proud to defer to someone else's advice if it provided a more expedient and safer solution. Lillian remembered the eeriest parts of the stories Matt and Granddad told them until late into the evening last night. They were much more gripping and chilling now, however, considering they were actually going to be out on the ocean today.

It was like watching a horror movie unfold while hating how scared it was making you feel. The story was so thrilling, it captured your interest and you became invested so you had to keep watching. You are frozen into thinking, "what's next?" but the horrifying images keep reeling around inside your head when you're all alone in the dark.

The stories Granddad and Matt told weren't fake. It really happened to them on the sea, where she was going to be today.

Dragging herself out to the kitchen, she found Matt filling a thermos with coffee over the sink. Glancing at her, he seemed as fresh and chipper as a co-worker on a lunch break, not in the wee hours of the morning, prior to the crack of dawn. Matt was used to it, of course, being his work hours as he often told her. Matt couldn't sleep past five in the morning, not even on his days off.

Yuck. Never happening for her.

When he saw her, they shared a long, piercing look. Sparks shone and flickered in both of their gazes and Matt had a lazy grin on his face. Feeling instantly at ease and comfortable, her face beamed as well.

"You want anything to eat?" Matt asked, breaking the spell.

"No. I'd better not before we get out on the ocean." She had no idea if she had "sea-legs" since river rafting was the sum total of her experiences on a boat.

He let out a short laugh. "Good point. Just coffee then?"

"Yes. I'll try a cup of that." She took the mug he handed her and blew off the steam before lowering it down to the table. "Is there a bathroom on the boat?"

"Yes. Of course."

"No, there's no *of course* for me; I have no idea what facilities to expect on a boat."

"Well, a commercial one like mine caters to paying clients who go out all day, so yes, we have a fully operational bathroom. It's called a head onboard."

"Right. Good. Then I can drink this safely."

"Drink up." He laughed. "Tides are high and winds are light; so it all looks good. You ready for this?"

She sipped at her coffee cautiously, and when it didn't burn her tongue, gulped it down. "No, not in the least, but we might as well get it over with."

"That is the most discouraging endorsement I've ever heard. Is it because we're killing fish?"

"It's more because of the treacherous bar that I don't care to capsize on."

"We won't. I won't. I've done it so many times and under every kind of conditions imaginable. If I could put in an order for the perfect day to cross it, it would be today."

"I have to trust you with our lives. Okay. Then…"

He walked towards her, still shaking his head and laughing. "I should never have let you convince me to tell you our scariest stories at sea."

"No. Last night, it was too much fun to stop, but these are the consequences."

She flopped into a chair by the table.

He eyed her up. "Can I ask you something?"

"Sure. But my brain isn't working on all four cylinders yet. Thanks to someone in this room."

He ignored the dig and the hot, sexy look she sent his way. Then he asked, "Are you good at your job?"

"The best," she replied without pause or hesitation.

"Well, that's how I am when it comes to being a charter boat captain. So, try to remember that."

She peeked at him, but he didn't glance towards her. Did he fear she didn't trust him? She really did trust him. But the elements were beyond his control and that made her anxiety grow exponentially. The ocean's water was so deep and vast, she couldn't begin to conceive of it. But she owed him her trust, knowing he did his job very well.

"Okay. Point taken. We're going fishing today."

Matt slid another side glance at her, beaming with approval and damn! Her heart sped up like a reflex. "Damn right we are. Vegetarians and pescatarians…"

She smirked and ignored his comment.

He blew on the steaming coffee before him. "Benny really liked Granddad."

"He did. But it's pretty hard not to."

"Yeah. That's the general consensus, isn't it?" He grinned.

She leaned forward, taking his hand. "Benny will see that in you too. He's just not sure how to catalogue you in his life."

"Yeah. I'm slowly beginning to understand that."

"It's a unique situation for all of us. But especially for him. I'm not sure if we handled it right, but when I analyze it from every angle, I still can't see any other possible solution."

"He just needs more time and space. It has to come naturally to him and all of us."

Lillian nodded as she replied, "Honestly? It feels—"

Her voice stopped dead. Should she admit that to him? From the start, she found it hard to keep anything that floated through her brain from him. He was way too easy to talk to. Matt somehow drew out her words. All her secrets. She hated to have secrets between them.

"Feels like… what?" His gaze was heavy on her.

Licking her lips, her eyes darted away. "It feels so natural to me to have you around. and to be around you. I dreaded the thought of sharing Benny with anyone, but now I am impatient for Benny to understand that you really are his dad and that's a good thing."

Matt exhaled and shuddered as he replied, "That means a lot to me. You thinking that. Despite the colossal failures on my part. But it's all been genuine. I really want to get to know him. And be part of his life and yours. I might never know how. But I'm always trying. I promise I will keep trying too, no matter what."

Her heart thumped in her chest and she wanted nothing more than to believe him. She pressed her lips and said, "It will work, Matt, it has to. You can keep trying, and I want you to. I want—" She sighed as she released her shoulders. "I want you in Benny's life. It shocks me to realize how strongly I feel this way."

His eyes bugged out and his gaze landed on hers, staring with his mouth open.

She smiled softly. "What?" she finally asked when he didn't speak.

His eyes shut and then opened as if it were a profound moment. "You can't imagine what that means to me, coming from you. Lillian, you're—"

"What?" she asked eagerly.

"The only woman I always hoped I could feel everything wonderful towards. You are someone I never really thought I could have. I can't get you out of my mind. I share a son with you, and barely know you, but then again, there is no one I understand better than you. I live in abject terror that I'll inadvertently mess it all up, because we have so much riding on it. I find it hard to believe you just said that."

"Well, don't you believe that I feel that exact way?"

"It's so unreal to me, I'd have bet my boat against the odds it were true."

Her head tilted. "Why? I mean… why is it so unreal?"

"Just look at you. Your life. Your family compared to mine."

She jerked back and straightened up. "No. We aren't going there. Neither our jobs nor our families decide who we are. Besides, Granddad is the best ever. So that's all horse shit."

"Yes, regarding Granddad, but what about me? You really

don't see the striking difference between your success in life and mine?"

She folded her arms across her breasts. "No. I don't. That wasn't my point."

His gaze was glued on hers before a slow smile and a nod broke it off.

"You're right, it wasn't your point. Which was: we're nothing less of fantastic together."

A huge smile overtook her face, and she could not restrain it. "We are definitely that. We are. It'll work with Benny. He just needs time. Seeing where you live and how you spend your time will help him feel like he knows you. Each element of your life is another puzzle piece for a picture that he's trying to put together in his mind, and he will. I have no doubt he will get there."

Matt glanced down at his coffee and then back up at her. She could not ignore the flecks of gold in his eyes that were also the same color as the coffee. She nearly groaned at the lame comparison and unusual musing, which rarely happened. She really had it bad for this guy.

Which was good since as he was her child's father. And also strange for the exact same reason.

And it just wasn't long enough! kept blaring through her head. But nothing could stop the burst of feelings that always began to flow through her whenever she was near him. Happy, bubbly, giddy sensations that Lillian Rydell never felt before. She tried to analyze how she felt since she had no control over them and could not stop it. Not that she actually wanted to.

Matt gulped down the rest of his coffee and grimaced. "Okay, I'll go wake Benny and Granddad. You sure you're ready for this?"

The butterflies in her stomach came from doing something so special for him, and for the adventure they were about to embark on in general.

"Ready as I'll ever be." Her doubts surged in her. "What if I don't get my sea-legs? What does that mean?"

His grin widened and he had to laugh. "It means you'll be seasick, and this will turn out to be the worst day of your life. But don't worry. I have some drugs that minimize the effects, so it won't be as bad as it could be," Matt replied cheerfully as he passed her and gave her shoulder a squeeze.

She glared after him and sent a silent prayer up, *please give me sea-legs.*

"So, Benny. What do you think? Ready to get your sea-legs?"

"So ready."

They stood at the top of the breezeway at the marina and gazed towards the mooring docks.

"Which one is it?" Benny asked as he looked out over the bobbing mass of boats and masts. The water had soft ripples. Sailboats and several charter boats and small personal water-crafts bobbed rhythmically in their slips.

"See that one? The one with the red line on the side? It says, 'Griffin Family Charters' that's it, that's my boat."

Benny jumped up and down as if something was blocking his view. His excitement was that infectious. They started down the ramp and quickly reached the side of the charter boat that would transport his *family* today. That was such a strange, new, and thrilling concept.

His family.

Plopping the gear onto the dock, Matt turned and took Benny's hand, swinging him over the gunwale and railing. Benny glanced around and his eyes grew huge with unmasked wonder. Obviously, this was a major adventure for Benny and Matt's heart nearly exploded with love. He was so happy to be doing this with *his son*. Loading the gear onto the boat, Matt started at the bow and identified to Benny everything he could think of. Benny asked streams of questions. From bow to stern, Benny asked the names and purposes of everything he could see or touch. Benny marveled at the compact head, the dining table and the booths on either side of it. He ducked under and jumped around the small bed stashed beneath the bow. He scrambled around the boat, snugly strapped into his life jacket and so eager to head out onto the ocean.

Matt and Granddad finished stowing the gear while Lillian listened attentively to Benny's narration of everything Matt explained to him. Matt grinned since Benny seemed unaware that Lillian was right there too, listening to it all. But she let him ramble on. Matt started to release the mooring lines. Hopping back to the boat from the dock, he rushed to the steering wheel, engaged the engines and cranked the wheel to keep the bow from hitting the dock. Spinning and turning the wheel, he guided the boat out of the slip, heading for the main channel of the marina. Benny was thrilled. He moved all around the boat and pointed at the diverse vessels they passed, including a few pleasure yachts that were so enormous they had to be moored on the west end of the marina.

He glanced at Lillian, sitting at the small table with two booths on each side. She was staring out the window, wide-eyed as she watched the passing scenery, water, boats and Matt's well-practiced actions. Her fingertips kept grazing over her life jacket as if she had to reassure herself it was still there.

"How are the nerves and your stomach?" Matt asked with a small smile at her.

"Nerves are ragged, stomach is fine."

"That's a good start. I've seen people get queasy just from stepping onto the boat. I can't even imagine how they feel, but it happens."

"No. It's fascinating to see how you steer this thing. It seems... impossible." She shuddered as they passed within a parking stall distance from a large crabbing boat that was tied to the wharf, waiting to be offloaded.

"This is my office, Lillian."

She nodded. "Right. It's much more adventurous and interesting than mine."

He glanced at her and then forward. "You save lives. Fixing broken bones and repairing tendons. The adventures here are strictly for fun."

"And fishing. You're a hunter and gatherer."

A sense of levity rushed over him. Despite being a true vegetarian, she was here and willing to have fun. Her humor never left her, even if she didn't condone killing for sport. She was so right for him although she didn't appear to be.

When they reached the channel, the waves were considerably bigger than in the protected marina. The swells rolled in incessantly no matter the weather.

"Remember, I'm very good at this," Matt reassured her without even looking at her. He was familiar with the timid reactions of newbies to the rough water, having experienced it plenty of times before. Especially the passengers who came from landlocked homes, like Lillian and his son. Crazy to think his son had never been on a boat before. Not a real boat out on the ocean.

But Benny wasn't acting scared or sick. He ran and jumped on the bench and his mother's apprehension made her mouth tighten. She was visibly worried and scared. Luckily, Granddad mesmerized Benny with his myriad tales of getting over the bar. Some should have probably not been repeated right then, not in front of Lillian and Benny right before they attempted to do the exact thing. The tides were high and there was little wave action from the wind. The currents were always a factor, but Matt planned to hit them at the best time.

"So, the bar is the place where the Pacific Ocean meets the harbor, right?" Benny asked.

"Yeah. The deep ocean meets the shallower water of the harbor mouth. When you add that to the tidal fluctuations, it can create spots that are dangerous," Granddad replied.

"I know what the tides are, but how do they affect us crossing it? I guess you have to judge them just right, huh?"

"Tidal movement that goes toward the shore or upstream is called the flood period of the tide, or high tide. Movement away from the shore or downstream is called the ebb, or low tide. The time between the two, when there is no movement, is known as slack water. We are hitting the slack tide, which is the safest crossing. You never want to hit an ebb tide, not even on a calm day, because it is surprisingly fast moving."

"Which is most dangerous? To cross the bar going to the ocean or coming in from it?"

"From the ocean. Swells approaching the stern of a boat reduce your maneuverability, which can cause the vessel to broach sideways."

"What's broach mean? Make it tip over?"

"Not quite, but it means losing control. If you catch a wave at the side, the rudder becomes ineffective. Usually happens during severe windstorms or extreme wave action. Loss of control can lead to capsizing," Granddad explained.

Matt gave Lillian a long look. "I know all these things sound scary, and all of them can happen. But the opposing influence is me. I know about all of them and how to best avoid them. I would not bring you out here if we didn't have peak conditions to cross the bar both now and later. I swear that to you, Lillian."

She nodded several times as if she took his words to heart. But her hands still remained clasped tightly and her fingertips turned white. He leaned over and squeezed her hands, which she held together like in prayer. "Many vessels, of all shapes and sizes, do it multiple times daily. They update the conditions every three hours. There is no reason to think this time will be different than every other time I've done it. I've crossed it in all kinds of conditions. I got this."

The grip on her own hands loosened and she slipped her hand in his. She also gave him a small nod and an appreciative look. "Okay. I trust you."

He smiled with relief at her confidence. He knew the topography of the sea and what lay beneath them. He knew his instruments and his vessel. He could read tide charts, currents and weather from his many decades of doing this.

The waves started to get larger. Over one side and down the other. Over and down. Chop, chop, chop, the boat bounced over the crests of waves. Lillian held onto the table's edge. It was pretty smooth in comparison to some days, but Matt didn't point that out. Lillian wasn't heaving over the side or whimpering with fear, so he counted it as a win. She smiled at Benny and nodded or made faces at Granddad's stories, but Matt doubted she was really listening. Granddad chatted away to Benny as if they were slowly cruising the harbor.

Lillian turned white when the boat dipped sharply. She glanced out the port side and unexpectedly lurched forward as they passed the jetty. As the waves swelled up, she saw the huge, massive black rocks, a wall-like fortress that could ground a boat. But Lillian didn't whimper or plead for him to turn around. That happened on the boat quite often too. People who shut their eyes, or started crying, or whimpering, or moaning. Matt even got threats from people who were too scared to continue. Lillian was obviously filled with anxiety, but she held it all in. Literally. No seasickness yet, but no sea-legs either.

He leaned over and squeezed her shoulder. "You're doing great. Today's all clear and smooth sailing. I swear."

She nodded as she flashed him an appreciative smile. Gulping, she said with a desperate grip of the counter, "I can't imagine when it's not all clear."

He gave her a cocky grin. "Long as you know your tides, listen to the latest bar report, watch the weather, and the swell direction, know where the rough bar signs are located, watch your speed, and of course, if the freaking fleet turns back, you don't even try it. You just go home in that case."

"Are there times when that happens? And when you say the fleet, who is that actually?"

He smiled with a quick, affectionate glance her way. "Yeah, it happens occasionally, and there's no official fleet, that's just what we call the regulars that go out often. Charter boats and crabbers mainly. If enough come back in, you don't bother to go out. But people cross the bar in small watercrafts as well all the time. It's a big deal but it doesn't have to be something that stops people from going out."

She shook her head with an eye-roll, and a gleam of appreciation for him. He suspected she watched how he kept working the throttle and the wheel to control the boat. Soon they were over the bar, free and clear, ready to confront the rolling swells of the open ocean. It was a lovely day in late September.

Lillian finally loosened her vise-like grip on the table. "What do people usually fish for out here?"

"Bottom dwellers like halibut, rockfish, and ling cod. We also get lots of requests for salmon and albacore tuna, just to name a few."

"And what are we aiming for?"

"Salmon fishing is open until the end of the month so we're hoping for those."

Matt checked his coordinates and located the fishing grounds that were hot yesterday by all reports. Whistling, he finally slowed down as they came into position. Usually, Matt set the auto pilot on course, but Granddad got up without a word. He came over to grab the wheel and troll them along while Matt got their lines into the water.

It was a matter of having the right bait, at the right depth, knowing the flow of currents, and trolling and current speeds, and of course, luck. Always the main factor of any fishing expedition. Matt hoped that they weren't just lucky but had a spectacular day.

The sky was a soft blue, streaked with white clouds. Sky and water were all that surrounded them. Nirvana. Heaven. This was Matt's favorite place and his first choice to be.

Not Lillian, he guessed. One look at her face, which was white as the clouds and not in a pretty way, and Matt hurried to be of assistance. Oh, shit. He feared the worst.

"Gonna be sick?"

"No. Just feeling things."

"Those sea-legs building?" He tried to tease her, but she did not respond, and her head stayed forward. She didn't move after that. But neither did she start to heave or complain. Tough cookie. He had to give her that.

Instead of allowing her to suffer, Matt dug out the bottle of seasick pills he kept onboard and gave her the prescribed amount. "This should help."

She gratefully took them before letting her head drop down on the table.

"It's better not to sleep—" Matt warned her.

"I thought you've never gotten it before?"

"Well, no, but they recommend that you stay upright."

"Right. Well, you don't know how nauseous I am and all I want to do is sleep so…"

So, screw off. He got it. He backed away and turned his head so she wouldn't see his grin. Not that her pain amused him. Seasickness made people absolutely miserable. Matt couldn't relate. He guessed when someone felt chipper while someone else felt sick, the sick one probably wanted to throw the chipper one overboard.

But Benny loved every moment. He pretended to rock back and forth with the boat as they hit wave after wave. The seas weren't too spectacular, but constant as they pushed the boat, up and down, up and down, or rocked it from side-to-side. And Benny enthusiastically bounced over each one. Then Matt brought out the bait and gear. Benny stood right beside Matt as he rigged up the fishing poles and released the lines into the water with the downriggers.

Matt stopped quite often to thoroughly explain to Benny what he was doing and why. He also let Benny try to do what he did, which enthralled Benny. It wasn't long before the tips of one of the reels started ratcheting up and down. Tug. Tug. Tug. "Fish on. Fish on!" Matt called out with a huge grin and unrestrained enthusiasm.

Benny started to run over but tripped as he turned back towards the pole holder. Matt grabbed Benny's arm before he fully landed on the boat deck. Benny was already starting to cry as he exclaimed, "The fish! The fish!"

"Are you okay?" Matt asked.

"The fish!" Benny all but screamed again, which Matt took as Benny's way of saying he was fine. Tears fell in streams from Benny's eyes.

"It's okay, buddy, we got it. We'll get it." Holy crap. Benny could go from being feverishly happy to bursting into tears. Heart-wrenching tears. Like the end-of-the-world kind of tears.

Matt plucked up the pole with the still tugging end and pulled hard, setting the hook. "We got it. We're hooked up! Come here now, Benny, if you want to reel it in."

Benny scurried forward and stared up at Matt with some apprehension. Matt smiled gently. "Just sit on it. Put this end between your legs and go for it. Reel as much and as hard as you can."

"But... what if I lose it?" Benny's eyes were glassy and filled with concern as he watched Matt strain and pull.

He shrugged. "Then you lose it. No biggie. We'll just get another one. Come on, it's the fight that counts. Try and reel it in." He was grinning as he encouraged Benny.

Benny nodded and came forward but remained cautious. Matt lowered the end of the rod so Benny could slide it under him. Matt encircled Benny with his arms, each hand still holding onto the pole.

Benny's face was right beside his. He looked at Matt and said, "Don't... don't let go, okay?"

Matt's heart grew as big as the ocean. He never had Benny, or anyone else for that matter, look at him with such trust and need and faith. Matt smiled gently, and the words he used to reply were about so much more than fishing. Matt's feelings were brand new and just as primitive and raw. "Never, Benny." His voice broke and he cleared his throat. "Only when you're good and ready."

Benny's voice quivered. "I'm not ready yet."

"Then we'll do it together. Ready?"

"Ready." Benny's clear apprehension shone in his eyes and quivering voice. Matt hoped he wasn't making too much of this. Benny seemed unreasonably stressed. Far more than the task warranted. Losing a fish was the last thing Matt cared about. He could always get more. He wanted Benny to have fun. And learn something he could enjoy. Without stress and fear. Maybe he failed to make that clear. Did he stress the kid out too much by being so eager to get him out there? Regret sliced through him like a razor. He hoped he wasn't instilling fear instead of excitement. What if Benny hated this?

Oh, damn, the exact opposite of what he wanted to happen.

But Matt remembered what happened in August, when Benny got stressed about catching the small river trout. Maybe that was just Benny and how he approached all new things.

Matt stayed crouched down, closer to Benny's height and used his arms to hold the pole above the reel. "Okay, buddy, after I pull up, you start reeling it in as I push the pole downwards, okay?"

Benny nodded, sucking on his lower lip, in total concentration. Almost like he was about to take a special test. Matt wanted to stop and reassure the boy it wasn't a test but strictly for fun.

Nothing looked fun about Benny's facial expression now.

If Matt stressed Benny out too much, he would have to deal with it later. There was no time now. Instead, Matt pulled up and Benny quickly reeled down. The first time, his brow quit furrowing.

The second time, his lip pulled free from his teeth.

The third time, his eyes widened with astonishment.

The fourth time, he reeled in harder. More confidently.

The fifth time, he smiled.

The sixth time, he said, "I'm doing it!"

The seventh time made Matt pretty sure the child stole his heart forever. Benny was trying so hard because he cared that much. Did Benny always perform new skills with so much perfection? Even the first time he did something? Even when it was something brand new to him? Matt began to believe that was the case. He appeared to be loving it as he started doing it right. But if he erred in his efforts, he got stressed and hated it and refused to do it again. At the tender age of six, did he already put that much pressure on himself? Interesting. Matt glanced at Lillian and wondered if she were like that as a kid.

At last, he found something he could offer Benny *and* Lillian. The joy of the work, not so much the end result. The satisfaction one gained from doing and trying. The getting better with practice was the point, and learning was far more encouraging than perfection. If Matt could convey all of those concepts, perhaps Benny's anxiety would vanish, and his performance would become a much better experience.

Matt didn't doubt that Lillian was completely goal-oriented in her approach to life, so it made sense that her son was too, obviously. Matt was more patient in his efforts to get there. The journey was the goal to him, not the final destination. That was where the growth occurred. Matt could definitely use the skills required in fishing to teach his son.

They kept pulling up and reeling down in a steady rhythm for a long while. There was soon more action at the end of the line. "Getting closer. We'll see it soon!" Matt's voice rose with eager anticipation. Benny's gaze stared out over the surface of the sea. He appeared hopeful. He rose onto his tiptoes, forgetting to reel down and allowing slack to get into the line. Matt jerked back but he was too late. Just enough reduction of tension to let the fish loose.

Ahh, darn. They worked so hard. But that's how it went. Matt started reeling the line in and Benny, still half cradled in his arms, looked up at him with curiosity.

"What… what happened? Where is it?"

"We lost it, buddy."

"It's just gone?" Benny blinked and stared vacantly at the empty line he reeled in. Matt released him to stand up fully and finish bringing in the line. He set the pole back in the holder.

"Hey, Benny, it happens all the time. That's why they call it fishing, not catching." How many times had that lame joke been circulated among his disappointed clients? Most were adults who handled the loss in stride, but occasionally, an adult had a temper-tantrum, yelling, swearing, and even hitting stuff. Kicking the side of the boat and all but breaking the gear. That happened once after a guy lost a salmon weighing more than thirty pounds. A rarity nowadays. The man lost his freaking mind while screaming, cursing and breaking the fishing pole in half. Of course, the man had to pay for the damages. So, it wasn't any surprise that Benny was so invested in bringing the fish in. Many adults went apeshit over a lost fish. Especially the ones they fought and *almost* landed on the boat, that were *right there,* or the "big ones that got away." So many things could go wrong. One guy fell on his knees and cried, full on sobbing. Sobbing!

Over a lousy fish.

Matt loved his job and the activity it required, as well as the special knowledge and skill. Experience helped too, but there was also the stubborn factor of luck, which always conspired to make the experience different and unpre-dictable, the good and the bad. Sometimes even when you did everything right, the big one still got away. Other times, when you did everything wrong, getting your fishing line tangled on the motor or caught in another boat's line or breaking something, and somehow, you manage to get the fish anyway.

Honestly, that's why Matt loved it so much. He was never fully in control of it. Long ago, Matt learned to let it roll off his back like a duck.

Matt guessed his son and Lillian didn't know how to roll

with life. They were used to grabbing it by the neck and choking it into submission.

Benny's lip was quivering, and his eyes were blinking. Matt's stupid joke intended to avoid a tantrum or freak-out, simply made Benny cry. Matt stepped forward without hesitation and put his arms around Benny, pulling his small body against him. "Hey, Benny, it's okay. It happens all the time. That's why we try again. If it were always successful, it would be too easy. Remember the trout hiding behind the rocks and losing them in your river? Well, there's a heck of a lot that could go wrong out here too."

"No. I loosened the line. You told me *not* to do that. I got excited—"

He rubbed Benny's curls. "Or I might have tied a lousy knot; or maybe there was a frayed line I didn't notice. Might be my fault. Would you yell at me for doing that? Or be mad? I'm the one who rigged it up, what if *I* did it wrong?"

"I…"

"Well, Benny?" he pressed. "Would you get mad at me?"

"No." Benny sniffled and became quieter. "No, I guess not."

"Well, I hope not. Fishing takes practice and not everything has to go perfectly to make it a great experience. And now that we know the fish are biting, who's to say we won't drop our lines and get another one just like that?" Matt snapped his fingers for emphasis.

Benny pushed a few inches away from him, leaning back as he rubbed his palm over his nose. "Really?"

"Really." Matt grinned. "Wanna help me rig it up this time? Then we can blame you if it gets loose." He cringed and shook his head. "No. Just kidding. Sorry. Fishermen do that a lot for fun."

"You do?" Benny looked at him with big eyes and nodded. "Does that mean I'm one of the fishermen?"

"Of course. You're fishing, aren't you?"

"Yes." Benny straightened up. "I sure am. Well, maybe I can rig it, so we *don't* lose the next one."

Matt's heart lurched with pride. Was Benny using sarcasm now? Was Benny kidding him too? Yeah, Matt was pretty sure he was. Benny's eyes gleamed, and he liked belonging to something. A new crowd? One of the fishermen? Matt put a fist out and waited to see if Benny reciprocated with a fist-bump. He did and grinned when he did it back to Matt. Then he turned around and headed to the back of the boat to open the bait box. He was ready to get going again. Thank goodness. No tears or tantrum. Mission accomplished.

Matt hurried to the back of the boat and helped Benny pull out the right stuff and figure out the rigging. Then they set the line back in the water with the three other lines. They still hadn't gotten a bite yet. He pushed his hands into his pocket. "Okay, hurry up and wait."

The ocean shimmered in shades of blue and the midmorning sun felt so damn pleasant. Matt stayed out on deck, letting the sun warm his bare arms in the pleasant-but-not-too-hot weather. It was a good hour before the back pole suddenly fell off the clip and started tugging hard.

"Fish! Fish! Fish!" This time, Benny was right there. Granddad put the boat in neutral and turned to watch. Lillian, still subdued from her semi-misery, watched as well.

Benny quickly yanked the pole to set the hook before they resumed the position. This time, however, they brought the fish all the way in. Granddad showed up with the net, and they lifted the pole as the fish fell into it, nose first. Granddad scooped it up. After a collective roar and loud exclamations from all three of them, Lillian had to smile.

"Yah!" Benny clapped.

"Whoo!" Granddad cheered.

"Damn right!" Matt didn't yell but he had a huge, satisfied grin. "Look at this monster." He took the long net pole from Granddad and set the floundering fish in the hold at the back of the boat.

Glancing behind her, Lillian covered her face.

Yeah, she might find it hard to forgive the next part.

They marveled some more around their prize from the sea. Matt couldn't deny the sense of pride and rush that filled all of them. Three generations, excluding his own dad, but Granddad fit that role, so who cared if Matt's father was absent? They had three generations right there, spanning four generations.

Then he reached down and grabbed the slippery fish's mouth, digging the hook out with pliers and doing some-thing he feared might have Lillian heaving over the side, when he took the fish bonker and slammed it to the fish's head to kill it.

Lillian flinched and he tossed her a regretful look. "It's the quickest and most humane way." Which even he realized sounded kind of hypocritical.

But Benny was still excited as he grabbed the now dead fish to hold it.

Matt went full tourist. He grabbed his cell phone and posed his son several times with the biggest catch of his young life. They took a few snaps together and with Grand-dad, until he felt a tap on his shoulder. "Okay, I'll take one of all three of you."

Lillian grimaced and rolled her eyes as she waved her hand at Matt to get into the scene. Grinning at her, his heart swelling with pride, Matt was so impressed. She was awesome, despite the vegetarian diet, her queasy stomach and her total inability to get her sea-legs.

Matt took the fish and knelt down beside Benny, who stood beside him and Granddad posed behind him. The fish was featured as the star attraction in front of all three of them. They smiled for several more pictures.

Happy talk and recapping their accomplishment continued between Granddad and Benny as Matt stowed the fish and cleaned up the back end of the boat. Wiping his hands on a rag, he finally rigged up and dropped the lines back in. Joining his little crew, he gave Benny a huge high-five.

"You did good, little dude." Benny beamed. He also nodded at Lillian, "So did you."

She gave him a stink eye, sticking her tongue out, and squinting a dirty look. Matt thought maybe he'd gone too far, until she burst into a smile. "I hate killing any animal, but it was neat to see the three of you so in tune and united in your purpose."

If they had been alone, Matt would have grabbed her and kissed her, never mind his fishy, bait-smelling hands. She probably wouldn't have allowed him to do that anyway, but he would have. He'd have kissed her repeatedly, being so damn happy to have her vegetarian, slightly seasick, little ass out on his boat. To have her anywhere near him. Even when she wasn't supposed to, she seemed to totally get and understand him. It didn't make sense. None of it.

Relaxing in the warm sunshine with his favorite people, Matt sighed and closed his eyes. A calm peace that only came from being on the water overtook him. Granddad was at the helm and Matt could close his eyes without worry. Drifting off felt so pleasant, he grew languid in the sunshine and the bobbing, combined with the lull of the motor and lapping water on the side of the hull soothed him. Until…

"Dad! Fish! Fish! Get it!"

CHAPTER 19

*M*ATT'S EYES FLASHED OPEN, and his brain did three things at once.

First, it registered that Benny yelled "Dad!" at him. Was that on purpose? Or by accident?

Second, Matt's body was already moving before he fully opened his eyes, and he stubbed his toe on the corner of one of the boxes they used for storage, which he should have known was there. He stumbled and righted himself before diving for the pole.

Third, he yanked on the fishing rod, and realized he needed to teach Benny what "set the hook" meant, but Benny was a pro now and they reeled this one in successfully.

Now that he was wide awake and fully engaged, Matt couldn't stop glancing down at the brown curls, which made his breath catch every time he relived the word that came out of his son's mouth at long last. *Dad.*

Matt really was a dad. For real and forever. That moment was the epiphany and catalyst that congealed to form the basis of his future. Matt was called *Dad* for the first time in his life. Did Benny slip up? Or did those puzzle pieces Lillian talked about finally start to fit together in Benny's head? The reason was irrelevant; it stood alone as the greatest moment of Matt's life now. And he wished he could capture it forever and bottle it like a rare perfume. But even though he couldn't do that, he knew he'd never forget it.

They landed a total of three fish before they stowed the gear and tightened down everything as they began to head to the harbor with the late afternoon sun behind them. It had just started to set, and the soft, glorious pastel pinks, oranges, yellows and golds stretched across the horizon. The boat began rocking as they started back and got even rougher closer to the harbor. Lillian curled up on the bench, closing her eyes tightly. Matt hoped her seasick pill would last until they got back to the marina.

But as for Benny, his son? Benny was holding onto a grip near the helm, right next to Matt and he freaking prattled and chirped like a parrot, reliving the entire day with Matt. He wasn't fazed by even a single wave over the bar on their way in. He talked so incessantly, Matt had to remind himself to concentrate. Benny had zero fear and was having a great time. Bending his knees and straightening his legs in rhythm to the movements of the waves, he was clearly loving it. So much that he narrated a soundtrack to it.

He asked more random questions about the kinds of fish Matt caught on his chartered excursions. How big were they? Which was the biggest fish? The questions Benny asked Matt in River's End all got a "no" answer from Matt. But now, he had knowledge of the subjects Benny discussed and plenty of answers. It felt nice to appear not so lame in his son's eyes.

Finally, the water calmed, and they aimed for the marina channel as Lillian's head popped up. She was cradling it in her arms. "We're back in the harbor, safe and sound," Matt announced with a soft smile of consideration towards her.

She nodded, still a bit pale. Finally, he aimed for his dock slip. He slowed the engines, shifting to neutral before Granddad took over. Then Matt grabbed the mooring ropes and soon had the boat all tied securely and the engines shut down.

Lillian hurried toward the dock and seemed to race up to the marina pavement. Matt almost expected her to kiss the ground. But she held her composure and stood and watched them. There was still lots of work to do and no bait boy to help him. Matt usually did it by himself.

"Come on, Benny, you're never too young to learn how to do this." Maybe Benny could be his future bait boy.

Matt pictured the day, maybe a whole summer, spent with Benny if he wanted to come there and be with him. They could do this together daily. Benny could go out on the guided trips. He could learn how to handle the boat, the gear and maybe even, the clients.

His head was spinning with excitement at seeing Benny's desire to help him and his natural ease at doing it.

Granddad was busy scrubbing and stowing the gear. Benny was beside him, having a great time getting elbow deep in fish guts and blood. Luckily, Lillian was far away.

But Matt's joy could not be diminished, and he could not stop imagining someday that this might happen. His boy just called him *Dad!* Matt resisted the urge to start doing spins and leaps.

"Well, Benny, you got yourself a great pair of sea-legs. Maybe the best and the fastest pair I've ever seen."

Benny started dancing around after flinging the fish carcass overboard. "I do?!" His huge, happy eyes gave Matt a glimpse of how much he liked hearing that. Then he asked, "Do you think I got my sea-legs from you?"

Matt's heart swelled even bigger. He let go of the fish and stared down at his son. His joy and hope were his best allies now. Yes, they had to figure a way to start being father and son. He nodded and smiled slowly. "I sure do think that. I mean, no one gets on a boat and faces big waves like we did without being daunted or scared unless they've got some sea water in their blood. And you, my boy, have many generations of sea water in your blood."

Everything appeared to crystalize in Benny's mind. His face beamed and he looked at Granddad, who wasn't listening to the conversation. He was at the bow, coiling up the extra line. Granddad felt Benny's gaze and glanced at them and smiled. Benny turned fully back to Matt. "I got your blood then?"

"Yep. You got some of me and my family and some of your mama and her family. I know it's kinda confusing. But I see now that you inherited some pretty strong sea water in your genes."

Benny jumped up and down again. He had so much energy. "I think I did too. Did you see how green Mom's face was? She couldn't even take the little bumps."

Matt laughed. "Don't rub that in though. She did really good, what with the fish guts and all. I mean, considering there's no sea water in her blood, right? We should try to be kind to her and not make fun of her about it." He put out his fist again.

Benny nodded and matched his fist-bump. "Right. It'll be our thing."

"Totally," Matt agreed with a freaking lump in his throat, and the moisture in his eyes made him blink. Damn. Oh, damn. What a day.

Once the boat was properly secured, Matt helped Granddad and Benny get off before he finally followed them up the ramp. Benny was first, of course, his restless, little legs sprinting ahead while Granddad walked at a much slower pace. Matt was last and he stopped next to Lillian.

She gazed up at him and his first desire, which he wanted

287

more than anything, was to simply slip his arm around her and lean in to kiss her. Even a hug from her would have sufficed, and he imagined kissing the top of her head as the setting sun faded from pink and gold into that twilight hue above the marina. The boats became black shapes that bobbed with perfect tranquility in the exquisite setting. Her eyes shone when she looked at him. He saw something big and gleeful there, and he knew he pleased her. No mistake about that.

"He called you *Dad*," Lillian said with a tender, loving smile.

Matt released a huge sigh of relief and replied, "I couldn't believe it either. That was so amazing. The best thing that could have possibly happened and what I didn't dare hope for."

Lillian sensed what he really wanted and stepped closer to him. Her head reached his chest, and she leaned her forehead against him while setting her small hands on his waist. He put his hands around her shoulders and rubbed them gently. She lifted her face up and collapsed into his embrace. Tucking herself into him, her hands and arms wound around his back and he pulled her tighter and closer, setting his chin on the top of her head. Damn. She felt good. This was the next best thing to being called *Dad*. The light lingered, faded and became a soft glow on the horizon. It seemed to gild the glittering marina and all the boats in it, including this woman, the most incredible woman he ever met, who now chose to snuggle in his arms.

Benny scampered about in the distance. He was unaware that they hugged, being so busy jabbering about the fish to Granddad.

Lillian lifted her face. "He really liked that."

"Yeah, we had a man-to-man discussion about his excellent sea-legs, and what a pity it was that you don't have them."

She let out a full laugh, raising her eyebrow and repeating, "Man-to-man?"

He pretended to puff out his chest. "Sorry, that's what guys do sometimes. And it's too bad you really don't have sea-legs."

She rolled her eyes. "I don't. I'm terrible. Just one pill from hurling my guts out. At least I wasn't totally curled up in a tight ball."

"Did you hate it?"

"No, I loved it."

He tilted his head and his eyebrows quirked in disbelief. "You were more green than white, and you couldn't stand up. You hated seeing all the guts and blood and killing and that's all there was to do."

She kept her face up and her gaze glued on his. "Oh, right. It was pretty gross. The constant bobbing and rocking? Well, I could swear I still am feeling that. I can't get over how you guys manage to keep your balance when the entire deck is shifting and rising and dropping—" She stuck a hand over her mouth. "Oh. No. Not too eager to relive that part."

"See? You did hate it."

Lillian stuck her hand over his mouth. "No. I loved seeing you at work. And Granddad too. Seeing you as the captain and the man in charge… Whew. Made me hot and bothered."

He chuckled and a blush crept into his cheeks. She noticed it and touched his neck. "I made you blush."

"Well, most women don't consider gutting a fish any kind of aphrodisiac."

"Just little, old, vegetarian me." She shrugged with a sexy laugh. Oh, how Matt loved her laugh. It went straight to his… well, to his heart and somewhere else. "I liked seeing you in your element. Seeing the man you are, doing what you love the most. It showed me so much about you. Even if I can't share the experience for health reasons, I'm so glad I got to see you doing it. Most of all, I loved how our son instantly fell in love with something his father loves so much."

He gripped her biceps and shut his eyes before he blinked them open again. "You felt that too? I thought the same thing. But I don't want to be an asshole that expects his son to mirror his own life or become a mini-me or anything. He seemed so genuine. Yeah, I'd love to spend more time doing all the stuff he loves and if they happen to be the same as what I like, well done. But what I found so amazing was that I never expected to have Granddad and Benny together on the boat with me. Doing what I love, what we love, and sharing it. That was the greatest part of my life with Granddad, who raised me, you know. I think maybe Benny and I might have finally begun to find our path…"

"You did. You guys found your common ground. You became the father to him that you've been trying so hard to be. You did it just like that. You took the lead and tried to make it right when Benny pushed himself too hard the first time and failed to get a fish. You cajoled him out of his snit and taught him the lesson. Lessons like that will stick in his mind forever."

"It was just…."

"Yeah. I know. I feel that way too." She smiled at him. He couldn't stop himself from leaning down and planting his lips on hers for a quick, soft kiss. He planned to make it casual and fast, but both of them were staring wide-eyed at each other and it felt more intimate than anything they ever shared before. Maybe it was because their son was playing only steps away. The warm and fuzzy qualities of being all together as a family unit were so bizarre to Matt and strange and new, he wondered how best to handle it. Growing up,

Grandma never went out on the boat. It was only him and Granddad who were always together, just the two of them. There weren't any vacations or time they spent away, that was when they were at home with Grandma. Obviously, Lillian wasn't his grandma.

"Lillian?" Matt's whisper was husky and deep and he trembled with emotions. "What are we going to do?"

She took in a deep breath and replied, "I'm not exactly sure."

"You felt all of it too, right? It's not just me? I was already buzzed from a great day on the water and finding a way to connect with Benny, but you? We shouldn't hook up again, not after that. Not with how different we both are. But…"

She sighed heavily. "Yeah, I feel that too. And no, I have no idea what to do with it or about it."

"There were so many times I wanted to grab you and kiss you—"

She smiled up at him, licking her lips. "You have no idea how much I wondered what you did with other women on your boat. Your big, empty boat."

"You are awesome and impossibly sexy. You're driving me nuts right now. But since we have a seventy-eight-year-old man and a six-year-old son with us right over there, I think I'll have to let that pass."

She laughed, sounding so young and free in contrast to her job as a doctor and her motherhood. He loved all her sides and wondered if he was one of the few who experienced her like this. Sexy. Hot. Fun. Naughty. Then her face became more neutral as she peeked over her shoulder at Granddad and Benny.

"I assume our stress is rooted in our mutual realization that we feel something stronger than being co-parents. We're already more than friends. But if it doesn't work, we can't just go our separate ways."

"The responsible thing is not to take the risk at all."

"Of course. That's all I ever tell myself." They shared a look and the steam of passion seemed to radiate from both of them. She sighed heavily. "Yes, well, it isn't working. Not at all for me. For neither of us."

"No. I agree. If you refused to go fishing maybe it would have been a little easier."

"Or if you criticized me for being a vegetarian, it would have cooled me right down."

"So, by not being assholes to each other, now we are here?"

"Seems like it." She smirked, lifting her hand and touching the side of his face. He leaned into the heat of her palm. "I'm not sure we can deny this. What if we just see where it goes? Take it slowly but don't end it. I mean, it's not like we live around the corner from each other anyway. So, we're already limited by the distance."

His heart lurched. Everything was limited by the distance. Access to his son, forming a deeper relationship, and getting to know him and Lillian better.

But he had to consider the boat. His job. The ocean. This place and lifestyle symbolized the man he was, it was not just a job to Matt. He lifted his hand to cradle hers before placing the back of her hand to his lips and kissing it. "If only I had some crappy, ordinary job I didn't care about in the least. That would be something I could easily leave."

She let out a startled laugh. "I wish I had a job I hated too."

"We are so different. But very much the same. Family business and family ties that we care so much about and don't want to lose. We both have jobs we love. Careers that we consider our calling. Jobs that must keep us apart. Though mine is on a much smaller scale…"

"That doesn't reduce its significance or the presence it

holds in your life. Maybe it makes it even bigger for the intimacy it brings. Granddad and his boat are your connection to your family and your past and the history that you share. I saw it out there, I saw how much you cherish it."

"Yeah. But it isn't you. You and Benny are the deal-breaker there."

"No. And I can't take care of any horses here. We are both limited by our circumstances. Can we agree this isn't going away? What we feel between the two of us is not imagined. So, we... what? Sneak around and try to see each other secretly? Behind our families' and our son's backs?"

"Well, yeah. Maybe so. A lot less stress and fewer opinions to consider then. And what son wants to know about their parents' sex life? So that's just a kinder thing to do right there."

She smirked. "True. But who mentioned sex?"

He released her. "I think we both know what we find hardest to resist."

"Yeah, it's pretty powerful." They fell into step with each other, heading towards the lot where his truck was parked. They all piled in, tossing the gear in the back with the fish in the ice chest.

When they returned to his house, Matt prepared the fish, and they ate fresh salmon with noodles. Only noodles for Lillian. Benny seemed to acquire a taste for fish as much as he did catching it. They lounged afterwards, recapping the wonderful day and finally settling in to watch a movie. It was a kid's cartoon that Matt never would have bothered to watch, but he found it less annoying than he expected. Animation had come a long way in all the years since he last watched a cartoon. Even the storyline was compelling and funny. It cracked Matt up more than once. When he found himself leaning forward at the end, he heard a snicker from his left side as Lillian whispered something in his ear. Her breath tickled his ear as she said, "Don't worry; the prince gets the princess in the end."

He gave her a sharp look and scowl. "Well, duh!" he spat out under his breath. "But we don't know *how*. So don't ruin it."

She had to laugh and leaned her head on his arm. He liked that more than the movie.

When Granddad retired for the night and it was time for Benny's bedtime, Matt stayed up to watch the local news. Lillian came back and sat beside him without speaking, so he was content, but unsure how to proceed from there.

Lillian rose to her feet, clicked the TV off, and put a finger to her lips. She was telling him to be quiet and simultaneously putting a hand out to him before he all but catapulted off the couch—quietly, of course—and set his hand in hers. They walked past the guest room and *closed* the door, going to his bedroom.

Once inside, the door was locked, and Lillian's mouth devoured his as she pulled off his shirt. He allowed her to start stripping him and tried to join in the efforts. It was very dark. They used their hands over each other's mouth to muffle the passionate moans and approving sighs of unparalleled ecstasy. When they were on his bed, he was fully inside her as he closed his eyes and ground his teeth to remain quiet. Matt fought the urge to howl at the freaking moon when the full swell of emotions swept through him.

Damn.

That's how they decided to continue.

For one weekend every month, Matt drove to visit them and the next month, Lillian and Benny drove out to him. They all spent the weekend together, sometimes adding an extra day depending on school and if Matt could arrange it. Benny and he spent more time together. They watched movies, played games, and sometimes just wandered around the Rydell River Ranch. Autumn finally came, and Matt got to see how incredible the Rydell Ranch truly was. The temperatures finally cooled, and the trees glimmered in the vivid colors of burnt yellows, oranges and reds. Stepping outside in the brisk air and breathing it in without the suffocating heat made it much more appealing to Matt.

Then it grew icy cold. Snowfall came. Matt experienced a whole new level of cold. It was just as extreme as the unbearable heat of the summer. They spent a lot of time indoors. Matt wasn't as bothered by the snow and cold as much as he was the heat. The family cult members started to grow on him too. When he had to go back home, Matt found comfort in the huge family that adored his son and *girlfriend*(!). He was glad they had so much love surrounding them.

It took a long while for Matt to refer to Lillian as a girl-friend. The title of "doctor" before her name was intimidating to him. But no one really knew because they downplayed their involvement. Of course, he stayed at her house and she stayed at his because she accompanied her child in the trips designed to get to know his father. Granddad was well aware of the situation, but he didn't comment or pry, which was much appreciated by both of them. Granddad even helped them by taking Benny on special outings to give Matt and Lillian a few hours alone. Sometimes they went straight to bed. Other times found them in deep conversation. It was always intense and fun. Their conversations fed Matt's soul and their time in bed fed his hungry body.

God, he liked this woman.

And her son.

His son.

Still working through that. Benny called him Dad, but it was usually infrequent. It hadn't become totally natural yet. As he grew accustomed to Matt's comings and goings, as well as the regular visits to the ocean, there was no doubt Benny did love their visits. No one could argue with that.

There were other firsts and breakthroughs. The first time Benny hugged Matt goodbye, the first time he spontaneously climbed into his lap, the first time he kissed Matt goodnight. He started asking Matt to tuck him into bed. He told Matt he missed him on the phone. Those times, Benny called Matt *Dad*.

The winter followed and their visits became more regular. Matt's heart was much more involved, and he looked forward to the visits and strengthening the bond they were building.

Love for his son and his son's mother. It never concerned Matt until now. How to make it work while living hundreds of miles apart? Neither of them had the answer to that yet.

CHAPTER 20

SPRING BROUGHT WITH IT the opening of the fishing season, which translated to less time for Matt to take off on weekends. He reverted to visiting Lillian and Benny on the weekdays, but of course, Benny was in school and Lillian was working. When they visited him, he was out all day on the ocean and usually worn out by the time he got home, so it wasn't as fresh or as much fun as it was during the winter.

"Mattie, I was thinking, could I go with you on one of your visits? I'd sure like to see that big ranch and resort home that Benny always tells me about," Granddad said to Matt one April day. Startled, Matt nodded automatically.

He was running halibut fishing trips at the time, and he replied with an easy smile, "Sure. Of course. Maybe we can stay a few extra days."

Weeks later, everything was arranged, and Matt and Granddad drove off to the Rydell River Ranch.

Granddad was far more impressed than Matt was the first time he saw it. In April, of course, it was a good twenty degrees or more cooler than in summer, and thus, much more tolerable to spend time outside. Spring exploded with wild daisies on the hillside, mixed with the pea-green sprouts of new grass and budding foliage. It had an entirely different vibe than the mid-summer broil.

Benny ran towards both of them with a huge grin, eager to give hugs and already jabbering about his latest adventure. He was a lot more natural when he greeted Matt now. They hugged tightly and fist-bumped. "How was your week?"

"Fine. I painted a bunch of rocks and made one a ladybug for you. Maybe you can take it on the boat." Benny chatted away as he grinned up at Matt. Then he turned to Granddad and exclaimed, "Wait 'til you meet Scissero. That's a horse. I told Great-Grandpa Jack that my other great-grandpa Jefferson was coming to visit, and you never, ever rode a horse before. He said he had just the horse for you to ride, if you could get on it."

Granddad bristled. "Of course, I can get on it. Show it to me and I'll show him."

Matt set a hand on his Granddad's arm. "Perhaps tomorrow. You don't need to break your neck the first day we arrive and force me to take you back home."

Granddad scowled and jerked his arm away. "If Great-Grandpa Jack can still ride, then so can I. Come on, Benny. Show me the way to the horse."

Lillian walked up and Matt stopped dead as they both got huge, dopey grins on their faces when they eyed each other. Meanwhile, Benny and Granddad busied themselves by taking stuff out of the car and into the house.

"I missed you," Matt said softly. Like always. That's how they started almost every conversation.

She set her hand on his. "I think I miss you a little more each time."

They didn't kiss and turned when Benny called them. "Come on. The Greats are going to meet."

"Is there some unspoken contest going on between them?"

He nodded. "I believe our angelic son might have started the competition with all the stories of derring-do he tells the other one."

"Did you know he was doing that?"

"Maybe he likes the attention he gets from watching them try to outdo each other without even getting introduced yet."

Lillian burst out laughing. "Oh, my God. Grandpa Jack would totally fall for that."

"Yeah, so would Granddad. So… wanna go watch the show if only to make sure Granddad doesn't get hurt or actually break something?"

"I think we best hurry if we want to catch the first act."

They released hands but walked close enough to feel each other's body heat. Quickly covering the distance in long strides, they overtook Benny and Granddad just as they were entering the Rescue Barn.

"Grandpa! He's here!" Benny screamed.

Grandpa Jack stepped out from one of the stalls. He had a slow stride, and his hat was drawn low over his forehead. His shirt was tucked into a faded pair of jeans and he was wearing his signature, well-worn, dirty, creased cowboy boots. Lillian sighed and all but rolled her eyes. "I think he's channeling Clint Eastwood right before a duel. Could be?"

"Could be." Matt leaned down to nuzzle her neck, and his smirk was impossible to contain.

"If he says, "Howdy, Pardner," I'm so outta here," she muttered.

Luckily, Grandpa Jack just said hello. Granddad gave him a once-over. "So, you're the Jack Rydell I heard all about."

His hand outstretched, Jack stepped forward. "And you're the Jefferson Griffin I heard a lot about."

"Dear God, it's a geriatric face-off."

Matt snickered as he replied, "Except there is nothing geriatric about those two. I'd hesitate to take either one of them on."

Lillian stared and squinted. "You're right, they're both tough, leathery, old bastards, aren't they? Must be their demanding lifestyles, different but also eerily similar, you know? Man against the elements and all that. And they came from the generation that really took that concept pretty seriously."

Matt had to turn away, so no one saw his effort to conceal his laughter at her hasty synopsis.

A stepstool was dragged next to a saddled horse, and Granddad climbed up on it and raised his leg over the horse's back, adjusting his weight as he landed squarely on the horse. He made a face. Matt started to run forward, preparing to grab him if he fell. He feared Granddad's rusty movements might get the best of him, but Granddad leaned forward in the saddle, narrowing his gaze on Jack as he said, "Okay, now show me what to do next."

"You sure? It's plenty hard on the joints and muscles to tenderfoots."

Granddad gave him an evil glare. "I can still walk, and I am not a 'tenderfoot' as you dared to call me. Now show me what the heck to do."

Matt was overcome with surprise. Granddad's tone was so strong and vigorous and commanding. He hadn't heard him sound so authoritative since the last time he captained the boat. Maybe Granddad needed a new hobby.

Or the company of others that were more like him.

It was a startling thought, one that Matt never considered until now.

Halfway through Granddad's lesson, Erin entered the barn. Granddad watched the interaction between Jack and Erin, while Matt observed an amused twinkle in his granddad's gaze. What was Granddad planning? It soon became obvious when he flirted with Erin. She was politely friendly, which only encouraged Granddad, who gave Jack a smug, little smile. Good lord. Was Granddad trying to make Jack jealous just for the fun of it?

But oddly enough, it seemed to break the ice and a quick rapport was instantly established. This went on for several days. Soon, Granddad made learning how to ride his daily routine. He hadn't been out of the arena yet, but he managed to stay on the horse's back and still walk after he dismounted. So that was a win to him. He left each afternoon to go out to the barns and came back full of comments about Jack and Erin whom he often found out there.

Later, Matt said to Lillian, "Is it just me or does Granddad seem a lot more energetic than when we first got here?"

"I thought so too. He seems more animated. More so than usual. He is with me as well. And it was good to see him sparring with my grandpa."

"At home, he detests most of the senior-oriented activities. The idea of assisted living or even visiting someone there also leaves him cold. Do you think he misses the company?"

"Maybe. It's not organized and artificial here. Grandpa and Grandma just live their active lives and that makes them happy. Maybe your Granddad would like that too."

"By horseback-riding?"

She gave him a shoulder bump. "People change. Everyone likes to try new things sometimes. A new interest could fit their lives now, even if it didn't in the past." She added a pointed look.

"That might be true. I just didn't expect it to be here."

"He seems oddly content here."

"He seems much more than content," Matt agreed. Granddad and Benny spent most of their time out in the barns or wandering around the ranch. They liked to go down to the river with their trout poles and hang out with whichever Rydells showed up. There was no denying how much they all welcomed Granddad, who was so invigorated by their company and the contrasting change in scenery, he seemed to thrive. Matt never could have guessed that would be his reaction.

Their visit was idyllic and even Matt had to admit it. Granddad was having so much fun. He spent time with everyone there and visibly enjoyed meeting the diverse types of people from all ages. Matt got claustrophobic sometimes, while Granddad was thrilled to join in all activities. He compared it to living in a campground or an RV park where there was always something to do if one chose to. There were people around when you wanted them and no people around when you didn't. Lots of people went to the beach or golfing or horseback-riding. Granddad never tried any of them before, but now he was eager to try all the ranch had to offer. Golfing? Yeah. He was terrible but still enjoyed it. He mostly liked driving the golf cart, which tickled Matt.

Long walks, gazing at the horses or feeding them, became Granddad's favorite pastimes. Matt knew that Jack's barns housed the horses that were hurt, sick and abused. To his surprise, Granddad seemed to enjoy spending most of his time in there.

Granddad also liked talking to Jack Rydell more than anyone else, even more than Matt sometimes. Their constant repartee indicated how much time they spent together. And Jack didn't hesitate asking Granddad to do the chores alongside him. It never occurred to Matt, but damn! Old Granddad still had a lot of spunk in his steps. The ranch experience injected him with a new lease on life and heightened energy. Granddad was busy there. But Matt predicted that would wear off with time. The novelty of any location always faded with enough time.

And it wasn't near the ocean. Granddad had never lived away from the coastline. No way could he be okay without access to his life-long love and passion, especially now, when he was in his seventies.

Matt was convinced of that.

He was grateful for how well their visit went, but Granddad seemed overly reluctant to leave. Unfortunately, there was no choice in the matter.

Benny's eyes were filled with tears when he came out to the truck with them. He gave Granddad a hug and a kiss as more tears slipped from his eyes. But after he came over to Matt and gave him a hug, Benny's tears wouldn't stop.

"Bye, Daddy."

Oh, lord. Matt clutched Benny next to him and knelt down, squeezing Benny to his chest. He kissed his silky, brown curls and his voice broke when he said, "Bye, Benny. It won't be too long."

Benny nodded and let him go. "I know. I'll just miss you guys so much. It was fun having everyone here. Like a great, big holiday."

Matt glanced up at Lillian who stepped behind Benny. Benny just stepped backwards and leaned against her legs without looking. The child simply assumed his mother would always be there for him. *Always.* Matt felt the heart-wrenching ache of something deep and real that Lillian, alone, possessed. She blew him away when she was so awesome. He was leaving his son again. It was getting harder and harder to do that.

To his delight, his son finally missed him.

Benny cried as he and Granddad started leaving.

Benny called him *Daddy* now.

"It was just like a great big holiday," Matt agreed with Benny. "I love you, Benny. I'll call you tomorrow, okay?"

Benny nodded glumly. "I love you too, Daddy."

Wasn't it good his son missed him and didn't want him to leave? It was light years from where they were last summer. They had both grown and learned to accept each other. Trial and failure. The awkward moments paled against the true triumphs. They were still trying to make this hard situation work; it was a labor of love.

Logically, the closer they all grew, the more real their bond became, and as a reasonable consequence, the harder their separations became. It begged for a change. A real solution.

If only Lillian could move her veterinarian practice to Westport. She could earn a living there. It was much easier than working as a charter boat captain in River's End.

But he knew Lillian cared most about her family. Her parents, sister, grandparents, aunts, uncles and cousins. They were everywhere. And very necessary to Lillian *and* Benny. She interacted with so many of them daily. She needed and longed for the safety and lifestyle of the land she was born and raised on. Just as Matt needed and longed for the sea on which he was pretty much born and raised.

But Benny wasn't a coastal resident. Benny belonged here with Grandpa Ben, Grandpa Jack, Grandma Jocelyn, Grandma Erin and Aunt Jade just to name a few of the list of relatives who loved Benny.

Matt also loved him now too.

As they pulled onto the highway, neither he nor Granddad spoke. After two hours, Granddad muttered, "That place *could* grow on me."

Really? Matt didn't know. He had a charter business to run. He couldn't just motor down and park his boat on the

Columbia River now, could he? He might manage to host a few salmon trips over the summer months or scrape out a living by offering trout expeditions on the handful of lakes nearby. But in reality? How could he make a living at it? No way. The fishing inland was as inferior to fishing on the ocean as much as a local Little League was in comparison to the World Series.

"I can't make a living there," Matt replied, and his tone was grumpy and defensive.

"I never said you could," Granddad responded gently.

He glared hard at his Granddad. "Well, then what *are you* saying?"

"I don't know. I just liked it. I like that little boy and a charter boat isn't a lifetime commitment, Mattie."

"A charter boat? Not when it's mine—and yours—and might I remind you, our entire history and the source of our living. It's who we are. What do you want me to do? Sell it and do what? What, Granddad? I don't know how to do anything else."

Granddad crossed his arms over his chest. "Well, no. But you could learn a new trade."

Matt refused to indulge that hypothesis. He was puzzled by Granddad's overreaction to their trip. He thought Granddad would like seeing Benny, but hate the place, like Matt did. But no, his seventy-eight-year-old grandfather was more flexible, adaptable and compliant than he was?

Damn it.

Matt's entire life lay in Westport.

The silence hung heavy. Even Matt knew there wasn't much life in Westport anymore. Not without Benny and Lillian. Not if Granddad—

After two hours of silence, Matt said sharply out of nowhere, "What? You'd just move to a landlocked spot in the middle of the state? At your age? You'd move away from the ocean? You really expect me to just start over and abandon our life's work like an old car? Sell out? Really?"

"I would in a heartbeat. Quit being so fatalistic about it, Matt. You could simply hire another captain or two to run the boat and take the profits wherever you can. Come back in the summer with the boy, when he's out of school, and run the charters then. That way, you'll be getting the best of both worlds."

Matt was stunned and his eyeballs darted to the corners of his eyes as his mouth gaped like a fish. "The road!" Granddad exclaimed when the truck's wheels rolled over the rumble strip, but Matt immediately corrected it. However, Matt's brain still buzzed with possibilities.

"They wouldn't spend their summers there."

"Lillian and Benny? They sure as heck would. No doubt of that in my mind. Best time to be on the coast. Mild season. Lovely, sunny days. And you'd escape that heat you hate the most at the ranch. I think you could tolerate the rest."

"Got an answer for everything, huh," Matt grumbled as he glared at the street. "And what trade shall I do there for nine months out of a year?"

Granddad shrugged. "I don't know. Work at the school district maybe. If you consult with Lillian, she probably makes enough to support a decent lifestyle for all three of you."

"Granddad! I'm not moving across the state to mooch off a woman who had to raise my son alone until the last nine months. I'm not moving there, period. Or..."

"Then you'd better get used to tear-filled goodbyes and never feeling satisfied. If you think that boat compensates for what we both experienced this week, then you're one dumb son-of-a-bitch."

The words he used were harsh and Granddad chose them deliberately. Their driveway lay ahead. Pulling to a stop,

Matt gaped at his granddad. "I can't believe you just called me that."

"No, I said *if you don't* realize it, since I don't know what you're thinking."

"So, you're calling me that if I don't do what you want?"

"Yeah. Kind of. That probably best describes it."

"Granddad, what do you prefer to do? Just move there? It's impossible. Impractical. I don't even know why you so easily decided it's what we should do."

Granddad was quiet for a long, profound moment. Matt wasn't sure if he even heard him. They were parked in the driveway, unmoving and staring at their closed garage door. "Matt, you have one son. I think I would have moved wherever I had to for you. Your worthless father left you with us but if your grandma and I had to move to take care of you, even if it meant moving inland, I'm sure we would have done it. And never looked back. Or regretted it. Benny's six years old how many times? Huh, Mattie? And you completely missed his first five years. No blame on you, I get that. But it doesn't change it for Benny."

The truth of his words hurt like icicles being thrown against his bare skin. What made it more painful was that it came from Granddad. The man who raised him and gave him a moral compass and a business that always supported him. Was he saying that Matt wasn't doing that for his son?

"I want to be with Benny. But I also love our life here. And I can't just—"

"You can do whatever you want to do. It's your choice. And a job isn't a son. Or a possible life partner."

"I can't move there for Lillian. We're barely dating. I don't even know if it would work if we lived in the same area."

"Of course, you don't move for a relationship, but you should move for your son."

Matt couldn't argue. He didn't want to look worse than he already did.

Sucking in air, he nodded. "I know. I just, I'm still working this all out."

"While you work it out, time is ticking by. He called you *Daddy*. He misses you. He needs you. Not Grandpa Ben or Grandpa Jack or me. He needs *you*, Mattie. You're his father."

The words rippled through Matt, starting from his head and jolting through his entire body. His heart was burdened by the effects. "You're right. He does need me." Matt hated to give up a way of life that he loved and valued, but he knew his grandfather was spot-on correct. A job wasn't a son.

Gripping the steering wheel, even though the car was parked, Matt leaned forward and rested his head on it. "I failed to understand the full magnitude of what having a son means. I didn't know what to do with him. I had to fully comprehend he was my son. I had a hard time figuring out what that meant. But I'm starting to now, and it's far more than a few words. Anyone can claim to be a father or have a son. They can swear that child means everything to them. That could all be lip service instead of real love and commitment. But I'm finally understanding what it means to a child; a father isn't just a word *but* a series of actions. Always being right there for them. Every day. No matter what. I can't do that from here."

"No. You can't. That might be enough for some. A phone-in father. A summer-time dad, but that isn't the Mathias Griffin I know. You attack your life in all its aspects and that matters because of your singular love and commitment. You love your job and lifestyle because that's what you know. It doesn't mean you can't find something else you love. A different way to work. Another career is like discovering another way of life. You can't find another child. Or experience a lost childhood over again. If you prolong this another five years, he'll be eleven. You've missed the best parts. All for what? You can come back here every summer. I really believe that. I think any compromise has to be in favor of spending more time with Benny."

"I know. It gets harder each time I leave, or when they leave here."

His granddad smiled as he patted Matt's leg. "I saw that as well, and it's not just a 'him' anymore, it's not just little Benny leaving, it's 'them.' Yeah, I really see that now. Maybe it's time that you recognized it. This has a lot to do with Lillian Rydell, doesn't it?"

"I don't deny any of it. I just worry what if I can't find something to do for work?"

"Then you'll have to keep looking until you do."

Matt's heart sunk before it swelled with hope. He wanted to work in the same location where his son and Lillian lived. It was hard but he wanted it more than anything.

"What... how do I do it?" Matt asked Granddad.

"Text them. Call. Go there. Just find a way to let them know."

"What about you?"

"Me? I'll still be here. Living and doing what I normally do. When you decide, I'll go with you. I got along okay with that Jack Rydell and I really liked his wife." Granddad raised his eyebrows in a little jiggle for emphasis.

Matt groaned. "Granddad..."

"I'm just kidding. But I did enjoy my time there... a lot. There's not a heck of a lot to do here, we're so far away from everything. I might enjoy the ranch life with so many things to do right there. Even people-watching and seeing the different guests drawn to their resort is a kick for me. I think I could get used to that."

Matt was not only stunned, but also sad that Granddad wasn't happy here. He never considered that he might be bored or lonely. Knowing how insistent Granddad was in his very vocal aversion to organized activities offered by the senior association, Matt assumed he was just too independent. Hearing how much he liked the ranch truly made Matt's jaw drop to the floor.

"I could really have some fun at that place with your son around to hang out with. Nothing keeps a man young better than being around young people. I wondered if you'd ever have kids and now that you do, heck, Mattie. Of course, I want to spend all the time I can with him."

"You'd really move there?"

"In a heartbeat. I really would. If you want me to go with you."

He blinked. "I always want you with me, Granddad."

"We can always come back here, Mattie, if we miss it. That's why this is so timeless. The ocean tides will come in and out whether you're there to keep an eye on them or not."

"Okay. I guess… Look out, landlubber, here I come." Matt quipped with a smile that was both nervous and relieved. He doubted he could have ever made a decision without Granddad's push and advice. He started to get out of the truck, but he grabbed Granddad's shoulder, who glanced at him with a curious expression. "Thank you, Granddad. I'm not sure what I might have done without you."

Granddad took his hand in his fist and they smiled in a compassionate moment. Their lifelong connection was something that Matt realized he now wanted to extend to his son. He wanted Benny to feel the same way about him when Matt was in his seventies. Nodding, Granddad squeezed the hand that rested on his shoulder before they released each other and got out of the truck. Now, new plans had to be made… people had to be told… and an entirely new life lay ahead of Matt and Granddad. One they were eager to build and explore.

That is, if Lillian wanted that too.

But how to broach the subject? How to make this happen? Just call her? Text her? The moment was too pivotal for casual communication. No. He needed to tell her in person.

Tonight.

He no sooner took Granddad and his belongings inside before he was repacking his bag with clean clothes. Granddad watched him with an amused smile. "Tonight?"

"Yeah. I guess so… why wait?"

Granddad nodded as he smiled with hope and joy. "That's exactly what I was hoping I'd hear from you." Then he slapped Matt on the shoulder. "See, Mattie? You're not a son-of-a-bitch at all."

Matt laughed to release some of the tension. "Well, that's a relief."

They exchanged a long gaze. With a nod, Matt turned and left. His heart felt like it was lodged in his throat; and he was fluttering with raw nerves and excitement, but most of all, hope.

Was he ready to start a family? Yes. No matter what, he and Benny were already family, but now he was thinking of the three of them: him, Benny and Lillian.

CHAPTER 21

*L*ILLIAN WALKED AROUND LISTLESSLY. Her mother found her leaning on the top rail of the paddock, watching the horses in the pasture. Something alarmed them and riled up a few that were gathering together in a beautiful display of power, speed and herd mentality. Her heart felt as restless as their skittering feet.

"Matt get off okay?"

"Yeah."

"Granddad liked it here. And I think Grandpa Jack found his new bestie. Those two had more fun together than I've seen Grandpa Jack have in years."

"They really did get along. I think Benny triggered their competitive desire to outdo each other. By the time they met, they were already in contention. Luckily, that sense of competition seems to fuel both of them."

Her mom stood beside Lillian and leaned against the fence, staring out at the horses as she did. Dwarfing her by several inches, Jocelyn said softly, "Have you ever considered making a move out there?"

She nodded glumly. "Yeah, I was just standing here contemplating that very subject."

Her mom nodded. "I know. That's why I asked. I could see it building all year. You really fell for him, didn't you?"

"I think I did the first night I met him."

"Yeah. I mean you don't act the same as you do with him."

She snorted. "You mean, slutty and stupid?"

"No. I think you have more fun and feel young and don't worry about being perfect. You're always the one who remains in control. The smartest person in any room. Matt welcomes that, of course, but he also encourages you to relax and be a different version of yourself."

"A fun version, you mean?"

"Among other things."

"I don't want to leave here. I wish I did. I wish I'd grown up here and had a burning desire to escape from it, get away and see the world at large. Not to end up loving the small town where I was raised. What I saw of the world made me want nothing more than to be back here, taking care of the animals, working with Dad and Grandpa and everyone else I come into contact with. I *love* it, Mom. And Benny loves his school. He has his own friends now, not just you guys. He needs those too."

"What about his father?" Jocelyn replied. "I wished he wasn't such a great guy at first. I didn't want to lose Benny to a complete stranger. I shared all of your worries, but time and observation have revealed his true self. I find him authentic. After meeting Granddad, I can see he was raised with good morals and plenty of love. And knowing how much he wants to be a good father, he should be. That's undeniable. I understand why you can't deny Benny all of that."

"But Matt can't run his big boat on a river."

"No. He can't."

313

"And I could take care of animals even in a small town."

"Yes. You could."

Lillian shook her head as tears slipped free. "It physically pains me to consider leaving here. But each goodbye that Benny and Matt experience gets worse. Harder. And the more Benny asks for him and misses him lets me know how torn he is, just like I am. But if we moved now, he'd probably adjust. Better than I would. And in time, Benny would just assume he was from there. As he grew up and made friends, he'd eventually accept the coast as his home. Better than not having Matt?"

"I agree."

"I wish you didn't so easily."

"Dad won't. It will break his heart in two. But if Benny needs to know his dad, how can we say that is wrong?"

"And me too. I love Matt. I've only ever been in love with him."

"That's a good thing, honey. Certainly nothing to justify the dread I hear in the tone of your voice."

A small laugh escaped Lillian. "I'm in love with my son's father. That's the best news ever, or it should be. It all works out so tidily. But I might start resenting him if I hate living in Westport. But then again I don't want to keep doing this, going back and forth."

"Then I think we both agree there is no other choice."

Sighing Lillian nodded and Jocelyn smiled softly as she slung an arm around Lillian. When her mom released her, she tilted her face up and asked, "How am I going to tell dad?"

Her mom laughed. "Carefully, very carefully." Then her grin faded. "He'll be happy for you, Lil, really he will."

She knew that even as her dread at telling him about leaving here, leaving him, made her stomach hurt. There was simply no easy answer for the situation and no matter what, someone had to make it. She had finally decided what that answer needed to be.

LILLIAN TURNED and saw her dad standing there. Ben's arms were crossed, and his gaze was deep, intense, and heartbroken. His mouth turned down. After a long stare at her, he said, "You're leaving, aren't you?"

"Benny needs his father."

"And I'm not his father."

"No," she said softly, sniffling as she rubbed her nose. "You're my father."

Ben simply opened his arms to her. In a second, she was against him, crying, as he held her and rubbed her back. He kissed the side of her head. "Ahh, my Annie. I will miss you every single day. It's been the greatest honor of my life to raise you, and then to have the magnificent opportunity to work alongside you. You're an incredible person. A father could never be prouder of his child than I am of you. And most of all? For doing this. For giving your son a full life with both parents, which is what he needs more than this place or us. He needs his father *and* his mother. I just selfishly don't want to let you guys go."

Crying, she muffled her sobs against him for a few moments before lifting her head. Her dad had a special nickname for her that went back to her baby days. He'd call her his Lilly-Anne and then often shorten it to Annie. No one else called her that. He'd only lessened the nickname in her older years. But anytime he was being sentimental, she was his Annie again.

"You really mean all that?"

"Every damn word," he said with a half smile and a more tender tone.

"I thought you'd be furious."

"I am inside. But not toward anyone. Just life and all its irony. You know? Wanting things to be too perfect doesn't happen. Kids grow up and move on. They have their own lives and respective responsibilities. You just need to fulfill yours now."

She sniffled and held back the tears. "You're right. I do. I need to. Benny deserves both of us. I was so worried for nothing that Matt would turn out to be a jerk. I feared losing time with Benny because he would try to infringe on it. Instead, Matt's the epitome of goodness and a totally positive influence. Benny's father deserves to know him and vice versa."

Ben rubbed his neck. "Damn. Don't I know it. I wanted to dislike him too and somehow not disrupt the way things were, but in the end, that's not the best solution for either of you."

"Either of us?" Startled, Lillian tilted her head towards her father. "You think I…"

"Love him? Yes. Annie, it's so obvious. I know how you tried to keep it to yourselves, but believe me, one glance at you two and even I could tell."

"Tell what?" She gave him a grumpy look.

"That the chemistry between you two was undeniable and you both cared about developing something much more than just friendship. I want that for you, Annie, I really do. I want you to experience the love that I have with your mom, and if Matt is where you find it, then I have nothing but respect for you both."

"You make it both harder and easier for me to leave. Telling me it's the right thing to do relieves such a burden that I can't describe. I don't know how I feel yet. It's so difficult to willingly leave my home, and my work and position here. But without your approval and encouragement, it might have been easier not to do it."

"Except it'll only get harder on Benny the longer time you wait. His life, his schooling, and us can't equate to his father. I agree. To all of it. No, I'll never want it to happen, but I totally agree."

She shut her eyes, letting her new reality sink in. "I guess I'll just join my child's father and start a new business and live in the constant rain and gray skies beside the ocean."

Her dad chuckled. "You'll kick ass, to all of it. You're my daughter, so that's just how it'll go."

She let out a hollow laugh. "I really hope that turns out to be the case."

"It always does with you. You'll slay your troubles without batting an eye."

She took his confident tone and tried to weave her own confidence when her nerves rippled through her. Damn, this was so hard.

"So, what do I do? Just show up there?"

"Well, you could call first. Make some temporary plans. Prudently come up with a goal and then go about executing it."

"That's super romantic and too epic in scope. I plan to move there after I set up my life perfectly and rearrange all my clients and—"

Ben gave her a sharp look. "Well, if you don't like my idea, you could simply go there now and show up unexpectedly. Just hope he feels the same and sweeps you up and…"

"Okay, okay. I see your point. I'll make a plan and be the adult. I won't play games. I have my son's wellbeing hinging on this."

Her dad stopped dead and scraped his boots on the barn floor. He frowned, shaking his head as he hung the rope he had in his hand on a hook. "No. Oh, no, that's not at all what

I'm saying to do. I was simply suggesting you could go there all crazy and hope he feels the same. It's risky and scary and really putting yourself out there but—"

"But what?"

"But why the hell not? He wants you and Benny. If you show up, he'll know you're willing to come there, and hell yeah! He'll be glad you came there in such a fashion. What a story to tell your grandkids. Maybe you *should* do that. Makes a much better story than the one I tell my children and grandchildren. Take advantage of it and go. Be bold. Make it an exciting adventure. Spontaneous and totally unplanned. You can make a hundred plans and lists later on."

"Dad, are you serious?" Lillian's jaw nearly landed on the floor.

"So beyond serious. Just go. Do it. Have a fun, drama-filled, romantic moment for once, Lillian. You're the most responsible, pragmatic and solid woman I've ever known. I admire it and adore you for your sense of discipline. But this is unique, and you have to go..."

Her heart leaped strangely. She'd never heard her father talk that way. Never. Not even once. She thought he'd try his hardest to convince her not to go or to do what her gut kept insisting had to happen. It took a while to get here. It started out a small seed that quickly sprouted and grew and grew. When it got too big inside her head, she gave it a voice and told her parents who both agreed with her gut feelings. Shocking. They encouraged her to go. Even if they loved her and would miss her dearly. Lillian did not want to go, not until she did.

Hearing her dad's advice, her heart rose higher. Maybe it wasn't so damn bad to start over somewhere new. How exciting and different to experience a life she never planned. Benny was also unplanned, and he turned out to be the best part of her life. So maybe this impulsive idea would turn out like that. She'd never know if she didn't try.

Nothing was permanent except taxes and death. So, what if it didn't work out? Naturally, she hoped that wouldn't happen, but if it did, so what? She'd come back home and fix it if she had to. But if it worked out, they could be a *family.*

She grabbed her dad's shoulder, planted a kiss on his cheek and grinned. "You're right. I've never been bold and crazy and wild. Never. Unlike my own mother even. I will be. Now. Here. Will you guys watch Benny? I mean, obviously, this is pretty symbolic. I'll have to shut down my practice and buy a place and that'll be a whole new thing for me. It'll take lots of time and planning and making lists. But I want to do it today. Today, I can have this moment. Where I can finally stake my claim. I am making a choice. I can try to do this. Have my moment."

Her dad laughed, squeezing her biceps as he nodded. "Yes. Have your moment."

She nodded and gave him one last hug before she ran from the barn. She almost fell down going into her house. *Purse. Change of clothes. Personal items.* She frantically grabbed them all. Benny would be fine with her parents. She believed it would finally work out. She'd tell Benny only after she knew for sure. He'd be sad to leave the ranch and his school and extended family.

But he would have Matt. The boat. The ocean. The fishing. That was something special for Benny. Mostly, though for his father.

Dad.

Daddy.

She stopped dead, clutching all her things close to her chest. Staring out, she sighed. Her son had a real dad and maybe someday, she'd have the complete picture like she always wanted. Shaking it off, she focused on her next step.

No. Time to go. To see. To be bold. To have a moment. Who'd have guessed her father would be the one to push her to truly do something so risky and adventurous? Smiling, she shook her head as she bolted out towards her car.

She backed out and headed down the road. It would be late, well after ten before she pulled in. He might even be in bed already. Her nerves rippled through her. No. He cared about her just as much as she did him. He wanted her too, just like this. Finding work in the same town would launch the trajectory of their relationship into something entirely different but doable. He wanted that just as much as she did. She had to believe it and embrace it.

Tightening her hands on the steering wheel, she nodded to herself. She deserved a damn moment where her life culminated into something rare and precious. She was about to get it. Lillian Rydell wasn't thinking about being a doctor or a mother or every other practical role that she previously filled. She was going to pull into Matt's house, late at night, surprising and shocking him and it would be awesome. Life-changing. And a new beginning. For all three of them.

Now? She just had to get there.

Grabbing a coffee, she filled up her car with gas, and started sipping the hot fluid before she set her music station and drove off across the state.

IT WAS JUST past ten o'clock at night when Matt pulled his truck back into the driveway he just left that morning. Surprised that Lillian's house was so dark already and even her porch lights weren't on, he hated to knock on the door and feared he would scare her. But he came this far tonight. So, he wasn't waiting to see her. Not tonight. Not after deciding he wanted to be with her permanently. The drive there made Matt realize he was giving up something to gain something. As the miles diminished between him and his small family, he felt considerably happier and lighter inside. This was what he truly wanted. It was the right thing to do and exactly where he belonged. Westport, the ocean, and his boat were where he belonged once. But Granddad was the only person he belonged to. Until now. Until this moment. His ultimate decision to make the move, and fully commit to it, he now sensed in his gut was right. He was ready to sacrifice his own needs for someone else's. Matt was ready to change and grow, and while that was scary and hard to comprehend, it was full of new potential. It could turn out to be the most fulfilling thing he ever did.

Now his stomach was clenching but not because of his nerves, it was due to the excitement inside him and his eagerness to tell Lillian. There weren't anymore doubts. She would welcome his decision. They could build their relationship and be a couple and parents in the same town. Only minutes apart instead of hours. They could establish a family life and make it work. Whatever it took, Matt was ready to give it all he had. He could never imagine himself moving inland or giving up his boat and his job if he weren't completely and fully committed. And he felt sure the woman he wanted to share this with was just as committed as he was.

He parked and turned off the truck. Fine. He'd just have to startle her awake. It was too late to turn back. And he sure as heck couldn't wait to tell her. He'd let Benny sleep. But he at least had to tell Lillian.

He knocked several times. No answer. No light came on. Hmm. Where could she be? At her parents? Maybe. He could text her. But that would ruin his surprise. He swung around. Well, heck, he wasn't scared of the dark. Jogging down her driveway, he started up the road towards her parents' apartment above the arena. Yep, she must have been there. The lights were on, and he could hear the television too as he got closer to the front door. Leaning his hand on the doorjamb, he was breathing hard when he knocked. Then he was waiting.

Please let Jocelyn or Lillian answer the door. Not Ben. Matt wondered why Lillian would be there so late? Where was Benny on a school night? Not like them to be out at night on a weekday. Still, don't let it be—

Ben. Oh, yeah, it had to be Ben. What would Matt say? That he forgot his phone or something innocuous as that to explain his late-night return after just leaving there this morning?

Ben's expression went from neutral to startled and then he appeared shocked. "What the hell are you doing *here?*"

Right. Always so welcoming. "Is Lillian here? Her house was empty when I knocked."

"Well, no shit. Say, Matt, have you talked to her since you left?"

"No." Why did he say *no shit?* What was going on? Why the strange tone?

Ben sighed, rubbing the spot between his eyes like it hurt. "Why are you back?"

"I know it's strange, but I'd rather speak to Lillian…"

Ben shut his eyes. "Are you here to announce something to her?"

Well, shit. Fine. But Matt didn't want to tell her father before he told her. A little privacy would have been nice. Plus, what would Ben say? Go back home? Don't do it? You're not welcome here?

"Matt, please answer me."

Matt sighed, digging his hands in his pockets, while his shoulders dropped in unconcealed disappointment. "Fine. Yes. I was. I realized I should come back here."

"Here? In River's End? With them?"

"Yeah."

"With Benny *and* Lillian?"

"Yes." Matt's frustration was audible in his voice.

Ben's face broke out into a huge smile. "Well, shit. This is amazing. And too bad. But really amazing. I hope you'll keep that in mind."

"What's going on?"

"At this very moment, or just about any moment, in fact, Lillian will be knocking on your door in Westport. She went there looking for you with the intention of moving with Benny over there to be with you."

Those were the last words Matt expected to hear from Ben Rydell's mouth. He jerked upright, pulling his shoulders back. His mouth popped open, and his eyes widened. What? Lillian? This moment was in Westport? To announce exactly the same thing as he was ready to tell her? Matt's knees almost buckled. It was so unbelievable and ironic.

Or was it? Today was hard. So much harder than it had been in the past. It was getting increasingly that way each time. Obviously, they both agreed and felt the same, which was huge. Wonderful. And amazing.

Then reality hit Matt. She was at his house? He was at her parents' house? Right now, they couldn't have been in a more wrong place.

His phone started ringing and her father smirked. "I'd say, she just spoke to Granddad."

Pulling the phone free of his pocket, Matt gave Ben a serious look. Chuckling, Ben shut the door with a little wave and left Matt alone. He sat on Lillian's parents' porch as he talked to her yet again on the phone.

Answering, he said simply, "Hello, Lillian. How was your trip?"

Her deep, breathy voice was soft in his ear. "Are you really at my house this moment?"

"No."

"Oh." She hesitated.

"I'm standing in front of your parents' house after having a quick chat with your dad."

She paused and then she started to laugh out loud. "I just had a chat with Granddad after he answered the door. Apparently, my persistent knocking dragged him out of bed."

His heart was deflating, and a sinking feeling of disappointment set in. He leaned against the wall behind him. "Yeah? And what did you two talk about?"

"First, why don't you tell me what you and my father discussed."

"He wanted to know why I came back, and I had to tell him…" His voice drifted off.

"What? What did you have to tell him, Matt?"

"Over the phone? Really, Lillian? After what we both tried to do tonight? Really?"

She laughed. "Really. We tried. There will always be that. Maybe this is even better. We were thinking at about the exact same changes, at the exact same moment, almost down to the minute. I was what? Ten minutes later than you?"

His heart lurched in surprise as he got her point. "Yeah. Just about."

"Then what did you tell my father?"

"How about I tell you a better version of it?" His voice dropped to a husky, deep tone.

"Why are you there?"

"For you. And Benny. I'm ready to move here so we can be a family. I don't mean to move in with you. But we could date, and I could get to see Benny more regularly. I have no fucking idea what I'll do for a job or where I'll live, but those are just little details. I just…"

"You just…" she pressed, sounding breathless.

He longed and ached for her to come back here. He never imagined he would have to say this over the phone but they both drove for hours. On the same day. The same afternoon. Only ten minutes apart before they came to the same conclusion. They were both willing to make any sacrifice for each other and for Benny.

They were pretty awesome that way, Matt decided.

He nodded as if she could see him, his decision made. "I just love you, Lillian Rydell. I want to be with you forever. I'm moving inland so I can be a father to my son, no matter how you respond to this. Know that. But I do want to be with you. I'm in love with you. There can never be anyone else for me but you. So…"

She was quiet. His heart swelled with affection. But all the driving. Ben said she drove across the state to say something similar to him.

"Say it again."

He shook his head with surprise at her words. "What? What part?"

"The part about Benny."

"Oh." Not my love for her? What did she expect from him moving to live in the same town? Just being co-parents? "I'm moving here no matter what happens with you and me."

"Because?"

"Because I need, and I want, to be a father to our child. Lillian…?"

She laughed and it made a soft, sexy, tinkling sound. "I just wanted to hear you say the sexiest words you could ever speak again."

"What?"

"Relocating your entire life for our child is pretty potent stuff. It says everything about you. But oh, Matt. I love you too and I have loved you for awhile. It terrified me at first, because of the distance. And no familiarity with co-parenting. I was so unwilling to give up things before. But I want you. And I love you too."

"You had me terrified during the last minute. Do you mean it?"

"I drove all this way to say it to your face. Instead, I told Granddad. He explained what you were doing."

He finally laughed with her and said, "Here I am, telling your father…"

"Matt. You can't give up the boat. There is no ocean where I live. So, you can't do your job in River's End. But I can do mine here."

"Benny is thriving here. We can't, and I won't, uproot him. Not when it's so unnecessary. I know. I'll probably miss my life there. But I want a life with you two far more than my life in Westport. Maybe compromise by spending summers there or small chunks of it so I could still charter the boat out. Hire a relief captain in the meantime and oh, those are minute details, Lillian. We'll figure all that out eventually. But for now, I'm moving here to be with you two. Do you want that?"

"I do, sure, but I am willing to move to Westport."

"I didn't do this to start an argument. I did it to end one."

"Me too," she said with conviction.

"Then let me do this. Benny trumps our careers. You just lucked out. Benny shouldn't leave the family he knows. His life is too intertwined with them. And being here. So, this wins."

"Oh, Matt. My guilt is ripping through me because you've made me so happy."

Suddenly the regret he felt stopped. Her words alleviated any remorse he might have felt. "I want to do this, Lillian. I was, and I am, choosing to do this. Granddad wants to come here too. It's happening. It's real. I want it. There is so much we still have to figure out, and we will, but this is what I want. To be with you and Benny."

"I want that too."

"Get some sleep now. You can stay at my house obviously and I'll use yours. Then come home. I'll wait here. We'll discuss the details. And so many other things. And we can do so, so many other things."

She sniffled. Was she a puddle of tears? He was sure of it. "I wanted a big gesture. A crazy story. And to finally not do things according to a plan. And there you are. Here I am. I'm going to sleep on it."

Matt sniffled a little too and the lump in his throat made him gulp. "Nah. This was epic. Far better than anything we could do. Like star-crossed destinies. We both knew what we wanted, and we did the same thing at the same time for the same reasons. God, Lillian, what more convincing do we need to know that this is right between us? This is everything. We are everything."

Her sniffles increased. "That was awesome. Okay, it's epic. Even if it feels a little lackluster to go to your empty bed in a few minutes."

"Let me get in your empty bed and I'll call you. When I'm not in front of your parents maybe we can... you know, make it not so lackluster..."

Her girlish giggle was more than enough to compensate for the disappointment of what almost was but wasn't, although it still had unlimited potential.

A life was starting. A life for all three of them together.

EPILOGUE

*S*O MATT STARTED OVER with zero skills as a ranch hand since his only calling was captaining a boat. That expertise was obsolete on a ranch. Interesting. Hard. To be honest, it didn't end like the fairytale it started out as. Sure, Matt found love with the mother of his long-lost child he never knew about, so that was a win. His son was the most amazing, sweet, funny, kind, smart... He could go on and on with all the positive attributes he saw in Benny, yet another score. Yes. Of course, it was worth everything he sacrificed.

But did he miss being the boss on his own boat? Yeah, that sucked. There was no comparison to how that made Matt feel. Nothing could come close to being on the sea with a spiritual sense of connection, human skill and unparalleled satisfaction. Matt arranged for a relief captain to run his charters when he wasn't there. The final plan was for Matt to spend two months of the summer season in Westport, during which he'd run the charters. Lillian would commute, spending three days in River's End and four days in West-port, during the times Matt was there. Benny would have the extraordinary opportunity to truly learn Matt's trade and become part of the crew, if he chose to. He could decide for himself whether he wanted to make it a job, in which case, Matt would give him the boat just as he had received it from Granddad.

It thrilled Matt every chance he had to teach and work with his son.

Even though it ate up most of the summer vacation.

Compromise was not always sexy. But Matt didn't mind it if he did not get exactly what he wanted.

In exchange, he now had a family. He had unconditional love. His companionship with Lillian and his son made him happier than anything else. The Rydells accepted them at once, including Granddad. Their hospitality and grace gave Granddad a brand-new lease on life. His physical activity and exercise aside, he also enjoyed a vigorous banter with Jack Rydell, which served to stimulate his mind, and Jefferson Griffin seemed to turn the clock back a decade in how much younger he suddenly appeared. He had company when he wanted it, plenty of people who cared for him, and he stayed busy. That kind of stimulation also increased his energy and verve. He was so busy doing new things that sometimes Matt had a hard time hunting down his Granddad. That tickled Matt until he was almost giddy. It made his heart swell to see his Granddad so industrious and happy, making the move all the more worth it.

Seeing his son everyday, however, was the reward that solidified it all for Matt. No way could Matt settle for infrequent visits and sporadic contact. They interacted together everyday. Matt saw so many small things by constantly being an influence in his young son's childhood. Always having easy access to him. He saw the small tears that Benny tried to hide and learned all the things that made him smile. He learned why Benny's favorite toy was so special, and who annoyed him most in his class. He got to read books with Benny instead of always rough-housing in the living room, throwing a ball. Matt liked exposing him to good foods that were healthy and figuring out ways to convince him to try them even when Benny stubbornly refused. Matt loved to sneak in little treats and surprises to delight Benny, which simply melted his own heart.

Matt found a small place to live across the river in River's End, which he rented from a family friend. He learned the apartment was once occupied by Lillian's cousins-once-removed, Iris and Rose. There was plenty of space for him and Granddad and Matt appreciated having more autonomy.

His new life justified his choice. Not seeing or smelling the ocean, or feeling the salty air on his face, Matt sorely missed his boat in the beginning. It was a bigger adjustment than he expected. But the support and fun and companionship of his new family compensated for his painful longing and he rarely thought about it as often.

Finding a job turned out to be the toughest part. He tried several things at the ranch, but nothing interested him.

It took him a few weeks to organize their great move to River's End. First, he had to find a reliable captain and crew to charter his boat when he wasn't there. He made it crystal clear that he could decide to pop over anytime unexpectedly and would not tolerate any riff-raff. He found an old friend of Granddad's who had a captain's license but struggled to find work because he had no boat of his own. Satisfied with his first win-win, Matt rented out his house to a couple. He and Lillian bought a trailer that they parked behind the house on Matt and Granddad's land. There was enough space to fence it off, for the tenants' privacy as well as theirs, and they beautifully landscaped the site around the trailer. When they were in town for the summer, it perfectly served their needs. Matt organized everything and downsized considerably before he permanently landed in River's End.

He had nothing to do on the ranch. He followed Lillian around for a few days mostly out of curiosity and intrigue. He wanted to see the professional veterinarian at work since she was so knowledgeable, competent, and practical. Whatever it was, she could get it done. Matt's admiration for her rose to a higher level. She was not only amazing but patient, compassionate, and efficacious.

"Did anything at school ever interest you? Did you like to go to school and learn new things? Maybe you could do something like that. There are so many online degree programs now and everybody has access, making it easier for people anywhere to earn a degree." Lillian was hoping to stimulate Matt's ambitious side. At the time, she was doing a rectal check on a cow to see if she was pregnant.

"No. But I have been thinking of doing something. Seriously considered it even."

"What?" she asked eagerly.

"I like assisting you."

"You do?" Her stare clung to his and her hand quit moving for a startled moment. He dropped his gaze to indicate she could keep working. With a shake of her head, she quickly finished up.

"I really do enjoy it. Once, you talked about needing a veterinarian assistant... why not me? If you don't think it's insane. I could learn what to do hands-on from you. There is no required degree, right? But I found a program online that takes eighteen months and then you take a test to get certified. Between that and you, what couldn't I learn? That is, if you don't hate the thought of working with me. It'll always be your practice, but maybe we could do it together. And of course, every summer, when I leave to make the bulk of my salary for the year as boat captain, we'd have to find someone else to help you. I can't find a job where I can be gone all summer and then come back when it's over. But this way..."

She nodded and bit her lip, withdrawing her arm and then her hand.

"If you hate the idea, just say so now. I mean, two people working together and living in each other's pockets more or less can be stressful. No private separation time. And it's your thing. I just like doing it with you. But maybe that'll fade with time. I wanted to keep busy initially but now I find it fascinating and actually like it. But you have to be honest, Lillian. We won't make it if you're not open and honest with me."

She smiled softly as she patted the cow's side and replied, "I'm always too honest with you, Matt Griffin. And I love all the time we spend together doing this. Yes. I'm just so happy to know you found something you don't hate. I know you miss the autonomy you used to have. But if you think it could work out, I would love to try."

"I think it will."

"Okay." She grinned and he mirrored hers with a matching grin. Always in sync. This gave it another dimension. "And I am happy to announce the cow is pregnant." She stated brightly as they walked out of the paddock to report her finding to the dairy farm rancher.

The following May, Matt and Benny took a pleasure trip, just the two of them, and went out fishing for halibut early in the season. They were sitting in the sun, staring out over the calm seas, cruising on autopilot, beneath the beautiful blue sky that glistened on the water and Matt said, "Benny, I've been thinking."

"About what?"

"What would you say if I asked your mom to marry me?"

"Like, being husband and wife?"

"Yeah."

"Duh. You're my parents. What took you so long?"

Matt leaned over and ruffled his hair. "Okay, okay. So, I have your support?"

"Dad, it doesn't matter what I say. You still have to ask her." He giggled and rolled his eyes before he pretended to run. Matt jumped to his feet, grabbing his son and tossing him over his shoulder like a sack of potatoes. Then he pretended to heave him out to the sea.

"I was just checking with you. But don't tell her yet. Let me ask her first."

"Can't I be part of it?"

Matt tilted his head; he never considered that option. After wracking his brain for a way to propose to Lillian, nothing felt right to him so far. Not until his son's question. Slowly lowering his feet onto the boat deck, Matt nodded as he smiled. A new idea started to take shape in his head. "I think you have a big role to play in it."

THE GUILT HAUNTED Lillian for making Matt give up his job and his calling. After weeks of debating back and forth, she finally acquiesced to Matt moving there instead of her moving to the beach. Of course, she preferred he come to her. She could keep her job, her house, her family ties, and basically her entire lifestyle as it was. Her son could stay in the school he knew and be near his friends and family, which served as the backbone of his life. So yes, this was what Lillian wanted deep down. But her guilt was undeniable, and she spent a lot of time nursing a stomachache. How could she demand that Matt give up his whole identity? She couldn't imagine giving up her practice. And yet, he had to abandon his?

Nobody's fault; it was simply so. But when he went to

his first big-animal call with her, she was pleasantly surprised. They had an amazingly mutually satisfying time. He listened to her without arguing. When she asked him to do a task, he simply obeyed her. He wanted to keep working with her. Hell, yeah. All the stars seemed to align perfectly for her.

Yes.

Simply, yes. Lillian agreed to all of it. She never had a connection like what she had with Matt. Sharing their lives, a son, her hometown, and a job was totally awesome. They were both building and adding to the happy life they were creating. Lillian was in charge, but that didn't seem to bother Matt in the least. When she got stressed, she barked orders at him like a dictator, and he followed her instructions as any employee might. But later? At dinner they discussed the details of the event. Matt asked endless questions. His interest was not only in her, but the subject matter; he loved picking her brain for all the knowledge she had. Matt never seemed intimidated by her higher earning capacity, or in her having the final decision. Matt practically celebrated her career. He still had his boat and his experience, his own small universe where he was the boss and the more knowledgeable one. It was easy to let her have her bailiwick since she deserved it.

Unfortunately, things like cleaning the toilet were still a major part of her life also. Leaning over it, she finished scrubbing and flushed it before she slipped her rubber gloves off. "Mom! Mommy! Come here!"

Throwing her gloves with her cleaning supplies at her feet, she walked into the living room. Startled, she found Benny standing next to Matt. Both of them were grinning from ear-to-ear and looked startlingly similar. Like the big and little version of the same person. Even their clothes were similar, if not exact replicas. She paused to lean a shoulder against the wall and cocked an eyebrow. "What have you two cooked up?"

"We have a surprise!"

"Okay…" She gave Benny a suspicious glance. Then a keener one to Matt. "What exactly? And why do I have the feeling I should brace myself?"

"It's in the laundry room!" Benny was all but bursting out of his shoes and the smile could not be wiped off his face.

What could possibly arouse so much interest in the laundry room?

"Okay. Should I go look in there?"

"Yes!" Benny broke from their obviously rehearsed stance and started dancing around, skipping, jumping and yelling, "Go look! Go look!"

She gave Matt a glance. He revealed nothing in his neutral expression and polite smile to her. Finally, she turned and headed towards the laundry where the door was shut. Opening it, she was almost bowled over when a wriggling, four-legged creature launched itself at her with maniacal excitement—reminiscent of Benny—and nearly blew her mind.

A dog? It registered finally and she observed it more closely, jumping around her, wiggling against her legs, going back and forth. Benny's face beamed with joy and ecstasy.

"Me and Dad got a dog! We rescued it! I helped him pick it out!"

"I see that." She smiled. Matt had come a long way. His initial aversion to animals had apparently done a one-eighty and now he downright enjoyed them. But they never discussed getting a pet. "Maybe we've been a good influence on him."

"What do you think?" Matt asked.

The dog was a patchwork of white, black and tan. The adorable face had big, sad eyes that shone brightly, and she could not determine the breed without a DNA sample. She laughed as the body slammed into her again. Leaning down, she started to pet him… no, it was a she, and Lillian couldn't stop giggling when the dog's tongue started licking her face. "I think she's a keeper. What's her name?"

"We'll decide that together," Matt said, his tone much calmer than Benny's unbridled joy. "And we'll only keep her if you say it's okay."

"I could have helped you decide, but she's awesome. Scooter and Skeeter won't love her, but cats have to make adjustments all the time."

Still Matt and Benny beamed at her. Lillian was glad she reacted the way they wanted her to, but she gave them a strange look and asked, "What?"

"Are you sure you want to keep her? Why don't you pet her first?" Matt replied.

"It's an animal, Matt. Of course, I'm sure."

"Mommy!" Benny tilted his head as if to somehow communicate something obvious or clear to her. But she failed to get it.

Puzzled, she knelt down and said, "All right, girl, come here." The excited, happy dog all but knocked her over and she leaned on Lillian, who scratched her back, tummy, head and ears. To her surprise, she felt a collar buried in the dense hair. "Oh, she has a tag. Maybe she has a name too."

Spinning the collar, she frowned. It felt strange. What was this? What?

Oh… oh… what?

Her heart slammed against her chest, and her breath hitched. No. Yes? Oh, crap. Shit. Really?

But yes.

Yes.

Matt approached her with a tender, warm, deep, loving look in his eyes. When their gazes collided, they held. He lowered himself beside her, avoiding the wiggling, eager canine.

"This is so unconventional. I know. But Benny wanted to participate. He wanted a dog. He thought this up and said it was perfect. So, I indulged him."

"It…" Her voice wavered before it failed altogether, and she shook her head. "It is. Is this… are you…?"

He leaned forward and set his strong, warm hand over hers. She clutched the diamond solitaire ring she found hooked to the dog's collar, in place of a tag or a license.

He grinned when her tears slipped free and rolled down her cheeks. They knelt before the ecstatic dog, wiggling again until the ring popped free of her hand and she was left holding Matt's hand. The dog dropped down and rolled over to expose her tummy, obviously seeking a belly rub. Her tail thumped loudly as she squirmed happily. Neither Matt nor Lillian released the other.

"Dr. Lillian Rydell, would you do me the honor of becoming my wife?"

Tears streamed like rain and she had to restrain a sob. But she nodded repeatedly when she finally gasped and said the only word she could. The best one. "Yes."

Matt grabbed her and they stayed on their knees, clasping and clinging to each other while she cried and clutched his chest, burying her face into his shoulder. He rubbed her head and smoothed her long hair. "I'm so happy," he said in her ear. "Happier than I ever dreamed I could possibly be."

"Me too," Lillian replied as she pulled back so they could stare at each other.

Then the dog reappeared, placing her head between them as Benny suddenly ran forward. He managed to grab the dog around the neck and slide between them.

"So… what are we going to name her?"

It was impossible for Lillian to resist the urge to grab

Benny even though he held onto the new dog and crushed him against her.

Benny squirmed against her tight hold. "Ahh... Mom. Stop crying. This is no big deal. We're already family and now we're a family with a dog."

Matt reached out and hugged Benny, the dog and Lillian, bringing them all closer to him. "That's right. But we'll finally be official. And that's a pretty big deal."

"With a dog."

Matt laughed and then sighed. "With a dog. Now let's see if I can't detach this ring before she runs off again..."

Lillian's heart swelled with all the joy filling it. Matt struggled to release the ring he'd hooked to the collar as their dog and son played together, punctuated with peals of Benny's laughter. No wine or roses; no romantic, candlelit dinner. No. Matt's proposal was filled with warmth, family, life and the sense of togetherness. And it was all about to get so much better, brighter and bigger.

"Mom! What about Tapioca? Like the pudding?"

Misty-eyed, she glanced at Benny. What? Benny wanted her to make pudding? But no. She realized he wanted to call the dog that. Rising to her feet, she paused before Matt gently lifted her hand and slipped the ring on her finger. She stared up at him as he leaned down and kissed the side of her face. She had a tender, soft, loving smile as she simultaneously said, "We are not naming the dog after pudding."

"Ahh... Mom... then what do you like?"

"What about Peppa?"

"No. No one likes that. Aspen," Matt interrupted.

"Never. It doesn't even sound like a girl's name."

Smiling when their gazes locked and more than a million intimate messages were exchanged, they bickered for the next ten minutes about what to name the new dog. Their newest family member.

It would not be their last dog. Or pet. Or child. In the years to come, many more would arrive and the quibbling and fighting and bargaining and begging would accompany them as they struggled to name each one.

They called the new dog *Jewel*. That was because she gave Lillian the best jewel she ever received and could never forget. The dog officially brought them together and received their undying love and adoration for over a decade as their beloved first pet.

No one needed to remind them of how they came to be a family. Each and every day they worked, lived, raised kids and pets together, and that pretty well solidified it. The infamous one-night stand turned out to be the best thing that ever happened to all of them.

From a one-night stand to forever. From the valley to the ocean, they were destined to be together.

And finally, they could be, and they were.

ABOUT THE AUTHOR

Leanne Davis has earned a business degree from Western Washington University. She worked for several years in the construction management field before turning full time to writing. She lives in the Seattle area with her husband and two children. When she isn't writing, she and her family enjoy camping trips to destinations all across Washington State, many of which become the settings for her novels.

Made in the USA
Monee, IL
09 September 2021